BYGONES

Also by LaVyrle Spencer

BYGONES

LaVyrle Spencer

G. P. PUTNAM'S SONS   NEW YORK

G. P. Putnam's Sons
Publishers Since 1838
200 Madison Avenue
New York, NY 10016

The author acknowledges permission to reprint lyrics from the following:
"Old Time Rock and Roll" © 1979 Muscle Shoals Sound Publishing.
"Good Lovin," by Rudy Clark and Art Resnick, © 1965 Alley Music Corp. and Trio
Music Co., Inc. Used by permission. All rights reserved.
"The Living Years," by Mike Rutherford and B. A. Robertson, © Hit & Run Music
(Publishing) Ltd. (PRS), Michael Rutherford Ltd. (PRS), R & BA Music Ltd. (PRS).
Administered by Hidden Pun Music, Inc. (BMI) in USA and Canada. International
copyright secured. All rights reserved. Used by permission.

Printed in the United States of America

My most sincere thanks to the following people
for their help during the research of this book:

Brenda Taylor
Katie Holdorph
Jennifer Severson
Gar Johnson
Dr. Don Brandt
LaVonne Engesether
Cheryl at the Stillwater Chamber of Commerce

and a special thanks to the following people for allowing me
to use their beautiful homes as settings for this book:

Ted & Lorraine Glasrud
Tom & Edna Murphy

This book is dedicated with love
to some of my oldest friends
and some of my newest—

Barb & Don Fread
and
Barb & Don Brandt

BYGONES

chapter 1

THE APARTMENT BUILDING resembled thousands of others in the suburban Minneapolis/St. Paul area, a long brick rectangle with three floors, a set of steps on each end and rows of bruised doors lining stuffy, windowless halls. It was the kind of dwelling where young people started out with cast-off furniture and bargain-basement draperies, where toddlers rode their tricycles down the halls and could be heard through the floors when they cried. Now, at 6 P.M. on a cold January night, the smell of cooking meat and vegetables sifted under the doors, mingled with the murmur of televisions tuned to the evening news.

A tall woman walked down the hall. She looked out of place, dressed in a classic winter-white reefer coat bearing the unmistakable cut of a name designer, her accessories—leather gloves, handbag, shoes and scarf—of deep raspberry red. Her clothing was expensive, from the fifty-dollar silk scarf looped casually over her hair to the two-inch high heels combining three textures of leather. She walked with an air of hurried sophistication.

Pulling the scarf from her head, Bess Curran knocked at the door of number 206.

Lisa flung it open and exclaimed, "Oh, Mom, hi. Come on in. I knew I could depend on you to be right on time! Listen, everything's all ready but I forgot the sour cream for the stroganoff, so I have to make a quick run to the store. You don't mind keeping your eye on the meat, do you?" She dove into a closet and came up with a hip-length jean jacket, which she threw on over her dress.

"Stroganoff? For just the two of us? And a dress? What's the occasion?"

Lisa headed back to the door, digging her keys from her purse. "Just give it a stir, okay?" She opened the door halfway and stopped to call, "Oh! And light the candles and put a tape on, will you? That old Eagles one is there that you always liked."

The door slammed and left Bess in a backwash of puzzlement. Stroganoff? Candles? Music? And Lisa in a dress and pumps? Unbuttoning her coat, Bess wandered into the kitchen. Beyond the galley-style work area that divided it from the living room, a table was set for four. She studied it curiously—blue place mats and napkins cinched into white napkin rings; the leftover pieces of her and Michael's first set of dishes, which she'd given Lisa when she left home; four of her own cast-off stem glasses; and two blue candles in holders she'd never seen before, apparently bought specially for the occasion on Lisa's limited budget. What in the world was going on here?

She went to the stove to stir the stroganoff, which smelled so heavenly she couldn't resist sampling it. Delicious—her own recipe, laced with consommé and onions. As she replaced the cover on the pan, she realized she was famished: she'd done three home consultations today plus two hours in the store before it opened, grabbing a hamburger on the run. She promised herself, as she did every January, to limit the home consultations to two a day.

Returning to the front closet, she hung up her coat and straightened a pile of shoes so she could close the bifold door. She found matches and lit the candles on the dinner table and two others in clear, stubby pots on the living-room coffee table. Beside these a plate from her old dinnerware held a cheeseball waiting to be gouged and spread on Ritz crackers.

The match burned low.

She flinched and flapped it out, then stood staring at the cheeseball. What the devil? She glanced around the room and realized the place was clean for a change. Her old brass-and-glass tables had been freshly dusted and the cushions plumped on the hand-me-down family sofa. The tapes were stacked neatly, and the junk on the bookshelves had been neatened. The jet-black Kawaii piano Lisa's father had given her for high-school graduation hadn't a speck of dust on it. Instead, the key cover was neatly closed, and on top of the piano a picture of Lisa's current boyfriend, Mark, shared the space with a struggling philodendron plant and five Stephen King books in a pair of brass bookends Lisa had received from her Grandma Stella for Christmas.

The piano was the only valuable thing in the room. When Michael had given it to Lisa, Bess had accused him of foolish indulgence. It made no sense at all—a girl without a college education or a decent car or furniture owning a five-thousand-dollar piano that would have to be moved professionally—to the tune of about a hundred dollars per move—how many times before she was finally settled down permanently?

Lisa had said, "But, Mom, it's something I'll always keep, and that's what a graduation present should be."

Bess had argued, "Who'll pay when you have to have it moved?"

"I will."

"On a clerk-typist's salary?"

"I'm waitressing, too."

"You should be going on to school, Lisa."

"Dad says there's plenty of time for that."

"Well, your dad could be wrong, you know! If you don't go on to school right away, chances are you never will."

"You did," Lisa had argued.

"Yes, I did but it was damned hard, and look what it cost me. Your father should have more sense than to give you advice like that."

"Mother, just once I wish the two of you would stop haggling and at least pretend to get along, for us kids' sake. We're so sick of this cold war!"

"Well, it's a stupid gift." Bess had gone away grumbling. "Five thousand dollars for a piano that could finance a whole year of college."

The piano had remained a sore spot. Whenever Bess came to Lisa's apartment unannounced, the piano held a film of dust on its gleaming jet finish and seemed to be used merely as the depository for books, scarves, hair bows and all the other flotsam of Lisa's busy two-job life. It was all Bess could do to keep from sniping, "See, I told you!"

Tonight, however, the piano had been dusted and on the music rack was the sheet music for Michael's favorite song, "The Homecoming." In years past, whenever Lisa sat down to play, Michael would say, "Play that one I like," and Lisa would oblige with the beautiful old television-movie theme song.

Bess turned away from the memory of those happier times and put on the *Eagles Greatest Hits* tape. While it played she used Lisa's bathroom, noting that it, too, had been cleaned for the occasion. Washing her hands, she saw that the fixtures were shining, the towels fluffy and freshly laundered. On the corner of the vanity was the apothecary jar of potpourri she'd given Lisa for Christmas.

Bess hung up the towel and glanced in the mirror at her disheveled streaky-blonde hair, gave it a pluck or two: after the day she'd put in she looked undone. She'd been in and out of the wind, the shop, her car, and hadn't taken time since morning to pause for cosmetic repairs. Her forehead looked oily, her lipstick was gone and her brown eyes looked stark with the eyeshadow and mascara worn away. There were lap creases across the skirt of her winter-white wool crepe suit, and a small grease spot stood out prominently on the jabot of her raspberry-colored blouse. She frowned at the spot, wet a corner of a washcloth and made it worse. She cursed softly, then found a lifter-comb in Lisa's vanity drawer. Just as she raised her arms to use it, a knock sounded at the opposite end of the apartment.

She stuck her head around the corner and called down the hall, "Lisa, is that you?"

The knock came again, louder, and she hurried to answer it, leaving the bathroom light on behind her.

"Lisa, did you forget your—?" She pulled the door open and the words died in her throat. A tall man stood in the hall, trim, black-haired, hazel-eyed, dressed in a gray woolen storm coat, holding a brown paper sack containing two wine bottles.

"Oh, Michael . . . it's you."

Her mouth got tight.

Her carriage became stiff.

He gave her a stare, his eyebrows curled in displeasure. "Bess . . . what are you doing here?"

"I was invited for supper. What are you doing here?"

"I was invited, too."

Their face-off continued while she curbed the desire to slam the door in his face.

"Lisa called me last night and said, Dinner at six-fifteen, Dad."

She had called Bess the night before and said, "Dinner at six, Mom." Bess released the doorknob and spun away, muttering, "Cute, Lisa."

Michael followed her inside and shut the door. He set his bottles on the kitchen cupboard and took off his coat while Bess hustled back to the bathroom to put herself as far from him as possible. In the glare of the vanity light she backcombed four chunks of hair hard enough to push them back into her skull root-first. She arranged them with a few chunks and stabs of the wire hair lifter, slashed some of Lisa's grotesque scarlet lipstick on her mouth (the only tube she could find, considering she'd left her purse at the other end of the apartment), glared at the results and at the dark blob on her jabot. Damn it. And damn him for catching me when I look this way. She raised her brown eyes to the mirror and found them flat with fury. And damn me for squandering so much as a second caring what he thinks. After what he did to me, I don't have to pander to that asshole.

She slammed the vanity drawer, rammed her fingers into her forelock and ground it into a satisfying mess.

"What are you doing back there, hiding?" he called irritably.

It had been six years since the divorce, and she still wanted to arrange his penis with a hot curling iron every time she saw him!

"Let's get one thing clear," she bellowed down the hall. "I didn't know a damned thing about this!"

"Let's get two things clear! Neither did I! Where the hell is she anyway?"

Bess whacked the light switch off and marched toward the living room with her head high and her hair looking like a serving of chow mein noodles.

"She went to the store for sour cream, which I'm cheerfully going to stuff up her nostrils when she gets back here."

Michael was standing by the kitchen table, studying it, with his hands in his trouser pockets. He was dressed in a gray business suit, white shirt and blue paisley tie.

"What's all this?" he threw over his shoulder as she passed behind him.

"Your guess is as good as mine."

"Is Randy coming?" Randy was their nineteen-year-old son.

"Not that I know of."

"You don't know who the fourth one is for?"

"No, I don't."

"Or what the occasion is?"

"Obviously, a blind date for her mother and father. Our daughter has a bizarre sense of humor, doesn't she?" Bess opened the refrigerator door, looking for wine. Inside were four individual salads, prettily arranged on plates, a bottle of Perrier water, and sitting on the top shelf in a red-and-white carton, a pint of sour cream. "My, my, if it isn't sour cream." She picked it up and held it on one hand at shoulder level the way Marilyn Monroe would have held a mink. "And four very fancy salads."

He came to have a look, peering over the open refrigerator door.

"What are you looking for, something to drink?"

The smell of his shaving lotion, which in years past had seemed endearingly familiar, now turned her stomach. "I feel as if I need something." She slammed the door.

"I brought some wine," he told her.

"Well, break it out, Michael. We apparently have a long evening ahead."

She took two glasses from the table while he opened the bottle.

"So . . . where's Darla tonight?" She held the glasses while he poured the pale red rosé.

Over the gurgling liquid he answered, "Darla and I are no longer together. She's filed for divorce."

Bess got as rattled as an eighteen wheeler going over a cattle guard. Her head shot up while Michael went on filling the second glass.

She hadn't spent sixteen years with this man not to feel a mindless shaft of elation at the news that he was free again. Or that he had failed again.

Michael set the bottle on the cupboard, took a glass for himself and met Bess's eyes directly. It was a queer, distilled moment in which they both saw their entire history in a pure, refined state, so clear they could see through it, way back to the beginning—the splendid and the sordid, the regards and the regrets that had brought them to this point where they stood in their daughter's kitchen holding drinks that went untasted.

"Well, say it," Michael prodded.

"Good, it serves you both right."

He released a mirthless laugh and shook his head at the floor. "I knew that's what you were thinking. You're one very bitter woman, Bess, you know that?"

"And you're one very contemptible man. What did you do, step out on her, too?"

He walked out of the room replying, "I'm not going to get into it with you, Bess, because I can see all it'll lead to is a rehash of our old recriminations."

"Good." She followed him. "I don't want a rehash, either. So until our daughter gets back we'll pretend we're two polite strangers who just happened to meet here."

They carried their drinks into the living room and dropped to opposite ends of the davenport—the only seating in the room. The Eagles were singing "Take It Easy," which they'd listened to together a thousand times before. The candles were burning on the glass-top table they'd once chosen for their own living room. The davenport they sat on was one upon which they'd occasionally made love and cooed endearments to each other when they were both young and stupid enough to believe marriage lasts forever. They sat upon it now like a pair of church elders, in their respective corners, resenting one another and the intrusion of these memories.

"Looks like you gave Lisa the whole living room after I left," Michael remarked.

"That's right. Down to the pictures and the lamps. I didn't want any bad memories left behind."

"Of course, you had your new *business,* so it was no trouble buying replacements."

"Nope. No trouble at all," she replied smugly. "And of course, I get everything at a discount."

"So how's the business going?"

"Gangbusters! You know how it is after Christmas—everybody looking at those bare walls after they've pulled down all the holiday paraphernalia, and wanting new wallpaper and furniture to chase away the winter doldrums. I swear I could do half a dozen home consultations a day if there were three of me."

He studied her askance, remaining silent. Obviously she was happy with the way things had worked out. She was a certified interior designer now, with a store of her own and a newly redecorated house.

The Eagles switched to "Witchy Woman."

"So how's yours?" she inquired, tossing him an arch glance.

"It's making me rich."

"Don't expect congratulations. I always said it would."

"From you, Bess, I don't expect anything anymore."

"Oh, *that's* funny!" She cocked one wrist and delicately touched her chest. *"You* don't expect anything from *me* anymore." Her tone turned accusing as she dropped the cutesy pose. "When was the last time you saw Randy?"

"Randy doesn't give a damn about seeing me."

"That's not what I asked. When was the last time you made an effort to see him? He's still your son, Michael."

"If Randy wants to see me, he'll give me a call."

"Randy wouldn't give you a call if you were giving away tickets for a Rolling Stones concert and you know it. But that doesn't excuse you for ignoring him. He needs you whether he knows it or not, so it's up to you to keep trying."

"Is he still working in that warehouse?"

"When he bothers."

"Still smoking pot?"

"I think so but he's careful not to do it in the house. I told him if I ever smell it in there again I'll throw him out."

"Maybe you should. Maybe that would straighten him up."

"And then again maybe it wouldn't. He's my son, and I love him, and I'm trying my best to make him see the light but if I give up on him, what hope will he have? He certainly never gets any guidance from his father."

"What do you want me to do, Bess?" Michael spread his arms wide, the glass in one hand. "I've offered him the money to go to college or trade school if he wants but he doesn't want anything to do with school. So what in the hell do you expect me to do? Take him in with me? A pothead who goes to work when he feels like it?"

Bess glared at him. "I expect you to call him, take him out to dinner, take him hunting with you, rebuild a relationship with him, make him realize he still has a father who loves him and cares about what happens to him. But it's easier to slough him off on me, isn't it, Michael? Just like it was when the kids were little and you ran off with your guns and your fishing rods and your . . . your mistress! Well, I can't seem to find the answers for him anymore. Our son is a mess, Michael, and I'm very much afraid of what's going to become of him but I can't straighten him out alone."

Their eyes met and held, each of them aware that their divorce had been the blow from which Randy had never recovered. Until age thirteen he had been a happy kid, a good student, a willing helper around the house, a carefree teenager who brought his friends in to eat them out of house and home, watch football games and roughhouse on the living-room floor. From the day they'd told him they were getting a divorce, he had changed. He had become withdrawn, uncommunicative and increasingly lackadaisical about responsibilities, both in school and at home. He stopped bringing his friends home and eventually found new ones who wore weird hairdos and army jackets and one earring, and dragged their boot heels when they walked. He lay on his bed listening to rap music through his headphones, began smelling like burned garbage and coming home at two in the morning with his pupils dilated. He resented school counseling, ran away from home when Bess tried to ground him and graduated from high school by his cuticles, with the lowest grade-point average allowable.

No, their marriage was certainly not their only failure.

"For your information," Michael said, "I have called him. He called me a son of a bitch and hung up." Michael tipped forward, propping his elbows on his knees, drawing gyroscopic patterns in the air with the bottom of his glass. "I know he's messed up, Bess, and we did it to him, didn't we?" Still hunched forward, he looked over his shoulder at her. On the stereo the song changed to "Lyin' Eyes."

"Not we. You. He's never gotten over you leaving your family for another woman."

"That's right, blame it all on me, just like you always did. What about you leaving your family to go to college?"

"You still begrudge me that, don't you, Michael? And you still can't believe I actually became an interior designer and made a success of it."

Michael slammed down his glass, leapt to his feet and pointed a finger at her from the far side of the coffee table. "You got custody of the kids because you wanted it, but afterwards you were so damned busy at that store of yours that you weren't around to be their parent!"

"How would you know? You weren't around, either!"

"Because you wouldn't let me in the goddamn house! *My* house! The house I paid for and furnished and painted and loved just as much as you did!" He jabbed a finger for emphasis. "Don't tell me I wasn't around when you're the one who refused to speak to me, thereby setting an example for our son to follow. I was willing to be sensible, for the kids' sake, but no, you wanted to *show* me, didn't you? You were going to take those kids and brainwash them and make them believe *I* was the only one in the wrong where our marriage was concerned; and don't lie to me and say different, because I've talked to Lisa and she's told me some of the shit you've told her."

"Like what?"

"Like, our marriage broke up because I had an affair with Darla."

"Well, didn't it?"

He threw up his hands and rolled his eyes to the ceiling. "God, Bess, take off your blinders. Things had soured between us before I even met Darla and you know it."

"If things soured between us it was because—"

The apartment door opened. Bess clapped her mouth shut while she and Michael exchanged a glare of compressed volatility. Her cheeks were bright with anger. His lips were set in a grim line. She rose, donning a veneer of propriety, while he closed a button on his suit jacket and retrieved his glass from the coffee table. As he straightened, Lisa rounded the corner into the living room. Behind her came the young man whose picture stood on the piano.

Had Pablo Picasso painted the scene, he might have entitled it *Still Life with Four Adults and Anger*. The words of the abandoned argument still reverberated in the air.

Finally Lisa moved. "Hello, Mother. Hello, Dad."

She hugged her father first, while he easily closed his arms around her and kissed her cheek. She was nearly his height, dark-haired and pretty, with lovely brown eyes, an attractive combination of the best features of both her parents. She went next to hug Bess, saying, "Missed hugging you the first time around, Mom, glad you could come." Retreating from her mother's arms, she said, "You both remember Mark Padgett, don't you?"

"Mr. and Mrs. Curran," Mark said, shaking hands with each of them. He had a shiny all-American face and naturally curly brown hair, crew-cut on top and trailing in thinned tendrils over his collar. He sported the brawn of a bodybuilder and a hand to match. When he shook their hands, they felt it.

"Mark's going to have supper with us. I hope you stirred the stroganoff, Mom." Lisa headed jauntily for the kitchen, where she went to the sink, turned on the hot water and began filling a saucepan. Right behind her came Bess, snagging Lisa's elbow and forcing her to do an about-face.

"Just what in the world do you think you're doing!" she demanded in a pinched whisper, covered by the sound of the running water and "Desperado" from the other side of the wall.

"Boiling noodles for the stroganoff." Lisa swung the kettle to the stove and switched on a blue flame, with Bess dogging her shoulder.

"Don't be obtuse with me, Lisa. I'm so damned angry I could fling that stroganoff down the disposal and you right along with it." She pointed a finger. "There's a pint of sour cream in that refrigerator and you know it! You set us up!"

Lisa pushed her mother's arm as if it were a turnstile and moved beyond it to open the refrigerator door. "I certainly did. How'd it go?" she asked blithely, removing the carton of sour cream and curling its cover off.

"Lisa Curran, I could dump that sour cream on your head!"

"I really don't care, Mother. *Some*body had to make you come to your senses."

"Your father and I are not a couple of twenty-year-olds you can fix up on a blind date!"

"No, you're not!" Lisa slammed down the carton of sour cream and faced her mother, nose-to-nose, whispering angrily. "You're forty years old but you're acting like a child! For six years you've refused to be in the same room with Dad, refused to treat him civilly, even for your children's sake. Well, I'm putting an end to that if I have to humiliate you to do it. Tonight is important to me and all I'm asking you to do is *grow up, Mother!*"

Bess stared at her daughter, feeling her cheeks flare, stunned into silence. From the countertop Lisa snagged a bag of egg noodles and stuffed them into Bess's hands. "Would you please add these to the water while I finish the stroganoff, then let's go into the living room and join the men as if we all know the meaning of gracious manners."

When they entered the living room it was clear the two men, seated on the sofa, had been doing their best at redeeming a sticky situation in which the tension was as obvious as the cheeseball meant to mitigate it. Lisa picked up the plate from the coffee table.

"Daddy? Mark? Cheeseball anyone?"

Bess stationed a kitchen chair clear across the room, where the living-room carpet met the vinyl kitchen floor, and sat down, full of indignation and the niggling bite of shame at being reprimanded by her own daughter. Mark and Michael each spread a cracker with cheese and ate it. Lisa carried the plate to her mother and stopped beside Bess's rigidly crossed knees.

"Mother?" she said sweetly.

"No, thank you," Bess snapped.

"I see you two have found something to drink," Lisa noted cheerfully. "Mark, would you like something?"

Mark said, "No, I'll wait."

"Mother, do you need a refill?"

Bess flicked a hand in reply.

Lisa took the only free seat, between the two men.

"Well . . ." she said brightly, clasping her crossed knees with twined hands and swinging her foot. She glanced between Michael and Bess. "I haven't seen either one of you since Christmas. What's new?"

They somehow managed to weather the next fifteen minutes. Bess, struggling to lose the ten extra pounds she consistently carried, refused the Ritz crackers with cheese but allowed herself to be socially manipulated by her daughter while trying to avoid Michael's hazel eyes. Once he managed to pin her with them while sinking his even, white teeth into a Ritz. You might at least *try,* he seemed to be admonishing, for Lisa's sake. She glanced away, wishing he'd bite into a rock and break off his damnable perfect incisors at the gums!

They sat down to eat at 7:15 in the chairs Lisa indicated, her mother and dad opposite each other so they could scarcely avoid exchanging glances across the candlelit table and their familiar old blue-and-white dishes.

Setting out the last of the four salad dishes, Lisa requested, "Will you open the Perrier, Mark, while I get the hot foods? Mom, Dad, would you prefer Perrier or wine?"

"Wine," they answered simultaneously.

The older couple sat obediently while the younger one got the bottled water, lime slices, wine, bread basket, noodles, stroganoff and a vegetable casserole, working together until everything was in place. Finally Lisa took her chair while Mark made the rounds, pouring.

When the glasses were filled and Mark, too, was seated, Lisa picked up her glass of Perrier and said, "Happy new year, everyone. And here's to a happier decade ahead."

The glasses touched in every combination but one. After a conspicuous pause, Michael and Bess made a final *tingg* with the rims of their old household stemware, a gift from some friend or family member many years ago. He nodded silently while she dropped her gaze and damned herself for disheveling her hair in an angry fit an hour ago, and for dropping ketchup on her jabot at noon, and for not stopping at home and putting on fresh makeup. She still hated him but that hate stemmed from a fiery pride, bruised at the moment. He had left her for someone ten years younger and ten pounds underweight, who undoubtedly never appeared at social functions with her hair on end, her forehead shiny and lunch on her jabot.

Lisa began passing the serving bowls and the room became filled with the sounds of spoons rapping on glass.

"Mmm . . . stroganoff," Michael noted, pleased, while he loaded his plate.

"Yup," Lisa replied. "Mom's recipe. And your favorite corn pudding, too." She passed him a casserole dish. "I learned to make it just like Mom. Be careful, it's hot." He set the dish beside his plate and took an immense helping. "I figured since you're living alone again you'd appreciate a good home-cooked meal. Mom, pass me the pepper, would you?"

Complying, Bess met Michael's eyes across the table, both of them grossly uncomfortable with Lisa's transparent machinations. It was the first point upon which they'd agreed since this unfortunate encounter began.

Michael tasted his food and said, "You've turned into a good little cook, honey."

"She sure has," put in Mark. "You'd be surprised how many girls today can't even boil water. When I found out she could cook I told my mother, I think I've found the girl of my dreams."

Three people at the table laughed. Bess, discomfited, hid behind a sip of rosé, recalling that one of the things Michael had criticized after she'd returned to college had been her neglecting the chores she'd always done. Cooking was one of them. She had argued, What about you, why can't you take over some of the household chores? But Michael had stubbornly refused to learn. It was one of many small wedges that had insidiously opened a chasm between them.

"How about you, Mark," Bess asked. "Do you cook?"

Lisa answered. "Does he ever! His specialty is steak soup. He takes a big old slab of sirloin and cubes it up and browns it and adds all these big hunks of potatoes and carrots, and what else do you put in it, honey?"

Bess shot a glance at her daugher. *Honey?*

"Garlic, and pearl barley to thicken it."

"Steak soup?" Bess repeated, turning her regard to Mark.

"Mm-hmm," Mark replied. "It's an old family favorite."

Bess stared at the young man who was shaped like Mount Rushmore. His neck was so thick his collar button wouldn't close. His hairdo was moussed on top and girlish on the bottom. And he thickened his steak soup with pearl barley?

Lisa grinned proudly at Mark. "He irons, too."

"Irons?" Michael repeated.

"My mother made me learn when I graduated from high school. She works, and she said she had no intention of doing my laundry till I was twenty-five. I like my sleeves and jeans with nice creases in them, so . . ." Mark raised his hands—his fork in one, a roll in the other—and let them drop. "I'm actually going to make some woman a pretty good housewife." He and Lisa exchanged a smile bearing some ulterior satisfaction, and Bess caught Michael adding it up before he swept his uncertain glance back to her.

Lisa said, "We might as well tell them, Mark." The two exchanged another smile before Lisa wiped her mouth, replaced her napkin on her lap and picked up her glass of sparkling water. "Mom, Dad . . ." With her eyes fixed radiantly on the young man across the table, Lisa announced, "We've invited you here tonight to tell you that Mark and I are going to get married."

In almost comical unison, Bess and Michael set down their forks. They gaped at their daughter. They gaped at each other.

Mark had stopped eating.

The tape player had stopped playing.

From an adjacent apartment the grumble of a TV could be heard through the wall.

"Well," Lisa said, "say something."

Michael and Bess remained speechless. Finally Michael cleared his throat, wiped his mouth on his napkin and said, "Well . . . my goodness."

"Daddy," Lisa chided. "Is that *all* you have to say?"

Michael forced an uncertain smile. "You caught me a little by surprise here, Lisa."

"Aren't you even going to congratulate us?"

"Well . . . yes . . . sure, of course, congratulations, both of you."

"Mother?" Lisa's eyes settled on Bess.

Bess emerged from her stupor. "Married?" she repeated disbelievingly. "But Lisa . . ." *We hardly know this young man. You've only known him for a year, or is it that long? We had no idea you were this serious about him.*

"Smile, Mother, and repeat after me, Congratulations, Lisa and Mark."

"Oh, dear . . ." Bess's gaze fluttered to her ex-husband, back to her daughter.

"Bess," Michael admonished quietly.

"Oh, I'm sorry. Of course, congratulations, Lisa . . . and Mark, but . . . but when did all this happen?"

"This weekend. We're really sold on each other, and we're tired of living apart, so we decided to commit."

"When is the big event?" Michael inquired.

"Soon," Lisa answered. "Very soon. Six weeks, as a matter of fact."

"Six weeks!" Bess yelped.

"I know that doesn't give us much time, but we've got it all figured out."

"What kind of wedding can you plan in six weeks? You can't even find a church in six weeks."

"We can if we're married on a Friday night."

"A Friday night . . . oh, Lisa."

"Now listen, both of you. Mark and I love each other and we want to get married but we want to do it the right way. We both want to have a real church wedding with all the trimmings, so here's what we've arranged. We can be married at St. Mary's on March second, and have the reception at the Riverwood Club. I've already checked and the club's not booked. Mark's aunt is a caterer and she's agreed to do the food. One of the guys I work with plays in a band that'll give us a pretty decent price. We're only going to have one attendant each—by the way, Randy has agreed to be one of them, and he even said he'll cut his hair. With only one attendant there'll be no trouble matching bridesmaids' dresses—Mark's sister can buy one anywhere; and as for the tuxes, we'll rent them. Flowers are no problem. We'll use silk ones and keep them modest. The cake we'll order from Wuollet's on Grand Avenue, and I'm pretty sure we can still find a photographer—having it on a Friday night, we're finding out, makes last-minute arrangements pretty easy. Well?"

Beleaguered, Bess felt her lips hanging open but seemed unable to close them. "What about your dress?"

A meaningful look passed between Lisa and Mark, this one without a smile.

"That's where I'll need your cooperation. I want to wear yours, Mom."

Bess looked dumbfounded. "Mine . . . but . . ."

"I'm pretty sure it'll fit."

"Oh, Lisa." Bess let her face show clear dismay.

"Oh, Lisa, what?"

Michael spoke. "What your mother is trying to say is that she isn't sure it's appropriate under the circumstances, isn't that right, Bess?"

"Because you're divorced?" Lisa looked from one parent to the other.

Michael gestured with his hands: that's how it is.

"I see nothing inappropriate about it at all. You were married once. You loved each other and you had me, and you're still my parents. Why shouldn't I wear the dress?"

"I leave that entirely to your mother." Michael glanced at Bess, who was still laboring under the shock of the news, sitting with her ringless left hand to her lips, her brown eyes very troubled.

"Mother, please. We can do this without your cooperation but we'd rather have it. From both of you." Lisa included Michael in her earnest plea. "And as long as I'm laying out our plans, I may as well tell you the rest. I want to walk down the aisle between you. I want my mom and my dad both there, one on either side of me, without all this animosity you've had for the past six years. I want to have you in the dressing room, Mom, when I'm getting ready; and afterwards, at my reception, I want to dance with you, Dad. But without tension, without . . . well, you know what I mean. It's the only wedding present I want from either one of you."

The room fell into an uneasy silence. Bess and Michael found it impossible to meet each other's eyes.

Finally Bess spoke. "Where will you live?"

"Mark's apartment is nicer than mine, so we'll live over there."

And the piano will need to be moved again. It took great control for Bess to refrain from voicing the thought. "I don't even know where he lives."

Mark said, "In Maplewood, near the hospital."

She studied Mark. He had a pleasant enough face but he looked terribly young. "I must apologize, Mark, I've been so taken off guard here. The truth is, I feel as though I barely know you. You do some kind of factory work, I think."

"Yes, I'm a machinist. But I've been with the same company for three years, and I make good money, and I have good benefits. Lisa and I won't have any problems that way."

"And you met Lisa—?"

"At a pool hall, actually. We were introduced by mutual friends."

At a pool hall. A machinist. A bodybuilder with a neck like a bridge abutment.

"Isn't this awfully sudden? You and Lisa have known each other— what?—less than a year. I mean, couldn't you wait, say a half a year or so and give yourselves time to get to know one another better, and to plan a wedding properly, and us a chance to meet your family?"

Mark's eyes sought Lisa's. His cheeks colored. His forearms rested on the table edge, so muscular they appeared unable to comfortably touch his sides.

"I'm afraid not, Mrs. Curran." Quietly, without challenge, he said, "You see, Lisa and I are going to have a baby."

An invisible mushroom cloud seemed to form over the table.

Michael covered his mouth with a hand and frowned. Bess drew a breath, held her mouth open and slowly closed it, staring at Mark, then at Lisa. Lisa sat quietly, relaxed.

"We're actually quite happy about it," Mark added, "and we hoped you'd be, too."

Bess dropped her forehead onto one hand, the opposite arm propped across her stomach. Her only daughter pregnant and planning a hasty wedding, and she should be happy?

"You're sure about it?" Michael was asking.

"I've already seen a doctor. I'm six weeks along. Actually I thought maybe you'd guess, because I'm drinking the Perrier instead of wine."

Bess lifted her head and encountered Michael, somber, his food forgotten. He met her dismayed eyes, straightened his shoulders and said, "Well . . ." clearing his throat. Obviously, he was at as great a loss as she.

Mark rose and went to stand behind Lisa's chair with his hands on her shoulders. "I think I should say something here, Mr. and Mrs. Curran. I love your daughter very much, and she loves me. We want to get married. We've both got jobs and a decent place to live. This baby could have a lot worse starts than that."

Bess came out of her stupor. "In this day and age, Lisa—"

Michael interrupted. "Bess, come on, not now."

"What do you mean, not now! We live in an enlightened age and—"

"I said, *not now,* Bess! The kids are doing the honorable thing, telling us their plans, asking for our support. I think we should give it to them."

She bit back her retort about birth control and sat simmering while Michael went on, remarkably cool-headed.

"You're sure this is what you want to do, Lisa?" he asked.

"Very sure. Mark and I had talked about getting married even before I got pregnant, and we had agreed that we'd both like to have a family when we were young, and that we wouldn't do like so many yuppies do, and both of us work until we got so independent that *things* began mattering more than having children. So none of this was nearly as much of a shock to us as it is to you. We're happy, Dad, honest we are, and I do love Mark very much."

Lisa sounded wholly convincing.

Michael looked up at Mark, still standing behind Lisa with his hands on her collar. "Have you told your parents yet?"

"Yes, last night."

Michael felt a shaft of disappointment at being last to learn but what could he expect when Mark's family was, apparently, still an intact, happy unit? "What did they say?"

"Well, they were a little surprised at first, naturally, but they know Lisa a lot better than you know me, so they got over it and we had a little celebration."

Lisa leaned forward and covered her mother's hand on the tabletop. "Mark has wonderful parents, Mom. They're anxious to meet you and Dad, and I promised them we'd introduce you all soon. Right away Mark's mother suggested a dinner party at their house. She said if you two are agreeable, I could set a date."

This isn't how it's supposed to be, Bess thought, battling tears, Michael and I practically strangers to our future son-in-law and total strangers to his family. Whatever happened to girls marrying the boy next door? Or the little brat who pulled her pigtails in the third grade? Or the one who did wheelies on his BMX bike in our driveway to impress her in junior high? Those lucky, simpler times were bygone with the era of transient executives and upward mobility, of rising divorce rates and single-parent homes.

Everyone was waiting for Bess to respond to the news but she wasn't ready yet, emotionally. She felt like breaking down and bawling, and had to swallow hard before she could speak at all.

"Your dad and I need to talk about a few things first. Would you give us a day or two to do that?"

"Sure." Lisa withdrew her hand and sat back.

"Would that be okay with you, Michael?" Bess asked him.

"Of course."

Bess deposited her napkin on the table and pushed her chair back. "Then I'll call you, or Dad will."

"Fine. But you aren't leaving yet, are you? I've got dessert."

"It's late. I've got to be at the store early tomorrow. I really should be going."

"But it's not even eight yet."

"I know, but . . ." Bess rose, dusting crumbs from her skirt, anxious to escape and examine her true feelings, to crumple and get angry if she so desired.

"Dad, will you stay and have dessert? I got a French silk pie from Baker's Square."

"I think I'll pass, too, honey. Maybe I can stop by tomorrow night and have some with you."

Michael rose, followed by Lisa, and they all stood awkwardly a moment, politely pretending this was not a scenario in which parents were running, distraught, from the announcement that their daughter was knocked up and planning a shotgun wedding, pretending this was merely a polite, everyday leave-taking.

"Well, I'll get your coats, then," Lisa said with a quavery smile.

"I will, sweetheart," Mark offered, and went to do so. In the crowded entry he politely held Bess's coat, then handed Michael's to him. There was another clumsy moment after Michael slipped his coat on, when the two men confronted each other, wondering what to say or do next. Michael offered his hand and Mark gripped it.

"We'll talk soon," Michael said.

"Thank you, sir."

Even more awkwardly, the young man faced Bess. "Good night, Mrs. Curran," Mark offered.

"Good night, Mark."

Unsure of himself, he hovered, and finally Bess raised her cheek to touch his gingerly. In the cramped space before the entry door Michael gave Lisa a hug, leaving only the mother and daughter to exchange some gesture of good night. Bess found herself unable, so Lisa made the move. Once Bess felt her daughter's arms around her, however, she clung, feeling her emotions billow, her tears come close to exposing themselves. Her precious firstborn, her Lisa, who had learned to drink from a straw before she was one, who had carried a black doll named Gertrude all over the neighborhood until she was five, and, dressed in feet pajamas, had clambered into bed between her mommy and daddy on Saturday mornings when she got old enough to climb out of her crib unaided.

Lisa, whom she and Michael had wanted so badly.

Lisa, the product of those optimistic times.

Lisa, who now carried their grandchild.

Bess clutched Lisa and whispered throatily, "I love you, Lee-lee," the pet name Michael had given her long ago, in a golden time when they'd all believed they'd live happily ever after.

"I love you, too, Mom."

"I just need a little time, please, darling."

"I know."

Michael stood waiting with the door open, touched by Bess's use of the familiar baby name.

Bess drew back, squeezing Lisa's arm. "Get lots of rest. I'll call you."

She passed Michael and headed down the hall, clasping her clutch purse under one arm, pulling on her gloves, her raspberry high heels clicking on the tiled floor. He closed the apartment door and followed, buttoning his coat, turning up its collar, watching her speed along with an air of efficiency, as if she were late for a business appointment.

At the far end of the hall she descended two stairs before her bravado dissolved. Abruptly she stopped, gripped the rail with one hand and listed over it, the other hand to her mouth, her back to him, crying.

He stopped on the step above her with his hands in his coat pockets, watching her shoulders shake. He felt melancholy himself, and witnessing her display of emotions amplified his own. Though she tried to stifle them, tiny mewling sounds escaped her throat. Reluctantly, he touched her shoulder blade. "Aw, Bess . . ."

Her words were muffled behind a gloved hand. "I'm sorry, Michael, I know I should be taking this better . . . but it's such a disappointment."

"Of course it is. For me, too." He returned his hand to his coat pocket.

She sniffed, snapped her purse open and found a tissue inside. Still with her back turned, mopping her face, she said, "I'm appalled at myself for breaking down in front of you this way."

"Oh, hell, Bess, I've seen you cry before."

She blew her nose. "When we were married, yes, but this is different."

With the tissue tucked away and her purse again beneath an arm she turned to face him, touching her lower eyelids with the fingertips of her expensive raspberry leather gloves. "Oh, God," she said, and emptied her lungs in a big gust. She drooped back with her hips against the black metal handrail and fixed her tired stare on the opposite railing.

For a while neither of them spoke, only stood in the murky hallway, helpless to stop their daughter's future from taking a downhill dive. Finally Bess said, "I can't pretend this is anything but terrible, our only daughter and a shotgun wedding."

"I know."

"Do you feel like you've failed again?" She looked up at him with red-rimmed eyes, shiny at the corners with a new batch of tears.

He drew a deep, tired breath and took stock of their surroundings. "I don't think I want to discuss it in the hallway of this apartment building. You want to go to a restaurant, have a cup of coffee or something?"

"Now?"

"Unless you really have to hurry home."

"No, that was just an excuse to escape. My first appointment isn't until ten in the morning."

"All right, then, how about The Ground Round on White Bear Avenue?"

"The Ground Round would be fine."

They turned and continued down the stairs, lagging now, slowed by distress. He opened the plate-glass door for her, experiencing a fleeting sense of déjà vu. How many times in the course of a courtship and marriage had he opened the door for her? There were times during their breakup when he'd angrily walked out before her and let the door close in her face. Tonight, faced with an emotional upheaval, it felt reassuring to perform the small courtesy again.

Outside, their breath hung milky in the cold air, and the snow, compressing beneath their feet, gave off a hard-candy crunch like chewing resounding within one's ear. At the foot of the sidewalk, where it gave onto the parking lot, she paused and half-turned as he caught up with her.

"I'll see you there," she said.

"I'll follow you."

Heading in opposite directions toward their cars, they started the long, rocky journey back toward amity.

chapter 2

THEY MET IN THE LOBBY of the restaurant and followed a glossy-haired, effeminate young man who said, "Right this way." Michael felt the same déjà vu as earlier, trailing Bess as he'd done countless times before, watching the sway of her coat, the movement of her arms as she took off her gloves, inhaling the faint drift of her perfume, the same rosy scent she'd worn for years.

The perfume was the only familiar thing about her. Everything else was new—the professionally streaked blonde hair nearly touching her shoulder, the expensive clothes, the self-assurance, the brittleness. These had all been acquired since their divorce.

They sat at a table beside a window, their faces tinted by an overhead fixture with a bowl-shaped orange globe and the pinkish glow of the phosphorescent lamps reflecting off the snow outside. The supper crowd had gone, and a hockey game was in progress on a TV above the bar somewhere around a corner. It murmured a background descant to the piped-in orchestra music falling from the ceiling.

Michael removed his coat and folded it over an empty chair while Bess left hers over her shoulders.

A teenage waitress with a frizzy hairdo came and asked if they'd like menus.

"No, thank you. Just coffee," Michael answered.

"Two?"

Michael deferred to Bess with a glance. "Yes, two," she answered, with a quick glance at the girl.

When they were alone again, Bess fixed her gaze on Michael's hands, wrapped palm-over-palm above a paper place mat. He had square, shapely hands, with neatly trimmed nails and long fingers. Bess had always loved his hands. They were, she'd said many times, the kind of hands you'd welcome on your dentist. Even in the dead of winter his skin never entirely paled. His wrists held a whisk of dark hair that trailed low and made his white cuffs appear whiter. There was an undeniable appeal about the sight of a man's clean hands foiled by white shirt cuffs and the darker edge of a suit sleeve. Oftentimes after the divorce, at odd, unexpected moments—in a restaurant, or a department store—Bess would find herself staring at the hands of some stranger and remembering Michael's. Then reality would return, and she would damn herself for becoming vulnerable to memory and loneliness.

In a restaurant, six years after their divorce, she drew her gaze from Michael's hands and lifted it to his face, daunted by the admission that she still found him handsome. He had perfect eyebrows above attractive hazel eyes, full lips and a head of gorgeous black hair. For the first time she noticed a few skeins of gray above his ears, discernible only under the direct light.

"Well . . ." she began, "this has been a night of surprises."

He chuckled quietly in reply.

"This is the last place I expected to end up when I told Lisa I'd come for supper," Bess told him.

"Me too."

"I don't think you're as shocked by all this as I am, though."

"I was shocked when you opened that door, I can tell you that."

"I wouldn't have been there if I'd known what Lisa had up her sleeve."

"Neither would I."

Silence for a moment, then, "Listen, Michael, I'm sorry about all that . . . well, Lisa's obvious attempt to revive something between us—our old dishes and the stroganoff and the corn pudding and the candlelight. She should have known better."

"It was damned uncomfortable, wasn't it?"

"Yes, it was. It still is."

"I know."

Their coffee came: something neutral to focus on instead of each other. When the waitress went away Bess asked, "Did you hear what Lisa said to me when we were alone in the kitchen?"

"No. What?"

"The gist of her message was, Grow up, Mother, you've been acting like a child for six years. I had no idea she was so angry about our antagonism, did you?"

"Only in retrospect, when she'd talk about Mark's family and how close and loving they are."

"She's talked to you about that?"

His eyes answered above his cup while he took a sip of coffee.

"When?" Bess demanded.

"I don't know—a couple different times."

"She never told me she talked to you so often."

"You put up barriers, Bess, that's why. You're putting up a new one right now. You should see the expression on your face."

"Well, it hurts to know she's talked to you about these things, and that Mark's family knows her better than we know Mark."

"Sure it hurts, but why wouldn't the two of them gravitate toward the family that stayed together? It's only natural."

"So what do you think of Mark?"

"I don't know him very well. I think I've only talked to him a couple of times before tonight."

"That's my point. How could this have happened when they've been dating such a short time that we've scarcely met the boy?"

"First of all, he's not a boy. You have to admit, he certainly faced the situation like a man. I was impressed with him tonight."

"You were?"

"Well, hell, he was there beside her, facing us head on instead of leaving her to break the news by herself. Doesn't that impress you?"

"I guess so."

"And by the sound of it, he comes from a good family."

Bess had decided something on the way to the restaurant. "I don't want to meet them."

"Aw, come on, Bess, that's silly—why not?"

"I didn't say I *won't* meet them. I will, if I have to, but I don't *want* to."

"Why?"

"Because it's hard to be with happy families. It makes our own failure that much harder to bear. They have what we wanted to have and thought we'd have. Only we don't, and after six years I still haven't gotten over the feeling of failure."

He considered awhile, then admitted, "Yeah, I know what you mean. And now for me, it's twice."

She sipped her coffee, curious and hesitant while meeting his eyes across the table.

"I can't believe I'm asking this, but what happened?"

"Between Darla and me?"

She nodded.

He stared at his cup, toying with its handle. "What happened was that it was the wrong combination from the beginning. We were each unhappy in the marriage we had, and we thought . . . well, hell . . . you know. We married each other on the rebound. We were lonely and, like you said, feeling like failures, and it seemed important to get another relationship going and to succeed at it, to sweeten the bitterness, I guess. What it really turned out to be was five years of coming to terms with the fact that we really never loved each other."

After some time Bess said, "That's what I'm afraid is going to happen to Lisa."

His steady hazel eyes held her brown ones while each of them pondered their daughter's future, longing for it to be happier than their own. From the bar around the corner came the whine of a blender.

When it stopped Michael said, "But the choice isn't ours to make for her."

"Maybe not the choice but isn't it our responsibility to make her consider all the ramifications?"

"Which are?"

"They're so young."

"They're older than we were when we got married, and they both seem to know what they want."

"That's what they told us but what else would you expect them to say, under the circumstances?"

He considered awhile then remarked thoughtfully, "I don't know, Bess, they seemed pretty sure of themselves. Mark made some points that had a lot of merit. If they had already talked about when they wanted to have babies, they were a jump ahead of about ninety percent of the couples who get married. And, frankly, I don't see anything wrong with their thinking. Like Mark said, they have good jobs, a home, the baby would have two willing parents—that's a pretty solid start for a kid. You have your kids when you're young, you have more patience, health, zest—and then when they're gone from home you're still young enough to enjoy your freedom."

"So you don't think we should try to talk them out of it?"

"No, I don't. What would the other options be? Abortion, adoption, or Lisa raising a baby alone. When the two of them love each other and want to get married? Wouldn't make much sense at all."

Bess sighed and crossed her forearms on the table. "I guess I'm just reacting like a mother, wanting a guarantee that her daughter will be happy."

His eyes told her what he thought about hoping for guarantees.

After a moment she said, "Just answer me this—when we got married, didn't you think it would be for life?"

"Of course, but you can't advise your child not to marry because you're afraid she'll make the same mistakes you did. That's not realistic. What you have to do is be truthful with her, but first of all you have to be truthful with yourself. If you—I guess I should be saying *we*—can admit what we did wrong and caution them to avoid the same pitfalls, maybe *that's* how we can redeem ourselves."

While Bess was pondering the point the waitress came and refilled their cups. When she went away, Bess took a sip of her steaming coffee and asked, "So, what do you think about the rest? About us walking down the aisle with her and her wearing my old wedding dress and everything?"

They sat silently awhile, their glances occasionally touching, then dropping as they thought about putting on a show of harmony before a couple hundred guests, some, undoubtedly, who'd been guests at their own wedding. The idea revolted them both.

"What do you think, Bess?"

Bess drew a deep breath and sighed. "It wasn't pleasant, getting chewed out by my own daughter. She said some things that really made me angry. I thought, How dare you preach to me, you young whelp!"

"And now?" Michael prodded.

"Well, we're talking, aren't we?"

The question gave them pause to consider the six years of silence and how it had affected their children.

"Do you think you could go through with it?"

"I don't know. . . ." Bess looked out the window at the cars in the parking lot, imagining herself walking down an aisle with Michael . . . again. Seeing her wedding gown in use . . . again. Sitting beside him at a wedding banquet . . . again. More quietly, she repeated, "I don't know."

"I guess I don't see that we have any other choice."

"So you want me to give her the go-ahead for this dinner at the Padgetts'?"

"I think we can fake our way through it, for her sake."

"All right, but first I want to talk to her, Michael, please allow me that. Just to make sure she isn't marrying him under duress, and to assure her that if she makes some other choice you and I will be supportive. May I do that first?"

"Of course. I think you should."

"And the dress, what should I say about the dress?"

This issue touched closer to home than all the others.

"What harm would it do if she wore it?"

"Oh, Michael—" Her eyes skittered away, suddenly self-conscious.

"You think just because you wore it and the marriage didn't last, the thing is jinxed? Or that somebody in the crowd might recognize it and think it's bad judgment? Be sensible, Bess. Who in that entire church besides you and me and possibly your mother would even know? I say let her wear it. It'll save me five hundred dollars."

"You always were putty in her hands."

"Yup. And I kind of enjoyed it."

"Need I mention that the piano will have to be moved again?"

"I'm aware of that."

"On their limited budget, it'll be a drain."

"I'll pay for it. I told her when I bought it I'd foot the bill for the piano-moving for the life of the instrument, or the life of me, whichever ended first."

"You told her that?" Bess sounded surprised.

"I told her not to tell you. You had such a bug up your ass about the piano anyway."

Bess almost laughed. They eyed each other, repressing grins.

"All right, let's back up, boy, to that remark you made about saving five hundred dollars. I take it from that that you're going to offer to pay for the wedding."

"I thought it was damned noble of the two of them not to ask for any help, but what kind of Scrooge would let his kid lay out money like that when he's earning a hundred thousand a year?"

Bess raised her eyebrows. "Oooo . . . you dropped that in there very neatly, just to make sure I'd know, huh? Well, it just so happens I'm doing quite well myself. Not a hundred grand a year but enough that I insist on paying half of everything."

"Okay, it's a deal." Michael extended his open hand above their coffee cups.

She shook it and they felt the shock of familiarity: the fit hadn't changed. Their expressions grew guilt-tinged and immediately they broke the contact.

"Well," Michael said, expanding his chest and touching his stomach. "I've had enough coffee to keep me awake until three."

"Me too."

"You ready to go then?" She nodded and they hitched their chairs back from the table. While they were donning their coats, he inquired, "How's your mother?"

"Indefatigable as always. Makes me breathless just listening to her."

He smiled and said, "Say hi to the old doll for me, will you? I've missed her."

"I'll do that. But if this wedding comes off, you'll undoubtedly be able to say hello to her yourself."

"And your sister, Joan. She still in Colorado?"

"Yes. Still married to that jerk and refusing to consider divorce because she's Catholic."

"Do you ever see her?"

"Not very often. We just don't have anything in common anymore. By the way, Michael . . ." She paused, her coat on. For the first time her eyes softened as she looked at him. "I was very sorry about your mother."

"And I was sorry about your dad."

They had each lost a parent since the divorce but she still had one left. He now had none.

"I appreciated your coming to the funeral. She always liked you," Michael told Bess. She had attended and had taken the children, of course, but had not spoken to Michael. Likewise, he had attended her father's funeral, but they had remained stubbornly aloof from one another, exchanging only the most perfunctory condolences. They had each liked the other's parents. It had been one of the connections hardest to sever.

"It was damned hard when Mother died," Michael admitted. "I kept wishing I had some brothers and sisters, but . . . aw, hell, what good are wishes? I'm forty-three years old. You'd think I'd have gotten used to it by now."

His whole life he'd hated being an only child and had talked about it often with her. She, too, had missed having a sister she was close to. There was a seven years' age difference between herself and Joan, which left them little in the way of childhood nostalgia regarding play, or friends, or even school. In her memory, Joan seemed more like a third parent than a sister. When she'd married and moved to Denver it had made little difference in Bess's life, and though they occasionally exchanged letters, these were merely duty missives.

It felt odd to both Bess and Michael, standing in the doorway of a restaurant, commiserating with each other about their loneliness and their loss of loved ones. They'd handled bitterness well, knew exactly how to handle it, but this empathy was an imposition. It made them eager to part.

"Well," Bess said. "It's late. I'd better be going."

She left the restaurant ahead of him and at the door felt the brief touch of his hand in the center of her back.

Memories.

In the parking lot at the point of parting, he said, "Chances are we aren't going to get through this whole wedding without having to contact each other. I've moved. . . ." He handed her a business card. "Here's my new address and phone number. If I'm not there, leave a message on the recorder, or call the office."

"All right." She put the card in her coat pocket.

They paused, groping for parting words while this present good-bye melded into a montage of a hundred others from their courting years— New Year's Eves, dances and parties, all followed by long passionate sessions on her doorstep. The flashback lasted only seconds before Michael spoke.

"You'll call Lisa, then?"

"Yes."

"Maybe I'll call her, too, just to let her know we're in agreement."

"All right . . . well, good night."

" 'Night, Bess."

Again came that momentary void, with neither of them moving, then they turned and went to their separate cars.

Bess started her engine and waited while it warmed. He had taught her that long ago: in Minnesota a car lasts longer if you let it warm in winter. That was in their struggling days, when they'd kept cars for five or six years. Now she could afford a new one every two years. Presently she drove a Buick Park Avenue. She waited to see what kind of car he was driving—her curiosity some odd possessive holdover she could not control. She heard the muffled growl of his engine as he passed behind her, and caught a glimpse of a silver roofline in the rearview mirror, turning only as he eased into a pool of illumination from a tall pole light to identify a Cadillac Seville. So it was true—he was doing well. She sat awhile attempting to sort out her feelings about that. Six years ago she would gladly have stuck pins in a voodoo doll of Michael Curran. Tonight, however, she felt an inexplicable touch of pride that once, long ago, she'd chosen a winner, and that now, faced with an impromptu wedding, there would be no need to stint their daughter.

Remembering Michael's card, she snapped on the overhead light and fished it from her pocket.

5011 Lake Avenue, White Bear Lake.

He'd moved to White Bear Lake? Back within ten miles of her? Why, when he'd lived clear over in a western suburb of Minneapolis for the past five years? Too close for comfort, she decided, stuffing the card back into her coat pocket and putting her car in gear.

Twenty minutes later she pulled into the horseshoe-shaped driveway of the house she and Michael had shared in Stillwater, Minnesota. It was a two-story Georgian on Third Avenue, high above the St. Croix River, a beautifully balanced home with a center door and bow windows on either side. The entry was guarded by four fluted round columns supporting a semicircular railed roof. From behind the sturdy railing a great fanlight overlooked the front yard from the second story. The place had a look of permanence, of security, the kind of house pictured in children's readers, Bess had told Michael when they'd found it, the kind of house where only a happy family would live.

They had fallen in love with it on sight; then they'd gone inside and had seen the magnificent view, clear across the St. Croix River to Wisconsin, beyond, and the lot itself, cresting the bluff, with its great, grand maple tree dead center out back, and the sparkling river lying below. They had seen the place and had gasped in mutual delight.

Nothing that had happened since had changed Bess's opinion of the house. She still loved it; enough to be making payments on Michael's legal half of it since Randy had turned eighteen.

She pulled into the double attached garage, lowered the automatic door and entered the service door to the kitchen. She'd redone the room since her business had flourished, had installed matte white Formica cabinets with butcher-block tops, a new vinyl floor in shades of seafoam blue and plush, cream-colored carpeting in the attached family room. The new furniture was a blend of smoky blues and apricots, inspired by the view of the river and the spectacular sunrises that unfolded beyond the tall east windows of the house.

Bess bypassed the U-shaped kitchen and dropped her coat onto a sofa facing the wall of glass. She switched on a shoulder-high floor lamp with a thick, twisted ceramic base and a cymbal-shaped shade and went to the window to draw up the blinds. The window treatments were lavish above, simple below: great billowing valances in a busy blue-and-apricot floral, paired with pleated horizontal blinds of pale apricot. The pattern of the curtains was repeated in two deep, chubby chairs; a coordinating splash of waves appeared on the long sofa with its baker's dozen of loose cushions.

Bess drew up the blinds and stood looking out the window at the winter view—the smooth yard, swathed in snow, sloping down to the sheer bluff covered by scrub brush; the granddaddy maple standing sentinel at the yard's edge; the great pale path of the wide river and, on the Wisconsin side, a half mile away, dots of window light glimmering here and there on the dark, high, wooded bank.

She thought of Michael . . . of Lisa . . . of Michael again . . . and of their unborn grandchild. The word had not been mentioned but it had been there in that restaurant between them as surely as their cups of steaming coffee.

My God, we're going to have a grandchild.

The thought thundered through her, brought her hand to her mouth and a lump to her throat. It was difficult to hate a man with whom you were sharing this milestone.

The lights across the river became starbursts and she realized there were tears in her eyes. Grandparenthood had been something that happened to others. It was symbolized by television commercials with sixty-five-year-old gray-haired couples with round, rosy cheeks baking cookies with youngsters; calling their grandchildren long distance; opening their doors at Christmastime and welcoming two generations with open arms.

This child would have none of that. He would have a handsome young grandfather, recently divorced, living in White Bear Lake, and a business-woman of a grandma too busy for cookie-making, living in Stillwater.

Many times since her divorce Bess had felt regret for the loss of tradition and an unbroken family line but never so powerfully as tonight, when facing the advent of the next generation. She herself had known grandparents, Molly and Ed LeClair, her mother's folks, who'd died when she was in high school. Recalling them brought a wistful expression to her face, for they'd lived right here in Stillwater through her younger years, in a house on North Hill to which she'd ridden her bike whenever she wanted, to raid Grandma Molly's cookie jar or her strawberry patch, or to watch Grandpa Ed paint his birdhouses in his little workshop out back. He'd known the tricks of attracting bluebirds—a house with a slanted roof, no perch and a removable bottom, he'd taught her—and always in the summer their backyard had bluebirds flitting above Grandma Molly's gardens and the open meadow beyond.

Times had changed. Lisa's child would have to visit his grandma in her interior design shop, and his grandfather only after he got old enough to drive a car.

Moreover, the bluebirds had disappeared from Stillwater.

Bess sighed and turned away from the window. She removed her suit and left it on the sofa. Dressed in her blouse, slip and nylons, she built a fire in the family-room fireplace and sat on the floor before it, staring, disconsolate. She wondered what Michael thought about becoming a grandfather, and where Randy was, and what kind of husband Mark

Padgett would make, and if Lisa truly loved him, and how she herself was going to survive this charade Lisa was asking of her. Already, after only one night with Michael, she was bluer than she'd been in months.

The telephone rang and Bess glanced at her watch. It was going on eleven. She picked up the receiver from a glass-top table between the two tub chairs.

"Hello?"

"Hi. Just checking in."

"Oh, hi, Keith." Lifting her face to the ceiling, she scooped her hair back from one temple.

"You got home late."

"Just a few minutes ago."

"So, how was the dinner with Lisa?"

Bess flopped onto one of the chairs with her head caught on the rounded back. "Not so good, I'm afraid."

"Why not?"

"Lisa invited me over for more than just dinner."

"What else?"

"Oh, Keith, I've been sitting here getting a little weepy."

"What is it?"

"Lisa is pregnant."

At the other end of the line Keith released a swoosh of breath.

"She wants to get married in six weeks."

"To the baby's father?"

"Yes, Mark Padgett."

"I remember you mentioning him."

"Mentioning him, that's all. Lord, she's known him less than a year."

"And what about him? Does he want to marry her, too?"

"He says he does. They want a full wedding with all the trimmings."

"Then I don't understand—what's the problem?"

That was one of the troubles with Keith. He often failed to understand her problems. She had been seeing him for three years, yet in all that time he'd never seemed sympathetic at the moments she needed him to. Particularly when it came to her children, he had an intolerant side that often irritated her. He had no children of his own, and sometimes that fact created a gulf between them that Bess wasn't sure could ever be bridged.

"The problem is that I'm her mother. I want her to marry for love, not for expediency."

"Doesn't she love him?"

"She says she does but how—"

"Does he love her?"

"Yes, but—"

"Then what are you so upset about?"

"It's not that cut-and-dried, Keith!"

"What? Are you upset about becoming a grandmother? That's a lot of bunk. I've never been able to understand people getting all freaked out about these things—reaching thirty, or forty, or becoming a grandparent. It's all pretty ridiculous to me. What really matters is keeping busy and healthy and feeling young inside."

"That's not what I'm upset about!"

"Well, what then?"

Reclining in the chair, with her chin on her chest, Bess picked up the soiled jabot and toyed with it.

"Michael was there."

Silence . . . then, "Michael?"

"Lisa set us up, she invited us both, then made an excuse to leave the apartment so we'd be forced to confront each other."

"And?"

"And it was hellish."

Silence again before Keith said, decidedly, "Bess, I want to come over."

"I don't think you should. It's nearly eleven."

"Bess, I don't like this."

"My seeing Michael? For heaven's sake, I haven't spoken a civil word to the man in six years."

"Maybe not, but it only took one night to upset you. I want to come over."

"Keith, please . . . it'll take you half an hour to get here, and I should go into the shop early in the morning to do some bookwork. Believe me, I'm not upset."

"You said you were crying."

"Not about Michael. About Lisa."

From his silence she anticipated his reaction. "You're pushing me away again, Bess. Why do you do that?"

"Please, Keith, not tonight. I'm tired and I expect Randy will be home soon."

"I wasn't asking to stay overnight." Though Bess and Keith were intimate, she had made it understood early in their relationship that as long as Randy lived with her, overnights at her house were out. Randy had been hurt enough by his dad's peccadillo. Though her son might very well guess she was having an affair with Keith, she was never going to verify it.

"Keith, could we just say good night now? I really have had a rough day."

Keith's silence was rife with exasperation before he released a sound resembling escaping steam. "Oh, all right," he said, "I won't *bother* you tonight. What I called for was to see if you wanted to go to dinner on Saturday night." His invitation was issued in an acid tone.

"Are you sure you still want me to?"

"Bess, I swear to God, sometimes I don't know why I keep hanging onto you."

Bess became contrite. "I'm sorry, Keith. Yes, of course, I'd love to go to dinner Saturday night. What time?"

"Seven."

"Shall I drive in?" Keith lived in St. Paul, thirty miles away. His favorite restaurants were over in that direction.

"Come to my place. I'll drive from here."

"All right, I'll see you then. And Keith?"

"What?"

"I really am sorry. I mean it."

Across the wire she could sense him expelling a breath and drooping his shoulders. "I know."

After Bess hung up she sat in her chair a long time, curled forward, elbows to knees, her toes overlapped, staring at the fire. What was she doing with Keith? Merely using him to slake her loneliness? He had walked into her store one day three years ago, when she'd been three years without a man, three years trying occasional dates that turned into sexual embarrassments, three years insisting that all men belonged at the bottom of the ocean. Then in walked Keith, a little on the plain side in the looks department, a little on the thin side in the hair department, but one of the best sales reps she'd ever encountered. Known in the trade as a rag man, he'd wheeled in a big 40 × 20-inch sample case and announced he was from Robert Allen Fabrics and that she had decorated the home of his best friends, Sylvia and Reed Gohrman; he liked the looks of her store; needed a Mother's Day gift for his mother; and if she would look through his samples while he perused her merchandise, they might each find something they liked. If not, he'd be gone and would never darken her door again.

Bess had burst out laughing. So had Keith. He'd bought a forty-dollar vase trimmed with glass roses, and when she was wrapping it she said, "Your mother will be pleased."

He replied, "My mother is never pleased with anything. She'll probably come in here and exchange it for those three frogs that are holding that glass ball."

"You don't like my frogs?"

He glanced at the three ugly brass frogs, covered with green patina, their forefeet raised above their heads, supporting what looked like a large, clear glass marble. He raised one eyebrow and quirked his mouth. "Now, that's a loaded question when you haven't told me what you think of my samples yet."

She had looked, and liked, and been assured by Keith that his company maintained careful quality control of its products, would not keep her on ice for three months then ship flawed fabric, provided *free* samples rather than the "book plan" (which required storeowners to sign a year's contract and agree to pay for all samples), offered delayed billing and followed up every order with a computerized acknowledgment and shipping date.

She was impressed, and Keith went away knowing so.

He'd called a week later and asked if she would like to go to Dudley Riggs's Brave New Workshop with him and his friends Sylvia and Reed Gohrman. She liked his style—live comedy for a first date, which she needed at the time, and mutual acquaintances as reassurance that she wouldn't have another wrestling match on her hands at the end of the evening.

He had been impeccably polite—no groping, no sexual innuendos, not even a good night kiss until their second date. They had seen each other for six months before their relationship became intimate. Immediately afterward, he'd asked her to marry him. For two and a half years she'd been saying no. For two and a half years he'd been growing more frustrated by her refusals. She had tried to explain that she wasn't willing to take that risk again, that running her business had become her primary source of fulfillment, that she still had her troubles with Randy and didn't want to impose them on a husband. The truth was, she simply didn't love him enough.

He was nice (an elementary word but true, when describing Keith) but when he walked into her shop she only smiled, never glowed. When he kissed her she only warmed, never heated. When they made love she wanted the light off, not on. And when it was over, she always wanted to go home to her own bed, alone.

And of course there was that thing about her children. He'd been married once, briefly, during his twenties but being childless he had remained marginally jealous of Lisa and Randy and slightly selfish in his approach to many conflicts. If Bess had to say no to him because of a previous commitment with Lisa, he became piqued. He held that her stand on his sleeping at her house was ridiculous, given that Randy was nineteen years old and no dummy.

Another thing—he coveted her house.

He had come into it the first time and stood before the sliding glass doors, looked out over the river valley and breathed, "Wow . . . I could put my recliner right here and never move."

First off, she hated recliners. Secondly, she felt a trickle of irritation at the very suggestion of him moving into *her* house. For the briefest moment she'd even had a flash of defense on Michael's behalf. After all, it was Michael who'd paid for the house and helped her furnish it. How dare this upstart stand there musing about usurping the spot that had always been Michael's favorite?

There were many facets of Keith that displeased her. So the question remained, why did she continue to see him?

The answer was plain: he had become a habit, and without him life would have been infinitely more lonely.

She sighed and went to the fireplace, screaked open the metal screen and turned the logs, watching sparks rise like inverted fireworks. She sat before it, with her arms crossed on her upraised knees. *Oh, Lisa, don't worsen the mistake you've already made. It's no fun watching a fire alone, wishing things had turned out differently.*

Her face grew hot, and the nylon slip covering her thighs seemed to catch the heat and draw it to her skin. She dropped her forehead onto her arms but remained where she was. The house was so silent and bleak. It had never been as satisfying after Michael left. It was home, and she would never give it up. But it was lonely.

Outside, most of the lights across the river had disappeared. She rose and wandered into the dining room—an extension of the family room—running her fingers over the backs of the unused chairs as she passed them, and on through an archway into the formal living room, which stretched across the entire east end of the house, from the river view at the rear to the street view at the front. At the rear corner, where two immense windows met, a grand piano stood in the shadows—black, gleaming, silent since Lisa had grown up and moved away. On it was a gallery of framed family pictures. On Thursdays the cleaning lady moved the pictures and dusted the piano. At Christmastime a huge arrangement of red balls and greenery ousted the five framed portraits. After New Year's the gallery came back and stayed until the following Christmas. It was the only thing the piano was used for anymore.

Bess sat down on the sleek ebony piano bench and slid across it in her nylon slip. She switched on the music lamp. Its rays shone down upon an empty music rest and a closed key cover. She touched the brass pedals, cold and smooth beneath her nylon-bound toes. She folded her hands and rested them between her thighs and wondered why she herself had given up playing. After Michael left she'd shunned the instrument just as she'd shunned him. Because he had liked piano music so much? How childish. Granted, her life had been busy, but there were moments such as these when the sound of the piano would have been comforting, when the feel of the keys would have soothed.

She rose and opened the bench, leafed through the sheet music until she found what she was looking for.

The cover of the bench clacked loudly as it closed. By contrast, the key cover made a soft, velvet thump as it opened. The music rustled, and her raspberry silk sleeves appeared in the thin band of light illuminating the keys.

The first notes shimmered through the shadowy room, harp-like and haunting as she found the familiar combinations and struck them.

"The Homecoming." Lisa's song. Her father's song. Why Bess had chosen it, she neither dissected nor cared. The compulsion had struck and she'd responded, rusty as she was on this instrument. As she played, the tentativeness left her fingers, the tension left her shoulders and soon she began to feel what a runner feels when he hits his stride, the immense sense of well-being at baring one's teeth to the wind and utilizing some capability that has lain dormant too long.

She was unaware of Randy's presence until she ended the song and he spoke out of the shadows.

"Sounding good, Mom."

"Oh!" She gasped and lifted an inch off the piano bench. "Randy, you scared the devil out of me! How long have you been there?"

He smiled, one shoulder propped against the dining-room doorway. "Not long." He sauntered into the room and sat down on the bench beside her, dressed in jeans and a brown leather jacket that looked as though a fleet of Sherman tanks had driven over it. His hair was black, like his father's, and dressed with something sheeny, spiked straight up and finger-long on top, slicked back over the ears and trailing in natural curls below his collar in back. Randy was an eye-catcher—her clerk at the store said he reminded her of a young Robert Urich—with a lopsided, dimpled grin; a way of letting his head dip forward when he approached a woman; a tiny gold loop in his left ear; perfect teeth and brown eyes with glistening black lashes that were longer than some men could grow their beards. He had adopted the rough-cut look of the unshaved young pop singer George Michael, and an unhurried manner.

Sitting beside his mother he played a low-register F, holding the key down until the note diminished into silence. Dropping the hand to his lap, he turned his head infinitesimally—all his motions were understated—and unleashed his lazy quarter-smile.

"Been a long time since you played."

"Mm-hmm."

"Why'd you stop?"

"Why'd you stop talking to your dad?"

"Why did you?"

"I was angry."

"So was I."

Bess paused. "I saw him tonight."

Randy looked away but allowed the grin to remain.

"How is the prick?"

"Randy, you're speaking of your father, and I won't allow that kind of gutter language."

"I've heard you call him worse."

"When?"

Randy worked his head and shoulders in irritation. "Mom, get off it. You hate his guts as much as I do and you haven't made any secret of it. So what's all this about? All of a sudden you're buttering up to him?"

"I'm not buttering up to him. I saw him, that's all. At Lisa's."

"Oh yeah, that's right. . . ." Randy dropped his chin and scratched his head. "I guess she told you, huh?"

"Yes, she did."

He looked at his mother. "So, you bummed out or what?"

"Yeah, I guess you could say that."

"I was, too, at first but now I've had a day to think about it and I think she'll be okay. Hell, she wants the kid and Mark's okay, you know? I mean, he really loves her, I think."

"How do you know so much?"

"I spend time over there." Randy ran his thumbnail into the vertical crack between two piano keys. "She cooks me dinner and we watch videos together, stuff like that. Mark's usually there."

Another surprise. "I didn't know that . . . that you spend time over there."

Randy gave up his preoccupation with the keys and returned his hand to his lap. "Lisa and I get along all right. She helps me get my head on straight."

"She said you've agreed to stand up for them."

Randy shrugged and let his eyes rove indolently his mother's way.

"And to cut your hair."

He made a chucking sound, sucking his cheek against his teeth. "There you go. You're gonna like that, huh, Ma?" His grin was back.

"The hair doesn't bother me as much as the beard."

He rubbed it. It was coarse and black and undoubtedly a turn-on for many nineteen-year-old girls. "Yeah, well, it's probably gonna go, too."

"You got some girl who's going to miss it?" she teased, reaching as if to pinch his cheek.

He reared back and brandished both hands, karate-fashion. "Don't touch the nap, woman!"

They poised as if on the brink of combat, then laughed together and hugged, with her smooth cheek against his prickly one, and the smell of his distressed leather jacket engulfing her. No matter the worries he caused her, moments like this were her recompense. Ah, there was something wonderful about an adult son. His occasional hugs made up for the loss of his father, and his presence in the house gave her someone to listen for, someone else moving about, a reason to keep the refrigerator stocked. It probably was time she booted him out of the nest but she hated losing him, no matter how seldom they exchanged banter such as this. When he left there would be only her in this big house alone, and it would be decision time.

He released her and she smiled affectionately. "You're an incorrigible flirt."

He covered his heart with both hands. "Mother, you wound me."

She let his high jinks pass and said, "About the wedding . . ."

He waited.

"Lisa asked your father and I to walk her down the aisle."

"Yeah, I know."

"And it looks as though there's going to be a dinner at Mark's parents' home to introduce the two families." When Randy made no reply, she asked, "Can you handle that?"

"Lisa and I have already got that covered."

Bess's lips formed a silent *oh*. These children of hers had a relationship that seemed to have left her several years behind.

Randy went on. "Don't worry, I won't embarrass the family." After a brief assessment of his mother's eyes, he asked, "Will you?"

"No. Your father and I had a talk after we left Lisa's. We both agreed to honor her wishes. The olive branch has been passed."

"Well then . . ." Randy raised his palms and let them slap his thighs. "I guess everybody's happy." He began to rise but Bess caught his arm.

"There's one more thing."

He waited, settling back into his customary nonchalance.

"I just thought you should know. Your father and Darla are getting a divorce."

"Yeah, Lisa told me. Big deal . . . old love 'em and leave 'em Curran." He gave a disgusted laugh and added, "I really don't give a shit, Mom."

"All right. I've told you." Bess flipped her hands in the air as if excusing him. "End of parental duty."

He rose from the bench and stood in the shadows nearby. "You better look out, Mom, the next thing you know he'll be knockin' on your door again. That's how guys like him work. . . . They gotta have a woman and by the sound of it he's fresh out of one. He made a fool of you once, and I sure as hell hope you don't let him do it again."

"Randy Curran, what kind of an airhead do you take me for?"

Randy swung away and headed for the dining-room archway. Halfway through it he used it to brake himself and turned back to her.

"Well, you were sitting there playing that song he always liked."

"It happens to be one I always liked, too!"

Leveling his gaze on her, he patted out a bongo rap on either side of the doorframe. "Yeah, sure, Mom," he remarked dryly, then gave himself a two-handed push-off and left.

chapter 3

T HE ST. CROIX RIVER valley lay under a cloak of winter haze the following day as Bess left home for her shop. It was a frigid, windless morning. To the south rose an inert white plume from the tall brick smokestack of the Northern States power plant, the immaculate cloud building in a thick, motionless bundle that hovered against a pewter sky. To the north, rime formed a jeweled frosting upon the lacy tie braces of the ancient black steel lift bridge that linked Stillwater with Houlton, Wisconsin, across the water.

Rivertown, Stillwater was called. It snuggled in a bowl of wooded hills, rivers, ravines and limestone bluffs that pressed it close against the placid waters of the river from which the town took its name. It had been a mecca for lumberjacks of the 1800s, who'd worked in the pineries to the north and spent their earnings in the town's fifty watering holes and six bordellos that had long since disappeared. Gone, too, were the great white pines that had once supported the town, yet Stillwater prized its heritage of former sawmills, loggers' rooming houses and Victorian mansions built by the wealthy lumber barons whose names still dotted the pages of the local telephone directory.

It appeared, at first glance, a city of rooftops—steeples, mansards, peaks and turrets of the whimsical structures built in another day—all of them dropping toward the small downtown that rimmed the west bank of the river.

Bess viewed it as she drove down Third Street hill past the old courthouse. A right on Olive and she was at Main: a half-mile strip of commerce stretching from the limestone caves of the old Joseph Wolf Brewery at the south to the limestone walls of the Staples Mill at the north. Main Street's buildings were of another century, ornate, red-brick, with arched second-story windows above, old-fashioned street lamps out front and narrow alleys out back. Steep cobbled sidewalks led down the side streets on their way to the riverfront one block beyond. In summer tourists walked its strand, enjoyed its rose gardens, sat in the shade of the town gazebo at Lowell Park or on the green lawns in the sun while licking ice-cream cones and watching the pleasure crafts nose through the blue water of the St. Croix.

They boarded the stern-wheeler *Andiamo* for scenic rides and sat on the decks of the riverside restaurants sipping tall pastel drinks, eating sandwiches and squinting at the rippling water from the shade of chic terry-cloth visors, musing how great it would be to live here.

That was summer.

This was winter.

Now, in droll January, the roses were gone. The pleasure crafts were dry-docked in the valley's five marinas. The *Andiamo* lay ice-bound at her slip. The popcorn wagon on Main Street was battened down and covered with a dome of snow. The ice sculptures in front of the Grand Garage had lost their fine edges and dwindled into crystal memories of the sailboats and angels they had been during the busy Christmas season.

Bess had her usual English muffin and coffee at the St. Croix Club restaurant beside the cheerful gas fire, took another coffee along in a Styrofoam cup and headed for her shop.

It was on Chestnut Street, two doors off Main, an ancient building with two blue window boxes, a blue door and a sign that said BLUE IRIS, HOMESCAPES, with a likeness of the flower underscoring the words.

Inside it was gloomy but smelled of the potpourri and scented candles she sold. The building was ninety-three years old, scarcely wider than a hospital corridor but deep. The front door faced north, creating a cool, shady aspect in summer. This morning, however, cold drafts filtered in.

The walls of the store were papered in shantung-textured cream to match the painted woodwork, and beneath the cove molding ran a border strip of blue irises the same shade as the carpeting. Blue irises also appeared on the signature art that hung behind the desk on the stair wall, and on the paper bags in which customers' purchases were wrapped.

Grandma Molly had grown blue irises in her yard on North Hill. Even as a child Bess had dreamed of owning her own business and way back then had known what it would be called.

Bess picked her way through the maze of lamps, art prints, easels, brass picture frames, small furniture and dried botanicals to the small checkout counter set midway down the left wall against an ancient, steep stairway that climbed to the tiniest loft imaginable. It was pressed close against the ceiling—so close the top of Bess's hair brushed the embossed tin overhead. In the town's heyday some accountant had spent his days up there, penning numbers in ledgers and taking care of cash receipts. It often occurred to Bess that the man must have been either a midget or a hunchback.

She checked at the cash register and found several messages left by Heather the day before, taking them and her coffee up the creaky steps. Upstairs it was so crowded she was forced to balance on one foot while leaning over the clutter of swatch and wallpaper books to switch on a floor lamp, then the fluorescent one on her desk. As an office, the loft was inadequate by anyone's standards, yet every time she considered giving up the store to get a bigger one, it was the loft that kept her here. Maybe it was mornings like this, when her cramped, high work space collected the rising heat and reflected the light off the cream-painted ceiling, and kept the aroma of her coffee drifting close about her head. Or maybe it was the view of the front window and door over her railing. Or maybe it was simply that the loft had character and history, and both appealed to Bess. The thought of a modern office in a sterile cubicle slightly repulsed her.

It was Bess's habit to come early. The hours between 7 and 10 A.M., when the phones were quiet and no customers around, were the most productive of her day. Once 10 A.M. hit and the front door was unlocked, power paperwork was out.

She uncapped her coffee, read Heather's messages, did paperwork, filing, made phone calls and got some design work done before Heather arrived at 9:30 and called upstairs, " 'Morning, Bess!"

" 'Morning, Heather! How are you?"

"Cold." Bess heard the basement door open and close as Heather hung up her coat. "How was your supper at Lisa's?"

Bess paused with the page of a furniture catalog half-turned. Heather knew enough about her history with Michael that Bess wasn't going to open that can of worms yet.

"Fine," she answered. "She's turning out to be a very decent cook."

Heather's head appeared beyond the railing and her footsteps made the loft stairs creak. She stopped near the top of the stairs—a forty-five-year-old woman with strawberry blonde broom-cut hair glazed into fashionable disarray, stylish tortoiseshell glasses and sculptured garnet fingernails bearing tiny rhinestone nail ornaments that flashed as her hand rested on the railing. She had wide cheekbones, a pretty mouth and dressed with insouciant flair, creating a positive first impression when customers walked into the store.

Bess employed three part-time clerks but Heather was her favorite as well as her most valued.

"You have a ten o'clock appointment, you know."

"Yes, I know." Bess checked her watch and began gathering her materials for the house call.

"And a twelve-thirty and a three."

"I know, I know."

"Orders for today?"

Bess handed Heather various notes, gave her instructions about ordering wallpaper and checking on incoming freight, and left the store confident that things would run smoothly while she was gone.

It was a hectic day, as most were. Three house calls left her little time for lunch. She grabbed a tuna-salad sandwich at a sub shop between house calls and ate it in the car. She drove from Stillwater to Hudson, Wisconsin, to North St. Paul and got back to the Blue Iris just as Heather was locking up for the night.

"You had nine calls," Heather said.

"Nine!"

"Four of them were important."

Bess flopped onto a wicker settee, exhausted.

"Tell me."

"Hirschfields, Sybil Archer, Warner Wallpaper and Lisa."

"What did Sybil Archer want?"

"Her wallpaper."

Bess groaned. Sybil Archer was the wife of a 3M executive who believed Bess had a wallpaper press in her back room and could produce the stuff at the snap of a finger.

"What did Lisa want?"

"She didn't say. Just said you should call her back."

"Thanks, Heather."

"Well, I'm off to the bank before it closes."

"How'd we do today?"

"Terrible. A grand total of eight customers."

Bess made a face. The bulk of her business came from her design work; she kept the store chiefly as a consideration for her design customers. "Did any of them buy anything?"

"A Cobblestone Way calendar, a few greeting cards and a couple of tea towels."

"Hmph. Thank God for summer in a tourist town, huh?"

"Well, I'll see you tomorrow, okay?"

"Thanks, Heather, and good night."

When Heather was gone, Bess pushed herself up, left her coat on the settee and headed for the loft. As usual, she hadn't spent nearly as much time as she had hoped on designing. It took an average of ten hours to design most jobs, and she'd barely put in three today.

Upstairs, she kicked off her high heels and scraped back her hair as she dropped to her desk chair, opened a turkey-and-sprout sandwich she'd picked up at Cub supermarket and popped the top on her Diet Pepsi.

Slowing down for the first time since morning, she realized how tired she was. She took a bite of her sandwich and stared at a stack of replacement pages that had been waiting well over two weeks to be inserted in one of the furniture catalogs.

While she was still staring the phone rang.

"Good evening, Blue Iris."

"Mrs. Curran?"

"Yes?"

"This is Hildy Padgett . . . Mark's mother?" A friendly voice, neither cultured nor crude.

"Oh, yes, hello, Mrs. Padgett. It's so nice to hear from you."

"I understand that Mark and Lisa had supper with you last night and broke the news."

"Yes, they did."

"Well, it seems those two are getting set to make us some kind of shirttail relatives or something."

Bess set down her sandwich. "Yes, it certainly does."

"I want you to know right up front that Jake and I couldn't be happier. We think the sun rises and sets in your daughter. From the first time Mark brought her home we said to each other, Now there's the kind of girl we'd like for a daughter-in-law. When they told us they were getting married we were just delighted."

"Why, thank you. I know Lisa feels the same way about both of you."

"Of course, we were a little surprised about the baby coming but both Jake and I sat down and had a long talk with Mark, just to make sure that he was doing what he wanted to do, and we came away assured that he had every intention of marrying Lisa anyway, and that they both wanted the baby and are quite excited about it."

"Yes, they told us the same thing."

"Well we think it's just wonderful. Both of those kids really seem to have their heads on straight."

Once again Bess felt a twinge of regret, perhaps even jealousy, because she knew Mark and Lisa as a couple so much less intimately than this woman seemed to.

"I have to be honest with you, Mrs. Padgett, I haven't met Mark many times but last night at supper he certainly seemed straightforward and sincere when he told us this marriage is what he wants, what they both want."

"Well, we've given them our blessings and now the two of them want very much for all of us to meet, so I suggested a dinner party here at our house and I was hoping we could get together on Saturday night."

"Saturday night . . ." Her date with Keith; but how could she put one ordinary date before this? "That sounds fine."

"Say seven o'clock?"

"Fine. May I bring something?"

"Lisa's brother, is all. All of our kids will be here, too—we've got five of them—so you'll get a chance to meet them all."

"It's very kind of you to go to all this trouble."

"Kind?" Hildy Padgett laughed. "I'm so excited I've been getting up nights and making lists!"

Bess smiled. The woman sounded so likable and breezy.

"Besides," Hildy went on, "Lisa volunteered to come over and help me. She's going to make the dessert, so all you have to do is be here at seven and we'll get those kids off to a proper start."

When she'd hung up, Bess sat motionless in her swivel chair, melancholy in spite of the plans she'd just made. Outside, dusk had fallen, and in the window downstairs the brass lamps were lit, throwing fern-shadow through a plant that hung above the display. In the loft only the desk lamp shone, spreading a wedge of yellow over her work and her half-finished sandwich on its square of white, waxy paper. Lisa was twenty-one, and pregnant, and getting married. Why did it sadden her so? Why did she find herself longing for the days when the children were small?

Motherlove, she supposed. That mysterious force that could strike at unexpected moments and make nostalgia blossom and fill the heart. She longed, suddenly, to be with Lisa, to touch her, hold her.

Ignoring the work that needed attention, she leaned forward and dialed Lisa's number.

"Hello?"

"Hi, honey, it's Mom."

"Oh, hi, Mom. Something wrong? You sound a little down."

"Oh, just a little nostalgic, that's all. I thought if you weren't busy I might come over for a while and we could talk."

Thirty minutes later Bess had turned her back on her best design time and was entering the setting of last night's confrontation with Michael. When Lisa opened the door Bess hugged her more tightly and a little longer than usual.

"Mom, what's wrong?"

"I guess I'm just being a typical mother, is all. I was sitting there at the store, getting all misty-eyed, remembering when you were little."

Lisa gave a foxy grin. "I was pretty fantastic, wasn't I?"

Lisa had the gift for creating effortless laughter but as Bess released the sound she was wiping a tear from the corner of one eye.

"Oh, Mom . . ." Lisa curved an arm around her mother and led her toward the living room. "I'm getting married, not cloistered."

"I know. I just wasn't prepared for it."

"Dad wasn't either." They sat on the davenport and Lisa put her feet up. "So how did it go when the two of you left here last night? I figured you went off to talk about everything in private."

"We went out and had a cup of coffee and actually managed to be civil to one another for the better part of an hour."

"So what did you decide about Mark and me?"

Bess's expression became wistful. "That you're my only daughter, and you're only getting married once . . . at least I hope it'll only be once."

"That's why you really came over, isn't it, to make sure I'm doing the right thing."

"Your dad and I just wanted you to know that if for any reason you decide marriage to Mark isn't what you want, we'll stand behind you."

It was Lisa's turn to display a wistful expression. "Oh, Mom, I love him so much. When I'm with him I'm more than I was. He makes me want to be better than the me I was before, and so I am. It's as if . . ." Sitting cross-legged, Lisa gazed at the ceiling in her intense search for the proper words, then back at her mother, gesturing with both hands as if she were singing a heartfelt ballad. ". . . As if when we're together all the negative stuff disappears. I see people around me in a more charitable light; I don't criticize, I don't complain. And the funny thing is, the same thing happens to Mark.

"We've talked about it a lot . . . about that night when we met. When he walked into that pool hall and we looked at each other, we suddenly didn't want to be in a pool hall anymore but someplace pure, a woods maybe, or listening to an orchestra someplace. An orchestra! Cripes, Mom!" Lisa threw up her hands. "I like Paula Abdul but there I was, with all my senses open and new avenues looking inviting.

"Something happened . . . I can't explain it. We just . . ." Silence awhile, then Lisa continued, softly. "We just felt different. There we were, living that crazy bar scene, hanging around in noisy, smoky places and swaggering and showing off and being loud and obnoxious at times, and then our two crowds bumped into one another, and he smiled at me and said, 'Hi, I'm Mark,' and from that night on we never felt like we had to be phony with each other. We can admit our weaknesses to one another and that seems to make us stronger. Isn't it weird?"

On her end of the sofa, Bess sat very still, listening to the most stirring description of love she'd ever heard.

"You know what he said to me one day?" Lisa looked radiant as she continued. "He said, 'You're better than any creed I ever learned.' He said it was a line from a poem he read once. I thought about it awhile—actually I've thought about it a lot since he said it—and I realize that's what we are to each other. We're each other's creeds, and *not* to marry someone you feel that way about would be the greatest shame of all."

"Oh, Lisa," Bess whispered, and moved to take Lisa in her arms, this very young woman who had found a love to believe in the way every woman hopes she will one day. It was at once shattering and gratifying to learn that Lisa had grown up in a short span of time while she, Bess, had not been as attentive as she should have been. How humbling it was to realize that Lisa had learned something at age twenty-one that Bess herself had not at age forty. Lisa and Mark had discovered how to communicate, they had found the proper balance between praising each other's virtues and overlooking each other's shortcomings, which translated not only into love but into respect, as well. It was something Bess and Michael had never quite managed.

"Lisa, darling, if you feel that way about him I'm so happy for you."

"Yes, be happy. Because I am." While they were still hugging, Lisa added, "There's just one more thing I want to say." She set Bess away from herself and told her point-blank, "I know you're probably wondering how an educated young woman of the eighties could possibly be so stupid that she got pregnant when there are at least a dozen ways to prevent it. Remember when we went skiing up at Lutsen before Christmas? Well, I forgot my birth control pills that weekend, and we realized we might very well be making a choice if we made love. So we talked about it beforehand. What if we risked it and I got pregnant? He told me then that he wanted to marry me, and that if I got pregnant that weekend, it was fine with him, and I agreed. So, you see, Mom, we're not just handing you a pile of gas when we say we're happy about the baby. What you're worrying about . . . well, you just don't have to. Mark and I are going to be great . . . you'll see."

Bess tenderly touched her daughter's face. "Where have I been while you did all this growing up?"

"You were there."

"Exactly . . . there. Running my business. But I suddenly feel as if I spent too much time at it and not enough with you during the past few years. If I had, I'd have seen this relationship between you and Mark blossoming. I wouldn't have been caught so off guard last night."

"Mom, you handled it okay, believe me."

"No, you handled it okay, and so did Mark. Your dad was totally impressed by him."

"I know. I talked to him today. So did Mark's mother. She said she was going to call you, too. Did she?"

"Yes, she did. She's delightful."

"I knew you'd think so. So everything is set for Saturday night? No objections?"

"Now that I know how you feel, none."

"Whew! That's a relief. So Dad said you two talked about the rest—the dress, and all of us walking down the aisle together, and you'll do it, huh?"

"Yes, we'll do it."

"And I can wear the dress?"

"If it'll fit you, yes."

"Hey, Mom? I know what you're thinking about the dress, that it might put some kind of hex on my wedding or something, but that's really a lot of crap. It isn't dresses that make weddings work, it's people, okay?"

"Okay."

"I just like the dress, that's all. I used to play in it when you weren't home. You never knew that, did you?"

"No, I didn't."

"Well, that's what you get for putting something so irresistible off limits. Someday I'll tell you some of the other stuff that Randy and I used to do when you guys were gone."

Bess's grin became suspicious. "Like what?"

"Remember that sex manual you used to keep hidden between the spare blankets in the linen closet in your bathroom? The one with all the drawings of all the positions? You didn't think we knew it was there, did you?"

"Why, you little devils!"

"Yup, that's us. And remember that vase that disappeared and you could never find it again? That white one with the pink hearts around the top? We broke it one night when we were playing monster in the dark. We used to turn off all the lights and one of us would hide and the other one would walk like Frankenstein, with his arms out, roaring, and one night—

chink!—over went your vase. We knew you'd be royally pissed if we told you, so we hid the pieces in a tomato-juice can we found in the garbage and pretended we didn't know anything about it. But I just knew, Mom, that one day you'd have more vases than the Monticello Flea Market, and sure enough, look at you now. You probably have twenty of them in your store as we speak."

How could Bess resist laughing at such flippancy?

"And all the while I was sending you to catechism classes and teaching you to be good, honest children."

"Well, we were, basically. Look at me today. I'm going to marry the boy I got into trouble and give his baby a name."

When Bess finished laughing, she said, "It's getting late. I should go. It's been a long day."

Rising from the sofa, Lisa said, "You work too hard, Mom. You should take more time to yourself."

"I take all I want."

"Oh, sure you do. But I have a feeling that when Mark and I have this baby we're going to lure you away from your little loft in the sky more often. Just feature that, would y'—my mom a grandma. What do you think about that?"

"I think my hair needs bleaching. The roots are beginning to show."

"You'll get used to the idea. What does Dad think about being a grandpa?"

"We didn't discuss it."

"Oo . . . I hear a cool note."

"You bet you do. Now that the emotional part is over I can tell you that was an underhanded trick you pulled last night."

"It worked though, didn't it?"

"We've drawn a truce for the duration of the wedding festivities, nothing more."

"Oh yeah? Randy said you were playing 'Homecoming' when he got home last night."

"Good heavens, have I no privacy at all?" The two of them moved to the apartment door.

"Think about it, Mom . . . Dad and you together again, coming to visit us and your grandchild. That'd be wild, huh? The two of you wouldn't have to fight about taking care of the housework and kids anymore, because we're all grown up and you have a housekeeper. And you're all done with college so he couldn't be barking at you about that. And he's got his own cabin now so you wouldn't have to stay behind when he goes hunting. And since he's all washed up with Darla—"

"Lisa, you're hallucinating." Bess drew on her coat with an air of finality.

"Yeah, well, think about it, I said." Lisa braced one shoulder against the wall.

"I *will not!* I'll treat him civilly but that's the extent of it. Besides, you're forgetting about Keith."

"Old bald-headed Keith the rag man? Don't make me laugh, Mom. You've been dating him for three years and Randy says you don't even spend nights with him. Take it from me, Bess, the rag man's not for you."

"I don't know what's come over you tonight, Lisa, but you're being intentionally outrageous." Bess opened the apartment door.

"I'm in love. I want the rest of the world to be, too." Lisa popped a kiss on her mother's mouth. "Hey, see you Saturday night, huh? You know how to get there?"

"Yes, Hildy gave me directions."

"Great. And don't forget my little brother."

Heading for her car, Bess had totally lost her melancholy mood of earlier. Lisa truly had a gift for making people laugh at their own foibles. Not that she, Bess, had any intention of reviving anything between herself and Michael. As she'd said, there was Keith to consider. The thought of Keith brought a frown: he wasn't going to be pleased about her breaking their date Saturday night.

She called him from the phone in her bedroom the moment she got her suit and hosiery off.

He answered after the fifth ring.

"Hello?"

"Keith, it's Bess. Did I get you away from something?"

"Just got out of the shower."

There wasn't and never had been any sexual innuendo following convenient lead-ins such as this. It was one of the things Bess missed in their relationship, yet she never felt compelled to start it and since he didn't, humorous and intimate repartee was missing.

"I can call back later."

"No, no it's fine. What's up?"

"Keith, I'm really sorry but I'm going to have to cancel our dinner date Saturday night."

In the pause that followed she imagined he'd stopped drying himself. "Why?"

"The Padgetts are having a dinner at their house so both sides of the family can meet."

"Didn't anyone ask you if you were busy?"

"Everyone else was able to make it. I hardly thought I could ask them to delay it for me alone, and given how short a time there is before the wedding, I thought it best if the two families met right away."

"I suppose your ex will be there?"

Bess massaged her forehead. "Oh, Keith."

"Well, won't he?"

"Yes, he will."

"Oh, fine, just fine!"

"Keith, for heaven's sake, it's our daughter's wedding. I can't very well avoid him."

"No, of course you can't!" Keith snapped. "Well, when you have time for me, Bess, give me a call."

"Keith, wait . . ."

"No . . . no . . ." he said sarcastically, "don't worry about me. Just go ahead and do what you have to do with Michael. I understand."

She detested this brittleness he adopted whenever he became jealous of her time with the children.

"Keith, I don't want you to hang up mad at me."

"I've got to go, Bess. I'm getting the carpet wet."

"All right but call me soon."

"Sure," he replied brusquely.

When she'd hung up, Bess rubbed her eyes. Sometimes Keith could be so insufferably childish. Did he always have to see these conflicts as a choice between her children and him? Once again she wondered why she continued seeing him. It would probably be best for both of them, she thought, if she broke it off entirely.

She dropped her arms and thought wearily of the design work she'd brought home and left downstairs on the dining-room table. She hated designing when she felt this way. Somehow it seemed her moroseness might creep into the design itself.

But she had three jobs waiting after this one, and customers eager to get her phone call setting up their presentations, and more house calls on her calendar in the days ahead.

With a sigh she rose from her desk and went downstairs to put in two more hours.

chapter 4

ON SATURDAY NIGHT Bess took pains with her hair. It was nearly shoulder-length, its shades of blonde as varied as an October prairie. She curled it only enough to give it lift, and pouffed it out behind her ears, where it billowed like the sleeves of a choir gown caught in the wind. Her makeup was subtle but applied with extreme care—twelve steps from concealer to mascara. The finished results enlarged her brown eyes and plumped her lips. She stared at her reflection in the mirror, sober, smiling, then sober once again.

Unquestionably she wanted to impress Michael tonight: there was an element of pride involved. Toward the end of their marriage, when she'd been caught up in the rigors of studying for her degree and maintaining a domicile and a family of four, he had said during one of their fights, "Look at you, you don't even take care of yourself anymore. All you ever wear is blue jeans and sweatshirts, and your hair hangs in strings. You didn't look like that when I married you!"

How his accusation had stung. She'd been burning the candle at both ends trying to achieve something for herself, but he'd failed to recognize that her output of time meant some cuts were necessary. So her hair had gone uncurled, her nails unpainted and she had forsaken makeup. Blue jeans and a sweatshirt were the easiest to launder, the quickest to grab, so they became her customary uniform. At the end of a six-hour school day she'd come home to face studying and housework while he'd grow obstinate about helping with the latter. He'd been raised in a traditional household where women's work was exactly that, where men didn't peel potatoes or wash laundry or run a vacuum cleaner. When she'd suggested that he try these, he'd suggested she take a few less credits per quarter and resume the duties she'd agreed to do when they got married.

His narrow-mindedness had enraged her.

Her continued lack of attention to herself and to the house eventually drove him out of it, and he found a woman with beautiful curled tresses, who wore high heels and Pierre Cardin suits to work every day and painted her nails and brought him coffee and dialed his clients for him.

Bess had seen Darla occasionally, most often at the company Christmas parties, where she wore sequined dresses and dyed-to-match satin pumps and lipstick that sparkled nearly as much as her dangly earrings. Had Michael simply left Bess, she might have acceded to maintaining a speaking relationship with him; but he'd left her for another woman, and a stunning beauty at that. The realization had galled Bess ever since.

After she'd gotten her degree, one of the first things she had done was lay out three hundred dollars for a beauty make-over. Under the tutelage of a professional she'd learned what colors suited her best, what clothing silhouettes most flattered her shape, what shades of makeup to wear and how to apply them. She'd even learned what size and shape of handbag and shoes suited her build and what style of earring most flattered her facial features. She'd had her hair color changed from muskrat brown to tawny blonde, its style lightly permed into the bon vivant wind-fluffed look, which she still wore. She'd grown her fingernails and kept them meticulously polished in a hue that matched her lipstick. And over a span of years she'd acquired a new wardrobe to which she added judiciously only those pieces which perfectly matched the color and style guidelines she'd learned from the professionals.

When Michael Curran got a load of her tonight there'd be no ketchup on her jabot, no shine to her makeup and no hair out of place.

She chose a red dinner suit with a straight skirt and an asymmetrical jacket sporting one black triangular-shaped lapel rising from a single black waist-button. With it she wore oversized gold door-knocker earrings that drew attention to her winged hairstyle and her rather dramatic jawline.

When the suit jacket was buttoned she pressed both hands to her abdomen and turned to view herself in profile. She needed to lose ten pounds—it was a constant struggle. But since her mid-thirties the pounds seemed to go on so much faster than they came off. She'd shaved off the four extra pounds she'd gained over the holidays but she had merely to *look* at a dessert to put it back on.

Ah, well—she was satisfied with one full hour's efforts at grooming, anyway. She switched out her bedroom light and went down two flights to Randy's room. When he was sixteen he'd chosen to hole up in an unfinished room on the walkout level because it was twice as large as the upstairs bedrooms and two walls were backfilled with yard so the neighbors wouldn't complain about his drums.

They filled one corner, his prized set of Pearls—twelve pieces of gleaming stainless steel, including his pride and joy, three graduated sizes of rototoms, whose pitch could be changed with a simple twist of the revolving heads. The two concrete-block walls behind the drums were painted black. Fanned on one were posters of his idols, Bon Jovi, Motley Crüe and Cinderella. From an overhead strip a half-dozen canister lights picked out the drums. One of the remaining walls was white, the other covered with cork that gave the room the perennial smell of charcoal. The corkboard was hung with pictures of old girlfriends, beer ads, band schedules and prom garters. Since the room had no closet, Randy's clothes hung on a piece of steel pipe suspended from the ceiling by two chains. The floor was littered with several years' issues of *Car & Driver* magazine, dozens of compact discs, empty fast-food wrappings, shoes and overdue video rentals.

There was a compact disc player, a television, a VCR, a microphone and a fairly sophisticated taping setup. Among all this, the water bed—sporting disheveled leopard sheets—seemed almost incidental.

When Bess came to the door Paula Abdul was blasting "Opposites Attract" from the CD player, and Randy was standing before his dresser adjusting the knot in a skinny gray leather tie. He was dressed in baggy, pleated trousers, a silvery-gray double-breasted sport coat and a plaid shirt in muted shades of purple, gray and white. He'd put something on his hair to make it glossy and though he'd had it cut, as promised, it still hung to his collar in natural ringlets.

Coming upon him this way, while he was engaged in tying his tie, looking spiffy for once, brought a catch to Bess's heart. He was so good-looking, and bright, and charming when he wanted to be, but the path of resistance he'd chosen to take had put so many obstacles between them. Today, however, entering his room Bess felt a shaft of uncomplicated love. He was her son, and he was getting to look more like his father every year, and in spite of her animosity toward Michael, he was undeniably a handsome man. The aroma of masculine toiletries drifted to Bess as she entered Randy's room. She had missed such smells since Michael's departure. For that brief moment it was almost like having a husband and a happy marriage back.

Without glancing his mother's way, Randy said to the mirror, "I promised Lisa I'd have it cut, and I did but this is as short as I go."

She went to the CD player, glanced at the flashing control panel and shouted, "How do I turn this thing down?"

He came and did it for her, dropping one shoulder with unconscious masculine grace. The music ceased. Randy straightened and let a grin lift one side of his mouth while his eyes scanned her outfit and hair. "Lookin' vicious, Mom."

"Thank you, so are you. New clothes?" She touched his tie.

"It's a hot deal—the elder sister tying the big knot."

"Where'd you get the money?"

"I *do* have a job, Mom."

"Yes, of course you do. Listen, I thought we could ride over together."

"Yeah, sure, whatever you say."

"I left my car in the driveway. We may as well take it."

She let him drive, deriving a secret maternal pleasure from being escorted by her full-grown son, something she had fantasized about when he was a young boy, something that happened all too infrequently since he'd become a man. They took highway 96 to White Bear Lake, ten miles due west. The ride led them through snow-covered countryside, past horse ranches and long stretches where no electric lights shone. The lake itself appeared, a blanket of blue-gray in the thin light of an eighth-moon, and rimming it, like a necklace of amber, the lights from lakeshore homes. The lake shared its name with the town that lay on its northwest curve, paling the night sky with its halo.

As they were approaching the city lights, with a bay of the lake on their left, Mark said, "That's where the old man lives."

"Where?"

"In those condos."

Bess looked over her shoulder and caught a glimpse of lights receding behind them, tall skeletal trees and an imposing building she'd often admired when driving past.

"How do you know?"

"Lisa told me."

"Your dad will be there tonight, you know."

Randy glanced her way but said nothing.

"See what you can do to act natural around him, okay?"

"Yes, Mother."

"For Lisa's sake."

"Yes, Mother."

"Randy, if you say yes Mother one more time I'm going to sock you."

"Yes, Mother."

She socked him and they both chuckled.

"You know what I'm saying about your dad."

"I'll try not to punch his lights out."

The Padgetts lived on the west side of town in a middle-class residential neighborhood as flat as an elephant's foot. Randy found the house without a misturn and escorted his mother along the edge of a driveway filled with cars to a sidewalk that curved between snowbanks and led to the front door.

They rang the bell and waited.

Mark and Lisa answered, followed by a short woman shaped like a chest of drawers, in a blue dress with a pleated skirt and a white collar. She had brown hair, frizzled in a bowl-shape, and a smile that put six dimples in her cheeks and made her eyes all but disappear.

Mark said simply, with an arm around her shoulder, "This is my mom, Hildy."

And Lisa said, "This is my mom, Bess, and my brother, Randy."

Hildy Padgett had a grip like a stevedore's and a contralto voice.

"Glad to meet you. Jake, come over here!" she called, and they were joined by Mark's father, straight, tall, thin-haired and smiling, with a hearing aid in his left ear. He was wearing brown trousers and a plaid shirt, open at the throat and rolled up at the cuff. No jacket.

There would be—Bess saw—no dog put on by the Padgetts, not even at a wedding. She liked them immediately.

The living room stretched off to the left, decorated like a country keeping room with blue-and-white plaid wallpaper and a plate rail running the perimeter of the room, a foot below the ceiling. The furniture was thick and comfortable-looking and filled with people. Among them, standing near the archway to the dining room, was Michael Curran.

At the sound of the doorbell Michael turned to watch Bess come in, looking very voguish, followed by Randy, looking surprisingly tall in an outsized overcoat with baggy shoulders and a turned-up collar. The sight of Bess coming in escorted by their son caught Michael in a vulnerable spot. Lord, Randy had grown up! The last time Michael had seen him was nearly three years ago in a busy shopping center. It was Easter, Michael recalled, and the mall had been turned into a miniature farm, with children everywhere, petting baby goats and chickens and ducks. Michael had just bought a spring jacket and come out of J. Riggings to find Randy moving toward him in the foot traffic, talking animatedly with another boy about his age. Michael had smiled and headed toward him but when Randy spied him, he'd halted, sobered, grabbed his friend's arm and done a brusque right-face, disappearing into a convenient women's clothing store.

Now here he was, three years later, taller than his mother and shockingly good-looking. His face had filled out and resembled Michael's own, though Randy was much handsomer. Michael felt a paternal thrill at the sight of that dark hair so much like his; the eyes, mouth and cheeks that had at last taken on the mature planes and curves they would keep into middle age.

He watched Randy shaking hands, giving up his overcoat, and finally Randy's deep brown eyes found Michael's. His hand stopped smoothing down his tie. The smile dropped from his mouth.

Michael felt his chest constrict. His heart flopped crazily. They stood for a light-year, across the room from one another while the past rushed forth to polarize them both. How simple, Michael thought, to cross the room, speak his name, embrace him, this young man who as a boy had idolized his father, had followed like a shadow beside him when he mowed the lawn and shoveled the driveway and changed the oil in the car and said, "Daddy, can I help?"

But Michael could not move. He could only stand across the room with a lump in his throat, trapped by his own mistaken past.

Someone came between them—Jake Padgett, extending his hand in welcome, and Randy's attention swerved to him.

Bess moved into Michael's line of vision. They forced smiles while he committed himself to his spot in the dining-room archway. He might have moved forward to speak to Randy while Bess was near at hand to act as a buffer but the hurt of Randy's last snub returned, sharp and real as if it had happened only yesterday. Bess's admonitions the other night at Lisa's rang clearly in Michael's head—Randy needs a father, be one to him.

But how?

The living room was filled with people—the other four Padgett children, all younger than Mark, as well as a grandmother and grandfather—requiring a round-robin of introductions that seemed to shift people like fog. But Randy made sure he remained far enough from Michael to avoid the risk of having to speak. Bess, however, shook hands with one after another and eventually reached her ex-husband.

"Hello, Michael," she said, remote as if their brief truce had never happened.

"Hello, Bess."

They trained their eyes on the people and lamps across the room, avoiding the risk of lingering glances. They struggled for polite inanities, finding none. Covertly he assessed her clothes, hair, jewelry and nails—mercy, had she changed. As much as Randy, if not more.

Bess clamped a black patent-leather clutch bag beneath one elbow and adjusted an outsized gold earring, looking over the crowd while speaking.

"Randy's grown up, hasn't he?"

"Has he ever. I couldn't believe it was him."

"Are you going to talk to him or just stand here as if he's a stranger?"

"You think he'd talk to me?"

"You can give it a try."

A memory flashed past of Randy at two, padding into their bedroom on Saturday mornings and climbing aboard his chest in his feet pajamas. *'Toons, Daddy,* he would say, and Michael would open his bleary eyes and tip him down for a kiss, then the two of them would whisper awhile before sneaking out to turn on cartoons and let Mommy have a morning in bed. He wanted to kiss him now, wanted to pin his arms at his sides and take him in a fatherly embrace and say *I'm sorry I screwed up, forgive me.*

Hildy Padgett came from the kitchen with a tray of canapés. Jake was passing around cups of mulled cider. Lisa was showing the grandparents her small diamond ring, and Mark was with her. Randy stood across the room with his hands in his trouser pockets, knowing no one, glancing occasionally at his father but determinedly keeping his distance.

One of them had to make the move.

It required a heroic effort but Michael took the risk.

He crossed the room and said, "Hello, Randy."

Randy said, "Yeah," his eyes casting about beyond Michael's shoulder.

"I wasn't sure it was you, you got so tall."

"Yeah, well, that happens, you know."

"How have you been?"

Randy shrugged, still avoiding his father's eyes.

"Your mother tells me you're still working in a warehouse."

"So?"

"Do you like it?"

"What's to like? You get up in the morning, you go put in your hours. It's just something to do till I get in with a band."

"A band?"

"Yeah, drums—with a band, you know, like *rrupp pup pup rrr . . .*"

"You pretty good?"

For the first time Randy looked squarely into Michael's eyes. An insolent expression twisted his face, and he released a sarcastic snort. "Spare me," he said and walked away.

Michael's stomach felt as if he'd leapt off a second-story roof. He watched Randy's shiny black curls as the young man moved off, and felt the clench of disappointment and failure. His face grew warm and a fist seemed to be closing over his windpipe.

He glanced over at Bess and found her watching.

She's right. I'm a failure as a father.

Lisa came to rescue him, capturing his elbow and hauling him across the room. "Dad, Grampa Earl was wondering about your cabin. He used to be a big hunter and I was just telling him you got a ten-point buck this fall. He wanted to hear more about it."

Earl Padgett was a big man with three chins and a florid face. He had a voice like a truck collision and endless hunting stories upon which to use it. His gestures were wide and sweeping, and when he pointed an invisible gun he might as well have been wearing a camouflage hunting vest lined with rows of shotgun shells. The hunting stories drew in Jake as well as the Padgett boys, who'd been hunting since they were old enough to take gun-safety classes. Of the men in the room, only Randy remained aloof.

Michael listened and added his own hunting anecdotes, all the time aware of Randy visiting with Bess, his back turned on Michael.

He'd bought Randy a .22 when Randy was twelve, and had dreamed of teaching the boy all about the woods and wildlife, and taking him on hunting trips. But his divorce had quashed that dream. Now he stood among a circle of fathers and sons whose enthusiasm had been passed from generation to generation, and his heart broke for what he and Randy had missed.

Hildy Padgett came in and announced dinner.

In the dining room, Michael and Bess were directed to seat themselves side-by-side at one end of the table, while Hildy and Jake presided at the opposite end. Mark and Lisa took chairs in the center of one long side, and the others were staggered around. Michael automatically pulled out Bess's chair. Her poise faltered momentarily while she shot him a wry glance, then she submitted to propriety and accepted his gesture of courtesy.

While Michael was seating himself he caught Randy watching sourly from diagonally across the table.

In an undertone he said to Bess, "I don't think Randy likes seeing me with you."

"Probably not," she replied, flipping her napkin onto her lap, glancing surreptitiously at Randy. "Did he say something about it?"

"No, just glared at me when I pulled out your chair."

"On the other hand, Lisa seems overjoyed. I've assured them both it's all for appearances. So . . . here we go." She picked up her glass of water and saluted him. "Let's see if we can't keep up the charade for our children's sake." He returned her salute and they sipped their water. A platter of ham was served, followed by bowls of vegetables, warm rolls, butter, bacon-and-lettuce salad and glorified rice, all passed around family-style. Passing a bowl to Bess, on his left, Michael remarked, "If someone had told me a week ago that I'd be sharing a dinner table with you twice in one week I'd have said no way."

"We did this a time or two with our own families, didn't we?" She watched him load his plate with au gratin potatoes and said, "Hildy really hit you in the taste buds, didn't she?"

He took an immense helping and answered, "Mmm . . . I still love 'em."

He always had. Watching him loading up on his old favorites brought back a sharp flash of nostalgia. Her mother had always said, *That Michael is fun to cook for. He knows how to eat.*

Bess glanced away from his plate—damn, she was thinking like a throwback. But it was difficult to sit beside a man with whom you've shared thousands of meals, whose table mannerisms are more familiar to you than your own, without those familiarities imposing themselves. She found herself anticipating his moves before he made them—how he held his fork, where he laid his knife, the order in which he tasted his food, the particular way he stroked one corner of his mouth with the pad of his right thumb after taking a drink, how he rested a wrist on the edge of the table while he chewed. Certain quiet sounds peculiar only to him.

"Did you have that talk with Lisa?"

She turned to find him watching her, chewing, his lips politely closed. There was an intimacy to chewing that had never struck her more profoundly than at that moment. He still had beautiful lips. She looked away. "Yes, I did. I went over to her apartment the next night."

"Do you feel better now?"

"Yes. Infinitely."

"Look at her," Michael said, poising with an elbow on the table, holding a glass of iced tea.

Bess studied their daughter. She appeared jubilant, laughing with her intended, the two of them unquestionably happy.

"Look at *them,*" Bess corrected. "She convinced me he's the right one for her. She almost had me in tears that night."

"And what about your wedding dress?"

"She's going to wear it."

Bess felt Michael's gaze on the side of her face and succumbed to the urge to meet his eyes. Webs of wistfulness drew them.

"It's hard to believe she's old enough, isn't it?" he said quietly.

"Yes. It seems like only yesterday we had her."

"Randy, too."

"I know."

"My guess is, he's watching us right now and wondering what's going on down here."

"Is something going on down here?"

He shocked her by replying, "You look great tonight, Bess."

She flushed and applied herself to cutting a piece of ham. "Oh, for heaven's sake, Michael, that's absurd."

"Well, you do. Is there any harm in my saying so? You've really changed since we divorced."

Her anger flared. "Oh, you're really smooth. You're without a wife—what? A month? Two?—and you're telling *me* how great I look? Don't insult me, Michael."

"I didn't mean to."

At that moment Jake Padgett stood up with a glass of iced tea and interrupted. "I think a toast is in order here. I'm not very good at this so you'll have to bear with me." He rubbed his left eyebrow with the edge of a finger. "Mark's our first to get married, and naturally we hoped he'd pick somebody we liked. Well, we sure got our wish when he brought Lisa home. We just couldn't be happier, and Lisa, honey, I know you're going to make him the happiest man in Minnesota when you marry him. We want to welcome you, and say how nice it is to have you and your family here with us tonight." He saluted Michael and Bess and nodded to Randy. "And so . . ." He raised his glass to the engaged couple. "Here's to a smooth road ahead for Lisa and Mark. We're behind you all the way."

Everyone joined in the toast. Jake resumed his seat and there passed between Michael and Bess a silent message, the kind husbands and wives of long standing can execute merely by the expression in their eyes.

Somebody should make a toast on our side.

You want to do it?

No, you.

Michael rose, pressing his tie to his shirt, lifting his glass.

"Jake, Hildy, all of you, thank you for inviting us. It's the proper way to start a young couple off, with the families united and showing their support. Lisa's mother and I are proud of her, and happy for her, and we welcome Mark as her husband-to-be. Lisa . . . Mark . . . you have our love. Good luck to you."

When the toast was complete, Michael sat down and Bess felt herself in an emotional turmoil. There wasn't a false word in his toast. It *was* the proper way to start the young couple off but how bittersweet, having their own immediate family reassembled for the first time amidst all these undercurrents. Earlier, when she'd watched Michael cross the room and approach Randy, her heart had leaped with hope. When Randy turned away, she had felt bereaved. Sitting beside Michael she'd been wafted first by nostalgia, then by bitterness and now, in the wake of the toasts, she simply felt muddled.

She was divorced and independent. She had proved she could live alone, build a business, keep a house and a car and a lawn and her own tax records. But the truth was, sitting beside Michael again, on this auspicious occasion, felt fitting. Having him stand and make a toast on behalf of them brought both a strong sense of security—imitation though it was—and a longing for what was gone: a father, a mother, their children, united as it had been in the beginning, as they had thought it would always be when they'd conceived those children who were now seated across the table.

Michael sensed himself being observed, turned and caught Bess regarding him.

She glanced away self-consciously.

Coffee and dessert were served—a layered concoction of angel food, strawberries, bananas and something white and fluffy. She watched Michael watching Randy while he ate. Randy ignored his father and visited with the Padgetts' seventeen-year-old daughter on his left.

"That was a nice toast you gave," Bess offered.

Michael took a forkful of dessert, which he held without eating. "This whole thing is turning out to be tougher than I thought."

She resisted the impulse to lay her hand on his sleeve. "Don't give up on him, Michael, please."

Cognizant of social obligation, surrounded as they were by people they'd just met, they assumed untroubled faces and pretended to be politely chitchatting.

"It hurts," he said.

"I know. It hurts him, too. That's why you can't give up."

He laid down his fork, picked up a cup of coffee and held it in both hands, looking beyond it at his son.

"He really hates me."

"I think he wants to but it's costing him."

He sipped his coffee, left his elbows propped on the table. In time he turned to study Bess. "What's your stake in all this? Why all of a sudden the push to see Randy and I reconcile?"

"You're his father, nothing more complicated than that. I'm beginning to see what harm we've done by forcing the kids into this cold war we've waged."

He set down his cup, released a weary sigh and settled his shoulders against the back of the chair.

"All right, Bess, I'll try."

On the way home from White Bear Lake, Randy acted surly.

Bess said, "Do you want to tell me what's on your mind?"

He cast her a glance, returned his eyes to the road and went on driving.

"Randy?" she prodded.

"What's going on with you and the old man?"

"Nothing. And don't call him the old man. He's your father."

Randy tossed a glance out his side window and whispered, "Shit."

"He's trying to make amends to you, can't you see that?"

"Great!" Randy shouted. "All of a sudden he's my father and I'm supposed to kiss his ass when for six years you haven't kept it any secret that you hate his guts."

"Well, maybe I was wrong. Whatever I felt, maybe I shouldn't have imposed those feelings on you."

"I've got a mind of my own, Ma. I didn't need to pick up vibes from you to realize that what he did was shitty. He was screwing another woman and he broke up our home!"

"All right!" Bess shouted and repeated, more calmly, "All right, he was but there's such a thing as forgiveness."

"I can't believe what I'm hearing. He's getting to you, isn't he? Pulling out your chair and making toasts and cozying up to you over the dinner table just as soon as his other wife throws him over. He makes me sick."

Guilt struck Bess for having instilled such hate in her son without a thought for its effect on him. Bitterness such as he felt could stultify his emotions in dozens of other ways.

"Randy, I'm sorry you feel this way."

"Yeah, well, it's a pretty quick switch, isn't it, Mom? Less than a week ago you felt the same way. I'd just hate to see him make a fool of you a second time."

She felt a surge of exasperation with him for voicing what she'd thought, and with herself for being culpable. After all it was true she had felt flashes of cupidity at given moments tonight.

Let this be a lesson, she thought, and if you mend fences between yourself and Michael, keep your distance while doing it.

The following day was Sunday. There was Mass in the morning, prefaced by a battle to make Randy get up and go, followed by a lonely lunch for two—a pair of sad, bald, diet chicken breasts and baked potatoes with no sour cream for Bess and very little table conversation out of Randy. He left immediately afterward, said he was going to his friend Bernie's house to watch the NFC playoff games on TV.

When he was gone the house grew silent. Bess cleaned up the kitchen, changed into a sweat suit and returned downstairs, where the silent, familyless rooms held a gloom that was only amplified by bright day beating at the windows. She did some design work for a while but found concentrating difficult and finally rose from the dining-room table to wander from window to window, staring out at the wintry yard, the frozen river, a squirrel's nest in the neighbor's oak tree, the blue shadows of her own maple branches on the pristine snow. She sat down to resume her work but gave up once more, distracted by thoughts of Michael and their sundered family. She meandered into the living room, played middle C on the piano and held it till it dissolved into silence.

Once more she returned to the window to stare out with her arms folded across her chest.

In a yard several doors down a group of children were sledding.

When Randy and Lisa were little she and Michael had taken them one Sunday afternoon much like this one—a sterling, bright, blinding day—to Theodore Wirth Park in Minneapolis. They'd taken red plastic boat-shaped sleds, sleek and fast, and chosen a hill with fresh, unbroken snow. On their first glissade down the hill Michael's sled had slewed one hundred and eighty degrees and had carried him the remainder of the way backwards. At the bottom he'd hit a slight hummock, gone tail over teakettle and rolled to a stop looking like a snowman. He'd grown a beard and moustache that year; they and his hair were totally covered with snow. His cap was gone. His glasses were miraculously in place but behind them his eyes were completely covered with white.

When he'd finally sat up, looking like Little Orphan Annie, they had all rolled with laughter, collapsing on their backs in the snow and hooting themselves breathless.

Years later, when their marriage was losing its mortar, he'd said disconsolately, "We never do anything fun anymore, Bess. We never laugh."

In the yard next door all the children had run away and left one small bundled-up individual behind, crying.

You and me, Bess thought, left behind to cry.

She turned away from the window and went into the family room, where the fireplace was cold and the Sunday *Pioneer Press Dispatch* was strewn on the sofa. With a sigh she picked up the sections and began aligning them. Disconsolately she abandoned the job and dropped to a chair with the papers forgotten in her hand.

In silence she sat.

Wondering.

Withering.

Wasting.

She was not a tearful person, yet her aloneness had magnitude enough to force a pressure behind her eyes. It drove her in time to pick up the telephone and dial her mother.

Stella Dorner answered in her usual cheerful two-note greeting. "Hello."

"Hello, Mother, it's Bess."

"Well, isn't this nice? I was just thinking of you."

"What were you thinking?"

"That I haven't talked to you since last Monday and it was time I called you."

"Are you busy?"

"Just watching the Minnesota Vikings get whipped."

"Could I come over? I'd like to talk to you."

"Of course. I'd love it. Can you stay for supper? I'll make some of those barbecued pork chops you love with the onion and lemon on them."

"That sounds good."

"Are you coming right away?"

"As soon as I get my shoes on."

"Good. See you soon, dear."

Stella Dorner lived in a townhouse on Oak Glen Golf Course on the western edge of Stillwater. She had bought it within a year after her husband died, and had furnished it with sassy new furniture, declaring she hadn't been buried along with him and wasn't going to act as if she had. She'd continued her job as an on-call operating-room nurse at Lakeview Memorial Hospital, though she was nearly sixty at the time; had taken up golf lessons and joined a ladies' league at Oak Glen, the church choir at St. Mary's and the African Violet Society of America, which met quarterly in various places all over the Twin Cities. She went as often as she pleased to visit her daughter Joan in Denver, and once took a trip to Europe (on a Eurail Pass) with her sisters from Phoenix and Coral Gables; she often went on organized bus tours to places such as the Congden Mansion in Duluth and the University of Minnesota Arboretum in Jonathan; spent time at least once a week visiting the old folks at the Maple Manor nursing home and baking cookies for them. She played bridge on Mondays, watched *thirtysomething* on Tuesdays, went to bargain matinee movies most Wednesdays and got a facial every Friday. She had once signed up with a dating service but claimed all the old farts she'd been paired up with couldn't keep up with her and she didn't want any ball and chain around her foot.

Her townhouse reflected her spirit. It had three levels, long expanses of glass and was decorated in peach, cream and glossy black. Entering it, Bess always felt a shot of vitality. Today was no different. In the ten minutes since Bess's call, Stella had the place smelling like baking pork chops.

She answered the door dressed in a sweat suit the colors of a paint rag—a white background with smears of hot pink, yellow, green and purple, all strung together with black squiggles and dribbles. Over it she wore a disreputable lavender smock. She had coarse salt-and-pepper hair, styled only by gravity. It fell into a crooked center part and dropped in two irregular waves to jaw level. She had a habit of pushing it back by making a caliper of one hand and hooking both temple waves at once. She did so as she greeted her daughter. "Bess . . . darling . . . this is wonderful. I'm so glad you called." She was shorter than Bess and reached up to hug her gingerly. "Careful! I don't want to get any paint on you."

"Paint?"

"I'm taking an oil-painting class. I was working on my first picture." She performed the caliper move on her hair once more while closing the door.

"How in the world do you find time?"

"A person should always find time for the things he likes." Stella led the way inside, where the west window light was strong but unreached yet by the afternoon sun, which lit the snow-laden golf course beyond. Facing the window was a long sofa upholstered in coral calla lilies on a cream background. One wall was filled with an ebony entertainment unit, where the football game was in progress on TV. The tables were ebony frames with glass tops. Before the sliding glass doors stood an easel with a partially finished rendering of an African violet.

"What do you think?" Stella asked.

"Mmm . . ." Removing her jacket, Bess studied the painting. "Looks good to me."

"It probably won't be but what the heck. The class is fun, and that's the object." Stella walked over and turned down the television volume. "Can I get you a Coke?"

"I'll get it. You keep on with your work."

"All right, I will." She pushed back her hair and picked up a paintbrush while Bess went into the kitchen and opened the refrigerator.

"Can I fix you one?"

"No thanks, I'm having tea." Beside Stella, a waist-high folding table held her mug and tubes of paint. She reached for the mug, drank from it while studying her artwork and called, "How are the kids?"

"That's what I came to talk to you about." Bess entered the room sipping her pop, slipped off her black loafers and propped her back against one end of the long sofa, drawing her feet up and resting her glass on her knees. "Well . . . part of what I came to talk to you about."

"Oh-oh. This sounds serious."

"Lisa's getting married . . . and she's expecting a baby."

Stella studied her daughter for several seconds. "Maybe I'd better put these paints away." She reached for a rag and began cleaning her brush.

"No, please don't stop."

"Don't be silly. I can do this any old time." The brush joined some others in a tin can of turpentine before Stella removed her smock and joined Bess on the sofa, bringing her cup of tea and hooking her hair back.

"Well . . . Lisa pregnant, imagine that. That'll make me a great-grandmother, won't it?"

"And me a grandmother."

"Spooky, isn't it?"

"Uh-huh."

"Which is the least important aspect of all this. I imagine you're in shock."

"I was but it's wearing off."

"Does she want the baby?"

"Yes, very much."

"Ah, that's a relief."

"Guess what else."

"There's more?"

"I've seen Michael," Bess told her.

"My goodness, you have had a week, haven't you?"

"Lisa set us up. She invited us both to her apartment to announce the news."

Stella laughed, throwing her chin up. "Good for Lisa. That girl's got style."

"I could have throttled her."

"How is she?"

"Happy and excited and very much in love, she assures us."

"And how is Michael?"

"Detached again, on his way to getting another divorce."

"Oh my."

"He said to tell you hi. His exact words were, 'Say hi to the old doll. I miss her.' "

Stella saluted with her mug—"Hi, Michael"—and sipped from it, studying Bess over the rim. "No wonder you wanted to talk. Where is Randy in all this?"

"Where he's always been, very resentful, shunning his father."

"And you?"

Bess sighed and said, "I don't know, Mother." She shifted her gaze to her knees, where it remained for a long time before she sighed, let her head drop back and spoke to the ceiling. "I've been carrying around all this anger for six years. It's very hard to let it go."

Stella sipped her tea and waited. Nearly a minute of silence passed before Bess looked at Stella.

"Mother, did I . . ." She paused.

"Did you what?"

"When we were getting the divorce you never said much."

"It wasn't my place."

"When I found out that Michael was having an affair, I wanted so badly for you to be angry for me. I wanted you to raise your fist and call him a bastard, take my side, but you never did."

"I liked Michael."

"But I thought you should be indignant on my behalf, and you weren't. There must have been some reason."

"And you're sure you're ready to hear it now?"

"Is it going to make me mad?"

"I don't know. That depends on how much you've grown up in six years."

"It was partly my fault, is that what you're saying?"

"It always takes two, honey, but when a man retaliates by having an affair, he's usually the one who gets all the blame."

"All right, what did I do?" Bess's voice grew defensive. "I went back to college to get my degree! Was that so wrong?"

"Not at all. But while you were doing it you totally forgot about your husband."

"I did not! He wouldn't let me forget about him. I still had to cook and do laundry and keep the house in shape."

"Those are superficialities. I'm talking about your personal relationship."

"Mother, there wasn't time!"

"Now there, I think you've put your finger on it." Stella let that sink in while she went to the kitchen to refresh her tea. When she returned to the living room, Bess was sitting with one elbow on the high sofa arm, her thumbnail between her teeth, staring out the window.

Stella resumed her seat and said, "Remember when you were first married how you used to ask Dad and me to take the kids occasionally so you and Michael could go off camping by yourselves? And the Christmas you bought him that shotgun that he wanted so badly, and hid it over at our place so he wouldn't find out? Remember all the trouble we went to, sneaking that thing into your house and hiding it on Christmas Eve? And then there was the April Fools' Day when you had that Fanny Farmer box delivered to his office and it was full of nuts and bolts."

Bess stared at the snowy golf course, her Coke forgotten.

"Those are the kinds of things that should never stop," her mother said.

"Was I the only one who stopped them?"

"I don't know. Were you?"

"I didn't think so then."

"You got awfully caught up in school, and after it was finished, in opening your store. When you'd stop over to see us you were always alone, never with Michael anymore, always rushing between two places. I know for a fact that you stopped having Dad and me over for meals, and that sometimes the kids would come over and act a little forlorn and abandoned."

Bess looked at her mother and remarked, "That's when Michael accused me of letting myself go."

"As I recall, you did."

"But I asked him for help around the house and he refused to give it. Isn't he partly to blame?"

"Maybe. But those kinds of things are a trade-off. Maybe he'd have helped you around the house if he hadn't fallen to the bottom of your priority list. How was your sex life?"

Bess looked out the window and answered, "Shitty."

"You didn't have time for it, right?"

"I thought once I got through school and had my own business, everything would fall back into place. I could get a housekeeper, maybe, and I'd have more time to relax with him."

"Only he didn't wait."

Bess got up and passed the easel to stand near the window with one hand on her hip. She drank her Coke, then turned to Stella. "Last night he told me I looked great, and do you know how angry it made me?"

"Why?"

"Because!" Bess flung up one hand. "Because . . . hell, I don't know. Because he's just sloughed off another wife and he's probably lonely and I don't want him crawling back to me under those circumstances. I don't want him crawling back to me at all! And Randy was watching us from the other end of the table! And I was upset with myself because I took an hour and fifteen minutes getting ready for that damned supper just to show him I could knock his socks off and . . . and . . . then when I did . . ." Bess covered her eyes with one hand and shook her head vehemently. "Hell, Mom, I don't know. It just seems like all of a sudden I'm so damned lonely and I'm caught in this wedding situation and I'm . . . I'm asking myself questions." She stared unseeingly outside and ended, more quietly, "I don't know."

Stella set her mug on the coffee table and went to her daughter. From behind, she finger-combed Bess's hair back to her nape, then massaged her shoulders.

"You're going through a catharsis that's been six years coming, that's what it is. All that time you've hated him and blamed him, and all of a sudden you're starting to explore your own fault in the matter. That's not easy."

"I don't love him anymore, Mother, I really don't."

"All right, so you don't."

"Then why does it hurt so much to see him?"

"Because he's making you take this second look at yourself. Here." Stella produced a wrinkled Kleenex and handed it to Bess.

It smelled like turpentine when Bess blew her nose in it. "I'm sorry, Mom," she said, drying her eyes.

"Don't be sorry. I'm a big girl. I can handle it."

"But coming here like this, spoiling your day."

"You haven't spoiled my day. Matter of fact, I think you've made it." Walking Bess back to the sofa with one arm around her shoulders Stella asked, "Feel better now?"

"Yes. Sort of."

"Then let me tell you something. It was all right for you to be angry at first, right after the divorce. Your anger is what got you through. Then you got efficient, businesslike, and threw all your energies into showing him you could make it on your own. And you did make it. But now you're going into another stage where you're going to do more questioning, and I suspect you might have a few more days like this. When you do, come over and we'll talk you through it, just as we did today. Now sit down, tell me about the wedding plans, and about Lisa's young man, and about what I have to wear to this shindig and if you think I might meet any interesting men there."

Bess laughed. "Mother, you're incorrigible. I thought you didn't want a ball and chain around your ankle."

"I don't. But you can only stand so much of hearing women's cackly voices before you need to hear a male one, and I've been playing an awful lot of bridge this winter."

Bess gave her mother an impulsive hug. "Mom, maybe I never told you this before, but you're my idol. I wish I could be more like you."

Stella hugged her back and said, "You're a lot like me. I see more of me in you every day."

"But you never get down."

"The heck I don't. But when it happens I just go out and join another club."

"Or look for a man."

"Well . . . there's nothing wrong with that. And speaking of the critters, how are you and Keith getting along?"

"Oh . . . Keith." Bess made a face and shrugged. "He got upset because I had to break a dinner date with him to go to the Padgetts' last night. You know how he is where the kids are concerned."

"I'll tell you something," Stella said, "since we're being honest with each other today. That man is not for you."

"Have you and Lisa been comparing notes or what?"

"Maybe."

Bess laughed. "Why, you two devils. If you think this wedding business is going to get me back together with Michael, you're wrong."

"I didn't say a word."

"No, but you're thinking it, and you can just forget it, Mother."

Stella lifted one eyebrow and asked, "How does he look? He still as handsome as ever?"

"Moth-er!" Bess looked exasperated.

"Just curious."

"It'll never happen, Mother," Bess vowed.

Stella put on a smug expression and said, "How do you know? Stranger things have."

chapter 5

T HAT SAME SUNDAY MORNING Michael Curran awakened, stretched and stacked his hands behind his head, loath to stir and rise. His stomach grumbled but he remained, staring at the ceiling, which took on a rosy glow from the bright sunlight bouncing off the carpeting. The bedroom was huge, square, with triple sliding glass doors facing the lake, and a marble fireplace. The room held nothing more than a television set and the pair of mattresses upon which Michael lay. They were pushed against the north wall to keep his pillows from falling off.

The ten o'clock sun, reflecting off the frozen lake, made a nebula of light patterns on the ceiling, broken by strands of shadow from the naked elm trees beyond the deck. The building was absolutely silent; it was designed to be. No children were allowed, and most of the wealthy tenants had gone south for the winter, so he rarely crossed paths with anyone, not even in the elevator.

It was lonely.

He thought about last night, about his encounter with Randy. He closed his eyes and saw his nineteen-year-old son, bearing so much resemblance to himself, and so much animosity. The impact of seeing him came back afresh, bringing a replay of last night's convoluted emotions: love, hope, disappointment and a feeling of failure that made his chest feel heavy.

He opened his eyes to the ceiling designs.

How it hurt, being disowned by one's own child. Perhaps, as Bess had accused, he'd been guilty of withdrawing from Randy's life emotionally as well as physically, but wasn't Randy at fault, too, for refusing to see him? On the other hand, if Bess could have felt the cataclysm he'd experienced when he'd seen Randy walk into that house last night, she would have been forced to reconsider her words.

That boy—that *man*—was his son. His son, whose last six vital growing years had been lost to Michael, largely against his choice. If Bess had encouraged, or if Randy had not been brainwashed, he, Michael, would have been seeing Randy all along. There were things the two of them could have done together, particularly hunting and enjoying the outdoors. Instead, Michael had been excluded from everything, even Randy's high-school graduation. He'd known, of course, that Randy was graduating. When no announcement came he'd called Bess and asked about it, but Bess had replied, "He doesn't want you here."

He'd sent money, five hundred dollars. It was never acknowledged, either by written or spoken word, except for Lisa who, when Michael had asked, told him on the phone some weeks later, "He put it down on a thirteen-hundred-dollar set of drums."

A set of drums.

Why hadn't Bess seen to it that the kid went to college? Or a trade school? Something besides that dead-end job in a warehouse. After the way Bess had fought to complete her own college education he'd have thought she'd have taken a strong stand on the issue with her own kids. Maybe she had, and maybe it simply hadn't worked.

Bess.

Boy-o-boy, how she'd changed. When she'd walked into that room last night the craziest thing had happened! He'd actually felt a little charge. Yeah, it was crazy, all right, because Bess had a sharp edge to her now, a veneer of hardness he found abrasive. But she was his children's mother, and a transformed lady, and in spite of the way she carefully distanced herself from him, they shared a past that would forever intrude upon their lingering dissatisfactions with one another. He'd bet any money she felt it, too, at times.

Sitting next to each other at the dinner table, looking over at Lisa and Randy, how could either of them deny the gravity of memory?

As he lay in his unfurnished condominium with the Sunday sun shifting through the room, recollections of their beginnings played back through his mind—when Bess was in high school, and he, already a sophomore in college, had gone back for homecoming and had discovered her all grown up, an underclassman he didn't even remember. The first time he'd kissed her they were walking back to his car after a University of Minnesota football game in the fall of '66. The first time they'd made love was toward the end of her senior year on a Sunday afternoon when a gang of them had gone to Taylors Falls with picnic food, Frisbees and plenty of blankets. They'd been married a year later, with him fresh out of college and her with three more years to go. They'd spent their wedding night in the bridal suite at the Radisson Hotel in downtown Minneapolis.

Her mom and dad had given them the room as a surprise, and a bunch of her girlfriends had bought her a lacy white nightgown with a thin thing that went over it. He recalled how, when she came out of the bathroom wearing it, he was waiting in his blue pajama bottoms, both of them as hesitant as if it were their first time. He'd thought he'd never forget the details of that night but over time they'd become blurred. What he did remember, clearly, was waking the next morning. It was June and sunny and on the dresser sat a basket of fruit from the hotel management, along with two fluted glasses from the night before, each half-full of bubbleless champagne. He'd opened his eyes to find Bess next to him, with her nightgown back on. He'd lain there wondering when she'd gotten up and put it on, and if she expected him to wear his pajamas all night, too, and if, in spite of their premarital sex, she'd turn out to be a prude. Then she'd awakened and smiled, indulged in a quivering, all-over stretch, lain on her side facing him with her hands joined near her knees, and he'd gotten a hard-on just looking at her.

When the stretch ended she'd said simply, "Hi."

"Hi," he'd answered.

They'd lain a long time, looking at each other, absorbing the novelty and wonder of sanctioned morning bliss. He remembered her cheeks had grown flushed and supposed his had done the same.

In time she'd said, "Just imagine, nobody can ever send you home at one A.M. again. We get to wake up together for the rest of our lives."

"It's wild, isn't it?"

"Yeah," she'd whispered, "pretty wild."

"You put your nightgown back on."

"I can't sleep without something on. I wake up and my arms are stuck to my sides. What about you?" The sheet covered him to his ribs.

"I don't have that problem," he'd answered, "but I've got another one."

She had put her hand on his hip—he remembered so vividly what had followed, for in all of his life to that point nothing had been as incredible as that morning. Sex before marriage had been frequent for them but it had carried restraints, nevertheless. That sunny June morning when she had reached out for him those restraints had dissolved. They *felt* married, they *belonged* to each other and there was a difference. The vows they'd spoken gave them license and they reveled in it.

He had seen her half-naked, nearly naked, had gotten her naked from the waist down a lot of times. They'd made love in the sunlight wrapped in a blanket, in the moonlight wrapped in shadows and in cars beneath streetlamps with their socks still on. Even on their wedding night they'd left only the bathroom light on to shed a dim glow from around a corner. But that morning, the day after their wedding, the east sun had been streaming in a broad, high window, and she'd taken off his sheet and he'd taken off her nightgown and they'd indulged their eyes for the first time. In that regard they'd been virgins, and nothing he'd experienced before or since had been any sweeter.

Their breakfast had been delivered on a rolling cart with white linen and a red rose. Over the meal they had studied each other's eyes and reaffirmed that they'd done the right thing, and that their joy was so intense it eclipsed any other they'd ever felt.

About that day he recalled most vividly the overriding sense of consecration they'd both felt. They had met in an era when more and more young couples were declaring, *Marriage is dead,* and were choosing to set up housekeeping together instead. They'd discussed doing the same thing but had decided no, they loved each other and wanted to commit for life.

After breakfast they'd made love again, then had bathed and dressed and walked to St. Olaf's for Mass.

June 8, 1968, their wedding day.

And now it was January 1990, and he was rolling off his mattresses in an empty condo, dressed in gray sweatpants, aroused once again from his memories.

Forget it, Curran. Horn in. She doesn't want you, you don't really want her and your own kid treats you like a leper. That ought to tell you something.

He shuffled to the bathroom, switched on the light, flattened one palm on the vanity top, examined his face and harvested some sand from his eyes. He swigged a mouthful of cinnamon-flavored Plax, swished it around for the recommended thirty seconds and brushed his teeth with a full one inch of red Close-Up. Bess had always harangued him about using too much toothpaste. *You don't need that much,* she'd told him, *half that much is enough.* Now, damn it, he used as much as he wanted and nobody nagged. He brushed for one whole minute, rinsed, then bared his teeth to the mirror and thought, Look at these, Bess, pretty damned nice for a forty-three-year-old, eh?

His flawless teeth were of curiously little consolation this morning in his big, empty, silent condo.

He wiped his mouth, threw down the towel and went to the kitchen. It was tiled in white, had white Formica cabinets trimmed with blond oak and was connected to a family room with sliding glass doors at its far end, facing a small park with a gazebo. His entire pantry stock, on an oversized island in the middle of the kitchen, looked like a city block from 30,000 feet. Instant coffee, a box of Grape-Nuts, a loaf of Taystee bread, a jar of peanut butter, another of grape jelly, a half-stick of margarine smeared on its gold foil wrapper, a handful of paper sugar packets and a plastic spoon and knife he'd kept from Hardee's.

He stood awhile, staring at the collection.

Two times I've let women clean me out. When am I going to learn?

A quick-flash came along: the four of them—himself, Bess, Randy and Lisa—during those fun years when the kids were old enough to sit at the table and swing their feet without their toes touching the floor. Lisa, fresh from church, with her hair in pigtails and her elbows on the table, picking apart a piece of toast and eating it in tiny increments (all the while with her feet swinging wildly): "I saw Randy pick his nose in church this morning and wipe it on the bottom of the pew. *Yuuuuukkkk!"*

"I dint neither! She's lying!"

"You did, too! I saw you, Randy, you're *so gross!"*

"Mom, she lies all the time." (This with a whine that verified his guilt.)

"I'm *never* sitting in that pew again!"

Bess and Michael exchanging glances with their lips pursed to keep from hooting before Bess remarked, "Randy picks his nose in church, his dad does it when he's sitting at stop lights."

"I do not!" Michael had yelped.

"You do, too!"

Then the whole family breaking into laughter before Bess delivered an admonition about hygiene and handkerchiefs.

Sunday breakfasts were a lot different then.

In his White Bear Lake condominium, Michael poured some Grape-Nuts into a white plastic deli-food container, covered them with milk from the otherwise empty refrigerator, tore open a sugar packet, took his plastic spoon and returned to his mattresses, where he propped his pillows against the wall, turned on the TV and sat down to eat alone.

He wasn't up to either evangelists or cartoons, however, and found his mind returning to the perplexing stringball of family relationships he was trying to unknot. For perhaps the ten thousandth time in his life he wished he had sisters and brothers. What would it be like to pick up the phone and say, "Hi, you got any coffee over there?" and sit down with someone who'd shared your past, and your parents, and some warm memories, and maybe a few scoldings, and the chicken pox, and the same first-grade teacher, and teenage clothing, and double dates and memories of Mom's cooking? Someone who knew all you'd put into your lifetime's struggles, and who cared about your happiness and how you felt today.

How he felt today was lonely. So damned lonely, and hurting some, and wondering where to go next in his life. How to be a father to Randy, and how to make it through this wedding, and what tack to take with Bess, and what to make of these nostalgic thoughts he'd been having about her. Even being a grandfather—he'd like to talk about that.

Alas, there was no brother, no sister, and he felt as cheated and isolated as ever.

He got up, showered, shaved and dressed, then tried working awhile at his desk in one of the other two bedrooms, but the silence and emptiness were so depressing he had to get out.

He decided to go shopping for some furniture. He sure as hell needed it, and at least in the stores there'd be people moving around.

He went to Dayton's Home Store on highway 36, thinking he'd simply pick a living-roomful and have it delivered, but discovered to his dismay that just about everything would have to be ordered and would take from six weeks to six months to arrive. Furthermore, he had no carpet samples, no wallpaper samples and no idea what he really wanted.

He went next to Levitz, where he walked the aisles between assembled rooms and tried to visualize pieces in his condo but found he had no concept of what would look good. Color, in particular, threw him, and size, of course, became a factor. He realized that all the places he'd ever lived in had been decorated primarily by women and that he had no eye for it whatsoever.

He went next to Byerly's grocery store, where he stared at the fresh chickens a long time, wondering how Darla had made that stuff called fricassee. He passed the pork chops—Stella was the one who knew how to make pork chops. They had onions on top, he recalled, and lemon slices, but how she got them red and barbecuey, he had no idea. Ham? Ham sounded simpler, though his foremost craving was not for it but for the mashed potatoes and ham gravy that went along with it, the way Bess used to fix it.

Aw, hell . . . he turned away and went back to the delicatessen, where he fixed a salad at the open salad bar and bought some wild-rice soup for his supper.

It was twilight when he headed home, a melancholy time of day with the sun setting in his rearview mirror and the empty condo ahead. He parked in the underground garage, took the elevator up and went straight to the kitchen, where he warmed his soup in the microwave and ate it seated on the cold tiles of the countertop.

The idea hit him while he was sitting there with his feet dangling a foot above the floor, eating soup out of a cardboard carton with a plastic spoon.

You need a decorator, Curran.

He knew one, too; knew a damned good one.

'Course, this could be nothing but an excuse to call her. He looked around, reconfirming that he hadn't so much as a kitchen table to eat at. Fat chance she'd believe he really needed his place furnished; she'd think he was nosing around for something else.

He could call another one. Yes, he could, he certainly could. But it was Sunday: you can't call an interior decorator on Sunday.

He stared at the view of the gloaming out the sliding glass door, picturing Bess. If he called her he'd look like a jerk. So he sat on the cold counter, beside the white telephone, tapping the plastic spoon on his knee.

It took him until eight o'clock to work up the courage to dial his old number. In six years it hadn't changed, and he remembered it by heart.

Bess answered on the third ring.

"Hi, Bess, it's Michael."

A long silence passed before she said, "Well . . . Michael."

"Surprised, huh?"

"Yes."

"Yeah, me too." He was sitting on the edge of his mattress with its messy blankets, fiddling with the material covering his right knee, wondering what to say next. "It was a nice supper last night."

"Yes, it was."

"The Padgetts seem like likable people."

"I thought so, too."

"Lisa could do worse."

"She's very happy, and after seeing Mark with his family I have no objection whatsoever to their marriage."

Each ensuing silence became more awkward. "So, how's Randy today?" Michael asked.

"I haven't seen much of him. We went to church and he left right afterwards to watch the game with his friend."

"Did he say anything last night?"

"About what?"

"About us."

"Yes he did, as a matter of fact. He said he hoped you wouldn't make a fool out of me again. Listen, Michael, is there something in particular you wanted, because I brought some work home to do this evening and I'd like to get back to it."

"I thought you wanted us to be civil to each other for the kids' sake."

"I did. I do but—"

"Then give me a minute here, will you, Bess! I'm making the effort to call you and you start slinging insults!"

"You *asked* me what Randy said and I told you!"

"All right . . ." He calmed himself. "All right, let's just forget it. I'm sorry I asked about him, and besides I called for something else."

"What?"

"I want to hire you."

"To do what?"

"To decorate my condo."

She paused a beat, then burst out laughing. "Oh, Michael, that's so funny!"

"What's so funny about it?"

"*You* want to hire *me* to decorate your condo?"

His mouth got tight. "Yes, I do."

"Are you forgetting how you railed against my going to school to get my degree?"

"That was then, this is now. I need a decorator. Do you want the job or not?"

"First of all, let's get one thing straight, something you apparently never caught the first time around. I'm not a decorator, I'm an interior designer."

"There's a difference?"

"Anybody who owns a paint store can call himself a decorator. I'm a U of M graduate with a four-year degree and I'm accredited by the FIDER. Yes, there's a difference."

"All right, I apologize. I won't make that mistake again. Madame Interior Designer, would you care to design the interior of my condo?" he asked snidely.

"I'm no fool, Michael. I'm a businesswoman. I'll be happy to set up a house call. There's a one-time forty-dollar trip charge for that, which I'll apply to the cost of any furniture you might order."

"I think I can handle that."

"Very well, my calendar is at the store but I know I have next Friday morning open. How does that sound?"

"Fine."

"Just so you'll know what to expect, the house call is primarily a question-and-answer period so that I can get to know your tastes, budget, life-style, things like that. I won't be bringing any samples or catalogs with me at this time. That'll all come later. During this initial visit we'll just talk and I'll take notes. Will there be anyone else living in the condo with you?"

"For God's sake, Bess—"

"It's part of my job as a professional to ask, because if there will be, it's best to have everybody present at this first consultation and get everybody's input at the start. It eliminates problems later when the one who wasn't there says, 'Wait a minute! You know how I hate blue!' Or yellow, or African masks or glass-top tables. Sometimes we hear things like, 'What happened to Great-Aunt Myrtle's lamp made out of the shrunken head?' You'd be surprised what rhubarbs can come up over taste."

"No, there won't be anyone else living here with me."

"Good, that simplifies matters. We'll make it Friday morning at nine, then, if that's agreeable."

"Nine is good. I'll tell you how to get here."

"I already know."

"You do?"

"Randy pointed it out to me."

"Oh." For a moment he'd flattered himself thinking she'd taken the trouble to look it up after he gave her his card. "There's a security system, so just call up from the lobby."

"I will."

"Well, I'll see you Friday, then."

"Yes." She ended the conversation without either stumble or halt. "Good-bye, Michael."

"Good-bye."

When he'd hung up Michael sat on the edge of his mattress, scowling. "Whoa! Madame Businesswoman!" he said aloud, eyeing the phone.

The place seemed quiet after his outburst. The furnace clicked on and started the fan quietly wheezing through the vents. The night pressed black against his curtainless windows. The ceiling fixture sent harsh light over the room. He fell back with his hands behind his neck. A knot of jumbled bedding created an uncomfortable lump beneath him. He moved off it, still scowling.

This is probably a mistake, he thought.

When Bess hung up, she thought about the infamous decorating Doris Day had perpetrated on Rock Hudson's apartment in *Pillow Talk*. Ah, those red-velour tassels, those chartreuse draperies, that moose head, the orange player piano, beaded curtains, fertility gods, potbellied stove and the chair made of antlers . . .

It was tempting.

Definitely tempting.

The following evening Lisa went home to Stillwater to try on her mother's wedding dress. It was stored in the basement in a windowless space beside the laundry room, inside a plastic bag hanging from the ceiling joists. They went down together. Bess pulled the chain on a light switch and a bare 40-watt bulb smeared murky yellow smudge over the crowded cubicle. Its walls were the backside of the adjacent rooms, giving a view of two-by-fours and untaped Sheetrock. It smelled like fresh mushrooms.

Bess glanced around and shivered, then looked up at the row of shrouded garments.

"I don't think either one of us can reach. There's a step stool in the laundry room, Lisa, would you get it?"

While Lisa went to find the stool, Bess began moving aside boxes and baby furniture, a badminton net, a case holding a twenty-five-dollar guitar they'd bought for Randy when he was twelve, before he'd discovered his true love was drumming. Some of the cardboard boxes were labeled— *Baby Clothes, Lisa's Dolls, Games, School Papers*—representing many years' accumulation of memories.

Lisa returned and while Bess forced the legs of the stool into the tight space among the boxes, Lisa opened one of them.

"Oh, Mom, look . . ." Lisa took out a cigar box and from it drew a school picture of herself. In it she was missing both incisors and her hair was parted on one side, slicked to the opposite side and held in place with a barrette. "Second grade, Miss Peal. Donny Carry said he loved me and put those little heart-shaped candies on my desk every morning, with a different message on every one. *Be mine. Cool babe.* I was a real heartbreaker, wasn't I?"

Bess viewed the picture. "Oh, I remember that dress. Grandma Dorner gave it to you for Christmas and you always wore it with red tights and patent-leather shoes."

"Dad used to call me his little elf whenever I wore it."

Bess said, "It's cold down here. Let's get the dress and go upstairs."

Bess carried the bridal gown and Lisa took the cigar box, glancing through report cards, old, curled pictures and notes from her childhood friends as the two women climbed the stairs. Bess went outside on the front stoop, stripped the dusty plastic bag off the wedding dress and gave it a shake. She carried it upstairs to find Lisa in her old room, sitting cross-legged on the bed.

"Look at this one," Lisa said, and Bess sank down beside her with the gown doubled over on her lap. "It's a note from Patty Larson. 'Dear Lisa, Meet me in the empty lot after lunch and bring your Melody doll and all your Barbies and we'll put on a concert.' Remember how Patty and I used to do that all the time? We had these little penlights and we'd pretend they were microphones, and we'd set up all our dolls as our audience and sing our lungs out." Lisa extended her arms, clicked her fingers and sang a couple of lines from "Don't Go Breaking My Heart." She ended with a laugh that softened to a nostalgic note. "I remember once when we put on a show for you and Dad wearing some of her sister's dance costumes. We made up little tickets and charged you admission."

Bess remembered, too. Sitting beside Lisa, freeing the buttons on the back of her wedding dress, she remembered altogether too well those happier days, before her and Michael's troubles had begun. Though she could feel nostalgic at moments such as this, she was a realist who knew these flashes were momentary. She and Michael would never be husband and wife again, much as Lisa wished it.

"Why don't you try the dress on, honey?" she said gently.

Lisa set aside the cigar box and got off the bed. Bess stood behind her and forced twenty satin loops around twenty pearl buttons up the back of the dress while Lisa studied the results in the dresser mirror.

"It's going to fit," Lisa said.

"I was a size ten back then. You're a size eight. Even if you get a little tummy in the next few weeks there shouldn't be any problem."

Both of them studied Lisa's reflection. The dress had a beaded stand-up collar above a V-shaped lace bodice that ended with a point on the stomach. It had elbow-length pouf sleeves, a full satin skirt and train trimmed with beadwork and sequins. Though it was wrinkled, it hadn't discolored. "It's still beautiful, isn't it, Mom?"

"Yes, it is. I remember the day my mother said I could buy it, how excited I was. Naturally, it was one of the most expensive ones in the store, and I thought she'd say no but you know Grandma. She was always so crazy about your dad she'd have said yes to anything once she heard the news that I was going to marry him."

Without warning Lisa spun from the mirror and headed for the door. "Wait a minute!" she called as she disappeared.

"Where are you going?"

"Be right back. Stay there!"

Lisa thumped downstairs in her stocking feet and returned in a minute making a high-energy entrance, then dropping to the bed in a swish of wrinkled satin with a photo album on her lap.

"It was right where it always used to be in the bookshelves in the living room," she said breathlessly.

"Oh, Lisa, not those old things." Lisa had brought Bess and Michael's wedding album.

"Why not these old things? I want to see them."

"Lisa, that's wishful thinking."

"I want to see how you looked in the dress."

"You want to see things the way they used to be but that part of our lives is over. Dad and I are divorced and we're staying that way."

"Oh, look . . ." Lisa opened the album. There were Michael and Bess, close up, with their cheeks touching and her bouquet and veil forming an aureole around them. "Gol, Mom, you were just beautiful, and Dad . . . wow, look at him."

The photo caught at Bess's heart while she sat beside her daughter searching for the perfect balance in her response to Lisa. She had been bitter too long and was learning the hurt it had caused her children. At this turning point in her life, Lisa needed this foray into the past. To deny her the freedom of exploring it was to deny a certain part of her heritage. At the same time, allowing her to believe there was a chance of reconciliation between her parents was sheer folly.

"Lisa, dear . . ." Bess took her hand. Lisa looked into Bess's eyes. "Your dad and I had some wonderful years."

"I know. I remember a lot of them."

"I wish we could have made a happier ending for you but it didn't work out that way. I want you to know, though, that I'm glad you forced us to confront each other. It's making me take a second look at myself, which I needed, and even though your dad and I aren't getting back together, it feels much better to be his ex-wife without so much animosity between us."

"But Dad said you looked great the night of the dinner."

"Lisa, darling . . . don't. You're pinning your hopes on nothing."

"Well, what are you going to do, marry *Keith?* Mom, he's such a dork."

"Who said anything about marrying anybody? I'm happy as I am. I'm healthy, the business is going good, I keep busy, I have you and Randy—"

"And what about when Randy decides to grow up? What about when he moves out?" Lisa gestured at the walls. "You going to stay in this big old empty house alone?"

"I'll decide that when the time comes."

"Mom, just promise me one thing—if Dad makes a play for you, or if he asks you out or something, you won't get all pissed off and slug him or anything, will you? Because I think he's going to do it. I saw how he looked at you the other night, while you two were sitting down there at your end of the table—"

"Lisa—"

"—and you're still quite a looker, Ma—"

"Lisa!"

"—and as for Dad, he's one of the truly excellent men around. Even when he was married to that dumb Darla I thought so. You know, Ma, you could do worse."

"I'm not going to talk about it, and I wish you wouldn't."

Lisa left soon thereafter, taking the dress with her to drop at the dry cleaner's. After seeing her out, Bess returned upstairs to turn out the light in Lisa's old room. There on the bed lay the wedding album, bound in white leather and stamped in gold: BESS & MICHAEL CURRAN, JUNE 8, 1968.

The room still seemed to retain the musty smell of the bridal gown and the cigar box, which Lisa had left behind. A fitting smell, Bess thought, for the marriage that had turned to must.

She dropped to the bed, braced a hand beside the album and slowly flipped its pages.

Thoughtful.

Nostalgic.

Alternately relishing and ruing while the diametrically opposed wishes of her two children tugged her in opposite directions—Randy, the bitter; Lisa, the romantic.

She closed the book and fell back on the bed with one wrist across her waist. Outside somebody's dog yapped to be let in. Down in the kitchen the automatic icemaker switched on and sent the hiss of moving water up the pipes in the wall. Out in the world all around her men and women moved through life two-by-two while she lay on her daughter's bed alone.

This is silly. I have tears in my eyes and a pain in my heart that wasn't there before I entered this room. I've let Lisa put ideas into my head that are based on nothing but her sentimentality. Whatever she thought she detected between Michael and me the other night was strictly her imagination.

She rolled her head and reached out to touch the wedding album.

Or was it?

chapter 6

SHE WENT TO THE BEAUTY SHOP on Thursday and had her roots bleached, her ends trimmed and her hair styled. She painted her nails that night and spent nearly fifteen minutes deciding what to wear the next morning, choosing a wool crepe dress in squash gold with a tucked waist, tulip-shaped skirt and a wide belt with an oversized gold buckle. In the morning she finished it off with a variegated scarf, gold earrings and a spritz of perfume, then shot a critical glance at the mirror.

You're still quite a looker, Ma.

If, at given moments in her life, Bess Curran had considered herself a *looker,* she had not done so in the six years since Michael had put her down on that score. The insult lived on each time she looked in a mirror, and no matter what efforts she put into her grooming, at the final moment she always found some detail less than perfect. Usually it was her weight.

Ten pounds, she thought today. Only ten and I'd be where I want to be.

Aggravated with Michael for creating this perennial dissatisfaction and with herself for perpetuating it, she slammed off the light switch and left the room.

She arrived in White Bear Lake with five minutes to spare and approached Michael's condominium doubly impressed, observing it at close range in broad daylight. The sign said CHATEAUGUET. The driveway curved between two giant elms and led through grounds dotted with mature oaks. Closer to the building, a pair of venerable spruce trees stood sentinel beside the doors, taller than the four stories they guarded. The structure itself was V-shaped and sprawling, of white brick and gray siding, studded with royal-blue awnings. It had underground garages, white balconies, brass carriage lanterns and a lot of glass. On the uppermost floor, the decks and patio doors were topped by roof gables inset with sunburst designs.

But more, it had the lake.

One was conscious of it even from the landward side, and Bess found herself speculating on the view she'd discover when she got inside.

The foyer smelled like scented carpet cleaner, had tastefully papered walls, an elevator and a small bank of mailboxes along with a security phone. She picked it up and rang Michael's unit.

He answered immediately, " 'Morning, Bess, is that you?"

"Good morning, yes it is."

"I'll be right down."

She heard the elevator hum before its doors split soundlessly and Michael stepped out, wearing gray/black pleated trousers with needle-fine teal stripes, a teal polo shirt with its collar turned up and a finely knit double-breasted sweater in white. His trousers had the gloss of costly fabric, and the polo shirt picked up the exact hue of the stripes. Since becoming an interior designer, Bess noticed things like that. She could spot cheap fabric at twenty paces and clashing colors at fifty. Michael's clothes were well chosen, even the tassled loafers of soft black leather. She wondered who'd chosen them, since Michael was all but color-blind and had always had difficulty coordinating his wardrobe.

"Thanks for coming, Bess," he said, holding the elevator doors open. "We're going up."

She stepped aboard and was closed into the four-by-six-foot space with him and the familiar smell of his British Sterling. To dispel the sense of déjà vu she asked, "How do you pronounce the name of this place?"

"Chateau-gay," he replied. "Back in the 1900s there was a big hotel here by that name, and it was also the name of a racehorse that won the Kentucky Derby years ago."

"Chateauguet," she repeated. "I like it."

They arrived at an upper hall shaped like the one below, and he waved her ahead of himself into the condominium whose door stood open to their right.

She wasn't three feet inside before exhilaration struck. Space! Enough space to make a designer drool! The entry hall was as wide as most bedrooms, carpeted in a grayed mauve. It was totally bare but for a large, contemporary chandelier of smoked glass and brass. Ahead, the foyer widened into a space where a second, matching chandelier created a rich corridor effect.

Michael took her coat, hung it behind a louvered door and turned back to her. "Well, this is it." He spread his hands. "These are guest bedrooms. . . ." Light came through two doors to their right. "Each one has its own bath." They were identical in size and had generous windows. One bedroom was empty, the other held a drafting table and chair. She glanced over the rooms as she followed Michael, carrying a clipboard, measuring tape and pen, leaving her purse on the floor in the foyer.

"Do these windows face due north?"

"More like northwest," he replied.

She decided to put off her note-taking and measuring until she'd moved through the entire place, to get a sense of each of its rooms in relationship to the whole. They advanced beyond the entry to an interior octagonal space in the center of which the second chandelier hung. It appeared to be the hub of the apartment, created of four flat walls and four doorways.

"The architect calls this a gallery," Michael said, stopping dead center in the middle of the octagon.

Bess turned in a circle and looked up at the chandelier. "It's very dramatic . . . or can be."

They had entered the gallery from the hall door. Michael indicated the others. "Kitchen, combination living room/dining room, and utility area and powder room off this small hall. Which would you like to see first?"

"Let's see the living room." She stepped into it to be washed in light and delight. The room faced south-by-southeast, had a marble fireplace on the northerly wall, another chandelier at the south end and two sets of sliding glass doors—a triple and a double—that gave onto a deck overlooking the frozen lake. Between the two doors the wall took a turn at an obtuse angle.

"It's just struck me, Michael, this place isn't rectangular, is it?"

"No, it's not. The entire building is arrow-shaped, and this unit is at the point of the arrow, so I guess you'd call it oblique."

"Oh, how marvelous. If you knew how many rectangular rooms I've designed you'd know how exciting this is." Though the two guest bedrooms were rectangular, this room was a modified wedge. "Show me the rest."

The kitchen was done in white tile and Formica with blond oak woodwork. It was combined with an informal family room, which had sliding doors giving onto the same deck that wrapped around the entire apartment on the lake side. The laundry area was in a wedge-shaped space beside a powder room, both leading off the gallery. The master bedroom led off the living room and shared its fireplace flue. Besides the fireplace, the bedroom had yet another set of glass doors leading onto the deck, a walk-in closet and a bathroom big enough to host a basketball game.

In the bathroom, the smell of Michael's cosmetics was as evocative as that of fresh-cut grass. A rechargeable razor sat on the vanity with its tiny red light glowing. Beside it lay his toothbrush and a tube of Close-Up. The shower door was wet and on a towel bar hung a horrendous beach towel with fireworks designs in gaudy colors on a black background. No washcloth. He'd always used his hands.

Shame on you, Bess, you're regressing.

In the bedroom her glance slid over his mattresses and returned for a second take, then moved on as if the sight of them lumped on the floor had not stirred old memories. He must have left Darla taking nothing. Even his blankets were new; the fold lines still showed. How ironic, Bess thought, I'll probably end up choosing his bedspread again. Already she was envisioning the room with the bed and window treatment matching.

"Well, that's it," Michael said.

"I must say, Michael, I'm impressed."

"Thank you."

They returned to the living room with its magnificent scope. "The way the building blends with the land, and how the architect utilized the mature trees, the contour of the lakeshore and even the little park next door—it all becomes a part of the interior design as well as the exterior. The outdoors is actually taken inside through these magnificent stretches of glass, while at the same time the trees lend privacy." Bess strode the length of the room, admiring the view through the windows while Michael stood near the fireplace with his hands in his trouser pockets. "It's interesting," Bess mused aloud, "clients are often surprised to learn that architects and interior designers rarely get along well at all. The reason is because very few architects design from the outside in the way this one did, consequently we're often called in to analyze the space use and handle the problems the architect left behind. In this case, that's not so. This guy really knew what he was doing."

Michael smiled. "I'll tell him you said so. He works for me."

From the opposite end of the room she faced him.

"You built this building?"

"Not exactly. I developed the property and arranged to have it built. The city of White Bear Lake came to me and asked me to do it."

"Ah . . ." Bess's eyebrows rose in approval. "I had no idea your projects had grown to this size. Congratulations."

Michael dipped his head, displaying an appealing mix of humility and pride.

She was no appraiser but the building had to be worth several million dollars, and if the city came to him and invited him to do the job, he must have established a sterling reputation. So both of them—Michael and she—had made great strides since their breakup. "Do you mind if we continue moving from room to room while we talk?"

"Not at all."

"It helps me recall where I've been and familiarize myself with the psychological impact of each room, how the light falls, the space there is to be filled and the space that should remain unfilled. It's kind of like kicking the tires on a car before you buy it."

They gave each other glancing grins and moved into the gallery, where they stopped directly beneath the chandelier. Bess braced her clipboard against her hip and said, "On with the questions. I've been doing all the talking and it's supposed to be the other way around during a house call. I'm here to listen to you."

"Ask away."

"Did you choose the carpet?"

She'd noted that the same carpet was used throughout, with the exception of the kitchen and baths. It wasn't a color she'd have expected him to like. From the gallery she could glance to the sunny or shadowed side of the condo and observe its subtleties change.

"No, it was here when I took over the place. Actually what happened was that this unit was sold to someone else, a couple named Sawyer, who intended it to be their retirement home. Mrs. Sawyer picked out the carpet and had it laid but before she and her husband could close on the place, he died. She decided to stay put, so I inherited the carpet."

"It's staying?"

"It should. It's brand-new and I'm the first tenant."

"You say that as if you have reservations."

He pursed his lips and studied the carpeting. "I can live with it."

"Make sure before we plan a whole interior around it, and be aware that color affects your energy, your productivity, your ability to relax, many things. You're as affected by color as you are by texture and light and space. You should surround yourself with colors you're comfortable with."

"I can live with it," he repeated.

"And I can tone it down, make it more masculine by bringing out its gray rather than its rose, perhaps using a deep gray and a pastel lavender as an accent, maybe bringing in some black pieces. How does that sound?"

"All right."

"Do you have a carpet sample I can take along?"

"In the entry closet on the shelf. I'll give you a piece before you leave."

"What are your thoughts on mirrored walls?"

"In here?" Michael looked up. They were still standing in the octagonal gallery.

"An interior space like this would benefit from them. It could be dramatic to relight the chandelier in four mirror panels."

"It *sounds* dramatic. Let me think about it."

They moved into the room with the drafting table. "Do you work here?"

"Yes."

"How much?"

"Primarily in the evenings. Daytime I'm in the office."

Bess wandered nearer the drafting table. "Do you work—" she began but the question died on her lips. Taped onto an extension lamp over the drafting table was a picture of their two children, taken when they were about seven and nine, in the backyard after a water fight. They were freckled and smiling and squinting into the hard summer sun. Randy was missing a front tooth and Lisa's hair was sticking up in a messy swirl where the force of the hose had shot it.

"Do I work . . . ?" Michael repeated.

She knew full well he'd seen her reaction to the picture, but she was a businesswoman now and personal byplay had no place in this house call. Bess regrouped her emotions and went on.

"Do you work every evening?"

"I have been lately." He didn't add, Since Darla and I broke up, but he didn't have to. It was obvious he sat here in this room regretting some things.

"Would you ever be needing a desk in this room?"

"That might be nice."

"File cabinets?"

"Probably not."

"Shelving?"

He wobbled a hand like a plane dipping its wings.

"In order of preference, would you place this room high or low in the decorating order?"

"Low."

"All right . . . let's move on."

They meandered to the other guest bedroom, and from there to the powder room, the gallery, the kitchen, ending up in the living room.

"Tell me, Michael, what's your opinion of art deco?"

"It can be a little stark but I've seen some I like."

"And glass—glass tabletops, for instance, as opposed to wood."

"Either is fine."

"Would you be entertaining in this room?"

"Maybe."

"How many might you want to seat at one time?"

"I don't know."

"A dozen maybe?"

"Probably not."

"Six?"

"I suppose so."

"Would that entertaining be formal or informal?"

"Informal, probably."

"Meals . . ." She moved to the end of the room where the chandelier hung, studying the change of light on the carpet, imagining it on furniture as she moved from the light-realm of one window to another. "Would you ever entertain at sit-down meals?"

"I have in the past."

"Will you use the fireplace or not?"

"Yes."

"Will you ever watch television in this room?"

"No."

"How about a tape player or CD player?"

"Probably I'd want that in the family room off the kitchen."

"Which do you prefer, vertical or horizontal lines?"

"What?"

She looked up at him and smiled. "That one usually throws people. Vertical or horizontal? One is restful, the other energetic."

"Vertical."

"Ah . . . energetic. Are you an early riser or a late riser?"

"Early." He always had been but she had to ask.

"And how about the tail end of the day? Do you watch the David Letterman show?"

"Do I what?"

"Are you a night person, Michael?"

He scratched his neck and grinned crookedly at the floor. "I remember a time when I was but it's funny how nature takes care of that for you when you reach middle age."

She smiled and went on to her next subject. "Give me your opinion of this chandelier." She looked up at the ceiling.

He wandered nearer and looked up, too. "It reminds me of grapefruit sections," he said.

She laughed. "Grapefruit sections?"

"Yeah, those pieces of smoky glass all standing on end like that. Aren't they shaped like grapefruit sections?"

"Skinny ones, maybe. Do you like it?"

"Mmm . . ." He studied it pensively. "Yeah, I like it a lot."

"Good. So do I."

She made a note about repeating smoked glass in the tables and another about café doors as she moved through a wide doorway into the family room/kitchen. In this room the view had curved away from the lake and focused instead on a tall stand of cottonwood trees—naked now in winter—and a small town park with a white gazebo. Thankfully there were no swing sets or playground equipment, which would be desirable for a young family, not for a building that catered to older, wealthier people.

"What happens in the park?" she asked.

"Picnics in the summer, I guess. That's about all."

"No band concerts, no boat launching?"

"No. Boats are launched over at the county beach or at the White Bear Yacht Club."

"Will you launch one?"

"Maybe. I've thought about it."

"A lot of sailboats on the lake, aren't there?"

"Yes."

"I imagine you're looking forward to watching them from both inside and out on the deck."

"Sure."

She made a note about vertical blinds and sauntered toward the kitchen island, where a jar of peanut butter, a loaf of bread and some throw-away containers created his bachelor's pantry. She glanced over the pitiful collection, then looked away because it brought a sharp desire to play housewife, and neither of them needed that.

"Will this be a working kitchen?" she asked, her back to Michael as she waited for an answer.

It took some time before he replied, "No."

She gathered her composure and turned to rest her clipboard on the island. "Are there any hobbies of yours I should know about?"

"They haven't changed since six years ago. Hunting and the outdoors but I go up to my cabin for that."

"Have you developed any allergies?"

His eyebrows puckered. "Allergies?"

"It has to do with fabrics and fibers," she explained.

"No allergies."

"Then I guess all that's left to ask about is the budget. Have you thought about a range you want me to work within?"

"Just do it the way you'd do it for yourself. You were always good at it, and I trust you."

"All of it?"

"Well . . ." He glanced around uncertainly. "I guess so."

"The guest bedroom, too?"

His eyes came back to her. "I hate empty rooms," he said.

"Yes . . ." she agreed, "and it is the first room a visitor sees when he steps into the foyer."

She had the illogical impulse to go to him, take him in her arms for a moment, pat his back and say, It'll be all right, Michael, I'll fill it with things so it isn't so lonely, though she knew perfectly well a home full of things could not substitute for a home full of people.

She looked down at her clipboard. "I'll need to take some measurements. Would you mind helping me?"

"Not at all."

"I've tried to sketch the layout of the unit but it's unusual enough to be difficult."

"I have some floor plans at the office that were done for the sales people. I'll send you one."

"Oh, that would be helpful. Meanwhile, shall we measure?"

They spent the next twenty minutes at opposite ends of a surveyor's tape, getting room and window dimensions. When they were all tidily written on her rough floor plan, she cradled the clipboard against her arm and reeled in the tape.

"What happens next?" he asked as they returned to the foyer, where he retrieved her coat and held it for her.

"I'll take all these dimensions and transfer them onto graph paper, room by room. Then I'll go 'shopping' through my catalogs and come up with a furniture plan, window treatments, fabric and wallpaper samples. I'll also have all the suggested furniture cut out to scale on magnetic plastic so they can be arranged on the floor plan. When all that is done I'll give you a call and we'll get together for the presentation. I usually do that at my store after hours because all my books and samples are there and it makes it easier without customers interrupting. Then, too, if you don't like something I've suggested we can go into other books and look for something else."

"So when will I hear from you?"

Her coat was buttoned and she drew on her gloves. "I'll try to get on it right away and get back to you within a week, since you're living in rather Spartan conditions. I don't see anything wrong with playing favorites and putting you ahead of some of my other clients, do you?"

She flashed him a professional smile and extended her gloved hand. "Thank you, Michael."

He took it, squeezing hard. "Aren't you forgetting something?"

"What?"

"Your forty-dollar trip charge."

"Oh, that. I initiated the trip charge merely to dissuade lonely people who only want company for an afternoon—and you'd be amazed how many of them there are. But it's obvious you need furniture, and you're not some stranger whose intentions I question."

"Business is business, Bess, and if there's a trip charge, I'll pay it."

"All right, but why don't I bill you for it?"

"Absolutely not. Wait here."

He went into the room with the drafting table, leaving her in the empty foyer. She watched him through the doorway, stretching her gloves on tighter. She picked up her clipboard, her purse, and watched him some more, then followed him into the room, where he was making out the check with one hand flat on the drafting table, his elbow jutting.

The photo was still there, compelling. She studied it over his angled shoulders and said quietly, "They were adorable when they were that age, weren't they?"

He stopped writing, looked at the picture awhile and tore out the check before turning to Bess. His gaze lingered on her, then traveled once more to the picture.

"Yes, they were."

The room remained silent while the two of them studied their son and daughter caught in a carefree day from their past. His gaze returned to Bess and she felt it on her cheek as one feels heat from a nearby fire, while she continued studying the picture.

"Michael, I . . ." Struggling for words, she met his eyes and felt a burning sense of imminence in the admission she was about to make. "I went to visit my mother on Sunday and we had a talk." She paused but he said nothing. "I told her how difficult it's been seeing you again, and she said that the reason is because you're making me take a second look at myself and my fault in the divorce."

Still he waited while she clung to her clipboard and willed the words forth.

"I think I owe you an apology, Michael, for turning the kids against you."

Something changed in his eyes—a quick transport of repressed anger, perhaps. Though he moved not a muscle he seemed more rigid, while his hazel eyes remained steady upon hers.

She looked down at her glove. "I swore I wouldn't do this—mix business with anything personal but it's been bothering me, and today when I saw their picture here I realized that . . . well, that you loved them, too, and how it must have hurt you, losing them." She met his eyes once more. "I'm sorry, Michael."

He thought about it for passing seconds before speaking in a low, throaty tone. "I hated you for it, you know."

She shifted her gaze to the drafting table. "Yes, I know," she said quietly.

"Why did you do it?"

"Because I felt hurt, and wronged."

"But that was another matter entirely, what was between us."

"I know that now."

They stared at each other until the silence in the room seemed to be compressing them.

"Mother said something else." Again Michael waited for her to go on while she struggled for courage to do so. "She said that when I went back to college you fell to the bottom of my priority list and that's why you found another woman." Nothing changed on his face so she asked, "Is that true, Michael?"

"What do you think?"

"I'm asking you."

"Well, I'm not going to answer. I don't see any point, not at this late date."

"So it is true."

He handed her the check. "Thanks for coming, Bess. I really should get down to my office now."

Her cheeks were hot as she accepted his check and said, "I'm sorry, Michael. I shouldn't have brought it up today. It's not the appropriate time."

She preceded him into the foyer, where he opened the door for her then changed his mind and held it closed for a moment.

"Why did you bring it up at all, Bess?"

"I don't know. I don't understand myself lately. It seems as if there were so many things between us that were never settled, all these . . . these ugly emotions that kept roiling around inside me. I guess I just need to deal with them once and for all and put them behind me. That's what apologies are all about, right?"

His eyes lit on hers, hard as chips of resin. He nodded stiffly. "All right, fair enough. Apology accepted."

She didn't smile; she couldn't. Neither could he.

He found her a carpet sample and ushered her out, at a respectable distance, and pushed the elevator button. The door opened instantly, while he was still speaking.

"Thanks for coming."

She stepped on, turned to offer a conciliatory smile and found him already stalking back into his condo. The elevator door closed and she rode downstairs, wondering if by her apology she'd made things better or worse between them.

chapter 7

*R*ANDY CURRAN DROPPED INTO a lopsided upholstered
rocker and reached into his jacket pocket for his bag of
pot. It was almost 11 P.M. and Bernie's mom was out, as usual. She was
a cocktail waitress so most nights they had the place to themselves. The
radio was tuned to Cities 97 and they were waiting for "The Grateful Dead
Hour." Bernie sat on the floor with an electric guitar on his lap, the amp
turned off as he picked along with a Guns N' Roses song. Randy had
known Bernie Bertelli since the eighth grade, when he'd moved to town
right after his parents got divorced, too. They'd smoked a lot of dope
together since then.

Bernie's place was a dump. The floors were crooked, and the walls had
a lot of plastic knickknacks hanging on them. The shag carpeting was the
color of baby shit and matted worse than the hair of the two old Heinz 57
dogs, Skipper and Bean, who were allowed to do pretty much anything
they wanted anywhere in the house. Skipper and Bean were presently
stretched out on the davenport, which in its younger days had been
upholstered in some cheap nylon plaid but now was covered with a flowered throw with soiled spots the shapes of the dogs at either end. The
coffee tables and end tables had screw-on legs and the drapery pleats
sagged between all the hooks. Against one wall a pyramid of beer cans
reached the ceiling, the top can wedged against the water-stained tile.
Bernie's mom had put the top one there herself.

Randy never sat on the davenport, not even when he was high or drunk.

He never got *that* high or *that* drunk! He always took the green rocker, a decrepit thing that looked as if it had had a stroke, because everything on it sagged to one side. The broken springs in the seat were covered with a folded rag rug to keep them from poking your ass, and the upholstered arms were covered with cigarette burns.

Randy fished out the Ziploc bag and his bat, a miniature pipe big enough for a single hit. Gone were the days of rolling smokes. Who could afford that anymore?

"This shit is getting expensive, man," he said.

"Yeah, what'd you pay?"

"Sixty bucks."

"For a quarter?"

Randy rearranged his expression and shrugged.

Bernie whistled. "Better be good shit, man."

"The best. Lookit here . . ." Randy opened the bag. "Buds."

Bernie leaned over, took a closer look and said, "Buds . . . wow, how'd you score that?" Everybody knew that buds gave you the most for your money—better than leaves or sticks or seeds. You could pack it tighter and get really loaded off a couple of hits.

Randy packed his pipe, missing the days when he'd tear off a Zigzag paper and roll a joint big enough to pass around. He'd seen a guy one time who could roll one with one hand. He'd practiced it himself at home a few times over a sheet of paper, but he'd dropped more than he'd rolled, so he'd settled for doing it deftly with two hands, which in itself was considered a mark of prowess among pot smokers.

Randy struck a match. The bat held less than a thimbleful. He lit up, took a deep drag and held it in his lungs until they burned. He exhaled, coughed and refilled the bat.

"Want a hit, Bernie?"

Bernie took a turn, coughing, too, while a scent like burning oregano filled the room.

It took two hits before Randy got the rush—the sweet chill that riffled through him and left him with a slow-growing euphoria. Everything became so exquisitely distorted. Bernie looked as though he was on the opposite side of a fishbowl, and the lights on the component set shimmered like a meteor shower that was taking ten years to fall. Someplace in the distance men coughed occasionally but the sound filtered down a long corridor, like shouting through a concrete culvert. The music from the radio became a major sensation that expanded his pores, his hair follicles, his fingers and his ability to perceive.

Words came to him and swirled through his vision as if they had mass and form—graceful, beckoning words.

"I met this girl," Randy said. "Did I say that already?" Seemed like he'd said it about one hour ago and it had taken till now for the words to drift down, landing on the dog Bean, bouncing off his red fur in slow motion, disturbing him so he rolled over onto his back with his paws up and his eyes closed.

"What girl?"

"Maryann. Some name, huh? . . . Maryann. Who names their kids Maryann anymore?"

"Who's Maryann?"

"Maryann Padgett. I had dinner at her house. Lisa is marrying her brother."

On the davenport Bean was snoring and his lip was fluttering. Randy became transfixed by the sight, which took on kaleidoscopic beauty, that dog lip, black on the outside, pink on the inside, flap-flapping in rhythm with his gentle snores.

"She scares the shit out of me."

"Why?"

" 'Cause she's a good girl."

Thirst came, exaggerated like everything else. "Hey, Bern, I got the dry mouth. You got some beer?"

The beer tasted like magic elixir, every sip a thousand times better than orgasm.

"We don't mess with good girls, do we, Bern?"

"Shit no, man . . . why should we?"

"Screw 'em and strew 'em, hey, Bern?"

"That's right. . . ." Two minutes later Bernie repeated, "That's right."

Ten minutes after that Bernie said, "Shit, man, I'm really fucked up."

"Me too," Randy said. "I'm so fucked up your nose even looks good. You got a nose like a goddamned anteater and I'm so fucked up your nose looks cute."

Bernie laughed and scattered sound down a jeweled corridor.

Many minutes later Randy said, "You can't get serious about girls, you know what I mean, man? I mean . . . hell . . . next thing you know you're marryin' 'em and you got kids and you're screwin' somebody else's old lady and walkin' out and your kids are bawlin'."

Bernie digested that a long time before he asked, "You bawl when your old man left?"

"Sometimes. Not where anybody could see me, though."

"Yeah, me too."

A while later Randy felt the lethargy lifting and the munchies coming on. He pitched forward in his chair and counted seven beer cans around him. He belched and Bean woke up, stretched and quivered, jumped off the couch and shook a fresh layer of dog hair onto the matted carpet. Pretty soon Skipper did the same. The two of them nosed at Bernie, whose eyes were as red as if he'd been fighting fires.

Randy gave himself some time, coming down. It was after midnight and the deadhead hour was in progress on Cities 97 and he had to be up at six. Actually, he was getting pretty tired of the Grateful Dead and of that stinking job at the warehouse. And of this pigsty of Bernie's and of the rising cost of marijuana. And of Bernie, who never could afford to buy his own. What the hell was he doing here in this lopsided rocking chair with the cigarette burns on its arms, looking at Bernie's big nose and counting the beer cans?

Who was he getting even with?

His father, that's who.

Problem was, the old man didn't really give a damn.

Bess received the floor plan from Michael on the Monday after she'd seen his condo. He'd mailed it, along with a note in his familiar handwriting, on a piece of notepaper with his company logo in blue at the top.

> *Bess, Here's the floor plan for the condo, as promised. I've thought about the mirrors for the gallery. Go ahead and plan them in. I think I'll like them. I've been thinking about what you said just before you left and it makes me realize there were areas where I needed to change and didn't. Maybe we can talk about it some more. It was nice seeing you again. Michael.*

She got a queer flutter at the sight of his handwriting. Funny about a thing like that, it was like studying his wet toothbrush and his damp towel, things he'd touched, held, worked with. She reread the entire message four times, imagining his beautifully shaped hand holding the pen as he wrote it. *Maybe we can talk about it some more.* Now that was a loaded suggestion, was it not? And had it really been nice for him, seeing her again? Didn't he feel the same tension she felt whenever they stood in the same room? Didn't he feel eager to escape, as she did?

Michael received a call from Lisa.

"Hey, Dad, how's it going?"

"All right. How's it going with you?"

"Busy. Cripes, I didn't dream there was this much stuff you had to do to plan a wedding. You free on Saturday afternoon?"

"I can be."

"Good, 'cause you men have to meet at Gingiss Formal Wear and pick out your tuxedos."

"Tuxedos, wow."

"You're gonna be a knockout, Dad."

Michael smiled. "You think so, huh? What time and where?"

"Two o'clock at Maplewood."

"I'll be there."

Randy hadn't thought about his dad being there. He walked into Gingiss Formal Wear at two o'clock the following Saturday afternoon, and there stood Michael, talking with Mark and Jake Padgett. Randy came up short. Mark spied him and came forward, extending his hand. "Here's our last guy. Hey, Randy, thanks for coming."

"Sure, no problem."

Jake shook his hand. "Hello, Randy."

"Mr. Padgett."

That left only Michael, who offered his hand, too. "Randy."

Randy looked into his father's somber eyes and felt a sick longing to go into his arms and hug him and say, "Hi, Dad." But he had not called Michael *Dad* in a long time. The word welled up and seemed to fill his throat, needing to be spoken, needing to be repressed. Michael's eyes so resembled his own it seemed like looking in a mirror while his father's hand waited.

At last he put his hand in Michael's and said, "Hello."

Michael flushed and gripped Randy's hand hard. Long after the contact ended Randy felt the imprint of his father's palm on his own.

A young blond clerk intruded. "Everybody here now, gentlemen? If you'll step this way."

They followed him into a rear room, carpeted and mirrored. Mark and his father went first, leaving Michael and Randy to exchange uncertain glances before Michael politely waved Randy through the doorway before him. The room held tuxedos in every conceivable color from black to pink, and smelled of a hot iron from a tailor's adjacent workroom. The clerk told Mark, "Sometimes the bride is in on this, too. Since yours isn't, I presume you've talked about colors."

"The bridesmaid's dress is coral. She said I could decide what color the tuxes should be."

"Ah, good. Then might I suggest ivory with coral cummerbunds—ivory is always tasteful, always elegant, and seems to be the trendy choice right now. We have several styles, the most popular are probably the Christian Dior and After Six."

The clerk prattled on while Michael and Randy remained intensely aware of each other, electrified by their encounter. With their emotions in turmoil they missed much of what was being said. They assessed jackets with satin lapels, pleated shirts, bow ties, cummerbunds and patent-leather shoes.

They removed their jackets, faced a wall of mirrors and had their measurements taken—neck, sleeve, chest, overarm, waist and outseam. They shucked off their pants and donned trousers with satin stripes up the sides, stood stocking-footed before a wall of mirrors and zipped up their flies, trading glances in the mirror before looking discreetly away.

They buttoned on pleated shirts, ruffled shirts, experimented with bow ties and thought about when they were a boy and a young father and Randy had put shaving cream on his face and shaved with a bladeless razor while his dad stood beside him and shaved with a real one; and times when they'd stood side-by-side and Randy had asked, wishfully, "Do you think I'll ever be taller than you, Dad?" And now he was, by a good inch—all grown up and capable of holding grudges.

"A forty-two long, sir," the clerk said. Michael slipped into a tuxedo jacket that smelled of dry-cleaning fluid, tugged the sleeves and collar into place while the clerk circled him, assessing the fit. Mark made some joke and Randy laughed. Jake said, "Never been in one of these monkey suits before, how 'bout you, Michael?"

"Just once." At his own wedding.

When the fitting was done they put on their street clothes again, zipping winter jackets as they shuffled from the store into the mall. Saturday shoppers moved past in twos and threes. The smell of baking cookies drifted through the hall from Mrs. Field's across the way. Mark and Jake headed straight toward the exit, leaving Michael and Randy to follow. Every step of the way Michael felt his chest contract as his chance slipped away. A question danced on his tongue while he feared Randy's rebuff.

Just before they reached the plate-glass doors, Michael spoke. "Listen, I haven't had lunch yet, have you?" He strove for an offhand tone in spite of the fact that his heart was in his throat.

"Yeah, I grabbed a burger earlier," Randy lied.

"You sure? I'm buying."

For a moment their gazes locked. Hope took on new meaning as Michael sensed Randy vacillating about changing his mind.

"No thanks. I'm meeting some friends."

Michael gave away none of the crushing disappointment he felt. "Well, maybe some other time."

"Yeah, sure . . ."

The gravity remained in both of them, exerting a force that distorted their heartbeats. But six years is a long time and some sins go beyond forgiving. So they left the shopping center by separate doors, went their separate ways and clung to their separate hurts.

Like a penitent toward Mecca, Randy drove straight into downtown Stillwater to his mother's store. He had no meeting with friends. He quite nearly had no friends. He had only a deep need to be in his mother's presence after dashing aside his father's halting offer of conciliation.

Heather was at the counter when he walked in, and there were customers browsing.

"Hi, Heather, is Mom here?"

"Up here, darlin'," Bess called. "Come on up."

He shuffled upstairs, dipping his head to avoid bumping the ceiling when he reached the top, and found her among the jumble that looked capable of eating her alive.

"Well, this is a surprise." She swiveled to face him, sitting in a wooden captain's chair with her legs crossed and a black high heel dangling from her toes.

He scratched his head. "Yeah, I guess it is."

She studied him more closely. "Is something wrong?"

He shrugged.

She bent forward and began thrusting books aside, flopping heavy binders of fabric samples off the top of a heap, eventually unearthing a chair of sorts.

"Here . . . sit down."

He sat.

"What's wrong?"

He slouched back in the chair, crossed an ankle over a knee and poked at the blue rubber edge of his Reebok.

"I just saw Dad."

"Oh . . ." Her eyebrows arched. The word escaped her in an extended syllable as she, too, sat back in her chair, studying Randy. Her forearms rested along the worn wooden arms and in one hand she held a yellow pencil with her thumb folded over the red eraser. "Where?"

"We tried on tuxedos together."

"Did you talk?"

Randy spit on one finger and rubbed some dirt off the edge of his shoe sole. "Not really." He rubbed some more. "He wanted to buy me lunch but I said no."

"Why?"

Randy forgot his shoe and looked up. "Why! Shit, Mom, you know why!"

"No I don't. Tell me. If you said no and it's bothering you so much, why didn't you go with him?"

"Because I hate him."

"Do you?"

Their eyes locked in silence.

"Why should I go with him?"

"Because it's the adult thing to do. It's how relationships are handled, it's how wrongs are righted, and because I think you want to. But after six years it takes a little swallowing of pride, and that's hard."

Randy's anger flared. "Yeah, well, why should I swallow my pride when I never did anything to him. He's the one who did it to me!"

"Hold your voice down, Randy," she said calmly. "There are customers downstairs."

Randy whispered, "He walked out on me, I didn't walk out on him!"

"You're wrong, Randy. He walked out on me, not on you."

"It's the same thing, isn't it?"

"No, it's not. It hurt him very much to leave you and Lisa. He made many efforts to see you over the years but I made sure that didn't happen."

"But—"

"And in all these years I wonder if you've ever asked yourself why he walked out on me."

"What do you mean why? For Darla."

"Darla was the symptom, not the disease."

Disgusted, Randy said, "Aw, come on, Mom, who put that idea in your head? Him?"

"I've had a long examination of conscience lately, and I've discovered that your dad wasn't the only one at fault in the divorce. We were very much in love once, you know. When we were first married, when we had you kids—why, there was no family that was happier. Do you remember those times?"

Randy was sitting the way losers sit on the sidelines during the last thirty seconds of a championship basketball game. He stared at the floor between his Reeboks and made no reply.

"Do you remember exactly when it started to change?"

Randy said nothing.

"Do you?" she repeated softly.

He lifted his head. "No."

"It started when I went back to college. And do you know why?"

Randy waited, looking disconsolate, studying his mother.

"Because I didn't have time for your dad anymore. I came home at the end of the day and there was a family to take care of and housework to do, besides studying, and I was so set on doing it all that I let the most important thing go—my relationship with your dad. I'd get upset with him because he wouldn't help me around the house, and, yes, he was at fault for that but I never *asked* him nicely, we never sat down and talked about it. Instead, I made cutting remarks occasionally, and the rest of the time I zoomed around the house with my mouth tight, feeling like a martyr. Then it became a bone of contention between us. He refused to help me and I refused to ask him to, and pretty soon it was left up to you kids, and you weren't old enough to do it well, so most of the time things were in a mess. Now, if all that was going on in the rest of the house, what do you think was going on in the bedroom?"

Randy only stared at his mother.

"Nothing. And when nothing goes on in the bedroom it sounds the death knell to a relationship between a man and a wife. And that was my fault, not your dad's. . . . That's why he found Darla."

Randy's cheeks grew pink. Bess tipped her chair forward and rested her elbows on her lap.

"You're old enough to hear this, Randy. You're old enough to learn from it. Someday you'll be married, and at first it'll be a bed of roses, and then the humdrum starts in and you forget to do the small things that made that person fall in love with you in the first place. You stop saying good morning, and picking up his shoes when he forgets to take them to his closet, and bringing home the one special kind of Dairy Queen he likes. After all, it's out of your way and you're in a hurry. When he says, Do you want to take a bike ride after supper? you say no because you've had a rough day, so he goes alone and you don't stop to realize that if you'd gone with him it would have made your day a little better. And when he takes a shower before bed, you roll over and pretend to be asleep already because, believe it or not, you begin to consider sex work. You stop doing these things, and then the other one stops doing them, and pretty soon you're substituting criticism for praise, and giving orders instead of making requests, and letting sex fall by the wayside, and in no time at all the whole marriage falls apart."

A long silence passed before Bess sat back in her chair and went on ruminating quietly.

"I remember once, just before we broke up, your dad said to me, We never laugh anymore, Bess. And I realized it was true. You've got to keep laughing, no matter how hard times seem to be. It's what gets you through, and if you really stop to analyze it, one person trying to make another one laugh is a way of showing love, isn't it? It says, I care about you. I want to see you happy. Your dad was right. We had stopped laughing."

Bess set her chair in motion. The spring beneath the seat made a tick with each slight undulation while Randy studied her crossed legs. From downstairs came the *tt-tt-tt-tt* of Heather closing out the cash register for the day; then she turned on the lamps in the front window and called, "I'm going now. I'll lock the front door on my way out."

"Thanks, Heather. Have a nice weekend."

"You, too. 'Bye, Randy."

" 'Bye, Heather," he called.

When she was gone, the sense of intimacy doubled with all quiet below, and the overhead lights darkened. Only the dim light from Bess's desk lamp spread a brandy-colored glow on her abandoned work. She went on speaking in the same quiet tone as before. "I had a talk with Grandma Dorner a while back. It was after I saw your dad at Lisa's. I asked her to tell me, after all these years, why she'd never taken my side during the divorce. She verified all these things I've just told you and more."

Randy met his mother's eyes again as her tone took on sudden passion. Once more she leaned toward him earnestly.

"Listen to me, Randy. I've spent six years telling you all the reasons you should blame your dad, and now I've spent a few minutes telling you why you should blame me. But the truth is, you shouldn't blame anyone. Your dad and I both had a part in the breakup of our marriage. Each of us made mistakes. Each of us got hurt some. Each of us retaliated. You got hurt, too, and you retaliated. . . ." She took his hand. "I understand that . . . but it's time to reassess, dear."

He fixed his eyes on their joined hands, rubbing his thumb over hers. He appeared sheer miserable. "I don't know, Mom."

"If I can, you can." She squeezed his hand in encouragement.

He remained passive, disconsolate, answering nothing.

After some time, Bess swiveled toward her desk and began clustering her work, though she had little spirit for it. She scooped together a few papers, then swung back to Randy.

"You get to look more like him every day. It really does things to my insides sometimes when I turn and catch a glimpse of you standing the way he used to, or grinning the way he used to." She reached out and took both his hands loosely, turning them palms up within her own. "You got his hands," she said. "And his eyes." She looked into them and let a moment of silence pass before smiling gently. "Try as you might to deny you're his, you can't. And that's what hurts most, isn't it, honey?"

He made no reply but the expression in his eyes told her this day had made a deep impression on him.

"Well!" With forced brightness she sat back and checked her watch. "It's getting late and I have a little more work to do here while it's quiet."

"You going home then?"

"In about an hour."

"What's so important that it keeps you here on a Saturday night?"

"Actually, it's some work for your dad. I'm doing the interior design work for his new condo."

"When did all this happen?"

"I went to see it this week."

"Are you two getting back together or something?"

"No, we're not getting back together. He hired me to decorate his place, is all."

"Do you *want* to get back together?"

"No, but it feels better treating him civilly than it did being enemies. There's something about being hateful that deteriorates a person. Well, listen, honey, I really should get back to work, okay?"

"Yeah, sure...." Randy rose and went down one step so he could stand erect. He turned back to his mother. "I'll see you at home, then. You fixing supper when you get there?"

A shaft of guilt struck Bess deep. "I'm afraid not. I have a date with Keith."

"Oh ... well ...."

"If I'd known you wanted to, I would have—"

"No, no ... hell, I'm no baby. I can find supper by myself."

"What will you do tonight, then?"

"I'll probably go up to Popeye's. There's a new band playing there."

"See you at home in an hour or so."

When Randy was gone Bess turned back to her graph paper but sat staring at it with the pencil idle in her hands. Tonight was one of those rare nights when Randy truly wanted to be with her, and she felt devastated for having turned him down. But how was a mother to know? He was nineteen, she forty. They lived in the same house but went their separate ways. Most Saturday nights he wouldn't have stayed home if she'd cooked a five-course meal.

But all the commonsense self-rebuttal in the world would not assuage her guilt. A thought came to accompany it, to add weight to the burden she already carried: if Michael and I had never divorced, we'd be there together on nights like this when Randy needs us. If we had never divorced, he wouldn't be going through this pain in the first place.

On the street a short distance from the Blue Iris, Randy slammed his car door, started the engine and sat staring at the windshield while it collected his breath and turned it to frost. The streets of Stillwater were deserted, the ice along the curbs was too dirty and pitted to reflect the red stoplights. Dark had fallen. By 6:30 the streets would be strung with cars as diners came out to enjoy the restaurants, but now at the close of the business day the whole town looked like the aftermath of a nuclear power leak—not a moving soul about. A semi lumbered up Main Street from the south. He could hear it coming, downshifting, rumbling. He watched it appear at the corner ahead and make a right-hand turn toward the lift bridge, heading east into Wisconsin.

He didn't want to go home.

He didn't want to go to Bernie's.

He didn't want to be with any girls.

He didn't want any fast food.

He decided to drive over to Grandma Dorner's. She was always cheery, and there was always something to eat over there, plus he liked her new place.

Stella Dorner answered his knock and swept him into her arms for a hug. "Well, Randy Curran, you handsome thing, what are you doing here on a Saturday night?"

She smelled like ritzy perfume when he hugged her. Her hair was combed fluffy and she had on a fancy blue dress. "Just came to see my best girl." When he released her she laughed and lifted her hands to her left ear to fit it with a pierced earring.

"You're a doggone liar but I love it." She turned a circle and her skirt flared. "There, how do I look?"

"You're a killer, Gram."

"I hope he thinks so. I've got a date."

"A date!"

"And he's darned good-looking, too. He's got all his hair, all his teeth *and* his gallbladder! A darned nice set of pecs, too, if I do say so myself."

Randy laughed.

"I met him at my exercise class. He's taking me dancing to the Bel Rae Ballroom."

Randy scooped her close and executed an Arthur Murray–style turn. "Stand him up and go with me instead."

She laughed and pushed him away. "Go find your own girlfriend. Have you got one, by the way?"

"Mmm . . . got my eye on one."

"What's the matter with *her?*" She gave his arm a love pat as she swung away, crescendoing as she walked toward her bedroom. "So how's everything with you?"

"Fine," he called, ambling into the living room. There were lights on all over the condo, with music playing on a component set and a painting on an easel by the sliding glass doors.

"I hear you're going to be in a wedding," Stella called from the far end of the place.

"How about that."

"And I also hear you're going to be an uncle."

"Can you believe it?"

"Do I look like a great-grandma to you?"

"Are you kidding? Hey, Gram, did you paint these violets?"

"Yes, how do you like them?"

"Jeez, they're good, Gram! I didn't know you could paint!"

"Neither did I! It's fun." The lights went off in the far bedroom, the bathroom, the hall, and Stella breezed into the living room, wearing a necklace that matched her earrings. "Did you find a band to play with yet?"

"Nope."

"Are you trying?"

"Well . . . not lately."

"How do you expect to find a band if you don't keep trying?" The doorbell rang and Stella said, "Oh, there he is!" She skipped once on her way to answer. Randy followed, feeling like the old one there.

The man who came in had wavy silver hair, shaggy eyebrows, a firm chin and a nice cut on his suit. His pecs didn't look too bad, either.

"Gil," she said. "This is my grandson, Randy. He just dropped in to say hello. Randy, this is Gilbert Harwood." The two shook hands, and Gil's grip was hearty. They made small talk but Randy could see the pair was eager to be going.

Minutes later he found himself back in his car, watching his grandma drive off with her date. Hungrier. Lonelier.

He headed back down McKusick Lane to the stop sign at Owens Street, where he sat observing the collection of cars around The Harbor across the street. He parked and went into the crowded beer joint, slid onto a bar stool and ordered a glass of tap beer. The place was smoky and smelled like the grill was in use. The customers were potbellied, gruff-voiced and had a lot of broken capillaries in their faces.

The guy beside Randy wore a Minnesota Twins billcap, blue jeans and an underwear shirt beneath a soiled, quilted vest. His forearms rested on the bar while he turned his head and glanced at Randy from beneath puffy eyelids. "How's it goin'?" he said.

"Good . . . good," Randy replied and took a swig from his glass.

They sat with their elbows two inches apart, sipping beer, listening to Randy Travis sing a two-year-old song on the jukebox, and the sizzle of cold meat hitting a hot grill in the kitchen, and occasional loud bursts of laughter. Somebody came in and the cold air momentarily chilled the backs of their legs before the door thumped closed. Randy watched eight faces above eight bar stools turn and check out the new arrivals before returning indifferently to their beers. He finished his own, got off the stool, fished a quarter from his pocket and used the pay phone to dial Lisa's number.

Her voice sounded hurried when she answered.

"Hey, Lisa, it's Randy. You busy?"

"Yeah, sort of. Mark is here and we're making spanakopita to take to an all-Greek supper over at some friends' of ours. We're in butter and filo to our elbows!"

"Oh, well, listen, it's no big deal. I was just gonna see if you wanted to watch a video or something. Thought I could pick one up and come over."

"Gosh, Rand, sorry. Not tonight. Tomorrow night, though. I'll be around then."

"Yeah, well maybe I'll stop over then. Listen, have a good time tonight and say hi to Mark."

"Will do. Call me tomorrow, then."

"Yeah, sure. 'Bye."

Back in his car, Randy started the engine, turned on the radio and sat awhile with his hands hanging loosely on the wheel. He hiccuped once, then belched and studied the lights of the houses on either side of the Owens Street hill. What were they all doing in there? Little kids having supper with their folks. Young married couples having supper with each other. What would Maryann Padgett say if he called her up and asked her out? Hell, he didn't have enough money to take her anyplace decent. He'd spent that sixty bucks on pot earlier this week, and his gas tank was nearly empty, and the payment on his drum set was due, and payday wasn't until next Friday.

Shit.

He rested his forehead on the wheel. It was icy and brought a sharp stab of cold that concentrated in the back of his neck.

He lifted his head and pictured his dad's reflection in the mirror today beside his own while they'd zipped up their flies and experimented with tying bow ties. He wondered where they'd have gone if he'd said yes to lunch, what they'd have talked about, if they'd be together now.

He checked his watch. Not even seven yet. His mother would still be home, getting ready for her date with Keith, and he'd just be in their way if he got there before they left; and his mother would get that guilty look on her face for leaving him after he'd opened his big mouth at the store and asked if she was making supper.

Everybody had somebody. Everybody but him.

He reached into his pocket, found his bat and the Ziploc bag of marijuana and decided, To hell with it all.

chapter 8

*B*ESS AND KEITH ATE AT LIDO'S at a table beneath a potted tree trimmed with miniature lights. The minestrone was thick and spicy, the pasta homemade and the chicken parmigiana exquisite. When their plates had been removed they sat over wine and spumoni.

"So . . ." Keith said, fixing his stare on Bess. He wore glasses thick enough to magnify his eyes. His face was round, his sandy hair thinning, allowing the tree lights to reflect from his skull between the strands. "I've been waiting all evening for you to mention Michael."

"Why?"

"Isn't it obvious?"

"No, it's not. Why should I mention Michael?"

"Well, you've been seeing him lately, haven't you?"

"I've seen him three times but not in the way you infer."

"Three times?"

"I hardly thought I'd get through Lisa's wedding with*out* seeing him."

"The night Lisa set you up, and the night of the dinner at the in-laws." Keith ticked them off on his fingers. "When was the third time?"

"Keith, I don't appreciate being grilled like this."

"Can you blame me? This is the first time I've seen you since he came back on the scene."

Bess pressed a hand to her chest. "I divorced the man, are you forgetting?"

Keith took a sip of wine, lowered the glass and remarked, "You're the one who seems to be forgetting. I'm still waiting to hear about the third time you saw him."

"If I tell you, will you stop haranguing me?"

He stared at her awhile before nodding stiffly and picking up his spoon.

"I went to see his condo. I'm going to decorate it for him. Now could we just finish our spumoni and go?"

With his spoon poised over his ice cream, Keith asked, "Are you coming over tonight?"

Bess felt him watching her minutely. She ate some spumoni, met his eyes and replied, "I don't think so."

"Why?"

"I have a lot of work to do at home tomorrow. I want to get up early for church. And something's come up with Randy that's on my mind. I think I should be there tonight."

"You put everything and everybody else before me."

"I'm sorry, Keith, but I . . ."

"Your kids, your work, your ex-husband, they all come before me."

She said gently, "You demand a lot."

He leaned closer to her and whispered fiercely, "I'm sleeping with you, don't I have a right?"

He was so close she could detect the subtle color shadings in his green-brown eyes. She found herself unmoved by his resentment, grown very tired of fighting this fight. "No. I'm sorry, but no."

He pulled back and his lips thinned.

"I've asked you so many times to marry me."

"I've been married, Keith, and I never want to go through that again."

"Then why do you keep seeing me?"

She considered carefully before answering. "I thought we were friends."

"And if that's not enough for me?"

"You'll have to decide."

His spumoni had melted into a sickly green puddle. He pushed it aside, took a deep breath and said, "I think we'd better go."

They rose and left the restaurant politely. At the coat check, he held her coat. At the entry, he held the door. At his car, he unlocked the passenger door and waited while she got in. Inside his car they buckled their seat belts and headed for his place in silence. She had left her car parked at the foot of his driveway. He passed it and stopped before the garage door, which he got out to open. When he'd pulled inside, when the headlights were off and the engine silenced, Bess unsnapped her seat belt but neither of them moved. The beam from the streetlight stopped short of the car, leaving them in blackness. Beneath the hood the engine ticked as it cooled.

The absence of warmth from the heater chilled Bess's legs. The absence of warmth in her heart chilled much more.

She turned to Keith and laid her hand on the seat between them. "Keith, I think maybe we should break it off."

"No!" he cried. "I knew this was coming but it's not what I want. Please, Bess . . ." He took her in his arms. Hampered by their heavy winter outerwear, the embrace was bulky. ". . . You've never given us a real chance. You've always held yourself aloof from me. Maybe it's something I've done and if it is I'll try to change. We could work things out, we could have a nice life together, I just know we could. Please, Bess . . ."

He kissed her heavily, wetting her mouth and spreading the taste of wine into it. She found herself slightly revolted and eager to be away from him. He released her mouth but held her head in both hands with his forehead against hers. "Please, Bess," he whispered. "We've been together for three years. I'm forty-four years old and I don't want to start looking for someone else."

"Keith, stop it."

"No . . . please, don't go. Please come inside. Come to bed with me . . . Bess, please."

"Keith, don't you see? We're a convenience for each other."

"No. I love you. I want to marry you."

"I can't marry you, Keith."

"Why? Why can't you?"

She had no desire to hurt him further. "Please don't make me say it."

As he grew desperate his voice became pleading. "I know why, I've known all along, but I can make you love me if you just give me the chance. I'll be anything you want . . . anything, if only you won't leave me."

"Keith, stop it! You're abasing yourself."

"I don't care. I'll even abase myself for you."

"But I don't want you to. You have a lot to offer a woman. I'm just not the right one."

"Bess, please . . ." He tried to kiss her again, groping for her breast.

"Keith, stop it. . . ." Their struggle became ferocious and she shoved him back, hard. *"Stop it!"*

His head struck the window. Their breathing beat heavily in the confined space.

"Bess, I'm sorry."

She grabbed her purse and opened her door.

"Bess!" he pleaded, "I said I'm sorry."

"I have to go," she said, scrambling from the car with her heart clubbing and her limbs trembling, welcoming the rush of cold air and the sight of her own car in the nearby shadows. She hurried toward it, running the last several yards after she heard his car door opening.

"Bess, wait! I'd never hurt you, Bess!" he called. Her car door cut off his last word as she slammed and locked it, then rummaged in her purse for her keys. The sound of all four automatic locks clacking down should have calmed her but she found herself shuddering and digging frantically, then peeling out of his driveway in reverse.

A quarter mile up the street she realized her hands were gripping the wheel, her back was rigid and tears were running down her cheeks.

She pulled to the curb, dropped her forehead to the steering wheel and waited for the tears and shakes to dissolve.

What had happened to her back there? She knew full well Keith would not hurt her, yet her revulsion and fear had been genuine. Was he right? Did his being her lover give him the right to expect more from her? She *had* always held herself aloof from him: this much was true. Her children *had* often come first, and she *had* frequently put him off in favor of business that could have been delayed.

Furthermore, she was beginning to suspect perhaps Michael did play a part in her rather sudden severing of ties with Keith. He had been the one calling out apologies as she'd run away, but perhaps it was she who owed them.

She thought of Michael too much during the week that followed. While she leafed through wallpaper and furniture catalogs she pictured his empty rooms and recalled their voices echoing off the white ceramic tiles of the empty kitchen. She saw his damp towel, his toothbrush, his mattresses on the floor—most often his mattresses on the floor. Though she was divorced from him it was impossible to divorce herself from the knowledge of him, and sometimes she pictured him moving about the rooms, in intimate disarray, the kind only a wife or lover can know, or in an equally intimate freshly dressed state, with his skin still flushed from a shave and his lips still shiny from the shower. She saw him in a suit with his tie in a Windsor knot, still in his stocking feet, picking up his change, money clip and flat, flat billfold that held little more than his driver's license and two credit cards (he hated bulging out his rear pocket). And last, before he donned his shoes, she saw him opening the penknife he always carried, standing in the bedroom beside the dresser and cleaning his fingernails. He did it every morning without fail; in all the years she'd known him she'd rarely seen him with dirt beneath his nails. It was part of the reason she so loved his hands.

She unconscionably worked on Michael's designs before seven others that had been in her files longer. She knew things he liked: long davenports a man could stretch out on, chairs with thick arms and matching ottomans, the *USA Today* with his breakfast, fires at suppertime, schefflera plants, things with rounded corners rather than squared, real leather, diffused lighting.

She knew things he disliked: scatter rugs, doilies, hanging plants, clutter, busy florals, the colors yellow and orange, twelve-foot telephone cords that got stretched out and testy, television playing at mealtimes.

It was hard to remember a job she'd enjoyed more or had designed with as much confidence. How ironic that she knew his tastes better now than she had when planning the house in which the two of them had lived together. Having carte blanche with his budget didn't hurt, either.

She called him on Thursday.

"Hi, Michael, it's Bess. I've got your design all worked up and wondered when you can come to the store and go over it with me."

"When would you like?"

"As I said before, I try to make the appointments at the end of the day so that we won't be interrupted. How's five o'clock tomorrow?"

"Fine. I'll be there."

The following day, a Friday, she went home at 3:30, washed her face, put on fresh makeup, touched up her hair, changed into a freshly pressed suit and returned to the store in time to lay out the materials for her presentation and dismiss Heather with ten minutes to spare.

When Michael came in the window lamps were lit, the place smelled like fresh coffee and at the rear of the store around the grouping of wicker furniture, the materials for Bess's presentation stood at the ready, fabrics draped, wallpaper books standing; textures, colors and photographs overlapped.

She heard the door open and he came in bringing the smell of winter and the sound of the five o'clock traffic moving on the street behind him. When the door sealed it off Bess went forward, smiling.

"Hello, Michael, how are you? I'll lock that now and turn over the sign." She had to shinny past him in the limited space between her floor stock. The profusion of tables, baskets and glassware filled up all but the most meager traffic paths. She locked the door, reversed the OPEN sign and turned to find him perusing the walls, which were hung with framed prints and wall decor clear up to the blue iris border strip just below the cove molding. He turned her way, still looking up, unbuttoning his coat and blocking the aisle. The store seemed suddenly crowded with his presence, its proportions so much better suited to women.

"You've done a lot with this place," he said.

"It's crowded, and the loft is unbearable in the summer, but when I think of getting rid of it I always seem to get nostalgic and change my mind. Something keeps me here."

His eyes stopped when they reached her and she became aware that he, too, had freshly groomed for this meeting: she could tell by the absence of four-o'clock shadow and the faint scent of British Sterling.

"May I take your coat?"

It was gray wool and heavy in her hands when he shrugged it off along with a soft plaid scarf. She had to say excuse me to get around him once more. Hanging the coat on the back of the basement door, she caught a whiff of scent from it, not simply a bottled scent but a combination of cosmetics and fresh air and his car and himself—one of those olfactory legacies a man leaves on a woman's memory.

She drew a deep breath and turned to conduct business. "I've got everything laid out here at the back of the store," she said, leading the way to the wicker seats. "May I get you a cup of coffee?"

"Sounds good. It's cold out there."

He waited, standing before the settee, until she set the cup and saucer on the coffee table and took an armchair to his right.

"Thanks," he said, freeing a button on his suit jacket as he sat. The furniture was low and his knees stuck up like a cricket's. He took a sip of coffee while she opened a manila folder and extracted the scale drawings of his rooms.

"We'll start with the living/dining room. Let me show you the wallpaper first so you can be picturing it as a backdrop for the furnishings as I describe them." Surrounded by samples, she presented his living room the way she envisioned it—subtle wallpaper of cream, mauve and gray; vertical blinds; upholstered grouping facing the fireplace; smoked-glass tables; potted plants.

"I seem to remember you liked our schefflera plant and watered it when I forgot to, so I thought it was safe to plan live plants into your furniture-scape."

She glanced at him and found him considering the collected samples. He shifted his regard to her and said, "I think I like it. Actually, I like the sound of everything so far."

She smiled and went on, laying out her suggestions.

For the formal dining area a smoked-glass Swaim table on a brass base, surrounded by fully upholstered chairs.

For the foyer, a large mirror sculpture above a sassy Jay Spectre console table, flanked by a pair of elegant LaBarge side chairs upholstered in tapestry.

For the gallery, mirrored walls and a single faux pedestal directly beneath the chandelier, highlighting the sculpture of his choice.

A desk, chair, credenza, feather lamp and bookshelves for his drafting room.

For the guest bedroom, an art deco bed and dresser in cream lacquer, and a heavier concentration of lavender in the fabrics.

For the master bedroom, art deco once again—a three-piece suite in black lacquer from Formations, along with torchères and an upholstered chair. She suggested that the bedspread, wallpaper and vertical blinds all match.

She'd saved the coup d'état for last. For the family room, sumptuous Natuzzi Italian leather on a loose-cushioned sofa of cream that stretched out into forever and turned two corners before it got there.

"Italian leather is the finest money can buy, and Natuzzi is the best in the industry," she told him. "It's expensive but worth it, and since you gave me carte blanche on the budget, I thought you might enjoy the sheer luxury."

"Mm, I would." Michael studied the colored brochure of the curved sofa. She recognized the look of covetousness on his face.

"Exactly how much is 'expensive'?"

"I'll tell you later but for now submerge yourself in fantasy. The sticker shock will come at the end of the presentation, so if you don't mind waiting . . ."

"All right, whatever you say."

"The sofa is available in cream or black, and either color would fit but I thought we'd go with cream in the family room. Besides, black shows dust. Here, let me show you the entertainment unit I think would be really wonderful."

It was double wide and could be completely closed to reveal a solid, sleek surface of whitewashed oak.

"Whitewashing is being used a lot. It's rich yet casual, and I've repeated it in this ice-cream table and bentwood chairs for the adjacent informal eating area."

There were more wallpapers, fabric samples, wood swatches and photographs to be considered, as well as furniture layout. By the time she'd covered the highlights it was 7:30 and she'd lost his eye contact and could see that he was suffering data saturation.

"I know I've given you a lot to consider but believe it or not, there's still more. We've barely touched on the accent pieces—floor urns, wall decor, lamps and smaller case goods, but I think we've covered enough tonight. Most people do a room at a time. Doing an entire home is Olympian."

He leaned back, flexed his shoulders and sighed.

She laid a paper-clipped sheaf of papers on the table before him.

"Here's the bad news you've been waiting for. A breakdown, room-by-room and item-by-item with an allowance for additional small decor, which I'll select as I go—always with your approval, of course. The grand total is $76,300."

Michael looked as if he'd been poleaxed. "Holy old nuts!"

Bess threw back her head and laughed.

"You think it's funny!" He scowled.

"I haven't heard that expression in years. You're the only one I ever knew who said it."

Michael ran a hand over his hair and puffed out his cheeks. "Seventy-six thousand . . . Crimeny, Bess, I said I trusted you."

"That's including the Natuzzi sofa, which by itself is eight thousand, and a custom-made five-by-seven rug for in front of the living-room fireplace. We could drop those two items and save you almost ten thousand. Also the mirrored walls in the gallery are fifteen hundred. I went with some pretty classy designers, too—Jay Spectre, LaBarge, Henredon—these are makers who set standards in the industry."

"And how much am I paying you?"

"It's all there." She pointed at the sheaf of papers. "A straight ten percent. Most independents will charge you the wholesale price plus ten percent freight, and seventy-five dollars an hour for their design and consultation time. And believe me, those hours can mount up. It's also important to realize that the term 'wholesale price' is arbitrary, since they can say it's whatever they want it to be. My price includes freight and delivery, and my one-time trip charge, you'll remember, was only forty dollars, which I'll apply toward the cost of the job if you decide to go with me. You're welcome to compare, if you wish."

She sat back, collected, with her eyes leveled on Michael while he looked over the list. He studied it in detail, only the rustle of the turning pages marking the passing minutes. She rose, refilled his coffee cup and returned to her chair, crossing her legs and waiting in silence until he finished reading and closed the sheets.

"The price of furniture has gone up, hasn't it?" he asked.

"Yes, it has. But so has your own social status. You own your own firm now, you're very successful. It's only right that your home should reflect that success. I should think that in time you'll have more and more clients into your home. Decorated as I've suggested, it will make a strong state-ment about you."

He studied her without blinking until she wanted to look away but resisted. The light from the floor lamp on his far side put a luster of silver on the hair above his left ear. It painted his cheek gold and put a shadow in the relaxed smile line connecting his nose and mouth. He was an unnervingly handsome man, so handsome, in fact, that she had associated that handsomeness with unfaithfulness, so had intentionally chosen an unhandsome one in Keith. She realized that now.

"How much did you say that leather sofa's going to cost?"

"Eight thousand."

He considered awhile longer. "How long before I get this stuff?"

"The standard wait for custom orders is twelve weeks. Natuzzi takes sixteen because it's shipped directly from Italy and it comes over by boat, which takes four weeks by itself. I'll be frank with you and admit there's been some trouble over there lately with dock strikes, which could delay it even longer. But on the brighter side, sometimes we call the manufac-turer and find out they have a piece already made up in the fabric we want and out it comes in six weeks. But figure twelve, on the average."

"And what about guarantees?"

"Against defects and workmanship? We're dealing with quality names here, not flea-market peddlers. They stand behind everything, and if they don't, I do."

"And what about the wallpaper and curtains? How long do I have to wait for them?"

"I'll place an order with the workroom immediately, and window treat-ments should be installed within six weeks. Wallpaper, much sooner. It's possible I could have paper hangers in here within two weeks, depending on their work schedule and the paper availability."

"You take care of all that?"

"Absolutely. I have several paper hangers who do my work. I contract them directly, so you never have to do any of that. All you have to do is make arrangements to have the door unlocked when they come to do the job."

Her estimate still lay on his lap. He glanced at the top sheet and his lower lip protruded.

She said, "I should warn you, I'll be in and out of your place a lot. I make it a point to check the wallpapering immediately after it's done, and I also accompany my installers when they come to put up window treat-ments. If there's something wrong, I want to find it myself instead of having you find it later. I also come out to see the furniture on site once it's been delivered, to make sure the color match is right. Do you have any problem with that?"

"No."

Bess began gathering up the floor plans and putting them into the manila folder. "It's a lot of money, Michael, there's no question about that. But any interior designer you hire is going to cost a lot, and I think I have one advantage any other wouldn't have. I know you better."

Their gazes met as she sat forward in her chair, with a stack of things on her knees, steadying them with both hands.

"You're probably right," he conceded.

"I know I'm right. The way you've always loved leather, you'll go crazy over that Italian sofa, and the rich rug in front of the fireplace, and the mirrors in the gallery. You'd love it all."

So would you, he thought, because he knew her well, too, knew these were colors, styles and designs she liked. For a moment he indulged in the fantasy that she had planned the place for both of them, as she had once before.

"May I have a while to think about it?"

"Of course."

She stood and he did likewise, while she bent to collect his cup and saucer.

Michael checked his watch.

"It's almost eight o'clock and I'm starved. How about you?"

"Haven't you heard my stomach growling?"

"Would you want to . . ." He cut himself off and weighed the invitation before issuing it in full. "Would you want to grab a bite with me?"

She could have said no, she should put away all these books and samples, but in truth she'd need them for ordering if he decided to sign with her. She could have said she'd better get home to Randy, but at eight o'clock on a Friday night Randy would be anywhere but at home. She could have simply used good judgment and said no, without qualifying it. But the truth was she enjoyed his company and wouldn't mind spending another hour or so in it.

"We could go to the Freight House," she suggested.

He smiled. "They still make that dynamite seafood chowder?"

She smiled. "Absolutely."

"Then let's go."

She locked up and they left the Blue Iris with the lamps softly illuminating the window display. Outside the wind was biting, swaying the streetlights on their posts, whipping the electrical wires like jump ropes.

"Should we drive?" he asked.

"Parking is always horrendous there on weekends. We might as well walk, if you don't mind."

It was only two blocks but the wind bulldozed them from behind, sending their coattails skipping and Bess hotfooting it to keep from toppling on her face in her high-heeled pumps.

Michael took her elbow and held it hard against his ribs while they hurried along with their shoulders hunched. They crossed Main Street against a red light and as they turned onto Water Street the wind shifted and eddied as it stole between the buildings and formed whirlpools.

His hand and his ribs felt both familiar and welcome against her elbow.

The Freight House was exactly what its name implied, a red-brick relic from the past, facing the river and the railroad tracks, backing against Water Street with six wagon-high, arch-top doors through which freight had been loaded and unloaded in the days when both rail and river commerce flourished. Inside, high, wide windows and doors faced the river and gave onto an immense wooden deck, which in summer sported colorful umbrella tables for outside wining and dining. Now, in bitter February the corners of the windows held ice, and the yellow umbrellas were furled fast, like a flotilla of quayside sails. It smelled wonderful and felt better, being in out of the chill.

Unbuttoning his overcoat, Michael spoke to the hostess, who consulted an open book on her lectern.

"It'll be about fifteen minutes. You can have a seat in the bar if you'd like, and I'll call you."

They kept their coats on and perched on hip-high stools on opposite sides of a tiny square table.

"It's been a long time since I've been here," Michael remarked.

"I don't come here often, either. Occasionally for lunch."

"If I remember right, this is where we came to celebrate our tenth anniversary."

"No, our tenth we celebrated down in the Amana colonies, remember?"

"Oh, that's right."

"Mother took care of the kids and we went down for a long weekend."

"Then which one did we celebrate here?"

"Eleventh, maybe? I don't know, they sort of all run together, don't they?"

"We always did something special though, didn't we?"

She smiled in reply.

A waitress came and laid two cocktail napkins on the table. "What would you like?" she asked.

"I'll have a bottled Michelob," Michael answered.

"I'll have the same."

When the girl went away Michael asked, "You still like beer, huh?"

"Why should I have changed?"

"Oh, I don't know, new business, new image. You look like somebody who'd drink something in a tall stem glass."

"Sorry to disappoint you."

"It's not a disappointment at all. We drank a lot of beer together over the years. It's familiar."

"Mmm . . . yeah, a lot of hot summer evenings when we'd sit on the deck and watch the boats on the river."

Their beers arrived and after a skirmish about who would pay, they each paid for their own, then eschewed glasses in favor of drinking straight from the bottle.

When they'd each taken a deep swallow, Michael fixed his eyes on her and asked, "What do you do now on hot summer evenings, Bess?"

"I'm usually busy doing design work at home. What do you do?"

He thought awhile. "With Darla, nothing memorable. We both worked long hours and afterwards just sort of occupied the same lodge. She'd be gone, grocery shopping or having her hair done. Sometimes, when Mom was still alive, I'd go over to her house and mow her lawn. It's funny, because I had a yard service that took care of my own but after she had her stroke she couldn't handle the mower anymore, so I'd go over once a week or so and do it."

"Didn't Darla go with you?"

Michael scratched the edge of his beer label with a thumbnail. He worked up a little flap that was sticky on the backside. "It's a funny thing about second wives. That extended family bonding never seems to happen."

He took another swig of beer and met her eyes over the bottle. She dropped her gaze while he studied the way her lipstick held a tiny circle of wetness after she drank from her own bottle. Beneath the table she had one high heel hooked over the brass ring on the bar stool and her knees crossed. It made a pleasant shadow in her lap where her skirt dipped. Man-oh-man, she looked good.

"You know how it is," Michael continued. "A good Catholic mother doesn't believe in divorce so she never actually recognized my second marriage. She treated Darla civilly but even that took an effort."

Bess lifted her eyes. Michael was still studying her.

"I imagine that was hard for Darla."

"Yup," he said, and snapped out of his regardful pose as if nudged on the shoulder by an elder. "Aw, hell . . . water over the dam, right?"

The hostess came and said, "We have a booth ready for you now, Mr. Curran."

The backs of the booths went clear up to the ceiling, sealing them into a three-sided box which was lit by a single hanging fixture. While Bess spent some time perusing the oversized menu, Michael only flipped his open, glanced for five seconds and closed it again. She sat across from him, feeling his eyes come and go while he finished his beer and waited.

She closed her menu and looked up.

"What?" she said.

"You look good."

"Oh, Michael, cut it out." She felt a blush start.

"All right, you look bad."

She laughed self-consciously and said, "You've been staring at me ever since we came in here."

"Sorry," he said but went on staring. "At least you didn't get mad this time when I told you."

"I will if you don't stop it."

A waitress came to take their orders.

Michael said, "I'll have a grilled chicken sandwich and a bowl of seafood chowder."

Bess's eyes flashed up: she'd decided on the same thing. This used to happen often when they were married, and they would laugh at how their tastes had become so alike, then speculate on when they might start looking alike, the way people said old married couples did. For a moment Bess considered changing her choice but in the end stubbornly refused to be cowed by the coincidence.

"I'll have the same thing."

Michael looked at her suspiciously.

"You won't believe it but I'd made up my mind before you ordered."

"Oh," he replied.

Their seafood chowder came and they dipped into it in unison, then Michael said, "I saw Randy last Saturday. I asked if I could take him to lunch but he said no."

"Yes, he told me."

"I just wanted you to know I'm trying."

She finished her chowder and pushed the bowl back with two thumbs. He finished his and the waitress came and took away their bowls. When she was gone Michael said, "I've been doing some thinking since the last time we talked."

Bess was afraid to ask. This was too intimate already.

"About fault—both of ours. I suppose you were right about me helping around the house. After you started college I should have done more to help you. I can see now that it wasn't fair to expect you to do it all."

She waited for him to add *but,* and offer excuses. When he didn't she was pleasantly surprised.

"May I ask you something, Michael?"

"Of course."

"If I'm out of line just say so. Did you ever help Darla with the housework?"

"No."

She studied him quizzically awhile, then said, "Statistics show that most second marriages don't last as long as first ones, primarily because people go into them making the same mistakes."

Michael's cheeks turned ruddy. He made no remark but they both thought about their conversation throughout the rest of the dinner.

Afterward they divided the check.

When they reached the door of the restaurant, Michael pushed it open and held it while Bess passed before him into the cold. To her back he said, "I've decided to give you the job decorating my condo."

She came up short and turned to face him while behind him the door swung shut.

"Why?" she said.

"Because you're the best woman for the job. What do I do, sign a contract or something like that?"

"Yes, something like that."

"Then let's do it."

"Tonight?"

"Judging from how you handle yourself as a businesswoman, you've got a contract all made up back at the shop, right?"

"Actually, I do."

"Then let's go." He took her arm quite commandingly and they headed up the street. At the corner, when they turned into the wind it whistled in their ears and almost knocked them off their feet.

"Why are you doing this?" she shouted.

"Maybe I like having you poke around my house," he shouted back.

She balked. "Michael, if that's the only reason . . ."

He forced her to keep walking. "Just a joke, Bess."

As she unlocked the door of the Blue Iris, she hoped it was.

chapter 9

FEBRUARY SPED ALONG. Lisa's wedding was fast approaching. The telephone calls from her to Bess came daily.

"Mom, do you have one of those pens with a feather at your store? You know . . . the kind for the guest book?"

"Mom, where do I buy a garter?"

"Mom, do you think I have to get plain white cake or can I have marzipan?"

"Mom, they need the money for the flowers before they make them up."

"Mom, I gained another two pounds! What if I can't get into the dress?"

"Mom, I bought the most beautiful unity candle!"

"Mom, Mark thinks we should have special champagne glasses engraved with our name and date but I think it's silly since I'm pregnant and can't even drink champagne anyway!"

"Mom, have you bought your dress yet?"

Since she hadn't, Bess set aside an afternoon on her calendar and called Stella to say, "The wedding is only two weeks away and Lisa threw a fit when she found out I don't have a dress yet. How about you? Have you got one?"

"Not yet."

"Do you want to go shopping?"

"I guess we'd better."

They drove into downtown Minneapolis, browsing their way from the Conservatory to Dayton's to Gavidae Commons, where they struck it lucky at Lillie Rubin. Stella, turning up her nose at the grandma image, found a hot little silvery white number with a three-tiered gathered skirt and perky sleeves to match, while Bess chose a much more sedate raw silk sarong suit in palest peach with a flattering tulip-shaped skirt. When they stepped out of their adjacent dressing rooms Bess gave Stella the once-over and said, "Wait a minute, who's the grandma here?"

"You," Stella replied, "I'm the great-grandma." Perusing her reflection in the mirror, she went on, "I'll be darned if I've ever been able to understand why the mothers of brides go to such great lengths to add fifteen years onto their age by buying those god-awful dowdy dresses that look like Mamie Eisenhower's curtains. Now *this* is how I feel!"

"It's very jaunty."

"Y' darned right it is. I'm bringing Gil Harwood along."

"Gil Harwood?"

"Do I look like a dancing girl?"

"Who's Gil Harwood?"

"A man who makes my nipples stand at attention."

"Mother!"

"I'm thinking of having an affair with him. What do you think?"

"Mother!"

"I haven't done any of that sort of thing since your father died, and I think I should before all my ports dry up. I did a little experimenting the last time Gil took me out, and it's definitely not his arteries that are hardening."

Bess released a gust of laughter. "Mother, you're outrageous."

"Better outrageous than senile. Do you think I'd have to worry about AIDS?"

"You're the outrageous one. Ask him."

"Good idea. How are things between you and Michael?"

Bess was saved from answering by the clerk, who approached and inquired, "How are you doing, ladies?" But she felt a flurry of reaction at the mention of his name and caught Stella's sly glance that said very clearly she knew something was stirring.

They bought the dresses and went on to search out matching shoes. When they were in Bess's car, heading east toward home, Stella resumed their interrupted conversation.

"You never answered me. How are things between you and Michael?"

"Very businesslike."

"Oh, what a disappointment."

"I told you, Mother, I'm not interested in getting tangled up with him again, but we did straighten out some leftover feelings that have been lingering since before we got the divorce."

"Such as . . ."

"We both admitted we could have worked a little harder at holding things together."

"He's a good man, Bess."

"Yes, I know."

Bess had little occasion to run into the good man between then and the wedding. The paper was hung in Michael's condo and though Bess went over to check it when the paperhangers were just finishing up, Michael wasn't there. She called him the next day to ask if he was satisfied.

"More than satisfied. It looks perfect."

"Ah, good."

"Smells like squaw piss, though."

Bess burst out laughing and even across the telephone wire felt a thrill of attraction that she'd been staving off ever since her last meeting with him. She had forgotten how genuinely funny Michael could be and how effortlessly he'd always been able to make her laugh.

"But you like it?"

"Yes, I do."

"Good. Listen, the invoices are starting to come in now on your furniture. So far it looks as though most things will be arriving in mid-May. No word yet on the Natuzzi from Italy but I'm sure that'll take longer. I'll let you know as soon as I hear."

"All right."

Bess paused before changing the subject. "Michael, I need to talk to you about the bills for Lisa's wedding. Some of them have already been paid and others are coming in, so how do you want to handle it? I've paid out eight hundred dollars already, so why don't you match it and add two thousand, and I'll add the same and Lisa can put it into her savings account and draw on it as she needs it? Then what's left over—if any is—we can split."

"Fine."

"I have the receipts for everything, and I'll be more than happy to send them to you if—"

"Heaven's sake, Bess, I trust you."

"Oh . . . well . . . thanks, Michael. Just send the check to Lisa, then."

"You really think we'll see any leftover money?"

Bess chuckled. "Probably not."

"Now you're thinking like a realist."

"But I don't mind spending it, do you?"

"Not at all. She's our only daughter."

The chance remark left the phone line silent while they reached back to their beginnings, wishing they could undo the negative part of their past and recapture what they'd once had. Bess felt an undeniable stirring, the urge to ask him what he'd been doing, where he was, what he was wearing, the kind of questions that signal infatuation. She quelled her foolhardiness and said instead, "I guess I'll see you at the rehearsal, then."

Michael cleared his throat and said in a curiously flat voice, "Yeah . . . sure."

When Bess hung up she tipped her desk chair back to its limit, drove both hands into her hair and blew an enormous breath at her loft ceiling.

Randy kept his car like the bottom of a bird cage. Whatever fell, stayed. The day of the groom's dinner and rehearsal he took the battered '84 Chevy Nova to the car wash and mucked 'er out. Fast-food containers, dirty sweat socks, empty condom packages, crumpled *Twin Cities' Readers*, unopened mail, unmailed mail, parking-lot receipts, a dried-up doughnut, empty pop cans, a curled-up Adidas, unpaid parking tickets— all got relegated to the bottom of a fifty-gallon garbage drum.

He vacuumed the floor, ran the mats through the washer, Armor Alled the vinyl, emptied the ashtrays, washed the windows, washed and dried the outside and bought a blue Christmas tree to hang from the dash and make the inside smell like a girl's neck.

Then he drove to Maplewood Mall and bought a new pair of trousers at Hal's, and a sweater at The Gap, and went home to put on his headset and play Foreigner's "I Want to Know What Love Is" and beat his drums and dream about Maryann Padgett.

The rehearsal was scheduled for six o'clock. At quarter to, when his mother asked if he wanted to ride to the church with her, he answered, "Sorry, Mom, but I've got plans for afterwards." His plan was to ask Maryann Padgett if he could drive her home.

When he walked into St. Mary's and saw Maryann, the oxygen supply in the vestibule seemed to disappear. He felt the way he had when he was nine years old and used to hang upside down on the monkey bars for five minutes, then try to walk straight. She was wearing a prim little navy-blue coat, and prim little navy-blue shoes with short, prim heels, and probably a prim little Sunday dress with a prim little collar, and talking to Lisa in prim, proper terms. She probably went to Bible camp in the summer and edited the school newspaper in the winter.

He'd never wanted to impress anyone so badly in his life.

Lisa saw him and said, "Oh, hi, Randy."

"Hi, Lisa." He nodded to Maryann, hoping his eyes wouldn't pop out of their sockets and bounce on the vestibule floor.

"Where's Mom?" Lisa asked.

"She's coming. We drove in separate cars."

"You and Maryann are going to be first up the aisle."

"Yeah? Oh, well, hey . . . how about that." *Bravo, Curran, you glib rascal, you. Really knocked her prim little socks off with that one.*

Maryann said, "I was just telling Lisa that I've never been in a wedding before."

"Me either."

"It's exciting, isn't it?"

"Yes, it is."

Inside his new acrylic sweater he was warm and quivering. She had this little pixie face with blue eyes about the size of Lake Superior; and pretty puffed lips and the teeniest, tiniest mole above the upper one but close enough that if you kissed her properly you'd kiss it, too; and not a fleck of makeup ruining any of it.

"Dressing up for first Communion is about as close as I've come to this," she remarked. The vestibule was crowded, and Lisa spied someone else she needed to talk to.

Left in a lull, Randy searched for something to talk about. "Have you always lived in White Bear Lake?"

"Born and raised there."

"I used to go to the street dances there in the summer during Manitou Days. They'd get some good bands."

"You like music?"

"Music is what drives me. I want to play in a band."

"Play what?"

"Drums."

"Oh." She thought awhile and said, "It's kind of a tough life-style, isn't it?"

"I don't know. I never had the chance to find out."

Father Moore came in and started getting things organized, and they all went inside the church and laid their coats in the rear pews, and sure enough, Maryann Padgett was wearing her Marion-the-librarian dress, some little dark-colored thing with a dinky white collar made of lace. Without mousse or squiggly waves in her hair, she was a throwback, and he was captivated.

Randy was standing in the aisle continuing to be dumbstruck by her when someone rested a hand on his shoulder blade.

"Hi, Randy, how's it going?"

Randy turned to encounter his father. He removed all expression from his face and said, "Okay."

Michael dropped his hand and nodded to the girl. "Hello, Maryann." She smiled. "Hi. I was just saying, this is the first wedding I've ever been in, and Randy said it is for him, too."

"I guess it is for me, too, other than my own." Michael waited, letting his eyes shift to Randy but when no response came, he drifted away, saying, "Well . . . I'll be seeing you."

As Randy's expressionless gaze followed Michael, he repeated sarcastically, "Except for his own . . . both of them."

Maryann whispered, "Randy, that was your father!"

"Don't remind me."

"How could you treat him that way?"

"The old man and I don't talk."

"Don't talk! Why, that's awful! How can you not talk to your father?"

"I haven't talked to him since I was thirteen."

She stared at Randy as if he'd just tripped an old lady.

Father Moore asked for silence and the practice began. Randy remained put out with Michael for intruding on what had begun as a conversation with some possibilities. After the whole day of thinking about Maryann Padgett, cleaning up his car for her, dressing in new clothes for her, wanting to impress her, the whole thing had been shot by the old man's appearance.

Why can't he just lay off me? Why does he have to touch me, talk to me, make me look like a jerk in front of this girl when he's the one who's a jerk? I walked in here, I was ready to show Maryann I could be a gentleman, make small talk with her, get to know her a little and lead up to asking her out. The old man comes over and screws up the whole deal.

During the practice Randy was forced to observe his mother and father walking down the aisle on either side of Lisa, then sitting together in the front pew. There were times when he himself had to stand up front and face the congregation and could hardly avoid seeing them, side-by-side, as if everything was just peachy. Well, that was bullshit! How could she sit there beside him as if they'd never split up, as if it wasn't his fault the family broke up? She might say she had faults, too, but they were minor compared to his, and nobody was going to convince Randy differently.

When the business at the church ended they all went to a restaurant called Finnegan's, where the Padgetts had reserved a private room for the groom's dinner. Randy drove alone, arrived before Maryann and waited for her in the lobby. The door opened and she stepped inside, speaking with her father and mother, a smile on her face.

She saw him and the smile thinned, her speech faltered.

"Hello again," he said, feeling self-conscious waiting there with such obvious intent.

"Hello."

"Do you mind if I sit with you?"

She looked straight at him and said, "You'd do better to sit with your father but I don't mind."

He felt himself blushing—blushing, for Christ's sake—and said, "Here, I'll help you with that," as she began removing her coat.

He hung it up along with his own and they followed her parents into the reserved room, where a long table waited to accommodate the entire wedding party. Walking behind her, he studied her round white collar, which reminded him of something a Mennonite would wear, and her hair, dark as ink and falling in tiers to her shoulders, the tips upturned like dry oak leaves. He thought about writing a song about her hair, something slow and evocative, with the drums quiet at the beginning and building toward a climax, then ending with sheepskin mallets doing a cymbal roll that faded into silence.

He pulled out her chair and sat down beside her, at the opposite end of the table from his parents.

While they ate, Maryann sometimes talked and laughed with her father, on her right. Sometimes she did the same with Lisa or Mark, across the table, or bent forward to say something to her mother or one of her sisters, down the line. She said nothing to Randy.

Finally he asked, "Would you please pass the salt?"

She did, and flashed him a polite smile that was worse than none at all.

"Good food, huh?" he said.

"Mm-hmm." She had a mouthful of chicken and her lips were shiny. She wiped them with her napkin and said, "My folks wanted something fancier for the groom's dinner but this was all they could afford, and Mark said it was fine, as long as Mom didn't have to do all the cooking herself."

"You all get along really well, I guess . . . your family, I mean."

"Yes, we do."

He tried to think of something more to say but nothing came to mind. He grinned and glanced at her plate.

"You like chicken, huh?" She had eaten all of it and little else.

She laughed and nodded while their eyes met again.

"Listen," he said, his stomach in knots. "I was wondering if I could drive you home."

"I'll have to ask my dad."

He hadn't heard that answer since he was in the tenth grade and had just gotten his driver's license.

"You mean you want to?" he asked, amazed.

"I kind of suspected you'd ask me." She turned to her father, sitting back in her chair so Randy could hear their exchange. "Daddy, Randy wants to drive me home, okay?"

Jake touched his hearing aid and asked, "What?"

"Randy wants to drive me home."

Jake leaned forward, peered around Maryann to study Randy a moment and said, "I guess that would be all right but you have things to do early tomorrow, don't you?"

"Yes, Daddy, I'll get in early." She turned to Randy and said, "Okay?"

He raised his right hand like a Boy Scout. "Straight home."

When the meal was over there was a jumble of good-byes at the door. He held Maryann's coat, then the heavy plate-glass door, and they walked across the snowy parking lot together.

"This one's mine," he said, reaching his Nova and walking around to open the passenger door for her, waiting until she was seated, then slamming it, feeling gallant and eager to extend every courtesy ever invented by men for women.

When he was sitting behind the wheel, putting his keys in the ignition, she remarked, "Boys don't do that much anymore . . . open car doors."

He knew. He was one of them.

"Some girls don't want a guy to open doors for them. It's got something to do with women's lib hang-ups." He started the engine.

"That's the silliest thing I ever heard. I love it."

He felt all glowy inside and decided if she could be honest, so could he. "It felt good doing it, too, and you know what? Other than for my mother, I don't do it much, either, but I will from now on."

She buckled her seat belt, something else he rarely did, but he fished around and found his buried buckle and engaged it. He adjusted the heater, stalling for time, judging he'd have her at her doorstep in less than ten minutes. The floor fan came on and twisted the blue Christmas tree around and around on its string.

"It smells good in here," she said. "What is it?"

"This thing." He poked the tree and put the car into reverse and headed toward White Bear Avenue. It would have been more direct to take I-95 to 61 and go around the west side of the lake but he headed around the east side instead, driving twenty miles an hour in the thirty-mile zone through the residential district.

When they were halfway to her house he said, "Could I ask you something?"

"What?"

"How old are you?"

"I'm a senior. Seventeen."

"Are you going with anybody?"

"I don't have time. I'm in girls' basketball and track, and I work on the school paper and I spend a lot of time studying. I want to do something in either medicine or law, and I've applied to Hamline University. My folks can't afford to pay their tuition fees so I'll need a scholarship if I'm going to go there, which means I have to keep my grades up."

If he told her how he'd skated through high school she'd ask him to stop the car and let her out right here.

"How about you?" she asked.

"Me? Nope, don't go with anybody."

"College?"

"Nope, just high school."

"But you want to be a drummer."

"Yes."

"In a rock band?"

"Yes."

"And meanwhile?"

"Meanwhile, I work in a nut house."

"A what!" She was already amused.

"It's a warehouse, actually. I package fresh roasted nuts—peanuts, pistachios, cashews—it's a big wholesale house. Custom orders that go out to places all over America. Christmas is our biggest season. It really gets crazy in a nut house at Christmas."

She laughed, as people always did, but the comparison between their ambitions was pointed enough to sound ludicrous, even to him.

They rode in silence awhile before Randy said, "Jesus, I really sound like a loser, don't I?"

"Randy, I need to say something right up front."

"Say it."

"I'd just as soon you didn't say 'Jesus' that way. It offends me."

That was the last thing he'd expected. He hadn't even realized he'd said it. "Okay," he replied, "you got it."

"And as far as being a loser—well, that's all just a state of mind. I guess I've always thought if a person feels like a loser he ought to do something about it. Go to school, get a different job, do something to boost your self-esteem. That's the first step."

They reached her house and he parked on the street, leaving the engine running. There was a bunch of cars in the driveway—her parents', Lisa's, Mark's. The lights were on throughout the house. The living-room draperies were open and they could see people moving through the room.

Randy hunched his shoulders toward the steering wheel, joined his hands between his knees and looked straight out the windshield at a streetlight twenty feet away.

"Listen, I know you think I'm a jerk because I don't get along with my dad but maybe you'd like to hear why."

"Sure. I'm a good listener."

"When I was thirteen he had an affair and divorced my mother and married somebody else. Everything just sort of fell apart after that. Home, school. Especially school. I kind of drifted through."

"And you're still feeling sorry for yourself."

He turned his head, studied her awhile and said, "He screwed up our whole family."

"You think so?" He waited, eyeing her warily. "You aren't going to like what I have to say but the truth is, each of us is responsible for ourself. If you started sloughing off in school, you can't blame him for that. It's just easier if you do, that's all."

"Jesus, aren't we smug?" he replied.

"You said 'Jesus' again. Do it once more and I'm leaving."

"All right, I'm sorry!"

"I said you weren't going to like what I had to say. Your sister made it through. Your mother seems to have done all right. Why didn't you?"

He threw himself back into the corner of the seat and pinched the bridge of his nose. "Christ, I don't know!"

She was out of the car like a shot, slamming the door, leaping over the snowbank onto the sidewalk and heading for the house before he realized what he'd said. He opened his door and shouted, "Maryann, I'm sorry! It just slipped out!" When the house door slammed, he slugged the car roof with both fists and railed aloud, "Jesus Christ, Curran, what are you doing chasing this uptight broad!"

He flung his body behind the wheel, gunned the engine with the ear-splitting thunder of an Indy-500 ignition, peeled down the street fishtailing for a quarter of a block, rolled down the window, yanked the smelly Christmas tree off the radio knob, cutting his finger before the string broke, and hurled the thing into the street, cursing a blue streak.

He slewed around a corner at twenty-five miles an hour, came within inches of wiping out a fire hydrant, ran two stop signs and shouted at the top of his lungs, "Well, fuck you, Maryann Padgett! Get that? Fuck you!"

He braked beside some strange house, got out his marijuana, had a couple good hits and waited for the euphoria to drift in and calm him.

He was smiling the last time he either said or didn't say, Yeah, fuck you, Maryann Padgett . . .

While Randy was escorting Maryann from the restaurant, Lisa was saying good night to her mother and father.

She gave Michael a hug first.

"See you tomorrow, Dad."

"Absolutely." He felt unusually sentimental and held her extra long, one of the last times he'd do so before she took another man's name. "I understand you're staying at the house tonight with Mom."

"Uh-huh. We moved all my stuff over to Mark's today."

"I'm glad. I like to think of you there with her tonight."

"Hey, Dad?" At his ear she whispered, "Keep up the good work. I think you're makin' points with Mom." She broke away and smiled. "See you at home, Mom. Good night, everyone!"

Michael hid his surprise while Lisa went out the door with Mark, leaving various stragglers behind. While helping Bess with her coat he remarked, "Lisa seems absolutely happy."

"I believe she is."

The rest of the Padgetts said good night and left. Michael and Bess were the last two in the place, standing near the plate-glass door, dawdling, putting on their gloves, buttoning their coats.

"It looks to me like something is cooking between Randy and Maryann," Michael remarked.

"They were together all night."

"I noticed."

"She's a pretty girl, isn't she?"

"I'll say."

"Why do mothers always make that remark first?" Bess said.

"Because they want pretty girls for their handsome sons, I guess. Fathers are no different. Hell, I'd just as soon see my kids end up with foxes instead of dogs."

Bess chuckled, meeting Michael's eyes while an unsettling quiet fell between them. They should go, should follow the others outside and say good night.

"She's very young, still in high school," Bess said.

"I noticed she asked her father's permission to go with Randy."

"Nice old-fashioned thing to see, isn't it?"

"Yes, it is."

A soft expression came into Bess's eyes. "They're a wonderful family, aren't they?"

"I thought it bothered you to be around wonderful families."

"Not as much as it used to."

"Why's that?"

She gave no answer. The restaurant was closing up. Someone was running a vacuum cleaner and their waitress came through, dressed in her winter coat, on her way home. They should walk out, too, sensibly, and end this cat-and-mouse game they were playing with their own emotions. Still, they stayed.

"You know what?" Michael said.

"What?" Bess said the word so softly it could scarcely be heard above the whining vacuum cleaner.

He'd intended to say, I wish I was going home with you, too, but thought better of it.

"I've planned a surprise for Lisa and Mark. I've ordered a limousine to pick them up tomorrow."

Bess's eyes widened. "You didn't!"

"Why? What's—"

"So did I!"

"Are you serious?"

"Not only that, I had to pay in advance for five hours, and it's non-refundable!"

"So did I."

They began laughing. When they stopped they were smiling into each other's eyes. The restaurant manager came along and said, "Excuse me, we're closing."

Michael stepped back guiltily.

"Oh, I'm sorry."

They went out into the chill night air at last and heard a key turn in the lock behind them.

"Well," Michael said, his breath a white puff in the frigid air, "what are we going to do about that extra limo?"

Bess shrugged. "I don't know. Split the loss, I guess."

"Or treat ourselves. What do you say—wanna go to the wedding in a white limo?"

"Oh, Michael, what will people say?"

"People? What people? Want me to take a guess what Lisa would say? Or what your mother would say? Matter of fact, we could give the old doll a thrill and swing by her place on the way and pick her up, too."

"She's already got a date. He's picking her up."

"She does! Well, good for her. Anyone I know?"

"No. Somebody named Gil Harwood. Claims she's going to have an affair with him."

Michael reared back and laughed. "Oh, Stella, you're a real piss cutter." When his laughter subsided, he angled Bess a flirtatious grin. "Now, what about you?"

She grinned. "Do *I* want to have an affair? Michael, hardly."

"Do you want to ride in a limo?"

"Ohhhh . . ." She drew out the word coquettishly, as if to say, Oh, that's what you meant. "Do I want to ride in a limo? Certainly. Only a dummy would say no to an invitation like that, especially since the thing is paid for with her own money."

"Good." He grinned, pleased. "We'll let yours take Lisa and mine will come and pick you up. Four forty-five. We'll get there in time for pictures."

"Fine. I'll be ready."

They started toward the parking lot.

"My car's this way," he said.

"Mine's that way."

"See you tomorrow, then."

"Yup."

They turned and walked at a forty-five-degree angle away from one another. The night was so cold it made their teeth hurt. Neither of them cared. Reaching their cars, they unlocked their doors and opened them, then stood looking at each other across the nearly empty parking lot while the halogen lights turned everything the color of pink champagne.

"Hey, Bess?"

"What?"

It was a moment as sterling and clear as the silent city night around them, the kind of moment lovers remember years after it happens, for no particular reason except that in the midst of it Cupid seemed to have released his arrow and watched to see what mischief it might arouse.

"Would you call tomorrow a date?" Michael called.

The arrow hit Bess smack in the heart. She smiled and replied, "No, but Lisa would. Good night, Michael."

chapter 10

To Lisa, spending her wedding eve in her childhood home seemed meet. Shortly after eleven, when she dropped her overnight bag on her bed, things were much as they'd been when she was a teenager. Randy was down in his room with his radio tuned low. Mom was in her bathroom cleansing off her makeup. It almost seemed as if Dad would shut off the hall light, stop in the doorway and say, "G'night, honey."

She dropped to the bed and sat looking at the room.

Same pale-blue flowered wallpaper. Same tiered bedspread. Same crisscross curtains. Same . . .

Lisa dumped her purse off her lap and radiated to the dresser. Into the mirror frame her mother had wedged her school pictures. Not just the second-grade one they'd laughed at the day she'd tried on the wedding dress but all thirteen of them, from kindergarten through twelfth. With her hands flat on the dresser and a smile on her face, Lisa studied them before turning to find, on the rocking chair in the corner, her Melody doll, and propped against its pink vinyl hand, the note from Patty Larson.

She picked up Melody, sat down with the doll on her lap and faced her closet doorway, where her wedding gown hung between the open bifold doors.

She was totally ready for this marriage. Nostalgia was fun but it failed to beckon her into those bygone days. She was happy to be altar-bound, happy to be pregnant, happy to be in love and happy she'd never taken up lodging with Mark.

Bess appeared in the doorway, dressed in a pretty peach nightgown and peignoir, rubbing lotion on her face and hands.

"You look all grown up, sitting there," she said.

"I feel all grown up. I was just thinking how absolutely ready I am for marriage. It's a wonderful feeling. And remember years ago when I asked you what you thought of girls moving in with guys, you said just try it and watch the shit hit the fan? Thanks for that."

Bess walked into the room, leaned over Lisa and kissed the top of her head, carrying with her the scent of roses. "I don't think I said it exactly like that but if the message stuck, I'm glad."

Lisa hugged her mother, her head nestled against Bess's breasts.

"I'm glad I'm here tonight. This is the way it should be."

When the hug ended Bess sat on the bed.

Lisa asked, "You know what I'm happiest about, though?"

"What?"

"You and Dad. It's so great to see you two sitting side-by-side again."

"We're getting along remarkably well."

"Any, ah . . ." Lisa made a hanky-panky gesture with a widespread hand.

Bess laughed quietly. "No. No *ah* anything. But we're becoming friends again."

"Well, hey, that's a start, isn't it?"

"Is there anything you want me to do for you tomorrow? I'm taking the whole day off so I've got time."

"I don't think so. It's hair in the morning and be at the church by five for pictures."

"Speaking of that, your father asked if he could drive you to the church. He said he'd pick you up here at quarter to five."

"Will you be here, too? And Randy? So we could all go to the church together?"

"I don't see why not."

"Wow, won't that be something . . . after six years. I can't wait."

"Well . . ." Bess said, rising. "It's early, and isn't that a miracle? I'm going to get a full night's rest and wake up bright and early with the whole morning to myself." She kissed Lisa's cheek. "Good night, dear." She looked into her happy eyes. "Sweet dreams, little bride. I love you."

"Love you, too, Mom."

The light over the kitchen stove was still on. Bess went down to turn it off. It was a rare occasion when Randy was home at this hour, so she indulged herself and continued down to the walkout level, where she knocked softly on his door. Music played low but no answer came. She opened the door and peeked inside. Randy lay on his side, facing the wall, both arms outflung, still dressed in the new clothes he'd worn earlier. On the opposite side of the room one dim lamp lit the top of his chest of drawers, and the ever-present lights on his component set spiked and fell like electronic graphs.

He always slept with the radio on. She'd never understood why or how he did so but no amount of nagging had changed his habit.

She approached the bed and braced a hand behind Randy while leaning over to kiss the crest of his cheek. So like his father he looked, young and innocent in slumber. She touched his hair; it even felt like Michael's, was the same dark color, the curl more pronounced.

Her son—so proud, so hurt, so unwilling to bend. She had seen Randy snub Michael tonight and thought him wrong. Her heart had gone out to Michael, and in that moment she'd felt a flash of bitterness toward Randy. Mothering was so complex: she didn't know how to handle this young man who hovered on a brink where an influence in either direction might decide his fate for years to come, possibly for life. She saw very clearly that Randy could be a failure in many regards. In human relations, in business and in that most important aspect of life, personal happiness.

If he fails, I'll be part of the reason.

She straightened, studied him a moment more, turned out the lamp and quietly slipped from the room, leaving the radio playing softly behind her.

When the door closed, Randy's eyes snapped open and he twisted to look back over his shoulder.

Whew, that was a close one.

He let his head drop to the pillow and rolled onto his back. He thought she'd come in to ask him some question, and all the while she'd been touching his hair he'd expected her to shake him and make him turn over. She'd have taken one look at his eyes and known, then he'd be out on his ass. He had no doubt she meant it the last time she'd warned him.

He was still loaded, the lights on the component set seemed threatening, as if they were attacking from the corner of his eye, and he was getting dry mouth and the munchies.

The munchies—God, they always got him, hard. And food never tasted so good as when he was high. He had to have something. He rolled from the bed and walked the mile and a half toward the door. Upstairs all was black. He felt his way to the kitchen, turned on the stove light and found a bag of Fritos. He searched the refrigerator for beer but found only orange juice and a covered jar of iced tea.

He drank some tea straight from the jar. It tasted like ambrosia.

Somebody whispered, "Hey, Randy, is that you down there?"

He nudged himself away from the cabinet and shuffled stocking-footed down the hall. Above him Lisa leaned over the rail.

"Hiya, sis."

"Whatcha got?"

"Fritos . . ." A long while later he added, "and iced tea."

"I can't sleep. Bring 'em up."

Climbing the stairs he mumbled, "Jesus, I hate iced tea."

Lisa was sitting Indian-fashion against her pillows, dressed in a gray jogging suit. "Come on in and shut the door."

He did as ordered and dropped to the foot of her bed, where he bounced forever, as if on a trampoline.

"Here, give me some," Lisa said, rolling onto her knees, reaching for the Frito bag. "Randy!" She dropped the bag and grabbed his face, pointing it toward herself. "Oh, Randy, you stupid ass, you've been smoking pot again, haven't you!"

"No," he whined. "Come on, sis—"

"Your eyes look like abortions! Gol, you're so damned dumb! What if Mom caught you? She'd throw you out."

"Are you going to tell her?"

"I should, you know." She looked as if she were considering it. "But I don't want to spoil my wedding day tomorrow. You *promised* me you weren't going to smoke that shit anymore!"

"I know but I just had a couple o' hits."

"Why?"

"I don't know." Randy fell to his back across the foot of Lisa's bed, one arm upflung. "I don't know."

She took the iced tea out of his hand, helped herself to a swig and stretched to set it on her bedside stand, then resumed her Indian pose and wondered how to help him.

"Man, do you know what you're doing to your life?"

"It's just pot; hey, I don't do coke."

"Just pot." She shook her head and sat awhile, watching him stare at the ceiling.

"How much you spend on it a week?"

He shrugged and flopped his head once.

"How much?"

"It's none of your goddamn business."

She stretched out a foot and rocked him. "Look at you. You're nineteen years old and you got a set of Pearls. Big deal. What else have you got? A decent job? A stick of furniture? A car anybody besides your mother paid for? A friend who's worth anything? Bernie, that anal aperture. God, I can't figure out for the life of me why you hang around with him."

"Aw, Bernie's all right."

"Bernie's a loser. When are you going to see it?"

Randy rolled his head and looked at her. She ate three Fritos. She leaned forward and put one in his mouth. She ate another one, then said, "You know what I think is wrong with you? You don't like yourself very much."

"Oh, listen to her, Lisa Freud."

She fed him another Frito. "You don't, you know. That's why you hang around with losers, too. Let's face it, Randy, you've dated some real pus bugs. Some of the girls you've brought over to my apartment, I mean I wanted to stretch a condom over my hand before I shook with them."

"Thanks."

She fed him two Fritos this time, then set the sack aside and brushed off her hands.

"You treated Dad like shit tonight."

"Yeah, well, you treat shit like shit."

"Oh, come off it, Randy, he's doing his damnedest to mend things between you. When are you going to be a big man and get past it? Don't you know it's eating you?"

"He's not what's bothering me tonight."

"Oh, yeah? Then what is?"

"Maryann."

"Struck out with her, too, huh? Good."

"Listen, I was trying. I was really trying!"

"Trying what? To get in her pants? You leave her alone, Randy, she's a nice girl."

"Boy, you really think a lot of me, don't you?"

"I love you, little brother, but I have to overlook a lot to do it. I'd love you more if you'd get your act together and give up that weed and get a job."

"I've got a job."

"Oh yeah, working in that nut house. What're you scared of, huh? That you're not good enough on those Pearls?" She stretched out one leg, put her foot on his ribs and wriggled her toes.

He rolled his head and looked at her.

"You gonna remember this in the morning?" she asked.

"Yeah, I'm all right now. I'm coming down."

"Okay then, listen, and listen good. You're the best drummer I've ever heard. If you want to drum, then by God, drum. But realize this—it's a high-risk job, especially when you go into it smoking grass. The next thing you know they'll have you on coke, then on crack, and before you know it you're dead. So if you're gonna be a musician, you get in with a straight band."

He stared at her a long time, then sat up. He drew one knee onto the bed. "You really think I'm good?"

"The best."

He grinned crookedly. "Really?"

She answered with a quirk of her head.

In time she said, "Okay, so what happened with Maryann? She didn't look too happy when she came charging into the house."

"Nothing happened." He dropped his gaze to the bedspread and ran a hand through his hair. "I cussed, that's all."

"I told you she was a good girl."

"And I apologized but she was already beatin' it inside."

"Next time watch your mouth around her. It won't hurt you, anyway."

"And I no sooner got inside the restaurant than she yelled at me for how I treated Dad."

"So other people notice it, too."

"I don't even know why I should like the girl!"

"Why do you?"

"I just said, I don't know."

"I'll bet I do."

"Yeah? . . . So tell me."

"She's no pus bag, that's why."

Randy chortled deep in his throat. He sat silently for some time before telling his sister, "The first time I saw her it was like wham! You know? Right there." He socked his chest. "Felt like I couldn't breathe."

Lisa gave a crooked grin. "Sometimes it happens that way."

"I put on my best manners tonight, honest, I did." He plucked at his sweater. "Even got these new clothes, and mucked out my car, and pulled out her chair at the table, and opened the car door for her but she's tough, you know?"

"Sometimes a tough woman is best. Same goes for friends. If you had tougher ones who demanded more of you maybe you'd be right for Maryann."

"You don't think I am?"

Lisa studied him awhile, then shrugged and reached for the nightstand.

"I think you could be but it'll take some work." She handed him the Fritos and the iced tea. "Go get some sleep, and your eyes better not look like guts when you walk down that aisle tomorrow, okay?"

He smiled sheepishly. "Okay." He rose from the bed and shuffled toward the door.

"Hey," she said quietly, "c'mere." She raised her arms. He came around the bed and plopped into them. They rocked and hugged a moment with the crackly Fritos bag and the cold tea jar against her back.

"I love you, little brother."

Randy squeezed his eyes shut hard against the sting. He really believed her and wished himself more worthy.

"I love you, too."

"You've got to end this thing with Dad."

"I know," he admitted.

"Tomorrow would be a good time."

He had to get out of there or he'd be bawling. "Yeah," he muttered and fled the room.

The day Bess had predicted would be relaxed was anything but. There was her own hair appointment in the morning, followed by nails. There were two calls from Heather with questions from the store. There were the white satin bows to be hung on the pews at St. Mary's, and the caterers to be contacted with notice of three late RSVPs, and a slotted box to be prepared for guests to drop their wedding cards into, and some odds and ends to be carted over to the reception hall, and the hall itself needed checking to make sure the cake had arrived and the table arrangements were the right color, and the guest register was set up and—how had she forgotten!—a wedding card to buy! And nylons—lord, why hadn't she thought to check her nylons earlier in the week?

By quarter to four Bess was frazzled. Lisa wasn't home yet and she was worried about the limo. Randy kept asking for things—an emery board, some mouthwash, a clean handkerchief, a shoehorn.

"A shoehorn!" she shouted over the railing. "Use a knife!"

Lisa returned, the calmest one of the trio, and hummed while putting on her makeup and donning her gown. She dropped her shoes and makeup into her overnight bag, collected her veil and arranged everything in the front hall for removal to the car when her father came.

He rang the bell at precisely 4:45.

Upstairs, Bess was crossing her bedroom and inserting a pierced earring when she heard it ring. Her footsteps halted. Her stomach went fluttery. She hurried to a window and held back the curtain. There in the street were two white limousines, and downstairs, Michael was entering the house for the first time since he'd collected his power tools and left for good.

Bess dropped the curtain, pressed a hand to her rib cage and forced herself to take one deep breath, then collected her purse and hurried out. At the top of the stairs her footsteps were arrested by the sight below. Michael, smiling, handsome, dressed in an ivory tuxedo and apricot bow tie, was hugging Lisa in the front entry, his trouser legs lost in the billows of her white lace. The door was open; the late afternoon sun slanted across the two of them and for that moment, it seemed Bess was looking down at herself. The familiar dress, the handsome man, the two of them smiling and elated as his hug curled Lisa's feet off the floor.

"Oh, Daddy, *really?*" she was squealing. "Are you serious?"

Michael was laughing. "Of course. You didn't think we'd let you ride to church in a pumpkin, did you?"

"But two of them!" Lisa wriggled from his embrace and danced outside, beyond Bess's sight.

"Your mother had the same idea, so they're really from both of us." Through the open door and the fanlight above it, the westering sun spread gold radiance into the house and upon Michael as he watched his daughter, then turned to look back inside at the place he'd once called home. From overhead, Bess watched his gaze take in the familiar terrain—the potted palm in the corner beside the door, the mirror and credenza, the limited view of the living room to the left of the entry, partially obscured by Lisa's bridal veil, which hung on the doorframe, and the family room straight ahead. He took three steps farther inside and stopped almost directly below Bess. She remained motionless, gazing at his wide shoulders in the exquisitely tailored tuxedo, at his thick hair, the tops of his dark eyebrows, his nose, the silk stripe down his right trouser leg, his cream-colored patent-leather shoes. He, too, stood motionless, taking in his surroundings like a man who's missed them very much. What memories called to him while he stood there so still? What pictures of his children returned? Of her? Himself? In those few moments while she observed him she felt his yearning for this place as keenly as she had many times felt his kiss.

Two things happened at once: Lisa came in from outside and Randy arrived from downstairs, coming to an abrupt halt at the sight of his father standing in the front hall.

Michael spoke first. "Hello, Randy."

"Hi."

Neither of them moved toward the other. Lisa stood watching, just inside the front door. Bess remained where she was. After a pause, Michael said, "You're looking pretty sharp."

"Thanks. So are you."

An awkward pause ensued and Lisa stepped in to breach it. "Hey, Randy, look what Mom and Dad ordered—two limos!"

Bess continued down the stairs and Lisa smiled up at her. "Mom, this is just great! Does Mark know?"

"Not yet," Bess answered. "And he won't till he gets to the church. Grooms aren't supposed to see their brides before the service."

Michael looked up and followed Bess's descent, taking in her pale peach suit and matching silk pumps, the pearls gleaming at her ears and throat, her hair flaring back and touching her collar, the soft smile on her lips. She stopped on the second to the last step, her hand on the newel post. The town idiot could have detected the magnetism between them. Their gazes met and riveted while Michael touched his apricot cummerbund in the unconscious preening gesture men make at such times.

"Hello, Michael," Bess said quietly.

"Bess . . . you look sensational."

"I was thinking the same thing about you."

He smiled at her for interminable seconds before becoming aware that his children were observing. "Well, I'd say we all look great." He stepped back to include the two. "Randy . . . and Lisa, our beautiful bride."

"Absolutely beautiful," Bess agreed, moving toward her. Lisa's hair was drawn back by two combs and fell in glossy ringlets behind. Bess turned her by an arm. "Your hair turned out just lovely. Do you like it?"

"Yes, miracle of miracles, I do."

"Good. Well, we should go. Pictures at five on the dot."

Michael said, "May I get your coat, Bess?"

"Yes, it's in the closet behind you, and Lisa's, too."

Lisa said, "No, I'm not going to wear mine. It'll only wrinkle my dress. Besides, it feels like spring out there."

Michael opened the closet door as he'd done hundreds of times, got out Bess's coat while Lisa took her veil from the living-room doorway and Randy picked up her overnight bag.

"How are we doing this?" Randy asked as they headed outside toward the two waiting cars with their liveried drivers standing beside them.

Michael was the last one out of the house and closed the front door. "Your mother and I thought we'd ride in one, and Randy, you can escort Lisa . . . if that's okay with you."

The limousine drivers smiled, and one tipped his visored hat and extended his hand as Lisa approached.

"Right this way, miss, and congratulations. You've got a beautiful day for a wedding."

Lisa put one foot into the car, then changed her mind and leaned back out as Bess was preparing to step into the second car.

"Hey, Mom and Dad," she called. Bess and Michael both looked over. "Tell Randy not to pick his nose while we're in church. This time the whole congregation will be watching."

Everyone laughed while Randy threatened to push Lisa face-first into the limo as he would have when they were children.

The limo doors closed everyone inside and in the lead car, Lisa reached over and patted Randy's cheek. "Nice job back there, little brother. And your eyes look better today, too."

He said, "Something's going on between those two."

Lisa said, "Oh, I hope so."

In the trailing car, Michael and Bess sat on the white leather seat a careful space apart, employing discipline to keep their eyes off each other. They felt resplendent, wondrous, radiant! Not only in solo but in duet, down to their color-coordinated clothing.

When the temptation became too great, he turned his gaze on her and said, "That felt just like when we used to leave for church on Sunday mornings."

She allowed herself to look at him, too. "I know what you mean."

The limo pulled away from the curb while their eyes lingered. It turned a corner and the driver said, "The bride is your daughter?"

"Yes, she is," Michael answered, glancing up front.

"Happy day, then," the driver ventured.

"Very happy," Michael replied, returning his gaze to Bess while the day became charged with possibilities. The driver closed a glass partition and they were alone. The climate was right, seductive even, and the trappings romantic. Neither of them denied that the past and the present were both at work, wooing and weakening them.

In a while Michael said, "You changed the carpet in the entry hall."

"Yes."

"And the wallpaper."

"Yes."

"I like it."

She looked away in a vain attempt to recall common sense. His image remained in her mind's eye, alluring in his wedding finery of apricot and cream.

"Bess?" Michael covered her hand on the seat between them. It took a great deal of self-restraint for her to withdraw it.

"Let's be sensible, Michael. We're going to be bumping up against nostalgic feelings all day long but that doesn't change what is."

"What is?" he asked.

"Michael, don't. It's just not smart."

He studied her awhile, with a pleasant expression on his face. "All right," he decided. "If that's the way you want it."

They rode the remainder of the distance without speaking but she felt his eyes on her a lot and her own pulse so close to the surface of her throat she thought it must show. It felt exhilarating, and bewildering, and oh so threatening.

At the church the Padgett family had already arrived. The appearance of the limousines set off an excited reaction. Mark, dressed in a tux identical to Michael's and Randy's, saw his bride arriving and smiled disbelievingly as he opened the back door and stuck his head inside.

"Where did you get this?"

"Mom and Dad rented it for us. Isn't it great?"

There were hugs and thanks and exuberations exchanged on the church steps before the entire party went inside, where the photographer was setting up his equipment and the personal flowers were waiting in flat white boxes in the bride's changing room. A full-length mirror hung on the wall there, too, and before it, Bess helped Lisa don her veil while the Padgett ladies fussed with their own last-minute adjustments. Bess secured the hidden combs in Lisa's hair and added two bobby pins for good measure.

"Is it straight?" Bess asked.

"It's straight," Lisa approved. "Now my bouquet. Would you get it, Mom?"

Bess opened one of the boxes. The green tissue paper whispered back and her hands became still. There, nestled in the waxy green nest was a bouquet of apricot roses and creamy white freesias that exactly duplicated the one Bess had carried at her wedding in 1968.

She turned to Lisa, who stood with her back to the mirror, watching Bess.

"No fair, darling," Bess said emotionally.

"All's fair in love and war, and I believe this is both."

Bess looked down at the flowers and felt her composure giving way, along with her will to keep things sensible between herself and Michael.

"What a cunning young woman you've become."

"Thank you."

Sentiment welled up within Bess, bringing the faint blur of tears.

"And if you make me cry and ruin my makeup before the ceremony even begins I'll never forgive you." She lifted the bouquet from the waxy green paper. "You took our wedding pictures to the florist, of course."

"Of course." Lisa approached her mother and lifted Bess's chin, smiling into her glistening eyes. "It's working, I think."

Bess said with a quavery smile, "You naughty, conniving, conscienceless girl."

Lisa laughed and said, "There's one in there for Daddy, too. Go pin it on him, will you?" To the other women in the room, she said, "Everybody, take the men's boutonnieres out and make them stand still while you pin them on, will you? Maryann, would you do Randy's?"

Randy saw Maryann walking toward him dressed like some celestial being. Her black hair hung in a cloud against a dress the color of a half-ripe peach. It had short sleeves as big as basketballs, which caught on the tips of her shoulders and seemed to be held there by a sorcerer's spell. Her collarbones showed, and her throat, and the entire sweep of her shoulders above a very demure V-neck.

Maryann walked toward Randy, thinking that in her entire life she'd never met anyone as handsome. His cream-colored tuxedo and apricot bow tie were created to be modeled against his dark skin, hair and eyes. She'd never cared much for boys who wore their hair past their collars but his was beautiful. She'd never cared much for swarthy coloring but his was appealing. She'd never hung around with underachievers but Lisa said he was bright. She'd certainly never gone with wild boys but he represented an element of risk toward which she gravitated as all habitually good girls will at least once in their lives.

"Hi," she said quietly, stopping before him.

"Hi."

His lips were full and beautifully shaped and had a lot of natural pigment. Of the few boys she'd kissed, none had been endowed with a mouth as inviting. She liked the way his lips remained parted while he stared at her, and the faint flare of pink that tinged his cheeks beneath his natural dark skin, and his long, black, spiky eyelashes framing deep brown eyes that seemed unable to look away.

"They sent me with your flower. I'm supposed to pin it on you."

"Okay," he said.

She pulled the pearl-headed pin from an apricot rose and slipped her fingers beneath his left lapel. They stood so close she caught the scent of his after-shave, and whatever he put on his hair to hold it in place and make it so shiny, and the new-linen smell of his freshly cleaned tuxedo.

"Maryann?"

She looked up with her fingertips still close to his heart.

"I'm really sorry about last night."

Was his heart racing like hers? "I'm sorry, too." She returned to her occupation with his boutonniere.

"No girl ever made me watch my mouth before."

"I probably could have been a little more tactful about it."

"No. You were right and I was wrong, and I'll try to watch it today."

She finished pinning on his flower and stepped back. When she looked into his face again a picture flashed across her mind, of him with drumsticks in his hands, and sweatbands on his wrists, and a bandanna tied around his forehead to catch the perspiration while he beat the drums to some outrageously loud and raucous song.

The image fit as surely as Mendelssohn and Brahms fit into her life.

Still, he was so handsome he was beautiful, and his obvious infatuation with her resounded within some depth of womanliness that had lain dormant in Maryann until now.

Today, she thought, for just one day I will bend my own rules.

Bess, too, had taken a boutonniere from the box and gone out in the vestibule to find Michael. Approaching him, she thought how some things never change. Males and females were made to move through the world two-by-two, and in spite of the Women's Movement, there would be tasks that remained eternally appropriate for one sex to do for the other. At Thanksgivings, men carved turkeys. At weddings, women pinned on corsages.

"Michael?" she said.

He turned from conversation with Jake Padgett and she experienced a fresh zing of reaction at his uncommon pulchritude. It happened much as it had when they were dating years ago. The moment his dark eyes settled on hers, embers were stirred.

"I have your boutonniere."

"Would you mind pinning it on for me?"

"Not at all." Performing the small favor for him brought back the many times she'd brushed a piece of lint off his shoulder, or closed a collar button, or any one of the dozens of niceties exchanged by husbands and wives. It brought her, too, the smell of his British Sterling at closer range, and the warmth of his body emanating from beneath his crisp lapel as she slipped her hand beneath it.

"Hey, Bess?" he said softly. She glanced up, then back at the stubborn stickpin that refused to pierce the wrapping around the flower stem. "Do you feel old enough to have a daughter getting married?"

The pin did its job and the boutonniere was anchored. She corrected its angle, smoothed his lapel and looked into Michael's eyes. "No."

"Can you believe it? We're forty."

"No, I'm forty. You're forty-three."

"Cruel woman," he said, with a grin in his eyes.

She backed up a step and said, "I suppose you noticed Lisa picked the same colors we had in our wedding."

"I wondered if it was just a coincidence."

"It isn't. Get ready for another one—she took our wedding pictures to the florist and got a bouquet just like mine."

"Did she really?"

Bess nodded.

"This girl is serious about her matchmaking, isn't she?"

"I have to admit, it did things to me when I saw it."

"Oh yeah?" He dipped his knees to bring his eyes level with hers, still grinning.

"Oh yeah, and don't get so smug. She looks absolutely radiant, and if you can look at her without getting misty I'll pay you ten bucks."

"Ten bucks I got. If we're going to bet, let's at least pick something that—"

Someone interrupted. "Is this the fellow who's been sending me Mother's Day cards for six years?" It was Stella, in her bright silvery tiers, coming at Michael with her arms spread.

"Stella!" he exclaimed. "You beautiful dame!"

They hugged with true affection. "Ah, Michael," she said, cheek-to-cheek with him, "if you aren't a sight for sore eyes." She backed up, commandeering both his hands. "Lord in heaven, you get better-looking every six years!"

He laughed and kept her hands in his larger, darker ones, then clicked his tongue against his cheek. "You, too." He looked down at her delicate satin pumps. "But is this any way for a grandma to dress?"

She kicked up one foot. "Orthopedic high heels," she said, "if it'll make you feel any better. Come on. You, too, Bess, I want you to meet my main man."

They had barely shaken hands with Gil Harwood when the bride appeared in full regalia. She stepped into the vestibule and both Michael and Bess lost communion with everything but her. They turned to her as one, and as she began moving toward them Michael's hand found Bess's and gripped it tightly.

"Oh, my God," he whispered, for both of them.

She was a pretty young woman, the synthesis of her mother and father, and as she moved toward them they were aware of many things—how nature had amalgamated the best features of both of them into her face and frame; how happy she was, smiling and eager for this wedding and her future life with her chosen; that she carried their first grandchild. But mostly they were aware of how carefully she had recreated aspects of their own wedding.

The dress rustled just as it had when Bess wore it.

The veil was a close match to Bess's own.

The bouquet might have been preserved intact from that day.

"Mom, Dad . . ." she said, reaching them, resting a hand on each of their shoulders and raising her face for a touch of cheeks. "I'm so happy."

"And we're happy for you," Bess said.

Michael added, "Honey, you look absolutely beautiful."

"Yes, she does," Mark spoke, coming to claim her.

The photographer interrupted. "Everyone, please! I need the wedding party at the front of the church right now. We're behind schedule!"

As Lisa moved away and the mélange of shifting began toward the front of the church, Michael's eyes found Bess's.

"Even though you warned me, it's still a shock. I thought for a second it was you."

"I know. It's very disconcerting, isn't it?"

During the next hour, while the photographer set up pose after pose, Michael and Bess seemed to be always together, whether in the picture or watching from the sidelines, intensely aware of each other's presence while recounting scenes from their own wedding.

Late in the photo session the photographer turned and called, "Now the members of the bride's family. Immediate family only, please."

There was a moment of hesitation on Michael's part before Lisa motioned him forward and said, "You too, Dad. Come on."

Moments later there they were—Michael, Bess, Lisa and Randy—on two steps in the sacristy of St. Mary's, the church where Michael and Bess had been married, where Lisa and Randy had been baptized, confirmed and received their first Communion, where they had gone as a family during all those happy years.

"Let's have Mom and Dad stand on the top step, and you two just in front of them," the photographer said, motioning them into position. "A little to your left . . ." He pointed to Randy. "And Dad, put your hand on his shoulder."

Michael placed his hand on Randy's shoulder and felt his own heart swell at touching him again.

"That's good. Now everybody squeeze in just a little tighter. . . ."

The photographer peered through his viewfinder while they stood close enough to feel one another's body warmth, touching where they were ordered.

And Lisa thought, Please let this work.

And Bess thought, Hurry or I'll cry.

And Randy thought, Dad's hand feels good.

And Michael thought, Keep me here forever.

chapter 11

*D*URING THE FINAL MINUTES while guests milled in the vestibule and the bride and her mother were having their photo taken in the dressing room, Michael turned and saw two familiar faces coming toward him.

"Barb and Don!" he exclaimed, breaking into a huge smile. The surprise stunned him even as he hugged the couple, who had been best man and maid of honor at his own wedding. During his years with Bess they had been dear friends but in the years since the divorce, some queer misplaced sense of unworthiness had prompted him to let their friendship flag. He had not seen them in over five years. Hugging Barb, he felt his emotions billow, and shaking Don's hand brought such a sharp pang of fraternity, it simply wasn't enough: he caught him in a quick embrace that was returned with equal heartiness.

"We've missed you," Don said at Michael's ear, squeezing so hard Michael's bow tie compressed his windpipe.

"I missed you, too . . . both of you."

The words brought a shaft of regret for the years lost, of pleasure for the friends retouched.

"What happened? How come we never heard from you?"

"You know how it is . . . hell, I don't know."

"Well, this segregation is going to end."

There wasn't time for more. Others found Michael—former neighbors, aunts and uncles from both sides, some of Lisa's old high-school friends and Bess's sister Joan and her husband, Clark, who had flown in from Denver.

Soon the ushers seated the last of the guests. The vestibule quieted. The bride prepared to make her entrance. While Maryann arranged Lisa's train, Michael found a moment to whisper to Bess, "Don and Barb are here."

Surprise and delight lit her expression. She quickly scanned the heads of the seated guests but of course, they were facing front, and furthermore, it was time for the ceremony to begin. The ushers unfurled the white runner. The priest and servers waited up front. The organ rumbled. The strains of *Lohengrin* filled the nave. Bess and Michael took their positions on either side of Lisa and watched Randy head up the aisle with Maryann on his elbow.

When their turn came, they stepped out onto the white runner with their emotions running as close to the surface as at any time since the plans for this day had begun. Bess's knees shook. Michael's insides trembled. They passed the sea of faces turned toward them without singling out any. They gave up their daughter to the waiting groom, then stood side-by-side until the traditional question was asked: "Who gives this woman?"

Michael answered, "Her mother and I do," then escorted Bess to the front pew, where they took their places side-by-side.

In a day laden with emotional impact, this hour was the worst. Michael and Bess felt themselves moved by it from the time Father Moore smiled benignly on the bride and groom and told the gathered witnesses, "I've known Lisa since the night she came into this world. I baptized her when she was two weeks old, gave her her first Communion when she was seven and confirmed her when she was twelve, so it feels quite fitting that I should be the one conducting this ceremony today." Father Moore's gaze encompassed the assembled as he went on. "I know many of you who have come as guests today to witness these vows." His eyes touched Bess and Michael and moved on to others. "I welcome you on behalf of Lisa and Mark, and thank you for coming. How wonderful that by your presence you do honor not only to this young couple who are about to embark on a lifetime of love and faithfulness to one another, but you express your own faith in the very institution of marriage and family, and the time-enriched tradition of one man, one woman, promising their fidelity and love to one another till death do them part.

"Till death do them part . . . that's a long, long time." The soliloquy went on, while Michael and Bess sat inches apart and took in every word. The priest told a lovely story about a very rich man who, upon the occasion of his wedding, so wanted to show his love for his bride that he imported a hundred thousand silk worms and upon the eve of his wedding had them released in a mulberry grove. In the pre-dawn hours the grove was laced with the efforts of their night's spinning, and before the dew had dried on the silken threads the groom ordered that gold dust be sprinkled over the entire grove. There, in this gilded bower by which the rich man attempted to manifest his love, he and his bride spoke their vows just as the sun smiled over the horizon, lighting the entire scene to a splendiferous, glittering display.

To the nuptial couple the priest said, "A fitting gift, most certainly, this gift the rich man gave his new bride. But the richest gold a husband can bring to his wife, and a wife to her husband, is not that which can be sprinkled on silk threads, or bought in a jewelry store, or placed on a hand. It is the love and faithfulness they bring to one another in the ongoing years as they grow old together."

From the corner of her eye Bess saw Michael turn his head to look at her. The seconds stretched on until she finally looked up at him. His expression was solemn, his gaze steady. She felt it as one feels a change of season on a particular morning when a door is flung open to reveal that winter is gone. She dropped her gaze to her lap. Still he continued watching her. Her concentration was besieged, and the words of the priest became lost on her.

She tried letting her gaze wander but always it returned to Michael, to the fringes of his clothing, which was all she'd allow herself to watch . . . to his knees . . . to the side seam of his tuxedo, which touched the edge of her skirt . . . to his cuffs, his elegant hands resting in his lap, the hands that had touched her so many times, that had held their newborn babies, and provided a living for them, and had rung the doorbell earlier today and had hugged Lisa and touched Randy so tentatively several times that she'd seen. Oh, how she still loved Michael's hands.

She emerged from her preoccupation to find everyone getting to their feet, and she followed suit, bumping elbows with Michael as he rose and jiggled his right knee to drop his pantleg into place. It was one of those little things that got her: Michael jiggling his pantleg down the way she remembered from a past when such a simple action meant nothing. Now it took on undue significance simply because it was happening beside her again.

They sat once more and Bess felt Michael's upper arm flush against hers. Neither of them drew away.

Father Moore spoke again, letting his eyes communicate with the congregation. "During the exchange of vows, the bride and groom invite all of you who are married to join hands and reaffirm your own wedding vows along with them." Lisa and Mark faced each other and joined hands.

Mark spoke clearly, for all to hear.

"I, Mark, take thee, Lisa . . ."

Tears rolled down Bess's cheeks and darkened two spots on her suit jacket. Michael found a handkerchief and put it in her hand, then, in the valley between them, where no one else could see, he found her free hand, squeezed it hard, and she squeezed back.

"I, Lisa, take thee, Mark . . ."

Lisa, their firstborn, in whom so many hopes had been realized, during whose reign as the center of their world they had been so unutterably happy. Lisa had them holding hands again.

"By the power invested in me by God the father, the son and the holy spirit, I now pronounce you man and wife. You may kiss the bride."

While Lisa raised her happy face for Mark's kiss, Michael's hand squeezed Bess's so hard she feared the bones might snap.

In consolation?

Regret?

Affection?

It mattered not, for she was squeezing his right back, needing that link with him, needing the firm pressure of their entwined fingers and their locked palms. She studied the back of Randy's head and said a silent prayer that his antipathy with Michael would end. She watched Lisa's train slide up three steps as she and Mark approached the altar to light the unity candle. A clear soprano voice sang "He has chosen you for me . . ." and still Michael's hand gripped hers, his thumb now drawing the pattern of an angel's wing across the base of her own.

The song ended and the organ played quietly as Lisa and Mark came toward their mothers, each carrying a long red rose. Mark approached Bess and Michael released her hand.

Over the pew, Mark kissed her cheek and said, "Thank you for being here together. You've really made Lisa happy." Shaking Michael's hand, he said, "I'll keep her happy, I promise."

Lisa came next, kissing each of them on the cheek. "I love you, Mom. I love you, Dad. Watch Mark and me and we'll show you how it's done."

When she was gone Bess had to use Michael's hanky once more. A moment later, as they were kneeling, he nudged her elbow and reached out a hand, palm-up. She placed the hanky in it and concentrated on the proceedings while he wiped his eyes and blew his nose, then tucked the handkerchief away in his rear pocket.

They celebrated the remainder of the Mass together, received Communion as they had in the past and tried to figure out what it had meant when they'd held hands during the vows while for the rest of the service they maintained a careful distance, touching no longer. When the organ burst forth with the recessional they were smiling, following their children from the church, Michael's hand holding Bess's elbow.

Lisa had insisted there be no receiving line at the church: it put a crimp in the festivities and made some people uncomfortable. So when the bridal party burst from the double doors of St. Mary's, their guests burst right behind them. The hugs and felicitations that happened on the church steps were spontaneous, accompanied by a quick shower of wheat and a retreat to the waiting limousines.

The bride and groom piled into the first car, the photographer snapped some pictures and Michael called, "Randy and Maryann, you can ride with us!"

Regretfully, Maryann replied, "I'd like to but I brought my own car."

Randy said, "I guess I'll ride with Maryann, then. See you there."

Bess touched Michael's arm. "I have to get Lisa's things from the changing room. I told her I'd bring them to the reception."

"I'll come with you."

They reentered the church and went to the brightly lit room where it was quiet and they were alone. Bess began collecting Lisa's street shoes, makeup, overnight bag. She was putting the smaller bag into the larger one when a great wave of melancholy struck. She released the handles of the duffel bag, covered her eyes and dropped her chin. Standing with her back to Michael she fished in the duffel bag for Kleenex while she felt a first sob building.

"Hey . . . hey . . . what's this?" Michael turned her around and took her gently in his arms.

"I don't know," she sniffled, with her hand between them, covering her nose with the tissue. "I just feel like crying."

"Ah, well, I guess it's allowed. You're her mother."

"But I feel like such a jerk."

"Doesn't matter. You're still her mother."

"Oh, Michael, she's all married."

"I know. She was our baby and now she doesn't belong to us anymore."

Bess gave in to the awful need to let the tears go. She put both arms around his shoulders and bawled. He held her loosely and rubbed her back. In his arms she felt less like a jerk. When her tears had stopped she remained against him. "Remember when she was little, how she used to put on shows for us?"

"And we thought for sure she was going to be the next Barbra Streisand."

"And how she always had to sit up on the cupboard when I was baking cookies and try to help me stir. Her head would always be in my way."

"And the time she tied her doll blanket around the light bulb in her playhouse and nearly burned the house down?"

"And the time she fractured her arm when she was ice skating and the doctor had to break it completely before he could put it in a cast? Oh, Michael, I'd sooner have had him break my own arm than hers."

"I know. Me, too."

They grew quiet, reminiscing. In time they became aware that they stood quite comfortably in a full-length embrace.

Bess drew back and said, "I've probably ruined your tuxedo." She brushed at his shoulder while his hands rested at her waist.

"We did all right by her, Bess." Michael's voice was quiet and sincere. "She's turned into a real winner."

Bess looked into his eyes. "I know. And I know she'll be happy with Mark, too, so I promise I'm done with these tears."

They remained awhile longer, enjoying the closeness, until she forced herself to step back. "I promised Lisa we'd make sure this room was cleaned up. Would you mind closing up the flower boxes while I fix my face?"

He dropped his hands from her and said, "Don't mind a bit."

When she got a load of herself in the mirror, Bess said, "Mercy, what a mess."

Michael looked back over his shoulder while packing up the floral tailings. Bess opened her purse and began repairing her makeup. Michael put the box on a chair by the door, zipped up Lisa's duffel bag and added it to the collection, then ambled back to Bess and stood behind her, watching in the mirror as she did mysterious things to her eyes.

"Don't watch me," she said, tipping her head to catch the light properly.

"Why?"

"It makes me nervous."

"Why?"

"It's personal."

"I've watched you do other things that were a lot more personal."

Her hand paused as she glanced at him in the mirror. He was exactly half a head taller than she. His bow tie and white winged collar showed above her shoulder, setting off his dark features and black hair to best advantage.

She went back to work, dotting green kohl beneath her eyes, smudging it with a fingertip, while he stood with his hands strung into his trouser pockets, defying her order and studying each move she made as though he enjoyed every minute of it. She tipped her head back and put mascara on her upper lashes, tipped it down to do the lower.

"I don't remember you going to all this fuss before."

"I took a class."

"In what?"

"Not a class, exactly. I had a beauty make-over."

"When?"

"Right after our divorce. Soon as I started earning money."

"You know what?" He let his lips hint at a grin and said quietly, "It worked, Bess." Their eyes met in the mirror while she made a grand effort to appear unruffled. When the effort failed, she dropped her mascara wand into her purse and snapped it shut.

"Michael, are you flirting with me?" She lifted her chin and fluffed at the hair behind her left ear.

He let the grin grow and took her elbow. "Come on, Bess, let's go celebrate our daughter's wedding."

The reception and dance were held at the Riverwood Club overlooking the St. Croix, out in the country on the Wisconsin side of the river. They rode there in the leather-wrapped privacy of the limousine, each on his own half of the seat, with not so much as their hems touching. Dark had fallen but as they descended the hill toward downtown Stillwater streetlights glanced into the car and swept across their shoulders, sometimes the sides of their faces. Occasionally they would let their eyes drift over one another, waiting for the sweep of lights to illuminate the other's face, and after it did, would turn their gazes out the windows with studied nonchalance.

They crossed the bridge to a whining note of tires on textured metal and left Minnesota behind as the car climbed the steep grade toward Houlton.

Finally Michael turned, letting his knee cross the halfway point on the seat.

"Bess?" he said.

She searched out his face on the other side of the seat. They had left the streetlights behind now and traveled through upland farm country.

"What, Michael," she said at last.

He drew a breath and hesitated, as if what he was about to say had taken great mulling.

"Nothing," he said at last, and she released her disappointment in a careful breath.

The Riverwood Club sprawled high above the banks of the river in a stand of knotty oaks. On the landward side it was approached by a horseshoe-shaped drive leading to an open-arms style entry reminiscent of a seventeenth-century Charlestonian mansion. The two arcs of its sweeping front stairs embraced a heart-shaped shrubbery garden filled with evergreens, trimmed at an angle to follow the descending steps. Above, six white fluted columns rose two floors, setting off the club's grand front veranda.

Michael helped Bess alight from the limo, took her elbow as they mounted the left stairway, opened the heavy front door, took her coat, checked it with his own and pocketed the number.

The entry held a chandelier the size of Maryland and a magnificent, free-flying staircase that led to the ballroom above.

"So this is what we're paying for," Michael remarked as they mounted the stairs, his knees lifting in perfect rhythm with Bess's. "Well, I don't know about you, but I intend to get my money's worth."

He started with the champagne. A fountain of it flowed just inside the entry to the ballroom, and beside it a cloth-covered table held a pyramid of stem glasses that a juggler would think twice about disturbing. Michael plucked one from the top and asked Bess, "How about you? Champagne?"

"Since we're paying for it, why not?"

With their glasses in hand they headed into the crowd to mingle. Bess found herself trailing Michael, stopping when he stopped, visiting with whom he visited, as if they were still married. When she realized what she was doing she drifted off in another direction, only to find herself searching him out across the room. Round tables with apricot-colored cloths circled a parquet dance floor. Above it, the mate to the entry chandelier hung in splendor, shedding whiskey-hued light over the gathering. Every table held a candle, their dozens of flames reflected in one entire wall of glass that looked out over the river, where the lights of Stillwater lit the sky to the northwest. It was a huge room, yet she could pick Michael out among the crowd within seconds of trying, his pale tuxedo and dark hair beckoning from wherever he stood.

She was studying him from clear across the room when Stella came up behind her shoulder and said, "He's easily the best-looking man in the place. Gil thinks so, too."

"Mother, you're incorrigible."

"Were you two holding hands during those vows?"

"Don't be absurd."

Heather came along with her husband in tow and said, "I loved the ceremony, and I *love* this room! I'm so glad you invited us."

They moved on and Hildy Padgett was there, saying, "Thank heavens I don't have to go through *that* every day."

Jake, beside her, said, "She cried all through the ceremony."

"So did I," Bess admitted.

Randy and Maryann showed up and began visiting with the group. Lisa and Mark appeared, holding hands, being hugged and kissed by everyone. Bess hadn't realized Michael had drifted up behind her until Lisa hugged him and said, "Wow, Daddy, you look good enough to be dessert. Speaking of which, I think they're ready to start serving dinner now. Mom and Dad, you're at the head table with us."

Once again Bess and Michael found themselves seated together while their food was served and Father Moore stood to say grace.

They dined on beef tips in wine sauce, wild rice and broccoli, relaxing even more with each other. The servers came around to refill their champagne glasses for the official toast.

Randy, as best man, stood to make it.

"Attention! Attention, everyone!" he said, buttoning his tuxedo jacket and waiting for the rustle of conversation to die. Several people clinked their glasses with spoons and the room quieted.

"Well, today I watched my big sister get married." Randy paused and scratched his head. "Boy, am I glad. She always used up the last of the hot water and left me with . . ." Laughter drowned out the rest of his recollection. He picked up again when he could be heard. "No, really, Lisa, I couldn't be happier for you. And you, too, Mark. Now you get to share the bathroom with her and fight for mirror time." Laughter again before Randy got sentimental. "Seriously, Lisa . . . Mark . . . I think you're both pretty great." He saluted them with his glass. "So here's to love and happiness, on your wedding day and for the rest of your lives. We hope you have plenty of both."

Everyone sipped and applauded, and Randy resumed his place beside Maryann.

She smiled at him and said, "That seems to come naturally to you."

He shrugged and said, "I suppose so."

"So you'll love it on stage when you get there."

He drank some champagne and grinned. "What, you don't think I'll get there?"

"How can I know? I've never even heard you play."

They ate awhile, then he said, "So tell me about these sports you're in. I suppose you've lettered."

"All three years."

"And you get straight A's."

"Of course."

"And you edit your yearbook."

"School paper."

"Oh . . . school paper, sorry." He studied her and asked, "So what do you do for fun?"

"What do you mean? All that is fun. I *love* school."

"Besides school."

"I do a lot with my church group. I'm thinking of going to Mexico this summer to help the hurricane victims there. It's all being arranged by the church. Fifty of us can go but we all have to raise our own money to pay our way."

"Doing what?"

"We raise pledges."

The concept boggled him. Church group? Hurricane victims? Pledges?

"So what'll you do there?"

"A lot of very hard work. Mix concrete, put roofs back on, sleep in hammocks and go without baths for a week."

"Pardon me, but if you go without baths those Mexicans are going to want you out of there long before a week is up."

She laughed, covering her mouth with a napkin.

"You smell good tonight, though," he said in his flirtiest fashion, and her laughter died. She lowered the napkin, blushed and transferred her attention to her plate.

"Is that the line you use on all the girls?"

"All what girls?"

"I figure there must be plenty of them. After all, you aren't exactly Elephant Man."

He told her the truth. "The last girl I dated seriously was Carla Utley and we were in the tenth grade."

"Oh, come on. You don't expect me to believe that."

"It's true."

"The tenth grade?"

"I've taken girls out since then, but none of them were serious."

"So what else? You do a lot of one-night stands?"

He leveled his dark, long-lashed eyes on hers and said, "For a beautiful girl you sure are vicious."

She blushed again, which pleased him.

She was the prettiest, freshest, most inviolable creature he'd ever had the pleasure of spending an evening with, and he thought with some astonishment that it was going to be the first time in years he kissed a girl without thumping her into bed.

Someone started tapping a champagne glass with a spoon, and the entire phalanx of wedding guests caught the cue and filled the ballroom with chiming.

Mark and Lisa rose to their feet and performed the ritual with gusto. They gave their guests a good one—a lusty French kiss that lasted five seconds.

While Maryann watched the proceedings, Randy watched her. She appeared transported while she took in the kiss with her own lips slightly parted.

When the bride and groom sat down the crowd burst into applause. All but Maryann. She dropped her eyes self-consciously, then, sensing Randy's unbroken regard, flashed a quick, embarrassed glance his way. It lasted only long enough for Maryann to grow more flustered but as her glance fled away, for the merest fraction of a second her eyes detoured to his lips.

The meal ended. Milling began and a band started setting up. Michael pushed back his chair and said to Bess, "Let's go mingle."

They did so together, catching up with relatives they'd each lost through divorce, with old friends, new friends, neighbors whose children had played with Lisa and Randy in their elementary-school days—a hall full of familiar people who politely refrained from asking their status as a couple.

They came at last to Barb and Don Maholic, who saw them approaching and rose from their chairs. The men clasped hands. The women hugged.

"Oh, Barb, it's good to see you," Bess said emotionally.

"It's been too darn long."

"It must be five years."

"At least. We were so happy to get the wedding invitation, and what a beautiful bride Lisa is. Congratulations."

"She is, isn't she? It's hard not to get teary-eyed when you watch one of your kids get married. So tell me about yours."

"Come on. Sit down and let's catch up."

The men brought drinks and the four of them sipped and talked. About their kids. About their businesses. About trips and mutual acquaintances and their parents. The band started up and they talked a little louder, leaning closer to be heard.

In the background, the bandleader called the bridal couple onto the floor as the group struck into "Could I Have This Dance." Lisa and Mark walked out beneath the chandelier and as they danced, captured the attention of everyone in the room, including Bess and Michael.

The bandleader called, "Let's have the other members of the wedding party join them."

Across the hall, Randy turned to Maryann and said, "I guess that means us."

Jake Padgett stood and said to his wife, "Mother?"

Over Mark's shoulder, Lisa pointed and gestured to Michael: *ask Mother!*

He glanced at Bess. She had her forearms crossed on the table and was watching Lisa with a wistful smile on her lips. At the turn of Michael's head, she turned her own.

"Dance, Bess?" he asked.

"I think we should," she answered.

He pulled out her chair and followed her onto the dance floor, conscious of Lisa's wide smile as she watched. He winked at the bride and turned to open his arms to Bess.

She stepped into them wearing a smile, wholly glad to be with him again. They had danced together for sixteen years, in a fashion that attracted the admiring gazes of onlookers, which happened once again as they struck the waltz position, waited out the measure and stepped into the three-quarter rhythm with flawless grace. There might have been no lapse, so at ease were they together. They danced awhile, smiling, making wide sweeping turns, before Bess said, "We always did this well, didn't we, Michael?"

"And we haven't lost it."

"Isn't it great to do this with somebody who knows how?"

"Boy, you said it. I swear, *no*body knows how to waltz anymore."

"Keith surely doesn't."

"Neither does Darla."

They did it properly, with the accent on the first beat. If there'd been sawdust on the floor they'd have scraped a wreath of neat little triangles through it.

"Feels good, huh?"

"Mmm . . . comfortable."

When they'd danced for some time, Michael asked, "Who's Keith?"

"This man I've been seeing."

"Is it serious?"

"No. As a matter of fact, it's over." They went on waltzing, separated by a goodly space, happy and smiling at each other without any undercurrents. What each of them said, the other took at face value.

Bess inquired, "How are things between you and Darla?"

"Uncontested divorces go through the courts quite fast."

"Are the two of you talking?"

"Absolutely. We never stopped. We never cared enough to end it with a war."

"Like we did?"

"Mm."

"We were so bitter because we still cared, is that what you're saying?"

"I've thought about it. It's possible."

"Funny, my mother said essentially the same thing."

"Your mother looks great. What a pistol she is."

They chuckled and danced in silence until the song ended, then remained on the floor for another song, then another and another. Finally walking her off the floor after four numbers, Michael said at her ear, "Don't go far. I want to dance some more."

The music got louder and faster as the night wore on. There was a predominance of young people present, and more drifted in as the night got older. The band catered to their wishes. The slower ballads—"Wind Beneath My Wings," "Lady in Red"—gave way to the kind of songs that lured even doubtful middle-agers out onto the floor: "La Bamba" and "Johnny B. Goode." When the crowd had caught the fire and were heating up, the band threw in "The Twist," followed by "I Knew the Bride," which filled the dance floor and got everybody sweaty, including Michael and Bess, who'd been partners the entire night.

Moods were high. Michael said, "You mind if I dance one with Stella?"

"Heavens no," Bess replied. "She'd love it."

To Stella he said, "Come here, you painted hussy. I want to dance one with you."

Gil Harwood snared Bess, and at the end of the song the foursome switched partners.

"You having fun?" Michael asked as he reclaimed Bess.

"I'm having a ball!" she exclaimed.

They danced another fast, hot one and when it ended, Michael had curled Bess up against his side, puffing. "Come on, I gotta get rid of this jacket." He hauled her by the hand to the table where they'd left their drinks and draped his jacket over the back of a chair. They were taking quick gulps of their cocktails when the band struck up "Old Time Rock and Roll." Michael slammed his glass down on the table, said, "Come on!" and towed her back toward the dance floor. Behind him, she snapped his suspenders against his damp shirt and shouted above the music, "Hey, Curran!"

He turned and dipped his ear to catch what she was shouting in the din.
"What?"

"You look pretty sexy in that tuxedo."

He laughed and said, "Yeah, well, try and control yourself, honey!"
They elbowed their way into the crowd and launched themselves into the
joie de vivre of the music once again.

It was easy to forget they were divorced, to join in the merriment,
raising their hands above their heads and clapping while beside them old
friends and family did the same thing and sang along with the familiar
words. . . .

I like that old time rock and roll . . .

When the song ended they were flushed and exuberant. Michael stuck
two fingers between his teeth and whistled. Bess clapped and thrust a fist
in the air, shouting, "More! More!" But the set was over and they returned
to Barb and Don's table, where all four of them collapsed into their chairs
at the same time.

Sapped, exhilarated, wiping their brows, reaching for their glasses, they
slipped back into the familiarity of their long-standing friendship.

"What a band."

"Aren't they great?"

"I haven't danced like this in years."

Barb's eyes glowed. "Gosh, it's good to see you two together again. Is
this . . . I mean, are you two seeing each other?"

Michael glanced at Bess.

Bess glanced at Michael.

"No, not really," she said.

"Too bad. On the dance floor you look like you've never been apart."

"We're having a good time, anyway."

"So are we. How many times do you think the four of us went out
dancing?"

"Who knows?"

"What happened anyway? Why did we all stop seeing each other?" Barb
asked.

They all studied one another, recalling the fondness of the past and
those awful months when the marriage was breaking up.

Bess spoke up. "I know one reason I stopped calling you. I didn't want
you to have to take sides or choose between us."

"But that's silly."

"Is it? You were friends to both of us. I was afraid that anything I said
to you might have been misconstrued as a bid for sympathy. And in a way,
it probably would have been."

"I suppose you're right but we missed you, we wanted to help."

Michael said, "I felt pretty much the same as Bess, afraid to look as if I wanted you to take my side, so I just backed off."

Don had been sitting silently, listening. He sat forward, working the bottom of his glass against the tabletop as if it were a rubber stamp.

"Can I be honest here?"

Every eye turned to him. "Of course," Michael replied.

"When you two broke up, you want to know what I felt?" He waited but no one said a word. "I felt betrayed. We knew you two were having your differences but you never let on exactly how bad they were. Then one day you called and said, 'We're getting a divorce,' and selfish as it sounds now, I actually got angry. We had all these years invested in a four-way friendship, and all of a sudden—pouff!—you guys were dissolving it. The absolute truth of it is, I never blamed either one of you more than the other. Both Barb and I looked at your relationship through pretty clear eyes, and we were probably closer to you than anyone else at that time. Anyway, when you said you were getting divorced from each other it felt as if you were getting divorced from us."

Bess reached over and covered his hand. "Oh, Don . . ."

Now that he'd said his piece, he looked sheepish. "I know I sound like a selfish pig."

"No, you don't."

"I probably never would have said that if I hadn't had a couple of drinks."

Michael said, "I think it's good that the four of us can talk this way. We always could, that's why we were such good friends."

Bess added, "I never really looked at our breakup from your viewpoint before. I suppose I might have felt the same way if you'd been the ones divorcing."

Barb spoke in a caring tone. "I know you said you haven't been seeing each other but is there any chance you two might get back together? If I'm speaking out of line, tell me to shut up."

Silence fell over the group before Bess said, in the kindest tone possible, "Shut up, Barb."

Randy and Maryann had danced the entire night long, talking little in the raucousness, playing eye games. When the second set ended she fanned herself with a hand while he freed his bow tie and collar button and said, "Hey, it's hot in here. Want to go outside and cool off?"

"Sure."

They left the ballroom, walked down the grand staircase and collected her coat.

Outside, stars shone. The fecund smell of thawing earth lifted from the surrounding grounds and farmlands. Someplace nearby, rivulets of melted snow could be heard gurgling toward lower terrain. The air was heavy with damp that had left the painted floor of the veranda slippery.

Randy took Maryann's arm and walked her to the far end, where they stood looking out over the driveway while the evergreens below them threw out a pungent scent like gin.

Now don't say Jesus, he thought.

"You're a good dancer," Maryann said as he released her arm and braced his shoulder against a fluted pillar.

"So are you."

"No, I'm not. I'm just average but an average dancer looks better when she dances with a good one."

"Maybe it's you making me look good."

"No, I don't think so. You must get it from your mom and dad. They look great out there on the dance floor together."

"Yeah, I guess so."

"Besides, you're a drummer. It makes sense—good rhythm, good dancer."

"I never really danced much."

"Neither did I."

"Too busy getting straight A's?"

"You don't like that, do you?"

He shrugged.

"Why?"

"It scares me."

"Scares you! You?"

"Don't look so surprised. Things scare guys, you know."

"Why should my straight A's scare you?"

"It's not just them, it's the kind of girl you are."

"What kind am I?"

"Goody two-shoes. Church group. National Honor Society, I bet."

She made no reply.

"Right?" he asked.

"Yes."

"I haven't been around many girls like you."

"What kind have you been around?"

He chuckled and looked away. "You don't want to know."

"No, I guess I don't."

They stood awhile, looking out over the horseshoe-shaped drive, surrounded by the burgeoning spring night, a moon as thin and white as a
daisy petal, and tree shadows like black lace upon the lawns. Once he
looked over at her and she met his gaze, Randy with his ivory tuxedo
sleeve braced upon the pale pillar, Maryann with her hands joined primly
on the veranda railing.

"So a guy like me just doesn't . . . you know . . . make a play for a girl
like you."

"Not even if you asked first and she said yes?"

Miss Maryann Padgett, in her proper little navy-blue coat, stood with
her shoes perched neatly side-by-side, her hands on that railing, waiting.
Randy drew his shoulder from the pillar and turned toward her, standing
close without touching. She, too, turned to him.

"I've been thinking about you a lot since I met you."

"Have you?"

"Yeah."

"Well, then . . . ?" Her invitation was just reserved enough to make it
acceptable.

He lowered his head and kissed her the way he used to kiss girls when
he was in the seventh grade. Lips only, nothing wet, nothing else touching.
She put her hands on his shoulders but kept her distance. He embraced her
cautiously, letting her make the choice about the proximity of bodies.
Close but not too close, she chose, resting against him the way chalk rests
on a blackboard: a touch and it'll disappear. He offered his tongue and she
accepted shyly, tasting the way she smelled—fresh, flowery, no alcohol or
smoke. As kisses went, it remained chaste, but all the while sweetness
coursed through him and he experienced a return to the innocent emotions
of first kisses, knowing he wanted more of this girl than he either deserved
or probably ought to dream about.

He lifted his head and kept a little space between them. Their fingertips
were joined at arm's length.

"Pretty wild, huh?" He smiled, lopsided. "You and me, and Lisa and
Mark?"

"Yeah, pretty wild."

"I wish I had my car tonight so I could drive you home."

"I have mine. Maybe I can drive you home."

"Is that an invitation?"

"It is."

"Then I accept."

She started to turn away but he stopped her. "One other thing."

"What?"

"Would you go out with me next Saturday? We could go to a movie or something."

"Let me think about it."

"All right."

He took a turn at turning away but she kept his hand and stood where she'd been. "I've thought about it." She smiled. "Yes."

"Yes?"

"Yes. With my parents' approval."

"Oh, of course." As if a parent had approved of him since he'd turned thirteen. "So what do you say we go dance some more?"

Smiling, they returned inside.

The band was blasting out "Good Lovin' " and the dancers were getting into it. His mom and dad were still on the floor, having a grand old time with their friends the Maholics and Grandma Stella and her date, who'd turned out to be a neat guy after all. Stella and the old dude were dancing the way old people do, looking ridiculous but enjoying it anyway. Randy and Maryann melded into the edge of the crowd and picked up the beat.

When the song ended, Randy heard Lisa's voice over the amplifiers and turned in surprise to see her standing on stage with a microphone.

"Hey, everybody, listen up!" When the crowd noise abated she said, "It's my special night so I get what I want, right? Well, I want my little brother up here—Randy, where are you?" She shaded her eyes and scanned the room. "Randy come up here, will you?"

Randy suffered some friendly nudging while panic sluiced through him. *Jesus, no, not without getting wrecked first!* But everyone was looking at him and there was no way he could slip outside and sneak a hit.

"A lot of you don't know it but my little brother is one of the better drummers around. Matter of fact, he's the best." She turned to the lead guitar man. "You don't mind if Randy sits in on one, do you, Jay?" And to the crowd, "I've been listening to him pounding his drums in his bedroom since he was three months old—well, that might possibly have been his heels on the wall beside his crib but you know what I mean. He hasn't done a lot of this in public, and he's a little shy about it, so after you hog-tie him and carry him up here, give him a hand, okay?"

Randy, genuinely embarrassed, was being encouraged to go onstage by a throng of his peers who circled him and Maryann.

"Yeah, Randy, do it!"

"Come on, man, hammer those skins!"

Maryann took his hand and said, "Go ahead, Randy, please."

With his palms sweating, he removed his tuxedo jacket and handed it to her. "Okay, but don't run away."

The drummer backed off his stool and stood as Randy leaped onto the stage and picked his way around the bass drum and cymbals. They did a little talking about sticks and Randy selected a pair from a quiver hanging on a drum. He straddled the revolving stool, gave the bass drum a few fast thumps, did a riff from high to low across the five drums circling him, tested the height of the cymbals and said to the lead guitar man, "How 'bout a little George Michael? You guys know 'Faith'?"

"Yo! 'Faith' we got." And to the band, "Give him a little 'Faith,' on his beat."

Randy gave them a lead-in on the rim and struck into the driving, syncopated beat of the song.

On the dance floor, Michael forgot to start dancing with Bess. She nudged him and he made a halfhearted attempt to do justice to both but the drumming won out. He bobbed absently while watching, entranced, as his son became immersed in the music, his attention shifting from drum to drum, to cymbal to drum, now bending, now reaching, now twirling a stick till it blurred. Some silent signal was exchanged and the band dropped off, giving Randy a solo. His intensity was total, his immersion complete. There were he and the drums and the rhythm running from his brain to his limbs.

Most of the crowd had stopped dancing and stood entranced, clapping to the rhythm. Those who continued dancing did so facing the stage.

At Michael's side Bess said, "He's good, isn't he?"

"My God, when did this happen?"

"It's been happening since he was thirteen. It's the only thing he really cares about."

"What the hell's he doing working in that nut house?"

"He's scared."

"Of what? Success?"

"Possibly. More probably of failure."

"Has he auditioned anywhere?"

"Not that I know of."

"He's got to, Bess. Tell him he's got to."

"You tell him."

The drum solo ended and the band picked up the last verse while on the floor Bess and Michael danced it out, reading messages in each other's eyes.

A roar of applause went up as Randy struck the cymbals for the last time and the song ended. He rested his hands on his thighs, smiled shyly and let the drumsticks slip back into the quiver.

"Good job, Randy," the band's drummer said, returning to the stage, shaking Randy's hand. "Who did you say you play with again?"

"I don't."

The drummer stopped cold, stared at Randy a moment and straddling his seat, said, "You ought to get yourself an agent, man."

"Thanks. Maybe I will."

On his way back to Maryann, he felt like Charlie Watts. She was smiling, holding his jacket while he slipped it on, then taking his arm, unconsciously resting her breast against it.

"You even look like George Michael," she said, still smiling proudly. "But I suppose all the girls tell you that."

"Now if I could only sing like him."

"You don't have to sing. You can play drums. You're really good, Randy."

None of the applause counted as much as her approval. "Thanks," he said, and wondered if it would still feel like this after twenty-five years of performing—the way Watts had been performing with the Stones all these years—the rush, the exhilaration, the high!

Suddenly his mother was there, kissing his cheek. "Sounds much better in a club than coming up the stairs." And his father, clapping his shoulder and squeezing hard, with a glint of immense pride in his smile.

"You've got to get out of that nut house, Randy. You're too good to squander all that talent."

If he moved, Randy knew, even half-moved toward his Dad he'd be in his arms and this stellar moment would be complete. But how could he do that with Maryann looking on? And his mother? And half the wedding guests? And Lisa coming at him with a big smile on her face, trailed by Mark? Then she was there and the moment was lost.

Jamming in somebody's basement had never been like this. By the time his praises had been sung by everyone who knew him and some who didn't, he still felt like a zinging neon comet and thought if he didn't smoke some grass to celebrate, he'd never have another chance to get the high-on-high. Christ, it'd be wild!

He looked around and Maryann was gone.

"Where's Maryann?" he asked.

"She went to the ladies' room. Said she'd be right back."

"Listen, Lisa, I'm kind of warm. I gotta go outside and cool off some, okay?"

Lisa mock-punched his arm. "Yeah, sure, little bro. And thanks again for playing."

He slumped his shoulders, gave her a crooked smile and saluted himself away.

"Any time."

Outside, he returned to the shadows at the far end of the veranda. The earth still smelled musty, and the runnels were still running, and the thump of the drums could be registered through the soles of his shoes. He packed his bat, lit it, took the hit and held it deep in his lungs, his eyes closed, blocking out the stars and the cars and the naked trees. It didn't take long. By the time he left the veranda he believed he *was* Charlie Watts.

He went inside to find Maryann. She was sitting at a table with her parents and some of her aunts and uncles.

"Hey, Maryann," he said, "let's dance."

Her eyes were like ice picks as she turned and took a chunk out of him. "No, thank you."

If he hadn't been stoned he might have done the sensible thing and backed off. Instead, he gripped her arm. "Hey, what do you mean?"

She jerked her arm free. "I think you know what I mean."

"What'd I do?"

Everyone at the table was watching. Maryann looked as if she hated him as she jumped to her feet. He smiled blearily at the group and mumbled, "Sorry . . ." then followed her out into the hall. They stood at the top of the elegant stairway down which they'd walked together such a short time earlier.

"I don't hang around with potheads, Randy," she said.

"Hey, wait, I don't—"

"Don't lie. I came outside looking for you and I saw you and I know what was in that little pipe! You can find your own way home, and as far as Saturday night goes, it's off. Go smoke your pot and be a loser. I don't care."

She picked up her skirts, turned and hurried away.

chapter 12

B ESS AND MICHAEL RECLINED in the backseat of the limousine, a faint sense of motion scuttling up from the trunk and massaging the backs of their heads through the supple leather. Michael was laughing, deep in his throat. His eyes were closed.

"What are you laughing about?"

"This car feels like a Ferris wheel."

She rolled her head to look at him. "Michael, you're drunk."

"Yes, I am. First time for months and it feels spectacular. How 'bout you?" He rolled his head to look at her.

"A little, maybe."

"How does it feel?"

She faced upward again, closed her eyes and laughed deep in her throat. They enjoyed some silence, and the purring, easy-chair ride, the subtle euphoria created by the dancing and drinking and the presence of each other. In time, he spoke.

"You know what?"

"What?"

"I don't feel much like a grandpa."

"You don't dance much like a grandpa."

"Do you feel like a grandma?"

"Mm-mm."

"I don't remember *my* grandpa and grandma dancing like that when I was young."

"Me either. Mine raised irises and built birdhouses."

"Hey, Bess, come here." He clamped her wrist, tipped her his way and put an arm around her.

"Just what do you think you're doing, Michael Curran?"

"I'm feelin' *good!*" he said, exaggerating an accent. "And I'm feelin' *baaad!*"

She laughed, rolling her face against his lapel. "This is ridiculous. You and I are divorced. What are we doing snuggling in the backseat of a limo?"

"We bein' *bad!* And it feel so good we gonna keep right on doin' it!" He leaned forward and asked the driver, "How much time have we got?"

"As much as you want, sir."

"Then keep driving till I tell you to head back to Stillwater. Drive to Hudson! Drive to Eau Claire! Hell, drive to Chicago if you want to!"

"Whatever you say, sir." The driver laughed and faced full front again.

"Now where were we?" Michael settled back and reclaimed Bess, nestling her close.

"You were drunk and being foolish."

"Oh, that's right." He threw up his arms and started singing a chorus of "Good Lovin'," adding a few hip thrusts for good measure.

". . . gimme that good, good lovin' . . ."

She tried to pull away but he was too quick. "Oh no you don't. You're staying right here. We gotta talk about this now."

"Talk about what?" She couldn't resist smiling.

"This. Our firstborn, all married up and off someplace to spend her wedding night, and you and me only months away from becoming grandparents, dancin' our butts off while our secondborn plays the drums. I think there's some significance here."

"You do?"

"I think so but I haven't figured it out yet."

She settled beneath his arm and decided to enjoy being there. He kept on singing "Good Lovin' " very softly, mumbling the words so they barely moved his lips. Pretty soon she was mumbling softly in counterpoint.

He'd mumble, "Good lovin' . . ."

And she'd mumble, "Gimme that mmm-mmm-mmm . . ."

"Good lovin' . . ."

"Mm-mm-mm mm-mm-mmm-mmm . . ."

"Mm-mmm . . ."

"Mm-mm mm-mm-mm-mm-mmm-mmm . . ."

He tapped out the drum rhythm on his left thigh and her right arm, then found her free hand and fit his fingers between hers, closed them and bent their elbows in lazy unison. She could feel his heartbeat beneath her jaw, could hear his humming resonate beneath her ear, could smell the diluted remnants of his cologne mingled with smoke on his jacket.

So quietly the sound of her own breathing nearly covered it up, he sang: "Good lovin' . . ."

"Mm-mm-mm mm-mm-mmm-mmm . . ."

Then nothing. Only the two of them, reclining on his half of the seat, holding hands and fitting their thumbs together and feeling and smelling one another while their arms wagged slowly down and up, and down and up . . .

He didn't say a word, just leaned forward, curled his hand around her far arm and kissed her. Her lips opened and his tongue came inside while she thought of the dozens of arguments she ought to voice. Instead she kissed him back, the leather seat soft against her head, his breath warm against her cheek, his taste as familiar as that of chocolate, or strawberry, or any of the flavors she had relished often in her life. And, my, it felt good. It was the familiarity of that first step on the dance floor magnified a thousandfold. It was each of them fitting into the right niche, melding to the right place, tasting the right way.

They kept it friendly, passionless almost, engaging themselves solely in the pleasure one mouth can give another.

When he drew away she kept her eyes closed, murmuring, "Mmm . . ."

He studied her face for a long moment, then reclined, removing his arm from around her, though she remained snug against his side with her cheek on his sleeve. They rode along in silence, thinking about what they'd just done, neither of them surprised it had happened, only wondering what it portended. Michael reached over and touched a button, lowering his window a couple of inches. The cool night air whisked in, scented by fertile fields and moisture. It threaded across their hair, their lips, bringing a near taste of thawing earth.

Bess interrupted their idyll as if rebutting thoughts they'd both been having. "The trouble is," she said quietly, "you fit in so remarkably well."

"I do, don't I?"

"Mother loves you. All the shirttail family thinks I was crazy to get rid of you in the first place. Lisa would sell her soul to get us back together. Randy's even coming around little by little. And Barb and Don—it felt like slipping into an old, comfortable easy chair to be with them again."

"Boy, didn't it."

"Isn't it strange, how we both gave them up? I thought you were probably seeing them all along."

"I thought *you* were."

"With the possible exception of Heather down at the store, I really don't have any friends anymore. I seem to have forsaken them since we got divorced—don't ask me why."

"That's not healthy."

"I know."

"Why do you suppose you did that?"

"Because when you're divorced you always end up feeling like the odd man out. Everyone else has a partner to be with and there you are trailing along like a kid sister."

"I thought you had that boyfriend."

"Keith? Mmmm . . . no, Keith wasn't one I took around and introduced to many people. When I did, most of them looked at me funny and got me in a corner and whispered, 'What in the world are you doing with *him?'* "

"How long did you go with him?"

"Three years."

They rode awhile before Michael asked, "Did you sleep with him?"

She gave him a mock slap on the arm and put distance between them. "Michael Curran, what business is it of yours?"

"Sorry."

Away from him, she felt chilled. She snuggled back against his arm and said, "Close the window, will you? It's cold."

The window made a whirr and thump and the chill breeze disappeared.

"Yes," Bess said after some time. "I slept with Keith. But never at home and never overnight so the kids would know."

It took some time before Michael said, "You want to know something funny? I'm jealous."

"Oh, that's rich. *You're* jealous?"

"I knew you'd say that."

"When I found out about Darla I wanted to scratch her eyes out, and yours, too."

"You should have. Maybe things would have ended up differently."

They spent time with their private thoughts before Bess told Michael, "My mother asked me if we were holding hands in church today and I lied."

"You *lied?* But you never lie!"

"I know but I did this time."

"Why?"

"I don't know. Yes, I do." She pondered a while and admitted, "No, I don't. Why were we?" She tilted her head to look up at him.

"It seemed like the right thing to do. It was a sentimental moment."

"But it had nothing to do with renewing vows, did it?"

"No."

Bess felt simultaneously relieved and disappointed.

Soon, she yawned and snuggled against his arm once more.

"Tired?"

"Mmm . . . it's catching up at last."

Michael raised his voice and told the driver, "You can head back to Stillwater now."

"Very good, sir."

On the way Bess fell asleep. Michael stared out the window at the blur of snowless, grassless land lit by the perimeter of the headlights. The wheels dipped into a low spot in the road and Michael swayed in his seat, Bess along with him, her weight heavy against his arm.

When they reached the house on Third Avenue, he touched her face.

"Hey, Bess, we're home."

She had trouble lifting her head, as much trouble opening her eyes.

"Oh . . . mmm . . . Michael . . . ?"

"You're home."

She forced herself upright as the driver opened the door on Michael's side. He stepped out and offered his hand, helping her out. The driver stood beside the open trunk.

"Shall I help you carry the gifts inside, sir?"

"I'd appreciate that."

Bess led the way, unlocking the door, turning on a hall light and a table lamp in the family room. The two men carried the gifts inside and stacked them in the family room on the floor and the sofa. The front door stood wide open. Michael followed the driver to it and said, "Thanks for your help. I'll be out in just a minute."

He closed the door and slowly walked the length of the hall to the family room, where he stopped with the sofa and a long table separating him from Bess, who stood among the packages.

Michael's glance swept the room.

"The house looks nice. I like what you've done with this room."

"Thanks."

"Nice colors." His glance returned to her. "I never was much good with colors."

She took two precariously perched boxes off the sofa and put them on the floor.

"Are you coming over tomorrow?"

"Am I invited?"

"Well, of course you are. You're Lisa's father, and she'll want you here when she opens her gifts."

"Then I'll be here. What time?"

"Two o'clock. There was food left over so don't eat lunch."

"You need any help? You want me to come early?"

"No, all I have to do is make coffee but thanks for offering. Just be here at two."

"It's a deal."

A lull fell. They weren't sure if Randy was home or not. If so, he was down in his room asleep. From outside came the faint note of the limousine engine. Inside, the room was dim, the window coverings drawn high, the night beyond the sliding glass door absorbing much of the light cast by the single burning lamp. Michael's tie was in his pocket, his collar button open, his cummerbund a splash of color as he stood on the opposite side of the furniture from Bess, with his hands in his pockets.

"Walk me to the door," he said.

She came around the sofa at a pace suggesting reluctance to see the evening end. Their arms slipped around each other as they sauntered, hip-to-hip, to the door.

Reaching it, he said, "I had fun."

"So did I."

She turned to face him. He linked his hands on her spine and rested his hips lightly against hers.

"Well . . . congratulations, Mom." He gave a smile of boyish allure.

She returned it, accompanied by a throaty chuckle. "Congratulations, Dad. We got us a son-in-law, didn't we?"

"A good one, I think."

"Mm-hmm."

Would they or wouldn't they? The questions glimmered between them as they stood together with every outward sign indicating they wanted to, and every inward voice warning it was unwise: that once in the limousine had been dangerous enough. He ignored the voice, dipped his head and kissed her, open-mouthed, tasting her fully and without restraint. Where his tongue went, hers followed, into all the familiar sleek caverns they'd learned during long-ago kisses. She tasted as he remembered, felt the same, the contours of her lips, teeth and tongue as familiar as during the uncountable kisses of their younger years. Their lips grew wet and he could tell by her breathing she was as turned on as he.

When he lifted his head she whispered, "Michael, we shouldn't."

"Yeah, I know," he replied, stepping away from her against all his basic instincts. "See you tomorrow."

When he was gone she shut off the downstairs lights and climbed the stairs in the dark. Halfway up she paused, realizing he had offered to help her in the kitchen. She was smiling as she continued toward her bedroom.

At 1:30 P.M. the following day Randy found Bess in the kitchen. He was dressed in jeans and a distressed leather bomber jacket. She, dressed in green wool slacks with a matching sweater, was arranging cold turkey and raw vegetables on a two-tiered platter. The room smelled strongly of perking coffee.

"I don't think I can make it today, Mom."

She glanced up sharply. "What do you mean, you can't?"

"I mean, I can't. I gotta meet some guys."

"You're a member of the wedding party. What *guys* are more important than your sister on her wedding weekend?"

"Mom, I'd stay if I could, but—"

"You'll stay, mister, and call your *guys* and tell them you'll make it another time!"

"Mom, goddamnit, why do you have to pick today to become Mussolini?" He thumped a fist on the cabinet top.

"First of all, stop your cursing. Second, stop rapping your fist on the counter. And third, grow up! You're Lisa and Mark's best man. As such you have social obligations that aren't done yet. This gift-opening today is as much a part of the wedding festivities as last night was, and she'll expect you to be here."

"She won't care," he jeered. "Hell, she won't even miss me."

"She won't, because you won't *be* missing!"

"What's got into you all of a sudden, Ma? Did the old man tell you you ought to get tougher on me?"

Bess flung a handful of raw cauliflower into a bowl of ice water. It splashed onto her sleeve as she spun to face him.

"I've had just about all the smart remarks about him I'm going to take from you, young man. He's making an effort, a real effort where you're concerned. And if he *did* tell me to get tough on you, and if that *were* the reason I am—which I'm not saying is true—maybe he'd be right! Now I want you back downstairs, out of that leather jacket and into some kind of respectable shirt. And when our guests get here I'd like you to answer the door, if that wouldn't be too much trouble," she ended mordantly, turning back to the raw vegetables.

He went downstairs, leaving her facing the kitchen sink with her face burning and her pulse elevated.

Mothering! Whoever said it got easier as they got older was a damned liar! She hated the indecisiveness—should she have lashed out or not?

Should she have given orders or not? He was an adult, so he deserved being treated like an adult. But he lived in her house, lived in it virtually scot-free at nineteen, when most boys his age were either attending college, paying rent or both. So she had a right to have expectations and make demands now and then. But did she have to take him on today of all days? Thirty minutes before a houseful of guests arrived?

She dried her hands, swiped the droplets of water off her sleeve and followed him downstairs. In his room the stereo was playing quietly and he was standing with his back to the door, facing the chain-and-metal bar that held his clothes, yanking off his shirt as if someone had called him a sissy. She went up behind him and touched his back. He got absolutely still, his wrists still caught in his inverted sleeves.

"I'm sorry I shouted. Please stay home this afternoon. You were wonderful on the drums last night. Dad and I were so proud of you." She slipped her arms around his trunk, gave him a swift kiss between the shoulder blades and left him standing there, his chin on his chest, his shirt still dangling from one wrist.

When the doorbell rang for the first time, Randy was there to answer it, dressed in a pressed cotton shirt and creased pants. It was Aunt Joan, Uncle Clark and Grandma Dorner, probably the easiest person to hug of all Randy knew, because with Grandma Dorner nothing was calamitous. She had a way of bringing everything into perspective. She hugged him in passing, said, "Nice job with those drumsticks," gave him her coat and continued toward the kitchen, asking what she could do to help.

Lisa and Mark came next, arriving at the same time as Michael, all of them swiftly followed by the Padgetts, who descended en masse. Randy's heart gave a little surge as he took Maryann's coat, but he might have been a hired doorman for all the truck she gave him. She handed him her coat, making sure it was off her shoulders so he need not touch her, turning away in conversation with her mother as they moved toward the family room, where a fire was burning in the fireplace and food was spread on the adjacent dining-room table.

He remained on the perimeter of the activity the entire afternoon, feeling like an outsider in his own home, standing back, watching and listening as gifts were opened and *oohed* over, studying Maryann, who never so much as glanced at him, watching his mother and dad, who remained carefully remote from each other at all times but whose eyes occasionally met and exchanged covert messages.

Damn weddings, he thought. If this is what they do to people, I'm never going to get married. Everybody goes crazy, they do things they wouldn't do for a thousand bucks on a normal day. Shit, who needs it?

When the giftwrap was shaped like a mountain and the table looked as though a grasshopper plague had just passed, the carry-through of weariness from three days of activity began to dull and slow everyone. Michael asked Lisa to play "The Homecoming" on the piano and she obliged. Half the guests left; half trailed into the formal living room while some of the women began repacking the gifts into their boxes and making neat stacks of them.

The music ended and the group thinned more. Randy caught Maryann just as she was about to leave and said, "Could I talk to you a minute?"

She found someplace to occupy her eyes: on her purse handle, untwisting it before threading it over her shoulder with a toss of her head. "No, I don't think so."

"Maryann, please. Just come in the living room a minute." He caught her sleeve and tugged.

Reluctantly she followed, refusing to meet his eyes. Outside, twilight had arrived. The room was dusky at the west end, where no lamps were lit. At the east end, the lamp on the abandoned piano made a small puddle of light. Randy led Maryann around a corner, away from the prying eyes of the departing guests, and stopped beside an upholstered wing chair with a matching ottoman.

"Maryann, I'm sorry about last night," Randy said.

She ran a thumbnail along the welting on the high back of the chair. "Last night was a mistake, all right? I never should have gone outside with you in the first place."

"But you did."

She gave up her preoccupation with the chair and flung him a reprimanding glare. "You're a talented person. It's obvious you come from a home with a lot of love, in spite of the fact that your parents are divorced. I mean, look at this!" She waved a hand at the room. "Look at them, and how they've made a solid show of support throughout this wedding. I know a lot more about you than you think I do—from Lisa. What are you fighting against?" When he made no reply she said, "I don't want to see you, Randy, so please don't call or anything."

She left to join her parents on their way out the door. He dropped onto the ottoman and sat staring at the bookshelves in the far corner, where the gloaming was so deep he could not discern the spines of the volumes.

People were making trips out to Mark's van, carrying the wedding gifts. Lisa and Mark were leaving. He heard her ask, "Where's Randy? I haven't said good-bye to him." He hid silently, waiting out the moments until she gave up calling down to his room and left the house without a good-bye. He heard Grandma Dorner say, "Joan and I will help you clean up this mess, Bess." And his father, "I'll help her, Stella. I've got nothing waiting at home but an empty condo." And Stella again, "All right, Michael, I'll take you up on that. It's just about time for *Murder, She Wrote* and that's one show I don't like to miss." There were more sounds of farewell, and cold air circling Randy's ankles, then the door closed a last time and he listened.

His mother said, "You didn't have to stay."

"I wanted to."

"What's this, a new side to Michael Curran, volunteering for KP?"

"You said it yourself. She's my daughter, too. What do you want me to do?"

"Well, you can carry in the dishes from the dining room, then burn the wrapping paper in the fireplace."

Dishes clinked and footsteps moved between the kitchen and dining room. The water ran, and the dishwasher door opened, something was put away in the refrigerator.

Michael called, "What do you want me to do with this tablecloth?"

"Shake it out and drop it down the clothes chute."

The sliding glass door rolled open and, a few seconds later, shut. Other sounds continued—Michael whistling softly, more footsteps, more running water, then the sound of the fire screen sliding open, the rustle of paper and the roar of it catching flame; in the kitchen the clink of glassware.

"Hey, Bess, this carpet is a mess. Scraps of paper everywhere. You want me to vacuum it?"

"If you want to."

"Is the vacuum cleaner still in the same place?"

"Yup."

Randy heard his father's footsteps head toward the back closet, the door opening, and in moments, the whine of the machine. While the two of them were distracted and the place was noisy, he retreated from his hiding spot and slipped down to his bedroom, where he put on his headphones and flopped onto his water bed to try to decide what to do about his life.

Michael finished vacuuming, put away the machine, went into the living room to turn off the piano light and, returning through the dining room, called, "Bess, how about this table? You want to take a leaf out of it?"

She came from the kitchen with one dishtowel tied backwards around her waist, drying her hands on another.

"I guess so. The catch is at that end."

He found the catch and together they pulled the table apart.

"Same table, I see."

"It was too good to get rid of."

"I'm glad you didn't. I always liked it." He swung a leaf into the air, narrowly missing the chandelier.

"Ooo, luck-y," she said, low-voiced, waiting while he braced the leaf against the wall.

"Not lucky at all, just careful." He grinned while they put their thighs against the table and clacked it back together.

"Oh, sure. And who used to break bulbs in the chandelier at least once a year?"

"I seem to remember you broke a couple yourself." He hefted the table leaf.

She was grinning as she headed back to the kitchen. "Under the family-room sofa, same place as always."

He put the table leaf away, snapped off the dining-room light and returned to her side by the kitchen sink. She had kicked off her shoes someplace and wore only nylons on her feet; he'd always liked the air-brushed appearance of a woman's feet in nylons. He took the dishtowel from her shoulder and began wiping an oversized salad bowl.

"It feels good to be back here," he said. "Like I never left."

"Don't go getting ideas," she said.

"Just an innocent remark, Bess. Can't a man make an innocent remark?"

"That depends." She squeezed out the dishcloth and began energetically wiping off the countertop while he watched her spine—decorated by the knotted white dishtowel—bob in rhythm with each swipe she made.

"On what?"

"What went on the night before."

"Oh, that." She turned and he shifted his gaze to the bowl he was supposed to be drying.

"That was Jose Cuervo talking, I think." She rinsed out her cloth and wiped off the top of the stove. "People do dumb things at weddings."

"Yeah, I know. Wasn't this bowl one of our wedding gifts?" He studied it while she went to the sink to release the water.

"Yes." She began spraying the suds down the drain. "From Jerry and Holly Shipman."

"Jerry and Holly . . ." He stared at the bowl. "I haven't thought about them in years. Do you ever see them anymore?"

"I think they live in Sacramento now. Last time I heard from them they'd opened a nursery."

"Still married, though?"

"As far as I know. Here, I'll take that." While she carried the bowl away to the dark dining room he took a stab at a cupboard door, opened the right one and began putting away some glasses. She returned, took off her dishtowel and began polishing the kitchen faucet with it. He finished putting away the glasses; she hung up her towel, dispensed some hand lotion into her palm and they both turned at the same time, relaxing against the kitchen cupboards while she massaged the lotion into her hands.

"You still like anything that smells like roses."

She made no reply, only continued working her hands together until the lotion disappeared and she tugged her sleeves down into place. They stood a space apart, watching each other while the dishwasher played its song of rush and thump, sending out faint vibrations against their spines.

"Thanks for helping me clean up."

"You're welcome."

"If you'd done it six years ago things might have turned out differently."

"People can change, Bess."

"Don't, Michael. It's too scary to even think about."

"Okay." He pushed away from the cabinet edge and held up his hands, surrendering to her wishes. "Not another word. It's been fun. I've enjoyed it. When is my furniture coming?"

He moved toward the front hall and she trailed him. "Soon. I'll call you as soon as anything arrives."

"Okay." He opened the entry coat closet and found his jacket, a puffy brown thing made of leather with raglan sleeves that smelled like penicillin.

"New jacket?" she asked.

Zipping it, he held out an elbow and looked down. "Yes."

"Did you stink up my closet with it?"

He laughed as the zipper hit the two-thirds mark and he tugged the ribbed waist down into place. "Cripes, a man just can't do anything right with you, can he?" His remark was made in the best of humor and they both chuckled afterward.

He reached for the doorknob, paused and turned back. "I don't suppose we ought to kiss good-bye, huh?"

She crossed her arms and leaned back against the newel post, amused. "No, I don't suppose we ought to."

"Yeah . . . I guess you're right." He considered her a moment, then opened the door. "Well, good night, Bess. Let me know if you change your mind. This single life can leave a man a little hard up now and then."

If she'd have had their glass wedding bowl, she'd have lobbed it at his head. "Jeez, thanks, Curran!" she yelled just as the door closed.

chapter 13

THE LAST OF THE MARCH snows had come and gone, late blizzards battering Minnesota with fury, followed by the sleety, steely days of early April. The buds on the trees were swollen, awaiting only sun to set them free. The lakes were regaining their normal water level, lost through the past two years of drought, and the ducks were returning, occasionally even some Canadian honkers. Michael Curran stood at the window of his sixth-floor St. Paul office building watching a wedge of them setting their wings for a landing on the Mississippi River. A gust of wind blew the leader and several followers slightly out of formation before they corrected their course with a rocking of wings and disappeared behind one of the lower buildings.

He'd called Bess, of course, twice in the past month, and asked her out but she'd said she didn't think it was wise. In his saner moments he agreed with her. Still, he thought about her a lot.

His secretary, Nina, poked her head into his office and said, "I'm on my way out. Mr. Stringer called and said he won't make it back in before the meeting tonight but he'd see you there." Stringer was the architect of the firm.

Michael swung around. "Oh, thanks, Nina." She was forty-eight, a hundred and sixty pounds, with a nose shaped like a toggle switch and glasses so thick he teased her she'd set the place on fire if she ever laid them in the sun on top of any papers. She kept her hair dyed as black as a grand piano and her nails painted red even though arthritis had begun shaping her fingers like ginseng roots. She came in and poked one into the soil of the schefflera plant beside his desk, found it moist enough and said, "Well, I'm off, then. Good luck at the meeting."

"Thanks. Good night."

" 'Night."

When she was gone the place grew quiet. He sat down at a drafting table, perused Jim Stringer's drawings of the proposed two-story brick structure and wondered if it would ever get built. Four years ago he had purchased a prime lot on the corner of Victoria and Grand, an upscale, yuppie, commercial intersection flanked by upscale, yuppie residential streets lined with Victorian mansions that had regained fashionable status during the last decade. Victoria and Grand—known familiarly throughout the Twin Cities as Victoria Crossing—had in the late seventies sported no less than three vacant corner buildings, each of them formerly a car dealership. The Minnesota Opera Company had rented one old relic nearby for its practice studio and had spread the lonely sound of operatic voices up and down Grand Avenue for a while.

Eventually Grand had been rediscovered, redone, revitalized. Now, its turn-of-the-century flavor was back in the form of Victorian streetlights, red-brick storefronts and flower boxes, three charming malls at the major intersection, along with variety shops that stretched along Grand Avenue itself.

And one vacant parking lot owned by Michael Curran.

Victoria Crossing had everything—ambience, an established reputation as one of the premiere shopping areas in St. Paul, even buses coming off the nearby Summit Avenue Historic Mansion Tours, disgorging tourists by the dozens. Women had discovered its gift shops and restaurants, and met there to shop and eat. Students from nearby William Mitchell Law School had discovered its fine bookstores and came there to buy books. Businessmen from downtown, and politicians from the State Capitol, found it an easy ride up the hill for lunch. Local residents walked to it pushing their baby carriages—baby carriages, no less! Michael had been down there last summer and had actually seen two old-fashioned baby buggies being perambulated by two young mothers. At Christmastime the storekeepers brought in English carolers, served wassail, sponsored a Santa Claus and called it a Victorian Walk. In June they organized a parade, street bands and ethnic food stalls and called it The Grand Old Days, attracting 300,000 people a year.

And all that clientele needed parking space.

Michael offset the edges of his teeth, leaned on the drafting table with both elbows and stared at the revised blueprints—including an enlarged parking ramp—remembering the brouhaha at last month's Concerned Citizens' Meeting.

Our streets are not our own! was the hue and cry of the nearby home-owners, whose boulevards were constantly lined with vehicles.

People can't shop if they can't park! complained the businesspeople till the issue ended in a standoff.

So the meeting had adjourned and Michael had hired a public relations firm to create a friendly letter of intent, including an architect's concept of the building blending with its surroundings; the results of the market analysis with demographics clearly indicating the area could bear the additional upscale businesses; additional demographics showing that the proposed parking ramp would hold more cars than the flat lot presently there; and assurance that Michael himself, as the developer, would remain a joint owner of the building, thus retaining an avid interest in its aesthetic, business and demographic impact not only now but in the future as well. Nearly two hundred copies of the letter had been distributed to business owners and homeowners in the vicinity of the proposed building.

Tonight they'd hash it over again and see if any minds had changed.

The meeting was held in an elementary-school lunchroom that smelled like leftover Hungarian goulash. Jim Stringer was there along with Peter Olson, the project manager from Welty-Norton Construction Company, who was slated to do the building.

The St. Paul city planning director called the meeting to order and allowed Michael to speak first. Michael rose, arbitrarily fixed his eyes on a middle-aged woman in the second row, and said, "The letter with the drawing of the proposed building that you got this past month was from me. This is my architect, Jim Stringer, who'll be co-owner of the building. And this is Pete Olson, the project manager from Welty-Norton. What we want all of you to think about is this. We've already had soil borings done on the lot and the land meets EPA standards—in other words, no contam-ination. With that obstacle aside, the truth is, that lot is going to be built on eventually, whether you like it or not. Now you can wait for some shyster to come along, who's going to build today and be gone tomorrow, or you can go with Jim and me. He designed it, I'm going to manage it, we'll both own it. Would we put up something unsightly or poorly con-structed, or anything that would clash with the aesthetics of Victoria Crossing? Hardly. We want to keep the same flavor that's been so carefully preserved because, after all, that's what makes the Crossing thrive. Jim will answer any questions about building design, and Pete Olson will answer those about actual construction. Now, since our last meeting, we've scaled down the number of square feet in the commercial building and increased the area for parking, and Jim's got the new blueprints here. That's our bid toward compromise but you people have to bend a little, too."

Someone stood up and said, "I live in the apartment building next door. What about my view?"

Someone else demanded to know, "What kind of shops will be in there? If we say yes to the building, we invite our own competition to put a dent in our business."

Another person claimed, "The construction mess will be bad for business."

Someone else said, "Sure, there'll be more parking spots but the extra businesses will bring in extra people and that means more cars on our side streets."

The discussions went on; most of the locals were outraged until after some forty-five minutes a woman stood up at the rear.

"My name is Sylvia Radway and I own The Cooks of Crocus Hill, the cooking school and kitchenwares shop right across the street from that lot. I was at the first meeting and never said a word. I received Mr. Curran's letter and did a lot of thinking about it, and tonight I've been listening to everything that's been said here, and I believe some of you are being unreasonable. I think Mr. Curran is right. That piece of land is too valuable and in too desirable a location to remain a parking lot forever. I happen to like the looks of the building he's proposing, and I think a half-dozen more tasteful specialty shops will be good for business all around. Another thing a lot of you haven't admitted is that when you moved here, you all knew Grand Avenue was a business street, whether you're a local resident or you own a business. If you wanted vacant lots, you should have been here in 1977. I say let him put up his building—it's darned nice-looking—and watch our property values rise."

Sylvia Radway sat down, leaving a lull followed by a murmur of low exchanges.

When the meeting ended, the concerned citizens had not yet voted to allow Michael's building but the tide of objection had clearly moderated.

Michael caught up with Ms. Radway in the school lobby just short of the door.

"Ms. Radway?" he called from behind her.

She turned, paused and waited as he approached. She was perhaps fifty-five, with beautiful naturally wavy hair of silver white, cropped in a soft pouf. Her face was gently grooved, roundish and attractive. The smile upon it looked habitual.

"Ms. Radway . . ." He extended his hand. "I want to thank you for what you said in there."

They shook hands and she told him, "I only said what I believe."

"I think it made a difference. They know you—they don't know me."

"Some people are against change, doesn't matter what it is."

"Boy, don't I know that. I run into them all the time in my business. Well, thanks again. And if there's anything I can ever do for you . . ."

She made her eyes wider and said, "If you take any cooking classes just make sure they're from The Cooks of Crocus Hill."

He thought about her on his way home, the surprise of her standing up in the meeting and speaking up on his behalf. You never know about people, he thought; there are a lot of good ones out there. He smiled, recalling her remark about cooking classes. Well, that was going a little far, but the next time he was up at the Crossing he'd stop in her store and buy something, by way of showing his appreciation.

That happened a week later. He had to meet a fellow from a land surveyor's office for lunch, and suggested Café Latte, which was just across the street from The Cooks of Crocus Hill. After lunch he wandered over to the shop. It was pleasant, with two levels and an open stairway, southern window exposure, hardwood floors and Formica display fixtures of clean, modern lines, everything done in blue and white. It smelled of flavored coffee, herbal teas and exotic spices. The shelves were loaded with everything for the gourmet kitchen—spatulas, soufflé dishes, popover pans, aprons, nutmeg graters, cookbooks and more. He passed some hanging omelette pans and approached the counter. Sylvia Radway stood behind it, reading a computer printout through half-glasses perched on the tip of her nose.

"Hello," he said.

She looked up and smiled like Betty Crocker's grandmother.

"Well, look who's here. Come to sign up for cooking class, did you, Mr. Curran?"

He scratched his head and winced. "Not exactly."

She picked up a jar off the counter and tipped her head back to read its label.

"Some pickled fiddlehead fern, then?"

He laughed and said, "You're kidding." She handed him the jar. "Pickled fiddlehead fern," he read. "You mean people actually eat this stuff?"

"Absolutely."

He glanced at the assortment of jars and read their labels. "Chutney—what in the world is chutney? And pecan praline mustard glaze?"

"Delicious on a baked ham. Just smear it on and bake."

"Oh yeah?" he said, taking a second look at the glaze.

"Steam a few fresh asparagus spears with it, a couple new potatoes with the skins on, and you have a meal fit for a visiting dignitary."

She made it sound so easy.

"Trouble is, I don't have anything to steam them in."

She turned with a flourish of the palm, presenting the whole of her shop. "Take your pick. Metal or bamboo."

He perused the store and felt out of his league. Pots and pans and brushes and squeezers and things that looked as if they belonged in a doctor's office. "I don't cook," he admitted, and for the first time ever, felt foolish saying so.

"Probably because nobody's ever turned you on to it. We have a lot of men in our basics classes. When they start they don't know which end of a spatula goes up, but by the time they finish they're making omelettes and quick breads and poached chickens and bragging to their mothers about it."

"Yeah?" He cocked his head and turned back to her, genuinely interested. "You mean anybody can learn to cook, even a dodo who's never fried an egg?"

"The name of our beginners' class is 'How to Boil Water 101.' Maybe that answers your question."

When they'd both chuckled, she went on. "Cooking has become a unisexual skill. I'd say we probably have an even mix of men and women in our classes now. People are marrying later in life, men leave home, get apartments of their own and get tired of eating out all the time. Some get divorced. Some have wives who work full-time and don't want to do the cooking. Voilà!" She threw up her hands and snapped her fingers. "The Cooks of Crocus Hill! The answer to the yuppie quandary at mealtime."

She was such an excellent saleswoman, he didn't even realize he was being pitched until she asked, "Would you like to see our kitchen? It's right upstairs."

She led the way past a tall, fragrant display of coffee beans in clear plastic dispensers to an open stairway of smooth, blond varnished oak. On the second floor more stock was arranged on neat white Formica cubes. Beyond it, at one end of the building, they emerged into a gleaming stainless-steel and white-tiled kitchen. A long counter with blue upholstered stools faced the cooking area. Above it hung a long mirror angled so that any demonstrations in progress could be viewed from the retail sales floor. When Michael hesitated she waved him in. "Come on . . . have a look." He meandered farther inside and perched on one of the blue stools.

"We teach you everything from basic equipment to how to stock your kitchen with staples, to the proper way of measuring liquid and dry ingredients. Our instructors demonstrate, then you actually prepare foods yourself. I take it you're single, Mr. Curran."

"Ah . . . yes."

"We have a lot of single men registering for classes. College graduates, widowers, divorcees. Most of them feel like fish out of water when they first come in here. Some are genuinely sad, especially the widowers, and act as if they need . . . well, nurturing, I guess. But do you know what? I've never seen one leave unhappy that he took the class."

Michael looked around, trying to imagine himself struggling with wire whips and spatulas while a bunch of people looked on.

"Do you have an equipped kitchen?" Sylvia Radway asked.

"No, nothing. I just moved into a condo a few months ago and I don't even have dishes."

"I'll tell you what," she said. "Since you and I are going to be neighbors, I'll make you a deal. I'll give you your first cooking class free if you buy whatever kitchenwares you need from the shop. I won't sell you a thing that's unnecessary. If you enjoy it—and I have a hunch you will—you'll pay for any extra classes you want to take. How does that sound?"

"How long do classes last?"

"Three weeks. One night a week, or afternoon, if you prefer, three hours each class. If you enjoy them, the second series continues for an additional three weeks."

It was tempting. He hated that empty kitchen at home, and eating out all the time had long ago lost its appeal. His evenings were lonely and he often filled them by working late.

"One other thing, Mr. Curran . . . speaking from a purely objective point of view, just in case you're interested, today's women love men who cook for them. That old stereotype has definitely done a turnaround. It is often the men who woo the women with their culinary expertise."

He thought about Bess and imagined the surprise on her face if he sat her at a table and pulled a gourmet supper out of the kitchen. She'd get up and search the broom closet for the cook!

"All I have to do is buy a couple kettles, huh?"

"Well . . . I'll be honest. It'll take more than a couple kettles. You'll need a wooden spoon or two and some staples at the grocery store. What do you say?"

He smiled. She smiled. And the pact was made.

*   *   *

On the night of his first class, Michael stood in his walk-in closet wondering what a person wore to cooking school. He owned no chef's hat or butcher's apron. His mother had always worn housedresses around the kitchen, and often had a dishtowel slung over her shoulder.

He chose creased blue jeans and a stylized blue-and-white sweatshirt with a ribbed collar.

At The Cooks of Crocus Hill, the class numbered eight, and five of them were men. He felt less stupid to find the other four men present, even less when one leaned close and quietly confided to him, "I can't even make Kool-Aid."

Their teacher was not Sylvia Radway herself but a plain-faced Scandinavian-looking woman around forty-five, portly, named Betty McGrath. She had a cheerful attitude and a knack for teasing in exactly the right way that made them laugh at their own clumsiness and revel in each small success. After a brief lecture they were given a list of recommended kitchen supplies, then they made applesauce muffins and omelettes. They learned how to measure flour and milk, crack and whip eggs, mix with a spoon—"Muffins should look lumpy"—grease a muffin tin, fill it two-thirds full, dice ham and onions, slice mushrooms uniformly, shred cheese, preheat an omelette pan, test it for readiness, fold the omelette and get the whole works cooking at the proper time. They learned how to test the muffins for doneness, remove them from the tin and serve them attractively in a basket lined with a cloth napkin, along with their nicely plumped omelette, all timed to end up on the table together—hot and pretty and perfect.

When he sat down to taste the fruits of his labor, Michael Curran felt as proud as the day he'd received his college diploma.

He furnished his kitchen with Calphalon cookware, oversized spoons and rubber scrapers. He bought himself some blue-and-white dishes and a set of silverware. He found to his delight that he enjoyed poking around Sylvia Radway's shop, buying a lemon squeezer for Caesar salad dressing, a French chef's knife for dicing onions, a potato peeler for cleaning vegetables, a wire whip for making gravy.

Gravy.

Holy old nuts, he learned how to make gravy! And cheese sauce on broccoli!

They did it the night of the second class, along with roasted chicken, mashed potatoes and salad. That night when the meal was done, the man who'd whispered he couldn't make Kool-Aid—his name turned out to be Brad Wilchefski—sat down at the table grinning and saying, "I don't believe this, I just damn well don't believe this." Wilchefski was built like a Harley biker and came close to dressing like one. He had frizzy red hair and a beard to match and wore John Lennon glasses. He looked like a man who'd be at ease walking around a campfire gnawing on a turkey drumstick and wiping his hands on his thighs.

"My old lady'd shit if she could see what I done," he said.

"Mine, too," Michael said.

"You divorced?"

"Yes. You?"

"Naw. She just took off and left me with the kid. Figured, what the hell, she was dumber'n a stump. If she could cook, I can cook."

"My wife always did all the cooking when we were first married, then she went back to college and wanted me to help around the house but I refused. I thought it was woman's work but you know something? It's kind of fun." It didn't occur to Michael that he hadn't even referred to his second wife, only his first.

Wilchefski chewed some chicken, tried some potatoes and gravy and said, "Any of the guys tease me and I'll serve 'em up their own gonads in cheese sauce."

Michael was amazed at how cooking had changed his outlook. Evenings, he left the office when everyone else did. He stopped at Byerly's and bought fresh meat and vegetables and hurried home to prepare them in his new cookware. One night he dumped some wine from his goblet into the pan when he was sautéing beef and mushrooms, delighting himself with the results. Another night he sliced an orange and laid it on a chicken breast. He discovered the wonders of fresh garlic, and the immediacy of stir-frying, and the old-fashioned delectation of meat loaf. More important, he discovered within himself a growing satisfaction with his life as it was and a broadening approval for himself as a person. His singleness took on a quality of peace rather than loneliness, and he began to explore other lone occupations that brought their own satisfaction: reading, sailing, even doing his own laundry instead of taking it to the cleaners.

The first time he took a load of clothes out of the dryer and folded them, he thought, Why, hell, that was simple! The realization made him laugh at himself for all the months he'd stubbornly refused to use the washer and dryer simply because he "didn't know how."

He hadn't seen Bess since the wedding but in mid-May she called to say the first of his furniture had arrived.

"What exactly?"

"Living-room sofa and chairs."

"The leather ones?"

"No, those are for the family room. These are the cloth-covered ones for the formal living room."

"Oh."

"Also, the workroom called to say the window treatments are all done and ready to install. Can we set up a date for my installer to come out and do that?"

"Sure. When?"

"I'll have to check with him but give me a couple of dates and I'll get back to you."

"Do I have to be there?"

"Not necessarily."

"Then any day is okay. I can leave the key with the caretaker."

"Fine . . ." A pause followed, then, in a more intimate voice, "How have you been, Michael?"

"Okay. Busy."

"Me too."

He wanted to say, I'm learning to cook, but to what avail? She had made it clear the kisses they'd shared had been ill-advised; she wanted no more of them or of him on a personal level.

They spoke briefly of the children, comparing notes on when they'd last visited Lisa, and how Randy was doing. There seemed little else to say.

Bess put a postscript on the conversation by ending, "Well, I'll get back to you about when to leave the key."

Michael hung up disappointed. What had he wanted of her? To see her again? Her approval of the strides he was making in his life? No. Simply to be in the condo when she came by with her workmen to bring furniture or trim windows. He realized he had been subconsciously planning to see her repeatedly during those times but apparently that was not to be the case.

On the day of the installation, Michael arrived home in the evening to find his living-room sofa and chairs sitting like boulders in a wide river, looking a little forlorn before the fireplace, but his windows sporting new coverings: vertical blinds and welted, padded cornice boards in the living room, dining room, family room and bedrooms; unfussy little things he immediately liked in the bathrooms and the laundry room.

On the kitchen counter was a note in Bess's handwriting.

Michael,
I hope you like the living-room furniture and the window treatments.
I hung the custom bedspreads in your entry closet until your beds

arrive. I think they're really going to look classy. The upholsterer who's covering the matching pair of chairs for your bedroom says those should be done next week. One of the vertical vanes in the living room (south window) had a smudge on it so I took it along and will return it as soon as the shop replaces it. I have shipping invoices on your guest-bedroom furniture and the family-room entertainment unit, which means they should be coming in next week, so I'll probably have to bug you to let me in again soon. It'll be exciting to watch it all come together. Talk to you soon. Bess.

He stood with his thumb touching her signature, befuddled by the emptiness created within him by her familiar hand.

He went to the entry closet and found the thick, quilted spreads folded over two giant hangers and got a queer feeling in his chest, realizing she'd been here, putting his house in order, hanging things in his closet. How welcome the idea of her in his personal space, as if she belonged there, where she'd been years ago. How unwelcome the thought of being no more to her than a client.

In those moments he missed her with a desolate longing like that following a lovers' quarrel.

He telephoned her, striving to keep his voice casual.

"Hi, Bess, it's Michael."

"Michael, hi! How do you like the window treatments?"

"I like them a lot."

"And the furniture?"

"Furniture looks great."

"Really?"

"I like it."

"So do I. Listen, things are going to be coming in hot-and-heavy now. I got some more invoices today from Swaim. All of your living-room tables have been shipped. Would you like me to hold them and bring them out all at once or keep bringing them out as they arrive?"

As they arrive, so I have more chances to bump into you. "Whatever's more convenient for you."

"No, I want to do whatever is more convenient for you. You're the customer."

"It's no bother to me. I can just leave word with the caretaker to let you in whenever you need to, and you can go ahead and do your thing."

"Great. Actually that does work out best for me because my storage space is really limited and at this time of year, after the post-Christmas rush, everything seems to be coming in at once."

"Bring it over, then. I'm only too glad to see the place fill up. Any sign of my leather sofa yet?"

"Sorry, no. I'd guess it'll be at least another month or more."

"Well . . . let me know."

"I will."

"Ah, Michael, one other thing. I can begin bringing in small accessories anytime. I just need to know if you want me to choose them or if you want to help. Some clients like to be in on these choices and others simply don't want to be bothered."

"Well . . . hell, Bess, I don't know."

"Why don't I do this. When I spot accessory pieces I think would fit, I'll bring them in and leave them. If there's anything you don't like just let me know and we'll try something else. How does that sound?"

"Great."

He grew accustomed after that to coming home and finding another item or two in place—the entry console, the living-room tables, a giant ceramic fish beside the living-room fireplace, a pair of framed prints above it (he loved how the snow geese on the right print became a continuation of the flock on the left), a floor lamp, three huge potted plants in containers shaped like seashells that suddenly made the living room look complete.

His divorce became final in late May and he received the papers feeling much as he did when a business deal was concluded. He put them away in a file drawer, thought, *Good, that's final,* and made out one last check for his lawyer.

He signed up for his third series of cooking classes and learned to plan menus and make a chocolate cake roll with fudge sauce. He met a woman in class named Jennifer Ayles, who was fortyish and divorced and relatively attractive, and who was looking for ways to alleviate her loneliness so had joined the class to fill her evenings. He took her to a Barry Manilow concert, and she talked him into using her son's golf clubs and trying golf for the first time in his life. Afterward at her house he tried to kiss her and she burst into tears and said she still loved her husband, who had left her for another woman. They ended up talking about their exes, and he admitted he still had feelings for Bess but that she didn't return them, or, maybe more accurately, wouldn't *let* herself return them and had warned him to stay away.

He bought a patio table and ate his evening meals on the deck overlooking the lake.

A torchère appeared in his bedroom and a faux pedestal in the center of his gallery with a note: *You sure you want me to pick out this piece of sculpture? I think this one should be strictly your choice. Let me know.*

He left a message with Heather at the Blue Iris: "Tell Bess okay, I'll look for the piece of sculpture myself."

Another time a message was left on his answering machine: "Get yourself some new sheets, Michael. Your bed is here! We'll deliver it tomorrow." He bought designer sheets that looked like blue-and-lavender rain had splashed across them driven by a hard wind, and slept in a fully decorated bedroom suite for the first time since separating from Darla.

And finally, in late June, the message he'd been waiting for: "Michael, it's Bess, Monday morning, eight forty-five. Just called to say your dining-room table is here and your leather sofa is on its way by truck from the port of entry on the east coast. Should be here any day. Talk to you soon."

He came home the following day at 4 P.M. and found her in his dining room removing the heavy plastic factory wrapping from his six fully upholstered dining-room chairs. A new smoked-glass table was centered beneath the chandelier, which was lit, even in the bright summer afternoon.

He stopped in the doorway and said, "Well . . . hello." It was the first time he'd seen her since Lisa's wedding.

She was on her knees beside an upturned chair, pulling oversized staples out of its four feet with a screwdriver and a pair of needle-nosed pliers. She lifted her head, used one whole arm to knock her hair out of her eyes and said, "Michael, I didn't think you came home this early."

He ambled inside and dropped his keys onto the glass top sofa table beside something that hadn't been there that morning—an arrangement of cream silk flowers stuck in a snifter full of clear marbles.

"I don't usually but I was clear up in Marine so I decided not to go back downtown to the office. How do they look?" he said of the chairs.

"So far so good." Only two chairs were unwrapped.

He removed his suit coat, tossed it onto the sofa and crossed to one of the sliding glass doors. "It's hot in here. Why didn't you open the doors?"

"I didn't think I should."

He opened the vertical blinds and both sets of wide doors, at the living and dining ends of the room. The summer air bellied in, then receded to a faint breeze that trembled the leaves of the new green plants and toyed with the vanes of the blinds.

He went to Bess. "Here, let me help you with that."

"Oh, no, this is my job. Besides, you're all dressed in your good clothes."

"Well, so are you." She was wearing a classy yellow sundress, its matching jacket draped over the back of the sofa beside his jacket.

"Here, give me those." He took the tools out of her hand, knelt and began pulling the remaining staples.

Still kneeling beside him, she looked at her hands and brushed them together with three soft claps. "Well . . . thanks."

"Something new over there." He nodded backwards at the silk bouquet.

She got to her feet, revealing black patent-leather pumps and giving off her customary aura of roses. "I kept it simple, only one kind of flower and very small, which tends to be a little more masculine."

"Looks nice. And if I get bored I can lay a string in a circle on the carpet and shoot marbles."

She laughed and began examining one of the unwrapped chairs. It was armless, with a solid upholstered back shaped like a cowboy's gravestone, covered in a subtle design of mauves and grays that reminded him of the seashore after waves have receded.

"Now these are smart. Michael, this place is coming together so beautifully! Are you pleased, or is there anything you don't like? Because the final okay has to be yours."

"No! No, I like it all. I have to hand it to you, Bess, you really know your business."

"Well, I'd better, or I won't have it long."

He finished with the chair and righted it, and she slid over another to be unwrapped while he reached up and loosened the knot in his tie and freed his collar button.

Setting back to work, he said, "You've got a suntan."

She lifted one elbow, glanced at it. "Mmm . . . a little."

"How did that happen?" He let his eyes flick to her, then back to his work. In all the years they'd been married she'd never taken time to lie in the sun.

"Heather's been scolding me for working too hard, so I've been knocking off a couple hours early once or twice a week and lying in the backyard. I have to admit, it's felt heavenly. It's made me realize that in all the years we've . . . I've lived in that house I never utilized the backyard the way I should have. The view from there is magnificent, especially with the boats out on the water."

"I've been doing the same thing from my deck." He nodded toward one of the sets of sliding glass doors. "I got myself that patio table and I sit out there in the evening and enjoy the water when I'm not on it."

"You're sailing?"

"A little. Fishing a little, too."

"We're slowing down some, aren't we, Michael?"

He lifted his gaze to find her studying him with a soft expression in her eyes.

"We deserve it, at our age."

He had stopped working. Their gazes remained twined while seconds tiptoed past and the screwdriver hung forgotten in his hand. Outside, a lawn mower droned, and the scent of fresh-cut grass came in, along with a faint breeze that ruffled the pages of a newspaper lying on the sofa. In the park next door children called, at play.

Bess studied Michael and recognized not age but a rekindling of feelings she had experienced years ago. In her imagination it was Lisa and Randy outside, and she and Michael thinking, *Hurry, while the kids are busy playing.* Sometimes it had happened that way—the rare hot summer day, the rare hot summer urge, the mad scramble with their clothing, the quickie with shirttails getting in the way, sometimes the two of them giggling, and the mad rush if the kids slammed the kitchen screen door before they had finished.

The memory hit like a broadside, while she became conscious of his attractiveness as he knelt beside the overturned chair, with his open collar casting shadows on his throat, and the breast pocket of his shirt flattened against his chest, and his trousers taut around the hips and his steady hazel eyes hinting he might be having much the same thoughts as she.

Bess's eyes dropped first. "I talked to Lisa yesterday," she said, breaking the spell and prattling on while they busied their eyes with more sensible pursuits.

He finished unwrapping the chairs while she folded and stacked the bulky packing material. When the entire dining-room set was in place, they stood at opposite ends of the table, admiring it in spite of the many blotchy fingerprints on the edge of the glass.

"Do you have any glass cleaner?" she inquired.

"No."

"I suppose it's futile to ask if you have any vinegar?"

"That I have."

She looked properly surprised, which pleased Michael as he went off to the kitchen to find it as well as a brand-new blue-and-white checked dishcloth and a roll of paper towels.

When he returned to Bess, she said, "You have to mix it with water, Michael."

"Oh."

He went away once more and returned in a minute with a blue bowl full of vinegar water. When she reached for it, he said, "I'll do it."

She watched him clean his new tabletop, watched him bend down at times while working at a stubborn smudge, catching a reflection across the glass. Sometimes his shirt would be stretched across his shoulder blades in a way that tightened her groin muscles. Sometimes the light from the chandelier would play across his hair and make her hands feel empty.

When he finished he returned the bowl to the kitchen while she went to the sofa table, confiscated the cream silk flowers and set them in the middle of the larger table. Once more they studied it, exchanging glances of approval.

"A raffia mat is all we need," she said.

"Mm . . ."

"Do you like raffia mats?"

"What's raffia?"

"Dried palm . . . you know, Oriental-looking."

"Oh, sure."

"I'll pick one up at the store and bring it out next time I come."

"Fine."

The table was polished, the chairs in place, the centerpiece centered; nothing more needed doing; they had no excuse to linger.

"Well . . ." Bess lifted her shoulders, let them drop and headed for her jacket. "I guess that's it, then. I'd better get home."

He was closer to the jacket and was holding it for her before she could reach it. She slipped it on and fluffed her hair free from the neck of the garment, picked up a black patent handbag and looped it over her shoulder. When she turned he was standing very near with his hands in his trouser pockets.

"How about having dinner with me on Saturday night?" he asked.

"Me?" she asked, her eyes wide, a hand at her chest.

"Yes, you."

"Why?"

"Why not?"

"I don't think so, Michael. I told you the other two times you called that I don't think it's wise."

"What were you thinking about a minute ago?"

"When?"

"You know when."

"Michael, you're so vague."

"And you're a damned liar."

"I've got to go."

"Running away?"

"Don't be ridiculous."

"What about Saturday night?"

"I said I don't think so."

He grinned. "You'll miss the chance of a lifetime. I'm cookin'."

"You!" Her expression of surprise lit him up inside.

He shrugged and raised his palms to hip level. "I took it up."

She had lost the ability to speak, giving him a distinct advantage.

"Dinner here, we'll christen my new table. What do you say?"

She seemed to realize her mouth was hanging open and shut it. "I'll have to hand it to you, Michael, you still have the ability to shock me."

"Six-thirty?" he asked.

"All right," she replied cockily. "This I've got to see."

"You'll drive over?"

"Sure. If you can cook, I can drive."

"Good. I'll see you then."

He walked her to the door, opened it and leaned one shoulder against the doorframe, watching her as she pushed the button for the elevator. When it arrived she began to step aboard, changed her mind and held the door open with one hand while turning to Michael. "Are you putting me on? Do you really know how to cook?"

He laughed and replied, "Wait till Saturday night and see," then went into his condo and closed the door.

chapter 14

MICHAEL'S CREAM LEATHER SOFA arrived on Friday and Bess moved heaven and earth to find a transport service to deliver it to his place Saturday morning. She wanted it there, wanted to walk in and see it in place that evening, wanted to sit on it herself with Michael in the room and rejoice with him over its sumptuousness. She was as giddy as if it were her own.

She was bound and determined that dressing for dinner with him was *not* going to take on the importance of a State visit. She wore white slacks and a short-sleeved cotton sweater of periwinkle blue with an unornamented gold chain at her neck and tiny gold loops in her ears. She'd had her hair cut and styled but that appointment had been made before Michael's invitation had been issued. She polished her nails but that happened twice a week. She wore perfume but it, too, was as routine as checking a watch. She shaved her legs but they needed it.

The only thing she couldn't dismiss was the new lacy underwear she'd splurged on yesterday, when she'd *just happened to be passing* Victoria's Secret. They were powder blue, with a deep plunge on the bra and plenty of hip showing inside the panties, and they'd set her back thirty-four dollars.

She put them on, looked in the mirror, thought, *How silly,* and took them off. Replaced them with plain white. Cursed and put on the sexy ones again. Grimaced at her reflection. *You want to get tangled up with a man you've already failed with once?* On, off, on, off, three times before defiantly putting the blue ones on and leaving them.

* * *

Michael had thrown himself upon the mercy of Sylvia Radway and admitted, "I want to impress a woman. I'm cooking for her for the first time and I want everything to be the way women like it. What should I do?"

The result was a pair of candle holders with blue tapers, a bowl of fresh white roses and blue irises, real cloth place mats and napkins, stem glasses and chilled Pouilly-Fuissé, a detailed menu plan and Michael's nervous stomach.

At ten to six on Saturday evening he paced around the table he'd just finished setting, surveying the results.

Obvious, Curran, disgustingly obvious.

But he wanted to knock her socks off. Well, hell, he admitted, he wanted to knock off a lot more than her socks. So what was wrong with that? They were both single and uninvolved with anyone else. Still, roses. Lord, roses. And he'd tied the napkins around the foot of the stemglasses just the way Sylvia had shown him. Sylvia said women most certainly appreciated details like that, but now that he'd set the stage Michael studied this invitation to thump and figured Bess would be back in her car before he could say Casanova.

He checked his watch, panicked and hit for the bathroom to shower and change.

Because the table suddenly looked so obviously overdone, he himself purposely set out to look underdone. White pleated jeans, a polo shirt in big blocks of primary colors and bare feet in a pair of white moccasins. A gold chain around his wrist. A little mousse in his hair. A splash of cologne. Nothing out of the ordinary.

So he told himself while he meticulously combed his eyebrows, wiped every water spot off the bathroom vanity, put away every piece of discarded clothing from his bedroom, smoothed the bedspread, dusted the furniture tops with his hands, closed the vertical blinds and left the torchère on beside the bed when he left the room.

She called from the lobby at precisely 6:30.

"That you, Bess?"

"It's me."

"Be right down."

He left his condo door open and rode the elevator down. She was waiting on the other side of the door when it opened, looking as studiedly casual as he.

"You didn't need to come down. I know the way up."

He smiled. "Blame it on good breeding." She stepped aboard and he stole a glance at her, remarking, "Nice evening, huh?"

Her return glance was as cautious as his. "Beautiful."

In his condo a strong draft from all the open patio doors made a wind tunnel of the foyer. It wafted the smell of Bess's rosy perfume into his nostrils as she entered ahead of him. He closed the door and the wind immediately ceased. Bess preceded him through the foyer toward the gallery, where she paused.

"Nothing for the pedestal yet?" she asked.

"I haven't had time to look."

"There's a wonderful gallery in Minneapolis on France Avenue, called Estelle's. I was looking at some Lalique glass pieces there and also some interesting hammered brass. Might be something you'd like."

"I'll remember that. Come on in." He passed her and led the way toward the kitchen and the adjoining family room, stopping in the doorway and deliberately blocking her view. "You ready for this sofa?" he teased, looking back over his shoulder.

"Let me see!" she said impatiently, nudging him on the back.

With his hands on the doorframe he barricaded the way. "Aw, you don't really want to see it, do you?"

"Michael!" she exclaimed, giving his shoulder blades a pair of good-natured clunks with both fists. "I've been waiting four months for this! I can smell it clear from here!"

"I thought you hated the smell of leather."

"I do but this is different." She pushed again and he let himself get thrust forward out of her way. She headed straight for the Natuzzi, five pieces of swank off-white leather that took two turns on its way around the perimeter of the room, dividing it from the kitchen and facing the new entertainment unit. She dropped onto the sofa dead center and snuggled deep. The supple cushions rose to envelop her like a caress.

"Ah . . . luxury. Sheer luxury. Do you like it?"

He sat down at a right angle to her. "Are you kidding? Does a man like a Porsche? A World Series ticket on the first-base line? A cold Coors on a ninety-degree day?"

"Mmm . . ." She nestled down deeper and closed her eyes. Momentarily they opened and she said, "I'll confess something. I've never sold a Natuzzi before."

"Why, you phony. Here all the time I thought you knew what you were talking about."

"I did. I just hadn't *experienced* it." Abruptly she popped up and began examining the sofa, working her way along its length. "I didn't get a chance to look at it before it was delivered. Is everything all right? No tears? No marks? Anything?"

"Nothing as far as I could see. Of course, I haven't had much time to look." She reached his knees and detoured around them as she prowled the sofa, eyeing its stitching and curves and welting. When she'd finished she stood with hands akimbo, looking at the thing. "It really does stink, doesn't it?"

He burst out laughing, sitting with his arms stretched out at shoulder level along the tops of the cushions, feeling the soft leather. "How can you say that about an eight-thousand-dollar sofa?"

"I'm just being realistic. Leather stinks. It's as simple as that. So how do you like the dining-room furniture by now?" She walked toward the doorway leading from the family room into the dining room while he remained where he was, waiting for her reaction.

The sight of the table stopped her the way the ground stops a thrown bronc rider. "Why, Michael!" She stared at his handiwork while he studied her back. "My goodness . . ."

He got himself out of the sofa and went up behind her. "I did invite you for supper, remember?"

"Yes, but . . . what an elegant table," she said in disbelief. "Did you do all this?"

"Not without a little advice."

"From whom?" She ventured closer to the table but not too close, still caught in the throes of disbelief.

"A lady who owns a cooking school."

She gaped at him in amazement. "You went to cooking school?"

"Yes, actually, I did."

"Why, Michael, I'm stunned." Half-turning, she swept a hand toward the centerpiece. "All this . . . roses, blue irises . . ." He could tell she was surprised by his sentimentalism, but he recalled very clearly how she associated blue irises with her grandmother. Her lips closed and her expression became wistful as she continued admiring the flowers, then the matching linens, the stemware.

"Would you like a glass of wine, Bess?"

"Yes, I . . ." She looked back at him but seemed unable to put coherent thoughts together. "Please," she finished.

"Be right back."

In the kitchen he checked the glazed ham in the oven, turned on the burner under the tiny red potatoes, checked to make sure his fresh asparagus was still waiting beneath a lid, centered the cheese sauce recipe directly beneath the microwave, consulted his careful list of starting times and finally opened the wine.

Returning to the living room, he found Bess standing before the sliding door, enjoying the view, with the breeze riffling the hair at her temples. She turned her head at his approach and he handed her a goblet.

"Thanks."

"Shall we go out?" he suggested.

"Mmm . . ." She was sipping as she answered. He slid the screen open, waiting while she stepped onto the deck before him.

They sat on either side of a small white patio table, angled toward the lake in cushioned chairs that bounced at the smallest provocation. The setting was lovely, the evening jewel-clear, their surroundings those of evocative movies, but suddenly they found themselves tongue-tied. Everything had changed with that dining-room table: there was no question anymore, this was a stab at a new beginning. Subjects of conversation were strangely elusive after their easy-fire repartee upon her arrival. They watched some sails on the water, the rim of trees outlining Manitou Island, waves washing up at the feet of some nearby cottonwoods. They listened to the soft slap of water meeting shore, the particular click of the cottonwood leaves against one another, the sound of themselves drinking, the metallic *bing* of their gently bouncing chairs. They felt the warmth of summer press their skins and smelled the aroma of someone lighting a barbecue grill nearby, and that of their own supper stealing outside.

But everything had changed and they understood this, so they sat unnaturally hushed, experiencing the uncertainties of forging into that second-time-around.

Finally Bess broke the silence, turning to look at him as she spoke.

"So when did you take this cooking course?"

"I started in April and took nine classes."

"Where?"

"Over at Victoria Crossing, place called The Cooks of Crocus Hill. I'm doing some developing over there, and I just happened to meet the woman who owns the cooking school."

"It's funny Lisa didn't mention it."

"I didn't tell Lisa." From the first, if only subconsciously, he'd been planning this day, planning to shock Bess. Funny, though, now that tonight was here all sense of smugness had fled. He felt nervous and afraid of failure.

"This woman . . ." Bess looked into her wine. ". . . is she someone important?"

"No, not at all."

His answer wrought only the subtlest change in Bess, but he detected it in the faint relaxing of her shoulders, of her lips just before she sipped her wine, of her eyes as she lifted them to the distant sails on the water. Too, she set her chair barely bouncing again, sending up a rhythmic *bing, bing, bing* that eased some tension in his belly.

He crossed his feet on the handrail and said, "I've been trying to do more things for myself lately."

"Like the cooking?"

"Yes. And reading and sailing, and I've even gone to a couple of movies. I guess I just came to the realization that you can't always rely on somebody else to take away your loneliness. You've got to do something about it yourself."

"Is it working?" She looked over at him.

"Yes. I'm happier than I've been in years."

She watched him study the wine in his glass while a slow grin stole over his lips. "You probably won't believe it, Bess, but . . ." His gaze shifted over to her. "I'm even doing my own laundry." She didn't tease as he'd expected.

"That's wonderful, Michael. That's growth, it really is."

"Yes, well . . . times change. A person's got to change with them."

"It's hard for men, especially men like you, whose mothers filled those traditional roles. You're in the generation that got caught in the cross fire. For the young guys like Mark it's easier. They grew up taking home ec class, with working mothers and a more blurred line between the obligations of the sexes, if you will."

"I never expected to like any of these domestic jobs but they're not bad at all, especially the cooking. I really enjoy it. Speaking of which . . ." He checked his watch and dropped his feet off the rail. "I've got some last-minute things to do. Why don't you just sit here and relax? More wine?"

"No, thanks. I'm going to be more sensible tonight. Besides, the view is heady enough."

He smiled at her and left.

She remained inert, listening to sounds drifting out from the kitchen—the clack of kettle covers, the bell on the microwave, running water—and wondered what he was making. The sun lowered and the lake looked bluer. The eastern sky became purple around the edges. Over on the public beach people began rolling up their towels and heading home. One-by-one the sails began disappearing from the water. The pastoral coming of evening, coupled with the wine and the sense of dissolving friction between herself and Michael, brought on a welcome serenity in Bess. She dropped her head back against the wall and basked in it.

After a full five minutes she took her empty wineglass and went inside, past the dining-room table to the kitchen doorway, against which she lounged with one shoulder. Michael had put on an audiotape of something New Age and keyboardish, and was measuring Parmesan cheese into a bowl, a blue-and-white dishtowel over his left shoulder. The picture he made was still so unexpected she felt a momentary thrill, as if she'd met this attractive stranger only tonight.

"Anything I can do to help?"

He looked around and smiled. "Nope, not a thing. Everything's under control . . ." He laughed nervously. ". . . I think." With a wire whisk he whipped an egg, then opened the refrigerator and took out a salad bowl filled with romaine.

"Caesar?" she inquired.

"Class number two." He grinned.

She raised one eyebrow and teased, "Do you trade recipes?"

"Listen, you're making me nervous, standing there watching me. If you want to do something, go light the candles."

"Matches?" she asked, boosting off the doorway.

"Oh, hell." He searched four kitchen drawers, came up with none, pawed through another and frantically lifted a lid off a simmering kettle before stalking toward his office. Finding none there, either, he hurried back to the kitchen. "Will you do me a favor? Check the pockets of my suitcoats. Sometimes I pick them up at restaurants. I've got to get these vegetables off the stove."

"Where are your suitcoats?"

"Master-bedroom closet."

She walked into his bedroom to find it impeccably clean, the torchère softly glowing, the bed neatly made. The room itself was engaging. All the decor items she'd chosen blended together in a wholly pleasing way: wallpaper, blinds, bedspread, matching chairs, art prints, a floor urn. The gleaming black bedroom furniture had a rich sheen, even in the reduced lighting. She particularly liked a unique, masculine piece called a dressing chest, and the headboard, shaped like a theater marquee from the thirties. Beside the bed the cover of a *Hunting* magazine displayed a stag with its rack in velvet. Michael's pocket tailings lay atop the chest of drawers— billfold, coins, somebody's business card, a ballpoint pen but no matches. Though she had planned the room and been in it countless times while decor items were being delivered, now that it was in use and occupied by his personal items, she felt like a window peeper in it.

She opened his closet door, searched for the interior light and switched it on. The closet smelled like British Sterling and him, a mixture so potent with nostalgia she felt her face heat. His shirts hung on one rack, jeans on another, suits on the third. A row of shoes toed the mopboard, one pair of Reeboks with worn white sweat socks poked inside. A rack of ties hung to the left of the door; one had slipped off and lay on the floor. She picked it up and hung it with the others, an insidiously wifely reaction that struck her only after the deed was done, and she whipped around to make sure he wasn't standing there watching her. He wasn't, of course, and she felt foolish.

Searching his jacket pockets proved nearly as personal as frisking the man himself. In one she found half of a theater ticket—*Pretty*, it said; presumably he'd seen the current hit *Pretty Woman*. In another was a used toothpick, in another an ad he'd torn out advertising a piece of land for sale.

She found some matches at last and scurried from the closet as if she'd just watched a porn movie in it.

The wine glasses were filled and their salad bowls on the table when she returned to it. She lit the blue candles while he came in with two loaded plates.

"Sit down," he said, motioning with a plate, "there." When she was seated, he placed before her a plate of steaming, savory food—glazed ham, tiny red potatoes in parsley butter and asparagus with cheese sauce. She stared at it, dumbfounded, while he seated himself at the opposite end of the table and watched for her reaction.

"Holy cow," she said, still staring at his accomplishment. "Holy old cow."

He laughed and said, "Could you be more specific?"

She looked up to find two candles and an iris directly in her line of vision, cutting his face in half. She craned to one side to see around them.

"Who really cooked this?" she asked.

"I knew you'd say that."

"Well, Michael, can you blame me? In the days when I knew you your idea of a three-course meal was chips, dip and a Coke, if you were doing the cooking." She looked down at her plate. "This is incredible."

"Well, taste it, go ahead."

She untied her napkin from around the stem of the wineglass, spread it on her lap and sampled the asparagus first while he held his fork and knife and forgot to use them, watching closely again for her reaction.

She shut her eyes, chewed, swallowed, licked her lips and murmured, "Mmm, fantastic."

He felt as if he'd just landed a job as head chef at the Four Seasons. He put his knife and fork to use as she spoke again.

"Whatever have you done to this ham? It's incredible."

He peered around the centerpiece and abruptly clacked down his silverware on his plate. "Aw, hell, Bess, I feel like I'm on *Dallas*. I'm coming down there." He picked up his wineglass and slid his place mat down to her end of the table, taking a chair at a right angle to hers. "There, that's better. Now let's get this meal off to a proper start." He lifted his wineglass and she followed suit. "To . . ." He thought a while, their glasses poised. "To bygones," he said, "and letting them be."

"To bygones," she seconded as their glasses chimed. They drank with their gazes fused and afterward, with their lips still wet, lingered in their absorption with one another until Michael wisely broke it.

"Well, try the salad," he said, and did so himself.

She was filled with praise, and he with pride. They spoke of cheese sauce, and real estate ventures, and pecan praline mustard glaze, and the smoothness of the wine, and the film *Pretty Woman,* which they'd both seen. He told her about the Concerned Citizens' Meeting and his hopes for the corner of Victoria and Grand. She told him about the American Society of Interior Designers and her hopes that they would get legislation passed to require licensing, thereby prohibiting the unschooled interlopers of the industry from calling themselves interior designers.

He said, "Hear, hear! You've made me a firm believer in interior designers."

"You're pleased, then?"

"Absolutely."

"So am I." She proposed a toast. "To our amicable business association, and its most successful outcome."

"And to the condo . . ." he added, toasting the newly decorated room, ". . . a much brighter place to come home to."

They drank and relaxed over their empty plates. Dusk had fallen and the candlelight created a halo. The scent of the roses seemed to intensify in the damper air of evening. Outside, the calls of the gulls hushed while those of the crickets commenced. Beneath the table Bess removed her shoes. Above it both she and Michael toyed lazily with their wineglasses.

"You want to know something?" he said. "Ever since I divorced you I've longed to live back in our house in Stillwater. Now, for the first time, that's not true anymore, and it feels great. This place suits me. I walk in here and I have no desire to leave." He looked very self-satisfied as he continued in a quiet tone. "Want to know something else?"

She sat with one fist propping up her jaw. "Hm?"

"Since I've bought this place I've finally managed to get over the feeling that I was ripped off when you ended up with the house."

"You felt that way all these years?"

"Well, yeah, sort of. Wouldn't you?"

She pondered a while. "I suppose I would have."

"With Darla it was different. I moved into her place so it never really felt like *ours*. All of her stuff was in it, and when I left it I felt as if I was only letting her have what was rightfully hers all along. I just sort of . . ." He shrugged. ". . . walked out and felt relieved."

"It really was that simple, leaving her?"

"Absolutely."

"And she honestly felt the same?"

"I think so."

"Hm . . ."

In silence they compared that scenario to their own upon divorcing, all the bitterness and anger.

"Sure different from you and me," Bess said.

He stared at his wineglass and rotated it on the place mat, finally lifting his eyes to hers. "Feels good to leave all that behind us, doesn't it?"

"Why do you suppose we were both so hateful?" she asked, recalling her mother's words.

"I don't know."

"It would be interesting to hear what a psychologist would have to say on that subject."

"All I know is, this time when I got my divorce papers, I just put them away in a drawer and thought, So be it, another item of business closed."

Bess felt a pleasant shock. Her eyes widened. "You've got them? I mean, it's final?"

"Yup."

"That was fast."

"That's how it is when it's uncontested."

For a minute they studied each other, trying not to let their total freedom cloud judgment.

"Well!" he said, breaking the spell, pushing back from the table. "I wish I could say I prepared a breathtaking dessert but I didn't. I thought I was pushing my luck to make as much as I did, so Byerly's is responsible for the chocolate-mint creme cake." He picked up their plates and said, "I'll be right back. Coffee?"

"I'd love some but I don't think I have room for dessert."

"Oh, come on, Bess." He disappeared into the kitchen and called from there, "Indulge with me. Can't be more than . . . oh, hell, eight hundred calories in one piece of this stuff."

He returned with two plates of the most sinful-looking green-and-brown concoction this side of Julia Child's kitchen. Bess stared at it with her mouth watering while he went off after the coffeepot.

When he was seated again he dug in and she continued vacillating.

"Damn you, Michael," she said.

"Oh, come on, enjoy yourself."

"May I tell you something?"

She was glowering at him less than affectionately.

"What?"

"Something that's been aggravating me for six, closer to seven, years now? Something you said to me just before we got divorced that's burned me up ever since?"

He set down his fork carefully, disturbed by her quick change of mood. "What did I say?"

"You said I'd stopped taking care of myself. You implied that I'd gotten fat and seedy, and all I wore were jeans and sweatshirts anymore; and see what it's done to me? I'm ten pounds overweight and it might as well be fifty. I look at a dessert and feel like a glutton if I eat it, and no matter what I put on or how my hair looks, I'm still critical of myself; and in all these years I've never stooped to putting on a pair of jeans again, no matter how badly I've wanted to. There, now I've gotten it off my chest, and I'm going to see if it feels better!"

He stared at her in astonishment.

"I said that?"

"You mean you don't remember?"

"No."

"Oh God!" She covered her face, threw back her head, then pretended to pound on the table with both fists. "I go through six years of obsessive self-improvement and you don't even remember the remarks?"

"No, Bess, I don't. But if I made them, I'm sorry."

"Oh, shit," she said gloomily, dropping her jaw to a fist and eyeing her dessert. "Now what am I going to do with this?"

"Eat it," he said. "Then tomorrow, go buy yourself a pair of jeans."

She looked across the corner of the table at him and put on her puckered, disgruntled mouth, lips all turned inside like a stripped-off sock. "Michael Curran, if you knew all the misery you've caused me!"

"I said I was sorry. And there's nothing wrong with your shape, Bess, believe me. Eat the damned cake."

She glanced at the cake. Glanced at him. Felt one corner of her mouth threaten to grin. Saw both corners of his do the same. Felt her grin break, and then they were both laughing and gobbling dessert and it felt so damned comfortable at one point she actually reached across the table and wiped one corner of his mouth with her own napkin.

They finished, leaned back and rubbed their bellies and sipped coffee.

At her first taste she looked with surprise into her cup. "What next? Is this raspberry-flavored?"

"Chocolate-raspberry. Sylvia sells it at the shop, fresh-ground. She said it goes well with dessert and that it would be bound to impress a woman."

"Oh, so you set out to impress me, did you, Michael?"

"Isn't that obvious?" he said, rising with their dessert plates, escaping to the kitchen. She stared at the empty doorway for some time, then finished her coffee and followed him. He was rinsing plates and putting them in the dishwasher when she entered the room. She set their cups and saucers down beside him and remarked quietly, "We've covered a lot of ground tonight."

He continued his task without looking at her. "You named it earlier. Growth."

She rinsed their cups and handed them to him. He put them in the dishwasher. She wiped off a cabinet top and he ran water into the roaster in which he'd baked the ham.

"Tell you what . . ." He closed the dishwasher door. "Let's lighten up a little bit. Let's go out and take a walk along the lakeshore. What do you say?"

Leaning his hips against the cabinet, he dried his hands on a towel then handed it to her. She wiped hers, too, then folded the towel over the edge of the sink.

"All right," she said.

Neither of them moved. They stood side-by-side, studying each other, their backsides braced against the edge of the countertop. They were doing a mating dance and both knew it. They might very well suspect the outcome but when it came to stepping close and bringing the dance to its logical conclusion, both backed off. They had loved and lost once before and were terrified of the same thing happening twice; it was as simple as that.

They walked over to the public beach, speaking little. They stared at the path of the moon on the water. He sidearmed a rock into it, distorting the moon's reflection, then watched it reform. They listened to the soft lick of the waves on the shore, and smelled the tang of wet wood from a nearby dock, and felt the sand close in around their shoes and hold them rooted.

They looked at each other, standing a goodly distance apart, uncertain, desirous and fearing. Then back at the lake again, knowing relationships did not come with guarantees.

In time they turned and walked back, entered the lobby and rode the elevator to the second floor in silence. Back in his condo, Michael stopped off at the bathroom while Bess continued to the family room and flopped onto her back on the leather sofa, staring at the ceiling, one leg stretched out, the other foot on the floor.

I can stay or go, risk it or risk nothing. The choice is mine.

The bathroom door opened and he entered the family room, crossed it and stopped several feet from her, his hands in his rear pockets. For moments he remained so, in the pose of deep reflection and indecision, concentrating on her without moving.

Cautiously she sat up and dropped her other foot to the floor in a last-ditch decision for common sense.

Taking his hands from his pockets, he moved toward her smilelessly, as if his decision had been made. "I liked you better lying down," he said, grasping her shoulders and pressing her against the pliant cream leather as she had been. In one fluid motion he stretched half-beside, half-upon her and kissed her, a soft, lingering question after which he searched her eyes and held her rounded shoulder in the cup of his hand.

"I'm not at all sure this is the right thing to do," he said, his voice gruff with emotion.

"Neither am I."

"But I've been thinking about it all night."

"Only tonight? I've been thinking of it for weeks."

He kissed her a second time, as if convincing them both it was the right thing to do, taking a long, sweet time while temptation began its work. They let it build slowly, opening their mouths to each other, touching and holding one another tentatively, finally ending the kiss to embrace full-length, the way old friends do, needing time before taking one more step.

"What do you think?" he asked.

"You feel good."

"Ahh, so do you."

"Familiar."

"Yes." Familiarity had caught him, too, bringing with it a rightness he welcomed. When he kissed her again the friendliness had fled, replaced by a first show of fire and demand. She returned both and they held strong, heart-to-heart, with their legs plaited and urgency beginning. With their caress gone full-length, the kiss became lush and stormy, wholly immodest as the best of kisses are, with arousal at last admitted and moderation denied. They hove together, searching for a dearer fit, tasting coffee and concupiscence upon one another's tongues, reveling in it while past and present welled up and became enmeshed in this embrace—desire, hope, amity, past failures and fear of repeating those failures.

Their breakdown marked the end of a long abstinence for both of them; passion was swift and complete. He found her breast, cupped and caressed it briefly through her clothing before delving beneath. He shinnied down her body, pushed her sweater up and kissed her through her brassiere and pressed his face between her breasts while pinning her hips flat with his chest. She arched, and cradled his head as a murmur of delight slid from her throat.

He shot up, sitting on one heel, and made short work of her clothing, then his own. Down he flung her again, and she was eager to receive his open mouth upon her naked breasts and belly. He uttered a single word while working his way down her body, to her midriff, stomach, and the warm familiar flesh below.

"Remember?"

She remembered—ah, she remembered—the shyness the first time they had done these things, the years it had taken to perfect them, to feel comfortable doing them. She closed her eyes as his mouth touched her intimately. Her nostrils dilated as he nuzzled her, calling back other nights, other times when, with hearts hammering as now, they'd explored these primal forces and allowed themselves to enjoy them. In three years of intimacy with another man she had allowed no such license. But this was Michael, whose bride she'd been, whose children she'd borne, with whom such intimacies had once been learned.

In time she returned the favor while he lay back with his head against the soft leather cushions as she knelt on the floor in the wishbone of his legs.

"Oh, Michael," she said, "it's so easy with you. It feels so right."

"Do you remember the first time we did this?"

"We'd been married two years before we dared."

"And even then I was scared. I thought you'd smack me and go sleep in the spare room."

"I didn't, though, did I?"

He smiled down at her as she resumed her ardent ministrations. Moments later he reached down to touch her head. "Stop." He groped for his white trousers, which lay on the floor, drawing a foil packet from his pocket. "Do we need this?" he asked.

Smiling, she stroked him and said, "So you planned on this."

"Let's just say I was hoping."

"Yes, we need that. Unless we want to risk having a baby who's younger than our own grandchild." She watched him put on the condom as she had uncountable times before, hoping for a thousand future times.

"Wouldn't the kids have something to say about that?"

"Lisa would be overjoyed."

"She'd be overjoyed anyway. This is what she was scheming for all along." The tone of his voice became sultry. His hair was messed and his grin was teasing as he reached for her. "Come here, Grandma." He laid her where he wanted her and arranged her limbs to best advantage. "Let's christen this Italian leather properly."

She lifted her arms in welcome and they ended six—nearly seven—years of separation.

She looked up at his face as he entered her, and touched his temples where the silver hairs gilded the black, and drew him down flush upon her. He made a sound, "Ahhh . . ." the way some men would after pushing back their plate after a satisfying meal. She'd been expecting it and it brought a smile. They held one another for a while without moving, letting familiarity and relief overtake them.

"It's wonderful," she said, "doing this with someone you know so well, isn't it?"

He pressed back to see her face and smiled softly. "Yes, it's wonderful."

"I knew you'd make that sound just now."

"What sound?"

"Ahh, you said, 'Ahh,' the way you always did."

"Did I always?"

"Always. At that moment."

He grinned as if this was news to him and kissed her lightly on the upper lip. Then her lower one. Then her full mouth while he began moving.

Her eyes closed, the better to enjoy what followed, and her hands rode low upon his hips.

Sometimes they kissed, softly, in keeping with veneration.

Sometimes they smiled for no single reason.

Sometimes he voiced questions, throaty and thick.

Sometimes she whispered a reply, gazing up into his eyes.

And once they laughed, and thought how grand they could do so in the midst of lovemaking.

When they reached their climaxes, Bess called out and Michael groaned, their mingled voices shimmering through the dimly lit rooms she had so newly trimmed for him. Ah, the dazzling disquiet of those few trembling seconds while they lost touch with all but sensation.

In the afterglow they lay on their sides, sealed to each other and the warmed leather. The welcome breath of early night drifted in to cool their skins. Moths beat against the screen. Through the archway the forgotten dinner candles washed the walls with amber light.

Bess's hair trailed over Michael's arm while his free hand idled over her breasts in a soothing, endless rhythm. She heaved a sigh of repletion and let her eyes close for a while. He knew these were the moments she savored best, afterward, when the souls took over where the bodies left off. Always she'd whispered, "Don't leave . . . not yet." He remained now, studying the faint tracery of creases at the corners of her eyes, the rim of her lips, which were so at rest they revealed a glimpse of teeth inside, the place on her throat where her pulse billowed and ebbed like the wings of a sitting butterfly.

She opened her eyes and found him studying her without the smile she'd expected.

"Just what do we think we're going to do about this?" he asked quietly.

"I don't know."

"Did you have any ideas before you came here?"

She wagged her head faintly.

"We could just keep having a torrid affair."

"A torrid affair? Michael, what have you been reading?"

He put his thumb beneath her lower lip and pulled down until her bottom teeth appeared.

"We're awfully darn good together, Bess."

"Yes, I know but be serious."

He gave up his preoccupation with her mouth and laid his arm along his hip. "All right, I will. How much do you think we've changed since our divorce?"

"That's a loaded question if I ever heard one."

"Answer it."

"I'm scared to." After a long pause she asked, "Aren't you?"

He studied her eyes for some time before answering, "Yes."

"Then I think what I'll do is just get up and put my clothes on and go home and pretend this never happened."

She rolled over and off him.

"Good luck," he said, watching her pick up her clothing and go. She used the guest bathroom off the gallery and felt reality return with every minute while she donned the brief blue underwear that had certainly done its job. Reality was the two of them, failures the first time around, starting up a carnal relationship again without rationalizing where it might lead. Dressed once more, she returned to the doorway to find him standing at the far end of the family room before the sliding glass door, barefooted, bare-chested, wearing only his white jeans.

"May I borrow a brush?" she asked.

He turned and looked back at her, silent for a stretch.

"In my bathroom."

Once again she went away, into his private domain, where she had probed once before. This time was worse—opening his vanity drawers and finding an ace bandage, dental floss, some foil packets of Alka-Seltzer and an entire box of condoms.

An entire box!

Looking at them, she found herself blush with anger. All right, so he was single, and single guys probably bought condoms by the dozen. But she didn't like being duped into believing this was an uncommon occurrence in his life!

She slammed that drawer and opened another to find his hairbrush at last. Some of his dark hairs were stuck in the bristles. The sight of them, and the feel of his brush being drawn through her hair, dulled her anger and brought a sense of grave emptiness, a reluctance to return to her lone life, where there was no sharing of brushes or of bathrooms or dinner tables or beds.

She did what she could with her hair, searched out mouthwash and used it, refreshed her lipstick and returned to the family room once more. He was still staring out at the darkness, obviously troubled by the same misgivings as she, now that the easy part was over.

"Well, Michael, I think I'll go."

He swung to face her.

"Yeah, fine," he answered.

"Thank you for supper. It was wonderful."

"Sure."

A void passed, a great terrifying void that reared up before both of them.

"Listen, Michael, I've been thinking. There are a few more empty walls in here, and you could use some more small items on the mantels and the tables but I think it's best if you find them on your own."

His expression grew stormy. "Bess, why are you blaming me? You wanted it, too. Don't tell me you didn't, not after those underclothes you were wearing. You were planning on it just as much as I was!"

"Yes, I was. But I'm not blaming you. I just think that we . . . that it's . . ." She ran out of words.

"What? A mistake?"

She remembered the condoms. "I don't know. Maybe."

He stared at her with a hurt look around his eyes and an angry one around his mouth.

"Should I call you?"

"I don't know, Michael. Maybe it's not such a good idea."

He dropped his chin to his chest and whispered, "Shit."

She stood across the room, her heart racing with fear because of what he had almost suggested. It was too terrifying to ponder, too impossible to consider, too risky to let it be put into words. They had changed a lot but what assurance was there? What fool would put his hand in the mill wheel after his finger had been cut off?

She said, "Thanks again, Michael," and he made no reply as she saw herself out and ran from the idea of starting again.

chapter 15

WHEN BESS GOT HOME the lights were on all over the house, even in her bedroom. Frowning, she parked in the driveway rather than waste time pulling into the garage, and had barely put foot inside the front door when Randy came charging down two steps at a time from the second story. "Ma, where you been? I thought you'd never get home!"

Terror struck. "What's wrong?"

"Nothing. I got an audition! Grandma's old dude, Gilbert, got me one with this band called The Edge!"

Bess released a breath and let her shoulders slump. "Thank heavens. I thought it was some catastrophe."

"Turns out old Gilbert used to own the Withrow Ballroom and he knows everybody—bands, agents, club owners. He's been talking to guys about me since Lisa's wedding. Pretty great, huh?"

"That's wonderful, Randy. When's the audition?"

"I don't know yet. The band's playing a gig out in Bismarck, North Dakota, but they're due back tomorrow. I've got to call them sometime in the afternoon. God, where were you, Mom? I've been hangin' around here all night, waiting to tell you."

"I was with your dad."

"With Dad?" Randy's ebullience fizzled. "You mean, on business?"

"No, not this time. He cooked dinner for me."

"*Dad* cooked dinner?"

"Yes. And a very good one at that. Come on upstairs with me and tell me about this band." She led the way to her bedroom, where the television was on and she could tell Randy had been lying on her bed. He must have been anxious, to have invaded her room. She snagged a robe and went into her bathroom, calling through the door as she changed into it, "So what kind of music does this band play?"

"Rock, basically. A mix of old and new, Gilbert said."

They went on talking until Bess came out of the bathroom with her face scrubbed, rubbing lotion on it while a headband held her hair out of the way. Randy was sitting on the bed, Indian-fashion, looking out of place in her boudoir, with its pastel stripes and cabbage roses, bishop sleeve curtains and chintz-covered chairs. Bess sat down in one and propped her bare feet on the mattress, crossing her terrycloth robe over her knees.

"Did you know about this?" Randy asked. "I mean, did Grandma tell you?"

"No. It's as much of a surprise to me as it is to you." From a skirted table Bess took a remote control and lowered the volume of the television, then pulled the band from her hair.

"Old Gilbert . . . can you believe that?" Randy wobbled his head in amazement.

"Yes, I can, the way he dances."

"And all because I played at that wedding."

"You see? Just a little courage and look what happens."

Randy grinned and slapped out a rhythm on his thighs.

"You scared?" his mother asked.

His hands stopped tapping. "Well . . ." He shrugged. "Yeah, I guess so, a little."

"I was scared when I started my store, too. Turned out good, though."

Randy sat looking at her. "Yeah, I guess it did." He fell pensive for some time, then seemed to draw himself from his thoughts. "So what's this between you and the old man?"

"Your dad, you mean."

"Yeah . . . sorry . . . Dad. What's going on between you two?"

Bess got up and walked to the dresser, where she dropped the headband and fiddled with some bottles and tubes before picking one up and uncapping it. "We're just friends." She squeezed some skin mask on her finger and put her face close to the mirror while touching selected spots.

"You're a lousy liar, you know that, Mom? You've been to bed with him, haven't you?"

"Randy, that's none of your business!" She slammed down the tube.

"I can see in that mirror and you're blushing."

She glared at his reflection. "It's still none of your business, and I'm appalled at your lack of manners."

"Okay! Okay!" He threw back his hands and clambered off the bed. "I just don't understand you, that's all. First you divorce him, and then you decorate his place, and now . . ." He gestured lamely as his words died.

She turned to face him. "And now, you will kindly give me the same respect I give you in personal matters. I've never asked about your sex life, and I don't expect you to ask about mine, okay? We're both adults. We both know the risks and rewards of certain choices we might make. Let's leave it at that."

He stared at her, torn by ambivalence about his father, one facet of him leavened by the possibility of her getting back together with him permanently; the other facet curdled by the idea of having to make peace with Michael at last.

"You know what, Mom?" Randy said, just before leaving the room, "You were never this touchy about Keith."

She studied the empty doorway when he was gone, realizing he was right. She dropped down and sat on the edge of the bed with her inner wrists together between her knees, trying to make sense of things. In time she flopped to her back, arms outflung, wondering what the outcome of tonight would be. She was being protective of herself because she was scared. That's why she had walked out on Michael, and why she had snapped at Randy. The risk of becoming involved was so great—hell, what was she saying? She was already involved again with Michael; to think anything else was self-delusion. *They* were involved, and more than likely falling in love again, and what was the logical conclusion of falling in love if not marriage?

Bess rolled to her side, drew up her knees, crossed her bare feet and closed her eyes.

I, Bess, take thee, Michael, for better or for worse, till death do us part.

They had believed it once and look what their gullibility had cost. All the anguish of breaking up a family, a home, joint finances, two hearts. The idea of risking it again seemed immensely foolhardy.

The audition was scheduled for Monday afternoon at two, at a club called Stonewings. The band had their equipment set up for their evening gig and were working on balancing sound when Randy walked in with a pair of drumsticks in his hand. The place was dark but for the stage, lit by canister lights from a ceiling strip. One guitarist was repeating into a mike, "Check, one, two," while another squatted at the rear of the stage, peering at the orange screen of an electronic guitar tuner.

Randy approached out of the darkness. "Hullo," he said, reaching the rim of light.

All sound ceased. The lead guitarist looked over, an emaciated man who resembled Jesus Christ as depicted on Catholic holy cards. He held a royal blue Fender Stratocaster with a burning cigarette stuck behind the strings near the tuning pegs. "Hey, guys," he said, "our man is here. You Curran?"

"That's right." Randy reached up, extending his hand. "Randy."

The man pushed his guitar against his belly and leaned over it to shake hands. "Pike Watson," he said, then turned to introduce the bassist. "Danny Scarfelli."

The keyboard man came over and shook hands, too. "Tom Little."

The rhythm guitarist followed suit. "Mitch Yost."

There was a sound-and-light man, too, moving around in the shadows, adjusting canisters from a stepladder.

Watson told Randy, "That's Lee out there, doing lights." He shaded his eyes and called, "Yo, Lee!"

Out of the darkness came a voice like a bastard file on babbitt. "Hey!"

"This is Randy Curran."

"Let's hear his stuff!" came the reply.

While the others drifted back to tuning and balancing, Watson asked Randy, "So what do you know?"

Randy's gesture flipped his drumsticks once, like windshield washers. "Anything. You name it—something with a shuffle beat or straight rock—doesn't matter."

"Okay, how about a little of 'Blue Suede Shoes'?"

"Great."

He had expected the simplest of songs, something everybody knew as well as they knew every nick and scratch on their own instruments. Simple songs were the best gauge of true talent.

The trap set was simple, five pieces—bass, snare, a floor tom, two ride toms and assorted cymbals, one, of course, a high hat. Randy settled himself behind them, found the foot pedals of the bass and a ride, rattled a quick riff across the skins and adjusted the height of a cymbal. He put both sticks in his left hand, drew the stool an inch forward, tested the distance again, looked up and said, "All set. I'll count it out, give you three for nothing and then we'll go into it on four."

Pike Watson blew smoke toward the ceiling, replaced the cigarette next to a tuning peg and replied, "Beat me, Sticks."

Randy tapped out the pickup beat on the rim of the snare and the band struck into the song with Watson singing lead.

For Randy, playing was therapy. Playing was forgetting anyone else existed. Playing was living in total harmony with two sticks of wood and a set of percussion instruments over which he seemed to have some sort of mystic control. It felt to Randy as if they put out sound at the command of his mere thought waves rather than his hands and feet. When the song ended, Randy was surprised, having little recall of playing it, measure-for-measure. It seemed, instead, to have played him.

He pinched the cymbals quiet, rested his hands on his thighs and looked up.

Pike Watson appeared pleased. "You got your chops down, man."

Randy smiled.

"How about another one?"

They played a little twelve-bar blues, then three more, typical musicians who, like the alcoholic, can never stop with just one.

"Nice licks," Scarfelli offered when they broke.

"Thanks."

Watson asked, "Do you sing?"

"A little."

"Harmony?"

"Yeah."

"Lead?"

"If you want."

"Well, shit, man, let's hear you."

Randy asked for the new Elton John hit, "The Club at the End of the Street," and although the band hadn't worked it up they ad-libbed expertly.

When the song ended, Watson asked, "Who have you played with?"

"Nobody. This is my first audition."

Watson raised one eyebrow, rubbed his beard and glanced at the others.

"What have you got for drums?"

"A full set of Pearls, rototoms and all."

"You must be into heavy metal."

"Some."

"We don't do much of that."

"I'm versatile."

"A lot of the club stages are smaller than this. Any objection to leaving a few of your Pearls at home?"

"No."

"Are you married?"

"No."

"Planning on it?"

"No."

"Got any kids?" Randy grinned and Watson added, "Well, hell, you never know anymore."

"No kids."

"So you can travel?"

"Yes."

"No other jobs?"

Randy chuckled and scratched the back of his head. "If you can call it that. I pack nuts in a warehouse." The whole band laughed. "If you guys take me on I'll be kissing that job good-bye."

"What have you got for wheels?"

"That's no problem." It was, but he'd face it if and when.

"You union?"

"No, but I will be if you say so."

"Whoever we hire will have to sit in on about six solid days of practices 'cause our drummer's leaving at the end of the week."

"No problem. I can blow off that pistachio palace in one phone call."

Pike Watson consulted the others with a glance, returned his gaze to Randy and said, "Okay, listen . . . we'll let you know, okay?"

"Okay." Randy lifted his hands, let them fall to his thighs, backed off the stool and shook hands all around. "Thanks for letting me sit in. You guys are great. I'd sell my left nut to play with you."

He left them laughing and stepped out into the midafternoon sun, longing for a hit of something to relax the tension. He tipped back at the waist, closed his eyes and sucked in half the blue sky; he jived toward his car, rapping out a rhythm against his thighs with one palm and the paired sticks. Sweet, the very sweetest—playing with real musicians. Hope pressed up against his throat and made his head buzz. He thought about spending the rest of his life playing music instead of weighing and packing nuts. The comparison was ludicrous. But it was a long shot; he realized that. The Edge had undoubtedly auditioned other guys with plenty of experience, guys who'd played with well-known bands from around the Twin Cities or beyond. What were his chances of competing with them?

He unlocked his car, slid in and rolled down the windows. No air-conditioning, so the interior was like a sauna, the vinyl seatcovers radiant, even through his jeans. Somewhere under the seat he'd left a fast-food container with part of an uneaten bun, and it smelled as yeasty as working beer.

He started the engine, turned the fan on, then off again when the blast of engine heat proved hotter than the motionless air had been. He put in a tape of Mike and the Mechanics and began pulling out of the parking lot.

Something hit the car like a falling rock.

Jesus, what was that?

He braked and craned around to find Pike Watson had thumped on the trunk to stop him. His bearded face appeared at the open window.

"Hey, Curran, not so fast."

"Was that you? I thought I ran over a kid or something." Randy turned down the stereo.

"It was me. Listen, we want you to be our rimshot."

Shock suffused Randy. It went through his body faster than a hit of marijuana. Felt better, too.

"You serious?"

"We knew before you went out the door. We just have this policy, we all talk it over, no one person decides. Wanna come back inside and get in a couple hours of practice?"

Randy stared, dumbfounded. He whispered, "Jesus . . ." and after a pause, "I don't believe this."

Watson wagged his head. "You're good, man. Believe it. But we've got only six days to work you into four hours' worth of music, so what do you say?"

Randy smiled. "Let me park this thing."

He parked the car and stepped onto the blacktop, wondering how he'd operate the foot pedals with his knees this weak, how he could do licks with his body trembling so. Pike Watson shook his hand as they headed back inside the club.

"You get that union card as quick as you can."

"Anything you say," Randy replied, matching him pace for pace as he headed toward paradise.

It had been three days since Michael's evening with Bess. At work, he had been withdrawn. In his car, he had ridden with the radio off. At home, he'd spent a lot of time sitting on the deck with his feet on the railing, staring at the sails on the water.

That's where he was on Tuesday evening when his phone rang.

He answered and heard Lisa's voice.

"Hi, Dad. I'm down in the lobby. Let me in."

He was waiting in his open door when she stepped off the elevator, looking quite ballooned, in blue shorts and a white maternity blouse.

"Well, look at you," he said, opening his arms as she hove up against him. "Getting rounder every day."

She rested a hand on her stomach. "Yup. Not unlike the St. Paul Cathedral." The church had a dome that could be seen for miles.

"This is a nice surprise. Come on in."

They sat on deck chairs, sipping root beer, watching evening slant in behind them and tint the tips of the trees golden. The water was jeweled and the smell of wild sweet clover drifted from nearby roadsides.

"How've you been, Daddy?"

"Okay."

"I haven't heard from you in a while."

"Been busy." He told her about the Victoria and Grand plans and the attendant hassle with the locals. He told her he'd been sailing some and had seen the new movie *Dick Tracy,* and asked if she and Mark had seen it. He mentioned his cooking classes and how he was enjoying his new skills.

"I hear you made dinner for Mother Saturday night."

"How did you hear that?"

"Randy called, about something else, actually, but he mentioned it."

"I suppose Randy wasn't too pleased."

"Randy's got other things on his mind right now. He auditioned for a band called The Edge, and they hired him."

Michael's face brightened. "Great!"

"He's blown away, rehearsing all morning with tapes and all afternoon with the band."

"When did all this happen?"

"Yesterday. Didn't Mother call you and tell you?"

"No, she didn't."

"But if the two of you were together on Saturday night . . ." Lisa let the suggestion hang.

"Things didn't go too well between us."

Lisa got up and went to the railing. "Damn."

Michael studied her back, her hair knotted in a loose French braid and tied off with a puckered circle of blue cloth.

"Honey, you've got to stop dreaming that Mom and I will get back together. I don't think that's ever going to happen."

Lisa flounced around to face him and rested her backside on the railing. "But why? You're divorced, she's free, you're both lonely. Why?"

He rose and caught her around the neck with one arm, turning her to face the lake. "It's not that simple. There's history between us that's got to be considered."

"What? Your affair? Mother can't honestly be hung up on that anymore, can she?"

Lisa had never used the word before. Hearing her speak it now, forth-rightly, throwing it out for honest examination, Michael discovered the two of them crossing some new plateau as a father and a daughter.

"We've never talked about it before, you and I."

She shrugged. "I knew about it all along."

"But you never held it against me the way the others did."

"I figured you had your reasons." He wasn't going to delineate them at this late date. Lisa added, "All I ever heard was Mom's side of the story but I remember things weren't so super around our house at that time, and part of it was her fault."

"Well, thanks for the benefit of the doubt."

"Dad?" Lisa looked up at him. "Will you tell me something?"

"Depends on what the question is." She bore so much resemblance to Bess as she looked straight into Michael's eyes.

"Do you still love Mom—I mean, even a little bit?" she finished hope-fully.

He dropped his arm from around her and sighed. "Oh, Lisa . . ."

"Do you? Because the way you were acting at my wedding, it seemed like both of you had some feelings for each other."

"Maybe we do, but—"

"Then, please don't give up."

"You didn't let me finish. Maybe we do but we're both a lot more cautious now, especially your mother."

"I think she loves you. A lot. But I can understand why she'd be scared to let you know. Heck, who wouldn't be when a guy has left you for another woman? Now, don't get upset that I said that. I *didn't* take sides when you left Mom but now I am. I'm taking both of your sides, because I want you back together again so badly, I just . . . I just don't even know how to say it." She turned to him with tears magnifying her eyes. "Give me your hand, Daddy."

He knew what she would do even as he complied. She placed his palm against her stomach and said, "This is your grandchild in here, some little thing who's probably going to come out looking like you and Mom in some way, right? I want him to have all the best advantages a child can have, and that includes a grandpa and grandma's house to go to at Christmastime, and the two of you together picking him up sometime and taking him to the circus, or to Valley Fair, or going to his school pro-grams, or . . . or . . . oh, you know what I mean. Please, Daddy, don't give up on Mother. You're the one who left her; you've got to be the one to go back and convince her it was a mistake in the first place. Will you try?"

Michael took Lisa in his arms and held her loosely.

"It's dangerous to idealize things so."

"Will you?"

He didn't answer.

"I'm not idealizing. I saw you two together. I know there was something between you the night of my wedding, I just know it. Please, Daddy?"

It had been far easier to promise her he'd have her piano moved forever.

"Lisa, I can't promise such a thing. If things had gone better between us the other night . . ."

The note upon which the night had ended had made mockery of his and Bess's sexual encounter. Since then Michael had viewed his actions as foolish and willful. Lisa's remarks only ripened his disillusionment into confusion. If Bess loved him as Lisa suspected, she had a strange way of showing it. If she didn't, her way was stranger yet.

Lisa drew herself out of his arms, looking forlorn.

"Well, I thought I'd try," she said. "Guess I better go."

He walked her to the door and rode the elevator with her down to the lobby, where she stopped and turned to him.

"There's something else I'd like to ask you, Dad."

"Ask away."

"It's about when the baby's born. I wondered if you'd like to be there during the delivery. We're inviting Mark's folks, too."

"And your mother, too, no doubt."

"Of course."

"Another attempt to work us back together, Lisa?"

Lisa shrugged. "Sure. Why not? But it might be the only chance you get to witness the awesome spectacle. I know you weren't there when Randy and I were born, so I thought . . ." She shrugged again.

"Thanks for asking. I'll think about it."

When Lisa was gone, Michael's thoughts returned to Bess, plunging him into a limbo of indecisiveness.

Ever since Saturday night he'd passed telephones the way sinners pass confessionals, wanting to reach out and dial Bess's number and say he was sorry, he needed absolution. But to call her was to place himself in a position of even greater vulnerability, so he resisted the urge once again.

The following day, however, he dialed the house at eleven o'clock in the morning, expecting Randy to answer.

To his surprise, Bess did.

"Bess!" he exclaimed, lunging forward in his desk chair and feeling his face ignite. "What are you doing home!"

"Grabbing a sandwich and picking up some catalogs I forgot before I head out for a noon appointment."

"I didn't expect you to be there. I called for Randy."

"He's not here, sorry."

"I wanted to congratulate him. I hear he's found a job with a band."

"That's right."

"I suppose he's really excited, huh?"

"Is he ever. He's quit his job at the nut house and he's practicing here every morning and with the band every afternoon. Today, though, he's out shopping for a used van. Says he's got to have one to haul his drums in."

"Has he got any money?"

"Probably not but I didn't volunteer any."

"What do you think? Should I?"

"That's up to you."

"I'm asking your advice, Bess. He's our son and I want to do what you think will be best for him."

"All right, then, I think it's best to let him struggle and find his own way to get a van. If he wants the job badly enough—and of course he does—he'll work it out."

"All right, I won't offer."

A lull fell. End of one subject, opening for another . . .

Michael picked up a stapler, moved it to a different spot on his desktop, moved it back where it had been. "Bess, about Saturday night . . ." She said nothing. He depressed the head of the stapler four times, not quite hard enough to release staples. "All week long I've been thinking I should call you and apologize."

Neither of them spoke for a long time. His fingertips lingered over the stapler, polishing it as if it were dusty.

"Bess, I think you were right. That wasn't a very smart thing we did."

"No. It only complicates matters."

"So I guess we shouldn't see each other anymore, should we?"

Again, no answer.

"We're only getting Lisa's hopes up for nothing. I mean, it isn't going to lead to anything, so why do we put ourselves through it?"

His heart was drumming hard enough to loosen the stitches on his shirt pocket. Sweet Jesus, it was just like when they used to talk this way on the phone in college, longing to be together yet summoning willpower to do the right thing, which they inevitably failed to do once they were together.

When he spoke again the words emerged in a ragged whisper. "Bess, are you there?"

Her voice, too, sounded strained. "The damned awful truth is that it's the best piece of sex I've had since the last good one you and I had together when we were still married. I've thought about it so much since Saturday night, about all those years of learning it took to get it right together, and how comfortable and easy it felt with you. Did it feel that way for you, too?"

"Yes," he whispered hoarsely while beneath the desk he felt himself grow priapic.

"And that's important, isn't it?"

"Of course."

"But it isn't enough. It's the kind of reasoning teenagers use, and we're not teenagers any longer."

"What are you saying, Bess?"

"I'm saying I'm scared. I'm saying I've been walking around thinking of nothing but you since Saturday night and it scares the living hell out of me. I'm scared of getting hurt again, Michael."

"And you think I'm not?"

"I think it's different for a man."

"Oh, Bess, come on, don't give me that double-standard crap. My feelings are involved here just like yours are."

"Michael, when I went into your bathroom to look for a brush I found a whole box of condoms in the drawer. *A whole box!*"

"So that's why you got all huffy and walked out?"

"Well, what would you have done?" She sounded very angry.

"Did you notice how many were used?" When she made no reply he said, "One! Go back and count them. One, which was in my pocket before you got there that night. Bess, I don't fuck around."

"Oh, that word is so offensive."

"All right then, screw. I don't and you know it."

"How can I know it, when six years ago—seven—it's a good part of what broke up our marriage."

"I thought we'd been through all that and agreed that it was both our faults. Now here we go again; we get together, we make love once and you're already slinging accusations at me. Hell, I can't fight this for the rest of my life."

"Nobody asked you to."

After a broad silence he responded in a sound of pinched anger, "All right. That's certainly clear enough. Tell Randy I called, will you? Tell him I'll try him again later."

"I'll tell him."

He hung up without a good-bye. "Shit!" He made a fist and banged the stapler. "Shit! Shit! Shit!" He banged it three more times, pumping out staples and jamming the contraption. He sat staring at it, scowling, his lips as straight and thin as a welt pocket. "Shit," he said again, quieter, spreading his elbows on the desk, joining his hands with the thumbs extended and pressed to his eyeballs.

What did she want of him? Why should he feel like the guilty one when she'd been as willing and eager as he last Saturday night? He hadn't done a damned thing wrong! Not one! He'd seduced his ex-wife with her total compliance, and now she was putting the screws to him for it. Damn women, anyway! And damn this one in particular.

He went up to his cabin the next weekend, got eaten up by mosquitoes, wished it were hunting season; got eaten up by deerflies, wished there were someone with him; got eaten up by wood ticks, wished he had a phone up there so he could call Bess and tell her what he thought of her accusations.

He returned to the city still fuming, picked up the phone on Sunday night and slammed it back into the cradle without dialing her number.

On Tuesday night he attended another "unreasonable citizens" meeting on the Victoria and Grand issue, came out of it angrier than ever because they wanted him to plant twenty-four good-sized boulevard trees all up and down Grand Avenue at a cost of probably a thousand dollars per tree (including concrete ironwork), which had nothing whatever to do with the building he wanted to put up but it appeared he was being legally extorted and would go along with it: twenty-four thousand dollars' worth of trees for his building permit and an end to their squawking.

He had tried to call and congratulate Randy three additional times, always without getting an answer, and that irritated him, too.

Every time he passed through the gallery, with its empty faux pedestal still waiting for a piece of sculpture, he railed against Bess for writing him off with the job unfinished.

She was at the root of his dissatisfaction with life in general, and he realized it.

Two weeks had passed and his disposition hadn't improved. Finally, one night in late July, when he'd overbroiled some fresh scallops for himself and gotten them rubbery, and had listened to roaring speedboats until he'd been forced to close the deck doors, and had picked up the television guide to find nothing but junk scheduled, and had sat at his drafting table for two hours without accomplishing a thing, he went into his bathroom, got the box of condoms, stormed down to his car, drove to her house, rang the bell and stood on her doorstep, waiting to tie into her.

After a delay the hall light came on, the door opened and there she stood, barefoot, wearing a thigh-length thing made of white terrycloth with an elastic neck hole and a tie at the waist. Her hair was wet and she smelled good enough to bottle and sell, which further piqued him.

"Michael, what in the world are you doing here?"

"I came to talk and I'm going to." He burst his way inside and closed the door.

She attempted to check her watch but her wrist was empty. Obviously she was fresh out of the shower. "It's got to be ten-thirty at night!"

"I really don't give a damn, Bess. Are you alone?"

"Yes. Randy's out playing."

"Good. Let's go into the family room." He headed that way.

"You go straight to hell, Michael Curran!" she shouted. "You come bursting into my house giving orders and bossing me around. Well, I don't have to put up with it. You can just get out and lock the door when you go!"

She caught her short skirt in her fingertips and headed up the stairs.

"Wait just a minute there, missus!" He charged after her, taking the steps two at a time, and caught her halfway up. "You're not going anywhere until you—"

"I'm not a missus, and take your hands off me!"

"That's not what you said that night in my apartment, is it? My hands were just fine on you then, weren't they?"

"Oh, so you came to throw that up in my face, did you?"

"No. I came to tell you that ever since that night everything's been horseshit. I walk around with a wad of anger in my throat, and I snap at people who don't deserve it, and I can't even get my own damn son to answer the phone so I can congratulate him!"

"And that's *my* fault?" She opened a hand on her chest.

"Yes!"

"What'd I do?"

"You accused me of screwing around, and I didn't!" He grabbed her hand and slapped the box of condoms into it. "Here, count 'em!"

She gaped at the box, dumbstruck.

"Count 'em! One missing, and that's all. I bought them that day! Count 'em, I said!"

She tried to give the box back to him. "Don't be absurd, I'm not going to count them!"

"Then how will you know I'm telling the truth?"

"It doesn't matter, Michael, because it's not going to happen again."

"The hell it isn't! I'm hornier than a two-peckered goat just standing here smelling you, and either you're by God going to count those rubbers or I will. You're not going to? All right, give them to me!" He grabbed the box and sat down on a step at her feet, opened it and started pulling them out. "One. Two. Three." He slapped them down on the carpet, counting clear to eleven, until they were scattered like petals at her feet. "There, you see?" He looked up at her, high above him. "One missing. Now do you believe me?"

She was leaning against the wall, covering her mouth with a hand, laughing. "You should just see yourself; you look absolutely ridiculous, sitting there counting those things."

"That's what you damn women do to us men, you play around with us until we do things that make us look like blithering idiots. Do you believe me now, Bess?"

"Yes, I believe you but for heaven's sake, pick them up. What if Randy happened to come home early?"

He grabbed her bare ankle. "Come on down here and help me."

"Michael, let go."

He gripped harder and with his free hand lifted her hem. "What have you got on under there?"

She slapped her skirt to her thighs. "Michael, you damned fool, stop it."

"My God, Bess, you're naked under that thing."

"Let my ankle go!"

"You horny, too, Bess? I'll bet you are. Why don't you invite me up to our old bedroom and we'll take one of these things and put it to good use?"

"Michael, don't." He was rising to his feet, one condom in his hand, climbing the two steps to reach her, then flattening her against the hand-rail, to which she clung with both hands.

"Bess, there's a lot of sex between you and me just waiting to be made. I think we found that out that night at my place, so let's get started."

She was trying hard not to be swayed by him. He looked devastating with his hazel eyes snapping and his hair in need of cutting, and he felt inviting, too, so near and warm and seductive. "You get out of here. You're plum crazy."

He kissed her neck and ground himself against her, breast to hips. "I'm crazy all right, crazy about you, missus. Come on, what do you say?"

"And what then? A replay of the last two weeks? Because it hasn't been any more fun for me than it's been for you."

He kissed her on the mouth once, more the strike of a wet tongue than an actual kiss, and whispered a suggestion in her ear.

She giggled. "Oh for shame, you dirty old man."

"Come on, you'll like it."

He was still grinding, and she was still amused but weakening.

"You're going to crush my pelvis on this handrail."

"But you'll be moaning so loud you won't even hear it crack."

"Michael Curran, your ego exceeds anything known to woman."

"Doesn't it, though." He had her skirt up and a two-handed grip on her buttocks. Then he had his lips on hers, and his tongue in her mouth, and her arms went around his shoulders and he was touching her inside where she was all liquid heat. The kiss grew rampant. Their breathing grew stressed.

Against his lips she mumbled, "All right, you devil, you win."

He hauled her by the hand, up the steps, along the hall, leaving the foil packets scattered on the stairs, into their bedroom, strewing flotsam as they went—his shirt, her belt, his shoes, her white cover-up—and hit the bed naked, already tangled.

They were laughing as they bounced onto the mattress on their sides. Abruptly the laughter fled, replaced by a gaze of pure passion.

"Bess . . ." Michael whispered, "Bess . . ." rolling with her, wanting his mouth everywhere at once. "I missed you."

"I missed you, too, and I thought about this. I wanted it . . ." She sucked in a quick breath and exclaimed, "Oh!"

They were giving and greedy, tender and tensile by turns. With hands and mouths they savored one another's bodies, each the perfect recipient of the other. The bedspread grew mussed, two pillows fell to the floor, several others bolstered them randomly, and in time not so randomly.

He told her, "You smell the way I remember."

She said, "So do you . . ."

Ah, the smells, the tastes.

"Your hands," she said once, examining them. "How I've always loved your hands. Here . . . they belong here . . ."

Later, he murmured, "You still like this, don't you?"

"Ohhh . . ." she crooned, her eyes closing, ending on a whisper, ". . . yes."

What they shared was universal. Why, then, did it feel unique? Triumphant? As if no one before them or after them would share these same feelings? They answered these questions themselves, when he entered her, levered her as close as possible with one heel and clasped her against his breast with her face in the cay of his neck.

"I think I've fallen in love with you again, Bess," he whispered against her damp hair.

She went still, all but her heart, whose beat seemed to suddenly fill her entire body, the entire room, the entire world.

"I think I've fallen in love with you, too."

For that trembling, precious moment each was afraid to speak further, to move. His eyes were closed, his wide hand cradling the back of her head where her hair felt cool. Her mouth had made a damp spot just below his whisker line.

Finally he drew back, tenderly brushing the hair from her face.

"Really?" His smile was delicate, surprised.

"Really."

They kissed with exquisite tenderness, touching each other in places that mattered as much as those joined below—napes, faces, temples, throats— each touch a reiteration of the words they'd spoken.

"These last two weeks apart were horrible. Let's not ever do that to each other again," he whispered.

"No," she agreed, so softly the word drifted back into her throat.

Then all that had begun so ribaldly ended in beauty, a man and a woman, cleaving, rhythmic, then gasping at the moment of cataclysm and smiling when it was over.

Afterward, she whispered, "Stay," and found a place for his hand, and another where her sole seemed to belong.

Later, they lay back-to-belly. The bedside lamp was on and an insect worried the shade with a *tick-tick* of wings. Bess's hair had dried and spread a floral scent upon their shared pillow. The bedspread, now snarled beneath them, rode up in rills here and there, creating a barrier between their legs. Michael flattened it with his calf and found Bess's bare toes with his own, invited hers to curl around his and closed his eyes.

He sighed.

She studied his left arm, stretching forth from beneath her ear; his hand hanging limply over the edge of the mattress; the pattern of dark hair ending along the soft inner arm, where white skin began; his gold watchband; the inside of his relaxed palm; ringless fingers.

She felt his lips on her hair, his breath warming it. She closed her eyes to enjoy the wondrous impuissance, the sense of well-being.

After many minutes he said quietly, "Bess?"

She opened her eyes. "Hm?"

"Are you ready to hear that M word yet?"

She thought for some time before answering. "I don't know."

He curled his arm toward her face and she turned to look back at him behind her.

"I think we'd better talk about it, don't you?" he said.

"I suppose so."

They settled on their backs. He removed his arm from beneath her.

"Okay," he said, "let's get it out in the open instead of dancing around it the way we have been. Do you think we could make it if we married again?"

Even forewarned, Bess was startled by the word. She said, "I've been spending a lot of time lately wondering. In bed we could."

"And out of it?"

"What do you think?"

"I think our biggest problem would be trust, because each of us has had others and . . ."

"Other. Just one, for me, anyway."

"Yeah, for me, too. But trust will still be a big factor."

"I suppose so."

"We'll each be meeting people, doing business with people, sometimes even in the evenings. If I tell you I'm going to a city council meeting, will you believe me?"

He picked up her near hand and placed it atop his, matching the curl of her fingers to his knuckles.

"I don't know," she answered honestly. "When I found that box of condoms, I really thought . . ." They both studied their hands, fitting and refitting them together. "Well, you know what I thought."

"Yeah, I know what you thought." He deserted her hand to double both his behind his head. "But we can't always be counting condoms, Bess."

She chuckled and turned on her side to study him, laying one hand on the hollow beneath his ribs.

"I know. I'm just being honest, Michael."

"You don't think you can ever trust me again?"

She only studied him, wondering herself. Soon he spoke again.

"I've been thinking about a lot of other things. The fact that both of us are working now—I think I've come to terms with that, and I'd be willing to share the housework, and not even fifty-fifty. Sometimes it might be sixty-forty, other times forty-sixty. I realize now that when both people are working it's got to be a cooperative effort that way."

She smiled. "I have a housekeeper now."

"Does she cook for you, too?"

"No."

"Well, there, you see? We can take turns cooking."

Bess was getting sleepy. "Know what?"

"What?"

"I like being convinced. Go on."

"I've even given some thought to my hunting. I know you used to get upset when I'd leave you to go hunting but now I have the cabin and you can come along . . . light a fire in the fireplace, bring a good book . . . how does that sound?"

"Mmm . . ."

"It'd be good for you to get away from the store, relax a little more . . ."

"Mmm . . ."

Her hand below his ribs lay heavy and motionless.

"Bess, are you sleeping?"

Her breathing was regular, her eyelashes at rest upon her cheek. He braced up on one elbow and reached beyond her, caught the side of the bedspread and flipped it over her, then did the same on his side. She murmured and snuggled deeper. He put a hand on her waist, drew a knee up against her belly, nestled on his side with his forehead near hers and thought, I'll only stay for a half hour or so . . . it's so nice here beside her . . . if I leave the light on it'll wake me up again in a while.

chapter 16

RANDY GOT HOME AT 2:15, pulled into the driveway and sat staring at the silver Cadillac Seville. *What the hell is he doing here?* He glanced up at his mother's bedroom window, found the light on, shook his head in disgust and slammed the van door behind himself.

Inside, the entry chandelier was aglow, as well as the lights in the upstairs hall. Something was scattered on the steps. He went up to get a closer look and discovered an empty box of condoms, along with its contents lying strewn all over two steps. He picked one up, studied it as it lay in his palm and glanced at the head of the stairs. He started up cautiously, passing a piece of clothing, and when he reached the top, peered around the corner along the hall. More clothing left a trail—a man's trousers, shoes, his mother's little white thing that she wore after her bath. At the far end of the hall her bedroom door was wide open and the light was on.

"Mom?" he called.

No answer.

He proceeded to the doorway, stopped just outside and called, "Mom, you all right?"

Again, no answer, so he stepped inside.

His mother and father were lying curled up together spoon-fashion, naked, with the bedspread haphazardly covering them to the hips. Michael's arm was looped over Bess's waist, his hand near her breast. From the looks of the room they'd had a wild one. Pillows lay scattered on the floor around the bed, which itself looked as though a twister had struck it. The empty packet from a condom lay on his father's side of the bed beside a soiled handkerchief.

Randy felt his face flame but just as he made a move to retreat, Michael came awake, lifted his head and discovered Randy in the doorway. He glanced sharply at Bess, still asleep, caught the edge of the bedspread and drew it up to cover her naked breasts. Once more he looked across the room at his son.

"Randy?"

"You got balls, man," Randy sneered, "coming here like this."

"Hey, Randy, just a min—"

But Randy was gone, his footfalls thundering angrily down the hall, down the steps.

Bess squinted awake and mumbled, "Michael? What time is it?"

"Two-fifteen. Go back to sleep."

She clambered onto her knees and began scraping the spread back. "Let's get under."

"Bess, Randy's home."

"Oh so what. So now he knows. Shut off the lamp and get under."

Michael shut off the lamp and got under.

In the morning he awakened to the sensation of being watched. He was. When he opened his eyes he found Bess with her head on the only pillow still remaining on the bed, her face turned his way, studying him.

"Hi," she said, looking quite pleased with herself.

"Hi."

"Where's your pillow?" His head was flat on the mattress.

"I seem to remember we threw it on the floor."

She smiled and said, "So we got caught, huh?"

"Did we ever."

"Did he come in here?"

"Uh-huh."

"Did he say anything?"

"He said, 'You got balls, man.' "

Her smile turned lurid. "Yeah, you do. Mind if I fondle them a little bit?"

He grinned, pushed her hand away and regretfully told her, "Listen, missus, our son's in the house, and he's royally pissed."

She gave up her pursuit and said, "So what are we going to tell him?"

"Hell, I don't know. You got any ideas?"

"How about, 'Forty-year-olds get horny, too'?"

"Cute. Very cute." Michael sat up on the edge of the bed, flexed his arms and stretched.

Bess braced her jaw on one hand and reached up to ruffle his tousled hair.

"He probably won't get up till nine or so."

"Then I'll stay till nine or so."

"You don't have to. I can talk to him."

"You're not the one he'll be angry with. It'll be me. I'm not leaving you here to do my dirty work while I slink off with my tail between my legs."

She let her palm ride down the center of his back. It was a good, straight back, still firm and tapered.

Michael looked back over his shoulder at her. "Did you ever think when we had him that we'd end up making excuses for something like this?"

She smiled.

He rose, fully naked, and she watched him move around the foot of her bed through the bathroom doorway on her left. He left the door open, which brought a smile to her lips and some pleasant memories of married life. After taking care of morning necessities, he leaned against the vanity top, inspecting his face, rubbing sandmen out of his eyes.

"You know how I knew you were having an affair?" she asked.

He said, "How?" opened a drawer, found her hairbrush and started using it.

"You started closing the bathroom door."

From her vantage point she saw the rear half of him, the front half cut off by the doorway. He stopped brushing, tipped back at the waist, peered into the bedroom and said, "Really?"

"Mm-hm." She was lying on her side, with her head cradled on a folded arm, wearing a soft smile. He left the bathroom and walked toward her, undeterred by his nakedness, dropped down to sit on the bed at her hip.

"There . . . you see?" He touched her nose with the back of the brush. "I left it open. Now doesn't that prove something?"

They smiled at each other a long time while he sat with one hand braced on either side of her, their bare hips separated by a single layer of sheet. It had rained during the night. The morning-cool air came through the open window bringing a faintly dank smell resembling mushrooms. Somewhere in a metal downspout droplets of water made a modulated *blip, blip, blip.* It was one of those sterling stretches of minutes that come along rarely in a relationship, certainly the most idyllic for Michael and Bess since their divorce. She hated to tarnish it.

"Michael, listen . . ." She rubbed her palms lightly up and down his arms. "I'm not going to lie to Randy and tell him you and I are getting married again, because it's just not true. I need some time to think things through. This . . . this affair we've started . . . well, it's just that, an affair, nothing more. If Randy has trouble adjusting to that, then so be it but I won't vindicate myself with a lie. Do you understand what I'm saying?"

He withdrew to the edge of the bed, turning his back on her. "Sure. You're saying I'm good enough for you in bed but not out of it."

She sat up, touched his back. "No, Michael."

He rose and found his underwear, stepped into it and followed the trail of clothing still decorating the hall and steps. When he returned he was half-dressed, carrying her white cover-up and a handful of condoms. He tossed them on the bed along with the empty box. "There." He buttoned his shirt and began stuffing it into his trousers with angry shoves. "Keep them handy, then, because I can promise you I'll be back. I won't be able to resist it but we'll be setting one hell of an example for our kids, won't we, Bess?"

"Michael, you came here! I didn't come to you, so don't blame me for what happened!"

"I want to marry you, damn it, and you're saying no, you'd rather have an affair; well what kind of—"

"That's not what I'm saying." She jumped up and grabbed her cover-up from the foot of the bed, flung it over her head. "I don't want to make the same mistake again, that's all."

"I can see the writing on the wall. We'll get together once, maybe twice a week, we'll make love, and afterwards we'll go through this same scene, me saying 'Let's make it honest' and you getting angry, and then both of us getting angry. Well, that's not what I want, Bess. I want what Lisa wants—the two of us back together for good."

She stood before him, a little angry, a little repentant, a lot afraid. No matter what they'd agreed about shared guilt during their first breakup, he'd been the philanderer and the hurt still clung.

"Michael," she said calmly, "I don't want to fight with you."

His shirt was on, his pants were zipped, his belt was buckled.

"Okay," he said. "I've called you twice. It's your turn next time. See how it feels to be the one who comes begging."

He strode toward the door.

"Michael . . ." The tone of her voice was tantamount to a reaching hand but he'd already disappeared around the door. She hurried to it and yelled down the hall, "Michael!"

He called back as he reached the top of the stairs, "Tell Randy I'll call him and explain."

Randy's voice came from below.

"You don't have to call him, he's here."

Michael's footsteps faltered, then continued more slowly to the bottom of the steps, where Randy stood, bare but for his blue jeans, which were zipped but unbuttoned. It startled Michael to see for the first time the dense pattern of hair on Randy's chest and around his navel, proof that he was as fully mature as Michael himself.

"Randy . . . I'm sorry we woke you."

"I'll just bet you are."

"I didn't mean it that way. I had every intention of talking to you about this. I wasn't going to skip out and leave it to your mother."

"Oh yeah? Well, that's the way it looked to me. Why don't you just leave her alone?"

"Because I love her, that's why."

"Love—Christ, don't make me laugh. I suppose you loved her then, too, when you had an affair with another woman and walked out on her. I suppose you loved me, and Lisa, too!"

Michael knew it would do no good to declare he did. He stood in silence. Randy replied as if Michael had answered.

"Well, that's some way to show your kids you love 'em. You want to know how it feels to have your father write you off? It hurts, that's how it feels!"

"I didn't write you off."

"Aw, fuck that, man, you left her, you left us! I was thirteen years old. You know how a thirteen-year-old thinks? I figured it must've been my fault, I must've done something wrong to make you leave but I didn't know what; then Mom finally tells me you had another woman and I wanted to find you and smash your face, only I was too little and skinny. Now here you are, crawling out of her bed—well maybe I should smash it now, huh?"

From the top of the stairs, Bess reprimanded, "Randy!"

His icy eyes looked up. "This is between him and me, Ma."

"You will apologize to him at once if for nothing more than your offensive language!"

"Like hell I will!"

"Randy!" She started down the stairs.

Randy's face wizened with disbelief. "Why are you taking his side? Can't you see he's just using you again? Comes down here saying he loves you—man, that's just bullshit! He probably said the same thing to that other floozy he married but he couldn't make that marriage stick, either! He's a loser, Ma, and he doesn't deserve you and you're a damn fool for letting him in here!"

She slapped Randy's face.

He stared at her in shock. Tears spurted into his eyes.

"I'm very sorry I had to do that. I've never done it before and I want you to know I hated it. But I cannot allow you to stand there berating your father and I. Neither one of us are blameless but there are proper, respectful ways in which to talk these things out. Now, I think, Randy," she said quietly, "that you owe us both an apology."

Randy stared at her. At Michael. Back at her before spinning and hitting for his downstairs bedroom without another word.

When he was gone Bess put her hands to her cheeks and felt them burning. She turned to Michael, who stood forlornly, studying the toes of his shoes. She put her arms around him. "Michael, I'm sorry," she whispered in a shaken voice.

"It's been coming for a long time."

"Yes, I suppose so but that doesn't make it hurt any less."

She held him awhile. Though his arms automatically went around her, they applied no pressure, only hung there like limp ropes.

Finally he pulled back and said in a strange, choked voice, "I'd better go."

"I'll talk to him when he's settled down."

Michael nodded at the floor. "I'll . . ." He didn't know what he'd do. Take another cooking course. Buy another piece of land to develop. Choose a sculpture for his gallery. Pointless, senseless, frantic scrambling by a man seeking to fill his life with meaning when the only meaning in life can come from people, not things.

"I'll see you, Bess," he said, and left, closing the door quietly behind him.

In his room, Randy sat on the edge of his water bed, doubled forward, holding his head in both hands.

Crying.

He wanted a dad, wanted a mom, wanted love like other kids. But why did it have to be so painful, getting it? He'd been hurt so much by their divorce. Why shouldn't he be allowed to vent this fury that had been building in him since the eighth grade, when they'd split? Couldn't they see what jerks they were making of themselves, falling back together this way for convenience? It wasn't as if they talked about getting married again—the word hadn't been mentioned. No, it was just plain lust, which made his mother as guilty as his father, and he didn't want her to be. Damn Lisa for stirring this all up. She was the one—Lisa!—who insisted they end the cold war. Now this.

It had been bad holding things inside all these years but letting them out hadn't felt much good, either. Seeing the look of pain on his dad's face when he had yelled, "It hurts!"—that was what he'd wanted, wasn't it? To hurt his old man for once the way the old man had hurt him. Wasn't that what he wanted? So why was he doubled over here, bawling like a baby?

Goddamn you, Dad, why did you leave us? Why didn't you stick with Mom and work it out?

I'm so confused. I wish I had somebody to talk to, somebody who'd listen and make me understand who I'm angry at and why. Maryann. Oh God, Maryann, I respected you so much. I was going to show you I could be different than my old man, I could treat you like some princess and never lay a hand on you, and show you I was worthy of you.

But I'm not. I talk like a gutter rat, and smoke pot, and drink plenty, and screw any girl who comes along, and my own father doesn't love me enough to stick around, and my own mother slaps me.

Somebody help me understand!

Shortly, Randy's mother came to his door. She knocked softly. He swiped his eyes with the bedsheet, hopped up and pretended to be busy at the controls of the CD player.

"Randy?" she called quietly.

"Yeah, it's open." He heard her come in.

"Randy?"

He waited.

"I'm sorry."

He watched the knobs on the control panel blur as his eyes refilled with tears. "Yeah . . . well . . . ." His voice sounded high, like when he was going through puberty and it was changing.

"Slapping you was wrong. I shouldn't have done it. Randy?"

He wouldn't answer.

She had come up silently and touched his shoulder before he realized she was there. "Randy, I just want you to know something. Your dad asked me to marry him again but I'm the one who said no."

Randy blinked and the tears dropped to his bare stomach, clearing his vision somewhat. He remained with his back to Bess, his chin on his chest.

"Why?"

"Because I'm afraid of getting hurt again, the same as you."

"I'm never apologizing to him. Never."

Her hand went away from his shoulder. She sighed. Time passed. Her hand returned, warm and flat on his bare skin.

"Randy, he loves you very much."

Randy said nothing. The damn tears plumped up again.

"I know you don't believe that but he does. And whether you believe it or not, you love him. That's why you're hurting so badly right now." Another pause before she continued. "The two of you will have to talk someday—I mean, really talk, without anger, about all your feelings. Please, Randy . . . don't wait too long, dear."

She kissed his shoulder and silently left.

He remained in his windowless room, willing away tears that refused his bidding. He touched a silver knob on his CD player, let his hand fall to his side. He imagined going to his father's place and knocking on his door and simply walking into his arms and hugging him hard enough to snap their bones. How did people manage to do that after they'd been hurt this bad?

The tape of The Edge was in the deck, the one he practiced with. He knelt down and replaced it with the rock group Mike and the Mechanics, fast-forwarded it to the song he wanted. Forward, back, forward again to the band between songs. The intro came on and he plugged in his earphones, put them on and sat at his drums, holding both sticks in his one hand, too bummed out to use them.

The words started.

> Every generation
> Blames the one
> before . . .

It was a song written by someone after his father had died. "The Living Years." A rueful, wrenching song.

> And all of their frustrations, come beating on your door . . .
> I know that I'm a prisoner to all my father held so dear
> I know that I'm a hostage to all his hopes and fears
> I just wish I could have told him
> In the living years.

Randy sat through it all, listening to the plaintive call of a son who waited until it was too late to make his peace with his father. He sat with his eyes closed, his drumsticks forgotten in his hand, tears leaking from the corners of his eyes.

That evening, The Edge was playing at a club called The Green Light. Randy was unusually quiet while they were setting up. Through the cacophony of tuning and balancing he let the others go about their BS'ing without him. There was always a lot of give-and-take at this time, part of the ritual of getting up for a performance.

When the lights were set and the instruments ready, the filler tape playing for the crowd and the amplifiers humming softly, the guys put their guitars in their stands and went off toward the bar to get drinks. All but Pike Watson, who stopped by Randy, still sitting behind his drums.

"Heya, Rimshot, you're a little low tonight."

"I'll be okay once we start playing."

"Got trouble with some of the songs? Hey, it takes time."

"No, it's not that."

"Trouble with your girl?"

"What girl?"

"Trouble at home, then."

"Yeah, I guess you could say that."

"Well, hell . . ." Pike let his thought trail away, standing with his hands caught on his bony hips. Brightening, he asked, "You need something to pick you up?"

"I got something."

"What, that jimmy dog you smoke? I mean something to really pick you up."

Randy came from behind the drums, heading for the bar. "I don't do that shit, man."

"Yeah, well, I just thought I'd offer." Pike sniffed. "Those drumsticks can get mighty heavy at times."

Randy had two beers and a hit of marijuana before they started the first set but the combination only seemed to make him lethargic and tired tonight. They played to a desultory audience, who acted as if the dance floor was off limits, and after the second set he tried more marijuana but it failed to do the trick. Even the music failed to lift Randy. The drumsticks felt very heavy, indeed. During the third break he went into the men's room and found Pike there, the only one in the room, sniffing a hit of cocaine off a tiny mirror through a rolled-up dollar bill.

"You really ought to try it." Pike grinned. "It'll cure whatever ails you."

"Yeah?" Randy watched as Pike wet his finger, picked up any stray powder and rubbed it on his gums.

"How much?"

"First hit is on me," Pike said, holding out a tiny plastic bag of white powder.

Randy looked at it, tempted not only to get out of this low but to spite his mother and father. Pike wiggled the bag a little bit as if to say, Go on, give it a try. Randy was reaching for it when the door burst open and two men came in, talking and laughing, and Pike swiftly hid the bag and mirror in his pocket.

* * *

After the night Randy discovered them in bed, Michael quit calling Bess, and though she missed him horribly, she, too, refused to call him. Deep summer came on: in Stillwater a time for lovers. They came by the hundreds, teenagers over from Minneapolis and St. Paul, flooding the town in their souped-up sports cars; the town's own teenagers, cruising the length of the quay on Friday nights; college kids off for the summer, dancing to the canned music at Steamers; boaters down for the weekends, setting the river agleam with the reflection of their running lights; sightseers out for an evening, walking the riverbank, holding hands.

At night, the volleyball court in front of the Freight House was a maze of tan, young arms and legs. The riverside restaurant decks were crowded. The old lift bridge backed up traffic several times an hour letting boats beneath it. The antique stores did a landmark business. The popcorn wagon put out its irresistible smell. The wind socks in front of Brick Alley Books waved a welcome to the cars streaming down the hill into town.

One hot Saturday Bess was invited to a pool party at Barb and Don's house. She bought a new bathing suit, expecting Michael to be there. He wasn't; he'd been invited but had declined when he'd learned Bess was coming.

A man named Alan Petrosky, who introduced himself as a horse rancher from over by Lake Elmo, kept up an irksome pursuit until she wanted to dump him into the pool, cowboy boots and all.

Don and Barb noticed what was going on and came to rescue her. Don gave her a brotherly hug and asked simply, "How have you been?" She found tears in her eyes as she replied, "Very mixed up and lonely."

Barb caught her by a hand and said, "Come up to the bedroom for a minute where we won't be disturbed." In the cool green bedroom with the curtains drawn and the party sounds distant, Barb asked, "So how are things between you and Michael?" and Bess burst into tears.

She broke down and called him in early August on the pretext of advising him about some nice pieces of sculpture on display at a gallery in Minneapolis. He was brusque, almost rude, declining to ask anything personal or to thank her for recommending the gallery.

She submerged herself in work; it helped little. She told Randy she wanted to come out some night and hear him play; he said no, he didn't think the kind of bars he played in would be her style. She attended a shower for Lisa, given by Mark's sisters; it only reminded her she would soon be a grandmother facing old age alone. Keith called and said he missed her, wanted to see her again; she told him no, smitten by a wave of mild revulsion.

Life felt humdrum to Bess while, by comparison, it seemed everyone around her was living it to the fullest, having the gayest summer of their lives. She found a batik piece depicting sandpipers that would have been stunning in Michael's dining room, but she stubbornly refused to call him for fear he'd again treat her as if she'd just peed on his shoe. Worse, what if she herself broke down and suggested their getting together for an evening?

Sexuality—damn the stuff. Bess would have thought, considering impending grandparenthood, that she'd be immune. She was not. She thought of Michael in a sexual regard as often as in a nonsexual. She fully admitted the reason she'd been repulsed by the idea of reviving anything with Keith was because, by comparison to Michael, he was a vacant lot. Michael, on the other hand, was a lush orchard—but hardly enough reason for a woman of forty to make a fool of herself gorging on ripe fruit. As she'd told him the night they'd last made love, they weren't teenagers anymore. Still, all the platitudes in the world couldn't prevent her from missing him immensely.

On August ninth Bess turned forty-one. Randy forgot all about it, didn't even give her a card before he left for a three-day gig in South Dakota. Lisa called and wished her a happy birthday but said she'd ordered something that hadn't arrived yet; it should be here by the weekend and they'd get together then. Stella was gone with three of her ladyfriends on a two-week vacation in the San Juan islands north of Seattle and had sent a birthday card that had arrived the day before, along with a postcard from the Burchart Gardens in Victoria, British Columbia: wish you were here.

Bess's birthday fell on a Thursday; she had appointments all afternoon long but rushed back to the store before Heather left for the day, asking if she'd had any calls.

"Four," Heather answered. But none were from Michael, and Bess climbed the stairs to her stifling loft telling herself she had no right to be disappointed. She was responsible for her own happiness, it was not the duty of others to create it for her.

Still . . . birthdays.

She found herself remembering certain ones while she'd still been married to Michael. The first one after they got married, when he'd taken her tubing on the Apple River and had pulled a Pepperidge Farm cake out of a floating cooler tied between them while they were bobbing down the stream on inner tubes, scraping their hinders on rocks and burning the tops of their knees and loving every minute of it.

The year she turned thirty, when he'd arranged a surprise party at Barb and Don's house and she'd sulked all the way there, thinking she was going to a birthday party for their daughter, Rainy, who was turning four the next day.

Another one—she'd forgotten exactly which. Thirty-two? Thirty-three?—when Michael had given her a particular bracelet she'd admired and had pulled it out of his vest pocket on their way out to dinner, the way rich men did in movies. It had been in a black velvet box, a simple gold serpentine chain, and she had it still.

No bracelets today, though. No black velvet boxes, no cards in the mailbox at home, nobody to float down a river with, or go out to dinner with, or surprise her with balloons and cheers.

She stopped at Colonel Sanders's on her way home and picked up two pieces of fattening chicken and some fattening potatoes and gravy and a cob of fattening corn and one of those little fattening lemon desserts, which she ate on the deck while watching the boats on the river and wishing she was on one of them.

Birthdays . . . oh, birthdays.

If there was any day when a lonely person felt more lonely, when a single person felt more single, when a neglected person felt more neglected, she wanted to know what it was.

With dusk approaching she puttered around the yard, plucking weeds in the rock-lined perennial beds she'd once tended meticulously but which had fallen into a state of neglect after she'd gone back to college. She broke a fingernail and got disgusted, went inside and took a long bath and gave herself a facial, examining her skin critically after washing the mask from it.

Forty-one—lord. And her skin getting a little droopy and soft like a maiden aunt's.

Forty-one and no gifts, no calls.

Tiny lines lurking at the corners of the eyes. A faint jowl beginning to show if she forgot to keep her chin high.

At 11 P.M. she turned off the television and lamp in her bedroom and lay with the windows open, listening to a thousand crickets and the bishop sleeves fluttering faintly against the sill, smelling the dampness of deep summer thread in from the yard, recalling nights like this when she was sixteen and went with mobs of kids to the drive-in theater. Always, there was company then.

The neighbors across the street came home, Elaine and Craig Mason, married probably forty years or more, slamming their car doors and talking quietly on their way into the house. Their metal screen door slammed and all grew quiet. Bess had stacked up her pillows as if knowing sleep would be reluctant, and reclined with her eyes wide open, intent upon the fretwork of shadows on the opposite wall, cast through the maples by the night light in the yard.

When the phone rang her body seemed to do an electric leap that shot her heart into fast time. The red light on the digital clock said 11:07 as she rolled over and grabbed the receiver in the dark, thinking, *Let it be Michael.*

"Hello, Bess," he said, his familiar voice at once raising a sting in her eyes.

"Hello." She went back against the pillows, touching the receiver with her free hand as if it were his jaw.

Outside, the crickets kept sawing away, their song throbbing in the summer night while on the telephone a lengthy silence hummed. She knew it meant he was not entirely pleased with himself for having broken down and called her after vowing he would not do so again.

"It's your birthday, huh?"

"Yes." She pointed one elbow to the ceiling, covering her eyes to stop them from stinging.

"Well, happy birthday."

"Thanks."

They remained silent for so long her throat began to ache. The crickets continued their rasping.

Finally Michael asked, "Did you do anything special?"

"No."

"Nothing with the kids?"

"No."

"Didn't Lisa come over or anything?"

"No. She said we'll get together soon, maybe this weekend. And Randy's playing out in South Dakota, so he's not around."

"Damn those kids. They should have done something for you."

She dried her nose on the sheet and forced her voice to sound normal. "Oh, what the heck. It's just one birthday. There'll be lots of others."

Please come over, Michael. Please come over and just hold me.

"I suppose so but they still should have remembered."

Another silence came and gripped them, and beat across the telephone wire. She wondered if he was in his bedroom, what he was wearing, if the light was on. She pictured him in his underwear, lying in the dark on top of the covers with one knee up and the balcony doors open.

"I ah . . . I got that mess straightened out down on Victoria and Grand." She formed an image of him watching his own fingernail scratching a groove into a sheet while he spoke. "Building's going to get under way soon."

"Oh, good!" she said, with false brightness. "That's . . ." Softer, she ended, ". . . that's good."

Why are we in separate bedrooms, Michael?

If she didn't invent some perky conversation soon, he'd surely hang up. She stared at the indigo leaf shadows on the opposite wall and searched for some clever dialogue to keep him on the line.

"Mom's gone on a trip to Seattle."

"Seattle . . . well." After a pause, "So she wasn't around today, either."

"No, but she sent a card. She's having a grand time with all her friends."

"She always seems to manage that, doesn't she?"

Bess turned on her side with the receiver pressed against the pillow, her position going slightly fetal while she coiled the phone cord around the tip of her index finger. Her chest felt ready to splinter into fragments. Oh God, she missed him so much.

"Bess, are you still there?"

"Yes."

"Well, listen, I . . ." He cleared his throat. "I just thought I'd call. Force of habit on this day every year, you know." He laughed. Oh, such a melancholy laugh. "I was just thinking about you."

"I was thinking about you, too."

He fell silent and she knew he was waiting for her to say, *I want to see you, please come over.* But the words stuck in her throat because she was afraid all she wanted to see him for were sexual reasons, and because she was so utterly lonely and it was her birthday, and she was forty-one and dreading the possibility of spending the rest of her life alone; and if he came over and they made love she'd be using him, and nice women weren't supposed to use men that way, not even ex-husbands, and then what would she say afterward, if he asked her again to marry him?

"Well, listen . . . it's late. I should go."

"Yes, me too."

She covered her whole face with one hand, her eyes squeezed shut, her lips bitten to keep the sobs from falling out, the telephone a hard knob between her ear and the pillow.

"Well, 'bye, Bess."

" 'Bye, Michael . . . Michael, wait!" She was up on one elbow, frantic, her tears at last running. But he'd hung up, leaving only the throb of the crickets to keep her company while she wept.

chapter 17

*L*ISA CALLED THE BLUE IRIS at 11 A.M. on August sixteenth and said she had gone into labor. Her water hadn't broken but she was spotting and cramping and had contacted the doctor. There was no reason for Bess to come to the hospital yet; they'd call when she should.

Bess canceled two afternoon appointments and stayed in the store near the phone.

Heather said, "It brings back the days when you were waiting for your own kids to be born, doesn't it?"

"It really does," Bess replied. "Lisa took thirteen hours but Randy took only five. Oh, I must call him and tell him the news!" She checked her watch and picked up the phone. Her relationship with Randy had been bumping along since the day she'd slapped him. She talked, he grunted. She made an effort, he made none.

He answered on the third ring.

"Randy, I'm so glad you're still home. I just wanted you to know that Lisa's gone into labor. She's still at home but it looks as though this is the real thing."

"Yeah? Well, tell her good luck."

"Can't you tell her yourself?"

"The band's heading out for Bemidji at one o'clock."

"Bemidji . . ." Her voice registered dismay.

"It's not the end of the world, Ma."

"No, I suppose not, but I hate your having to travel so much."

"It's only five hours."

"Well, be careful, dear, and be sure you get some sleep before you head back."

"Yeah."

"And no drinking and driving."

"Aw, come on, Ma, jeez . . ."

"Well, I worry about you."

"Worry about yourself. I'm a big boy now."

"When will you be back?"

"Sometime tomorrow morning. We're playing in White Bear Lake tomorrow afternoon."

"I'll leave a note at home if the baby is here. Otherwise call me at the store."

"Okay. Ma, I gotta go."

"All right, but listen . . . I love you."

He paused too long before replying, "Yeah, same here," as if pronouncing the actual words was more than he could manage.

Hanging up, Bess felt forlorn. She remained with her hand on the phone, staring out the front window, feeling like a failure as a mother, understanding how Michael had felt all these years, wondering how to mend these fences between herself and Randy.

"Something wrong?" Heather asked. She was dusting the shelving and glassware, working her way along the west wall of the shop.

"Ohhh . . ." Bess released a deep sigh. "I don't know." After a while she turned to Heather and asked, "Do you have one child who's harder to love than the others? Or is it just me? Because I feel very guilty sometimes but I swear, that younger one of mine is so distant."

"It's not just you. I've got one who's the same way. My middle one, Kim. She doesn't like being hugged—never mind kissed—never wanted to do anything with the family after she reached age thirteen, disregards Mother's Day and Father's Day, criticizes the radio station I listen to and the car I drive and the movies I like and the clothes I wear and only comes home when she needs something. Sometimes it's really hard to keep on loving a kid like that."

"Do you think they eventually grow out of it?"

Heather replaced a bowl on the shelf and said, "Oh, I hope so. So, what's wrong between you and Randy?"

Bess shot Heather a glance. "The truth?"

Heather continued her dusting indifferently. "If you want to tell me."

"He caught me in bed with his father."

Heather started laughing silently, her mouth open wide, the sound at first only a tick in her throat until it crescendoed and resounded through the store. When the laugh ended she twirled the dustrag through the air above her head. "Hooray!"

Bess looked a little pink around the edges. "You're spreading dust all over the stuff you just cleaned."

"Oh, big deal. So fire me." Heather returned to her task, smiling. "I figured it was getting serious between you two. I knew you weren't spending all that time on business, and I for one am glad to hear it."

"Well, don't be, because it's only caused problems. Randy's been bitter about the divorce ever since it happened, and he finally told his father so but I stepped in and things got out of hand. I slapped Randy and he's been withdrawn and unaffectionate ever since. Oh, I don't know, Heather, sometimes I hate being a mother."

"Sometimes we all do."

"So what did I do wrong? His whole life long I loved him, I told him so, I kissed and hugged him, I went to school conferences, I did everything the books said I should but somewhere along the line I lost him. He just pulls farther and farther away. I know he's drinking, and I think he's smoking pot but I can't get him to admit it or to stop."

Heather left her dustrag on the shelf and went around behind the counter. She took Bess in her arms and held her caringly. "It's not always us doing something wrong. Sometimes it's them, and we just have to wait for them to grow out of it, or confide in us, or hit bottom."

"He loves this job so. His whole life long he's wanted to play with a band but I'm so afraid for him. It's a destructive way of life."

"You can't make his choices for him, Bess, not anymore."

"I know . . ." Bess held Heather tighter for a second. "I know." She drew away with glistening eyes. "Thanks. You're a dear friend."

"I'm a mother who's tried her damnedest, just like you but . . ." Heather raised her palms and let them drop. ". . . all we can do is love 'em and hope for the best."

It was hard to concentrate on work knowing Lisa was in labor. There were designs to be finished in the loft but Bess felt too restless to be confined upstairs. She waited on customers instead, tagged some newly arrived linens and hung them on an old-fashioned wooden clothes rack for display. She went outside and watered the geraniums in the window box. She unpacked a new shipment of wallpaper. She checked her watch at least a dozen times an hour.

Mark called shortly before 3 P.M. and said, "We're at the hospital. Can you come now?"

Bess barely took time to say good-bye before hanging up, grabbing her purse and running.

Lakeview Hospital was less than two miles from her store, up to the top of Myrtle Street hill and south on Greeley Street to the high ground overlooking Lily Lake. Though there were other hospitals closer to Lisa and Mark's apartment, her pregnancy had been confirmed by the physicians she'd known all her life, so she'd stayed with the familiar names and faces who practiced right here in town. Bess found it comforting to be approaching the hospital where Lisa and Randy had been born, where Lisa's broken arm had been set, where both of them had been given their preschool physicals, and countless throat cultures, and where their height and weight and periodic infirmities had been recorded and were still safely filed away in metal drawers. Here, too, the whole family had seen Grandpa Dorner for the last time.

The OB wing of the hospital was so new it still smelled of carpet fiber and wallpaper. The hall was indirectly lit, quiet, and led to a hexagonal nurses' station surrounded by a circle of rooms.

"I'm Lisa Padgett's mother," Bess announced to the nurse on duty.

The young woman led the way to a birthing room, where both the labor and birth would be carried out. Lisa and Mark were there, along with a smiley nurse wearing blue scrubs, whose nametag read JAN MEERS, R.N. Lisa was lying on the bed holding up a wrinkled patient's gown while Jan Meers adjusted something that looked like a white tube top around her belly. She picked up two sensors, slipped them beneath the bellyband, patted them and said, "There. That'll hold them." Their leads dropped to a machine beside the bed, which she rolled nearer.

Lisa saw Bess and said, "Hi, Mom."

Bess went to the bed, leaned over and kissed her. "Hi, honey, hi, Mark, how's everything going?"

"Pretty good. Getting me all hog-tied to this machine so we can tell if the baby changes his mind or something." To the nurse, Lisa said, "This is my mom, Bess." To Bess, "This is the lady who's going to put me through the seven tortures."

Ms. Meers laughed. "Oh, I hope not. I don't think it'll be so bad. Look here now . . ." She moved aside and rested a hand on the machine where an orange digital number glowed beside a tiny orange heart that flashed in rhythm with a sound like a scratchy phonograph record. "This is the fetal monitor. That's the baby's heartbeat you hear."

Everyone's eyes fixed upon the beating orange heart while beside it a white graph paper began to creep into sight, bearing a printout of the proceedings.

"And this one"—Ms. Meers indicated a green number beside the orange one—"shows your contractions, Lisa. Mark, one of your jobs will be to watch it. Between contractions it'll read around thirteen or fourteen. The instant you see it rising you should remind Lisa to start breathing. It'll take about thirty seconds for the contraction to reach its peak, and by forty-five seconds it'll be tapering off. The whole thing will last about one minute. Believe it or not, Mark, you'll often know there's a contraction starting before she will."

Ms. Meers had scarcely finished her instructions before Mark said, "It's going up!" He moved closer to Lisa, his eyes on the monitor. Lisa stiffened and he reminded her, "Okay, relax. Here we go now, remember, three pants and one blow. Pant, pant, pant, blow . . . pant, pant, pant, blow . . . okay, we're fifteen seconds into it . . . thirty . . . hang on, honey . . . forty-five now and nearly over . . . good job."

Bess stood by uselessly, watching Lisa ride out the pain, feeling her own innards seizing up while Mark remained a bastion of strength. He leaned over Lisa, rubbed the hair back from her forehead and smiled into her eyes. He whispered something and she nodded, then closed her eyes.

Bess checked the clock. It was 3:19 P.M.

The next contraction came fifteen minutes later and by the time it arrived, so had Mark's mother. She greeted everyone, giving Mark a quick squeeze.

"Is Dad coming?" Mark asked her.

"He's at work. I left a note on the kitchen table for him. Hi, Lisa-honey. Today's the day you get your waistline back. I'll bet you're happy." She kissed Lisa's cheek and said, "I think it's going to be a boy. I don't know why but I have the strongest feeling."

"If it is we're going to be in trouble because we haven't thought of a boy's name yet. But if it's a girl it'll be Natalie."

The contractions came and went. It was hard for Bess to watch Lisa suffer. Her child. Her precious firstborn, who had, as a youngster of five, six, seven, mothered her baby brother the way little girls do: held his hand when they crossed the street together; lifted him up to reach the drinking fountain; soothed and cooed when he fell down and scraped a knee. And now she was a grown woman and would soon have a baby of her own. No matter that the pain was the means to eventual happiness and fulfillment, watching one's own child bear it was terrible.

At moments Bess wished she'd decided to delay coming here until the baby was safely born, then felt guilty for her selfishness. She wished she were needed more, then felt grateful that Mark was the one Lisa needed most. She wished Lisa were a little girl again, then thought, No, how foolish; I really wish no such thing. She was enjoying having an adult daughter. Nevertheless, often during those minutes of travail, she pictured Lisa as a kindergartner, walking bravely up the street alone for the first time—absurd, how fragments of those bygone years kept insinuating themselves into this hour that was so far removed from the days of Lisa's childhood. Perhaps it was peculiar to the stepping-stones of life that at those times an underlying sadness was rekindled.

Sometimes when the contractions ended, both Bess and Hildy released their breaths and let their shoulders slump, then glanced furtively at each other, realizing they'd been copying Lisa's breathing pattern as if doing so could make it easier on her.

At 6:30 Jake Padgett arrived, and Bess left the birthing room for a while because it was getting too crowded. She walked down to the pop machine by the cafeteria, got a can of Coke and took it to the family room, adjacent to Lisa's birthing room, a spacious, restful place with comfortable chairs and an L-shaped sofa long enough to stretch out and nap on. It had a refrigerator, coffeepot, snacks, bathroom, television, toys and books.

Bess found her mind too preoccupied to be interested in amusements.

She returned to the birthing room at five to seven and watched two more contractions, before rubbing Mark's shoulder and suggesting, "Why don't you sit down awhile. I think I can do this."

Mark sank gratefully into a recliner and Bess took his place beside the bed.

Lisa opened her eyes and smiled weakly. Her hair was stringy and flat, her face looked slightly puffy. "I guess Dad's not coming, huh?"

Bess took her hand. "I don't know, sweetheart."

From his chair, Mark murmured sleepily, "I called his office a long time ago. They said they'd give him the message."

Lisa said, "I want him here."

"Yes, I know," Bess whispered. "So do I."

It was true. While she had watched Lisa laboring she'd wanted Michael beside her as strongly as ever in her life. It appeared, however, that he was avoiding the hospital, knowing she was there, just as he had the pool party at Barb and Don's.

By ten o'clock there'd been no change, and the anesthesiologist was called in to administer an epidural, which made Lisa woozy and a slight bit giddy. The baby was big, probably close to ten pounds, and Lisa was narrow across the pelvis. The epidural, it was explained, would not stop the contractions, only make Lisa unaware she was having them.

Mark was napping. The Padgetts had their eyes closed in front of the TV, and Bess went out to find a pay phone and call Stella, who said she wouldn't clutter up the proceedings but wanted to know the minute the baby was born, even if it was the middle of the night. After the phone call, Bess returned to the obstetrics wing and ambled around the circular hall. On the far side she wandered into the solarium, an arc-shaped room with a curved bank of windows overlooking the treetops and Lily Lake across the street. Only a glimpse of the night-dark water was visible and from inside, where climate was carefully controlled and trees were potted, it was impossible to tell if the night was warm or cool, still or noisy, if crickets were chirping, water lapping or mosquitoes buzzing.

The thought of mosquitoes brought the memories of warm summer nights when Lisa and Randy were little and the whole neighborhood resounded with the sounds of squeals from a dozen children playing starlight-moonlight and kick the can. When they were called for bedtime, the kids would whine, "Come on, Mom, just a little while longer, pleeeeze!" When they were finally coerced inside, their bare legs would be welted with bites, their hair sweaty, their feet dirty. Then she and Michael would bathe and dry them and put them in clean pajamas. How good they would smell then, with their faces shiny and their pajamas crisp. They would sit at the kitchen table and gobble cookies and milk and scratch their mosquito bites and protest that they weren't a bit tired.

But once in bed they'd be asleep in sixty seconds, with their precious mouths open and their sunburned limbs half above, half under the sheets. She and Michael would study them in the wedge of light from the hall as it picked out their lips and noses and eyelashes, and often their bare toes protruding from pajama legs rucked up about their knees.

Remembering, Bess felt her eyes grow misty.

She'd been standing a long time, staring out the window, weighted by the bittersweet tug of nostalgia, too weary to uncross her arms, when someone touched her shoulder.

"Bess."

She turned at the sound of Michael's voice and felt an overwhelming sense of relief and the awful threat of full-fledged tears.

"Oh, you're here," she said, as if he had materialized from her fantasy. She stepped into the calm harbor of his arms as she had longed to step into that shadowy bedroom where her younglings slept. The pressure of his embrace was firm and reassuring, the smell of his clothing and skin familiar, and for a minute she pretended the children were young again, they had tucked them into bed together and at last were stealing a moment for each other.

"I'm sorry," he said against her temple. "I'd flown to Milwaukee. I just got back and my answering service gave me the message." The strength of Bess's embrace surprised Michael. "Bess, what's wrong?"

"Nothing, really. I'm just so glad you're here."

His arms tightened and he let out a ragged breath against her hair. They had the solarium to themselves. The indirect lighting created a soft glow above the black windows. At the nurses' station beyond the door, all was quiet. For a while time seemed abstract, no rush nor reason to refrain from embracing, only the utter rightness of being together again, bolstering each other through this next stepping-stone in their daughter's life and their own.

Against Michael's shoulder Bess confessed, "I've been thinking about when the children were little, how simple everything was then, how they'd play games after dark with all the neighborhood kids and come in all full of mosquito bites. And how they looked in bed when they fell asleep. Oh, Michael, those were wonderful days, weren't they?"

"Yes, they were."

They were rocking gently. She felt his hand pet her hair, her shoulder.

"And now Randy is out on the road somewhere with some band, probably high on pot, and Lisa is in there going through all this."

Michael drew back but held Bess by the upper arms while looking into her eyes. "That's how it is, Bess. They grow up."

For a moment the expression in her eyes said she wasn't ready to accept it. Then she said, "I don't know what's come over me tonight. I'm usually not so silly and sentimental."

"It's not silly," he replied, "it's understandable on this particular night, and you know something else? Nostalgia looks good on you."

"Oh, Michael . . ." She drew away self-consciously and dropped into a chair beside a potted palm. "Did you stop by Lisa's room?"

"Yes. The nurse explained they gave her something to help her rest for a little while. She's been here since three, they said."

Bess nodded.

He looked at his watch. "Well, that's only seven hours. If I remember right she took thirteen getting here." He smiled at Bess. "Thirteen of the longest hours of my life."

"And mine," Bess added.

He sat down in a chair beside her, found her hand and held it on the hard wooden arms between them, rubbing her thumb absently with his own. They thought about their time apart, their stubbornness that had brought them both nothing but loneliness. They studied their joined hands, each of them grateful that some force outside themselves had brought them here and thrust them back together.

After a while Bess said quietly, "They said the baby is really large, and Lisa might be in for a hard time."

"So we'll stay, for as long as it takes. How about Stella? Does she know?"

"I called her but she decided to stay home and wait for the news."

"And Randy?"

"He knew she was in labor before he left. He'll be home tomorrow."

They waited in the solarium, alternately dozing and waking. Around midnight they went for a walk around the wing, discovering a new shift had come on, gazing into the empty nursery, passing the family lounge, where Jake Padgett was stretched out on the sofa, sound asleep. In the birthing room Hildy was the only one awake. She was sitting in the wooden rocking chair doing cross-stitch and waved at them silently as they paused in the doorway.

Lisa's new nurse came by and introduced herself. Marcie Unger was her name. She went into Lisa's room to check the digital readings, came back out and said, "No change."

By two o'clock things had picked up. Lisa's contractions were coming every five minutes and the anesthesiologist was called to cut off the epidural.

"Why?" Lisa asked.

"Because if we don't, you won't know when to push."

The birthing room came to life after that. Those who wanted to witness the birth were asked to don blue scrubs. Marcie Unger stayed beside Lisa every moment and Mark, too, holding Lisa's hand, guiding her through her breathing.

Jake Padgett decided to wait in the family lounge but Hildy, Bess and Michael donned sterile blue scrubs.

For Bess it was a curious sensation, looking up to find only Michael's attractive hazel eyes showing above his blue mask. She felt a momentary current the way she had when she was first falling in love with him. His eyes—stunning beyond all others she'd ever known—still had the power to kick up a reaction deep within her.

His mask billowed as he spoke. "How do you feel?"

"Scared, and not at all sure I want to go in there. How about you?"

"The same."

"We're just being typical parents. Everything will go fine. I'm sure of it."

"If I don't faint on the delivery-room floor," Michael said.

Her eyes crinkled. "Birthing room, and I'm sure you'll do just great."

"If we don't want to go in there, why are we doing it?" Michael said.

"For Lisa."

"Oh, that's right. That darned kid asked us to, didn't she?"

The interchange took the edge off their nervousness and left them smiling above their masks. Bess could not resist telling him, "If we're lucky, Michael, this baby will have your eyes."

He winked one of them and said, "Something tells me everything's going to be lucky from here on out."

When they entered the birthing room again, Lisa's knees created twin peaks beneath the sheet. The head of her bed was elevated at a 45-degree angle but her eyes were closed as she panted and labored through a contraction, her face glistening with sweat and her cheeks puffing as she breathed.

"I've g . . . got to p . . . push," she got out between breaths.

"No, not yet," Marcie Unger said soothingly. "Save your strength."

"But it's time . . . it's . . . I know it's . . . oh . . . oh . . . oh . . ."

"Keep breathing the way Mark tells you."

Beside her, Mark said, "Deeply this time, in and out, slow."

Bess's eyes sought Michael's and saw reflected there the same touch of anguish and helplessness she herself felt.

When the contraction ended, Lisa's eyes opened and found her father's, above the blue mask. "Dad?" she said with a weak smile.

"Hi, honey." His eyes crinkled with a smile as he moved to her side to squeeze her hand. "I made it."

"And Mom," she added in a whisper, searching for and finding her mother's eyes. "You're both here?" She gave a tired smile and closed her eyes while Bess and Michael exchanged another glance that said, This is what she wanted, this is what she set out to do. They took their places on Lisa's left while Mark and his mother stood on her right.

A second nurse appeared, all sterile and masked. "The doctor will be here in a minute," she said. She looked down into Lisa's face and said, "Hi, Lisa, I'm Ann, and I'm here to take care of the baby as soon as it arrives. I'll measure him, weigh him and bathe him."

Lisa nodded and Marcie Unger moved to the foot of the bed, where she removed the sheet from Lisa, then the end cushion of the bed itself, before tipping up a pair of footrests. She told Lisa, "These are for your feet if you want them. If not, fine." On the side rails she adjusted two pieces that looked like bicycle handles with plastic grips, and placed Lisa's left hand on one. "And these are for you to hang onto when you feel like pushing."

Mark said, "Here comes another one . . . come on, honey, show me that beautiful breathing. Pant, pant, pant, blow . . ."

Lisa moaned with each blow. In the middle of the contraction the doctor swept in, dressed like all the others in blue scrubs and skull cap. She spoke in a feminine voice. "Well, how are things going with Lisa?" Her eyes darted to the vital signs, then she smiled down at her patient.

"Hello, Doctor Lewis," Lisa said with as much enthusiasm as she could muster. Her voice sounded weak. "Where've you been so long?"

"I've been in touch. Let's see if we can't get this baby into the world and have a look at him. I'm going to break your water, Lisa. After that, everything will happen pretty fast."

Lisa nodded and rolled a glance at Mark, who held her hand folded over his own, smoothing her fingers.

While Dr. Lewis broke Lisa's water, Michael glanced away. The doctor was giving Lisa a monologue on what she was doing but Lisa made small sounds of distress. Under cover of the doctor's voice, Bess whispered to Michael, "Are you all right?"

He met her eyes and nodded but she could tell he was not, especially when he observed the faint pinkish fluid that ran from Lisa and stained the sheets beneath her. She found his arm and rubbed it lightly while from across the room she caught Hildy watching. Hildy's eyes smiled and the two women, who'd both borne children of their own, exchanged a moment of silent communion.

Lisa's next pushing contraction brought even greater sounds of distress. She cried out, and her body and face quaked as she clasped the handles and tried mightily to push the baby from herself.

The contraction ended with no results, and when it ebbed Bess bent over Lisa and said, "You're doing fine, honey," worried herself but hiding it. She lovingly wiped Lisa's stringy, wet bangs back from her brow and thought, *Never again, I'll never watch this again!*

She straightened to find Michael's eyebrows furrowed with concern, his breath coming fast, luffing his mask in and out.

The next contraction seemed worse than the last and racked Lisa even harder. Her head lifted from the bed, and Bess bolstered her from behind while Michael stared at the swollen shape of the baby's head engaged in the birth canal and repeated along with Mark, "Pant, pant, pant . . . push."

Still the baby refused to emerge, and Bess glanced at Michael's eyes to find them bright with tears. His tears prompted some of her own and she glanced away, wanting to be strong for Lisa's sake.

The doctor ordered, "Get the mighty vac."

Marcie Unger produced it: a tiny cone-shaped device at the end of a rubber tube and hand pump.

"Lisa," the doctor said, "we're going to give you a little help here. This is just a miniature suction cup we're going to put on the baby's head so the next time you push, we can pull a little, too, all right?"

"Will it hurt him?" Lisa asked, attempting to lift her head and see what was going on below.

"No," the doctor replied while Mark pressed his wife back against the bed, leaning over her, soothing her, urging her to rest as much as possible between pains. Bess did likewise from the opposite side of the bed, cooing comforting words, softly rubbing the inside of Lisa's knee.

Lisa murmured, "I'm so hot . . . don't touch me . . ."

Bess dropped her hand and felt Michael secretly grope for it in the folds of their blue scrubs. She gripped his hand and squeezed it all the while the tiny cone was inserted, and the hand pump worked by Marcie Unger, all the while Lisa moaned and wagged her head deliriously against the mattress.

With the next contraction the mighty vac began helping but midway through the suction broke and the cup flew free, spraying blood across six sets of scrubs and striking terror into the eyes of Mark, Hildy, Bess and Michael.

"It's okay," Marcie Unger reassured. "No harm done."

It seemed to take hours for them to get the suction cup reapplied.

But with the next pain, it worked.

Dr. Lewis said, "Here it comes . . ." and all eyes were fixed upon Lisa's dilated body. She pushed and the doctor pulled, and out of her swollen flesh emerged a tiny head with bloody, black hair.

Bess gripped Michael's hand and stared through her tears while he did likewise, both of them wonder-struck by what was happening before their eyes.

Between breaths Lisa managed to ask Mark, "Is it born yet?"

Dr. Lewis answered. "Halfway but one more push and it'll be here. Okay, Mark, help her through it."

The next pain did, indeed, bring the full birth. Michael and Bess watched it happen, still clinging to each other's hands, smiling behind their masks.

"It's a girl!" the doctor announced, catching the infant as it slipped forth.

Lisa smiled.

Mark cried, "Yahoo!"

Hildy rubbed Mark's back.

Bess and Michael looked at each other and found telltale dark splotches on their blue masks. Michael shrugged a shoulder to an eye and left another dark spot, and Bess felt her heart go light with joy.

The nurse named Ann came immediately with a soft blue towel, scooped the infant into it and laid her on Lisa's stomach. The doctor clamped the cord in two places and handed a pair of scissors to Mark.

"How about it, Daddy, do you want to cut the cord?"

The baby was wriggling, testing out its arms in the confines of the towel while Bess bolstered Lisa up so she could see the baby's head and touch it.

"Wow . . ." Lisa breathed, ". . . she's really here. Hey, Natalie, how you doing?" Then to the doctor, "Isn't she supposed to cry?"

"Not as long as she's breathing, and she's doing that just fine."

Lisa sank back and discovered there was more work to do—afterbirth to be delivered, and stitches to be tolerated.

Meanwhile, Natalie Padgett was being passed around from hand to hand—to her father, her grandmothers, her grandfather, whose dark eyes beamed above his mask while he, too, welcomed her with "Hi, Natalie." She was about as pretty as a baby bird, still plastered with afterbirth and working her head and arms with the diminutive motions of a slow-motion film, trying to keep her eyes open while her fists remained tightly shut.

Hildy said, "I'd better go tell the news to Jake." While she was gone Bess and Michael had one lavish minute to appreciate their grandchild themselves. She lay in the soft blue towel, squirming, held in Michael's wide hands, with Bess cupping the warm flannel around her tiny, smeared head.

The instinct to kiss her was irrepressible.

Tears kept welling in their eyes and blurring her image while a well-spring of love encompassed them both.

Michael said, "How awful that I missed this when our own were born. I'm so glad I was here this time." He passed the baby to Bess, who held her far too short a time before she was claimed by her father, then by Ann, for weighing and measuring. Hildy returned with Jake in tow, and the birthing room became crowded, so Bess and Michael left for a while, repairing to the family room next door. There, all was quiet and they were alone. They turned to each other, pulled down their masks and embraced, wordless for a long time, the birth they'd just witnessed melding with the birth of Lisa in their memories.

When Michael spoke his voice was gruff with emotion.

"I never thought I'd feel like this."

"How?" she whispered.

"Complete."

"Yes, that's it, isn't it?"

"A part of us, coming into the world again. My God, it does something to you, doesn't it, Bess?"

It did. It brought a lump to her throat and a yearning to her heart as she simply stood in Michael's arms, softly rubbing his shoulders through the ugly blue scrubs, disinclined to ever leave him again.

"Oh, Michael . . ."

"I'm so glad we're together for this."

"Oh, me too. It was awful before you got here. I kept thinking you weren't coming, and I didn't know how I'd get through it without you."

"Now that I've been through it, I wouldn't have missed it for the world."

They remained locked in an embrace until their emotions calmed and weariness made itself known, then Michael asked, against her hair, "Tired?"

"Yes. You?"

"Exhausted."

He set her away and looked into her face. "Well, I guess there's no reason for us to stay. Let's go see the baby once more and say good-bye to Lisa."

In the room next door the new parents created a heartwarming tableau with their clean, red-faced infant between them, wrapped now in a pink blanket, Lisa and Mark radiant with love and happiness. So radiant, it seemed a transgression to interrupt and bid them good-bye.

Bess did so first, leaning over Lisa as she rested in bed, touching her hair and kissing her cheek, then the baby's head. "Good night, dear. I'll see you later on this afternoon. Thank you so much for letting us be a part of this."

Michael went next, kissing them, too, deluged with the same emotions as Bess. "I didn't really want to come in here tonight but I'm so glad I did. Thank you, honey."

They congratulated and hugged Mark and left the hospital together.

Outside it was nearly dawn. Sparrows were beginning to cheep from the nearby trees. The sky had begun its fade from deep blue to lavender. The night dew seemed to have lifted into the air and hung damp all around. The visitors' parking lot was nearly empty as Bess and Michael walked across it with lagging footsteps.

As they approached Bess's car, Michael took her hand.

"That was really something to go through, wasn't it?" he said.

"I feel as if I had the baby myself."

"I bet you do. I never had one, and *I* feel like I just did!"

"The funny thing is when I was the one giving birth I don't think the wonder of it struck me so hard. I suppose I was too busy to dwell on that part of it."

"Same for me. Waiting in another room—I wish things had been different in those days and I could have been in the delivery room like Mark was."

They reached her car and stopped but Michael kept her hand. "Can you believe it, Bess? We're a grandpa and grandma."

She smiled up at him wearily and said, "A couple of very tired ones. Do you have to work today?"

"I'm not going to. How about you?"

"I was supposed to but I think I'll let Heather handle it alone. I'll probably sleep for a few hours then come back up to see Lisa and the baby again."

"Yeah, me too."

There seemed little else to say. It was time to part, time for him to go to his condominium and for her to go to her house on Third Avenue.

They had been through an exhausting night. Their eyes hurt. Their backs hurt. But they stood in the parking lot, holding hands until it made no sense anymore. One of them had to move.

"Well . . ." she said, "see y'."

"Yeah," he repeated, "see y'."

She pulled free as if someone were dragging her against her wishes, from the opposite direction. She got into her car while he stood with both hands crooked over the open door, watching as she put her keys in the ignition and started the engine. He slammed the door. She shifted into reverse and waggled two fingers at him through the window, wearing a sad expression on her face.

He stepped back as the car began to roll, slipped his hands into his trouser pockets and remained behind feeling empty and lost as he watched her drive away.

When she was gone, he sighed deeply, tipped his face to the sky and tried to gulp down the lump in his throat. He went to his own car, got in and stuck his keys into the ignition, then sat motionless with the engine unstarted and his hands hanging limply on the wheel.

Thinking. Thinking. About himself, his future and how empty it would remain without Bess.

It began deep down within him, a bubbling rebellion that said, Why? Why must it be that way? We've both changed. We both want, need, love each other. We both want this family back together. What the hell are we waiting for?

He started his engine and tore out of the parking lot doing a rolling stop at the stop sign, then wheeled out onto Greeley Street on Bess's trail, doing a good fifteen miles an hour above the speed limit.

At the house on Third Avenue he screeched to a halt and opened the car door even before the engine stopped running. Her car was already put away in the garage, the door was down. He jogged up the sidewalk to the front door, rang the bell, thumped on the door with his fist several times, then stood waiting with one hand braced on the doorframe at shoulder level. She must have gone upstairs already. It took her some time to get back down and answer.

When she did, surprise dropped her jaw.

"Why, Michael, what's wrong?"

He burst inside, slammed the door and scooped her into his arms. "You *know* what's wrong, Bess. You and me, living in two separate houses, being divorced from each other when we love each other the way we do. That's no way for us to act, not when we could be together and happy. I want that . . ." He gripped her harder. ". . . oh God, I want that so much." He interrupted himself to kiss her—hard, brief, possessive—before wrapping his arms around her firmly and holding her to his breast. "I want Lisa and Mark to bring that baby to our house and the two of us waiting with outstretched arms, and keeping her overnight sometimes, and all of us together on Christmas mornings after Santa Claus comes. And I want us to try to make up for what we did to Randy. Maybe if we start now we can turn him around." He drew back, holding her face in both hands, pleading, "Please, Bess, marry me again. I love you. We'll try harder this time, and we'll compromise, for both us and the kids. Can't you see, Lisa was right? This is the way it should be!"

She was crying long before he finished, the tears coursing down her cheeks. "Aw, don't cry, Bess . . . don't . . ."

She dove against him and threw her arms around his neck. "Oh, Michael, yes. I love you, too, and I want all those things, and I don't know what's going to become of Randy but we've got to try. He still needs us so much."

They kissed the way they'd wanted to in the hospital parking lot, sealed together full-length, earnest with passion while at the same time too tired to know if they were standing on their own power or supporting one another. Their lips parted, their gazes locked but even so, they floundered in their attempt to impart the depth of emotions coursing through them.

He kissed the crests of her cheeks, sipping up her salty tears, then her mouth, softly this time. "Let's get married right away. As soon as possible."

She smiled through her tears. "All right. Whatever you say."

"And we'll tell the kids today. And Stella, too," he added. "We're going to make her the second happiest woman in the whole USA."

Bess kept smiling. "The third, maybe . . . behind me and Lisa."

"All right, third. But she'll be smiling."

"She'll be doing cartwheels."

"I feel like I could do a few myself."

"You do? I'm falling off my feet."

"On second thought, so am I. Should we go to bed?"

"And do what? Get caught again by Randy? He's due home, you know."

Michael took her breasts in both hands and went on convincing her. "You'll sleep better afterwards, you always do."

"I won't have any trouble sleeping at all."

"Cruel woman."

She drew back and smiled lovingly. "Michael, we'll have plenty of time for that, and I really am tired, and I don't want to antagonize Randy any more. Let's do the sensible thing."

He caught her hands and stepped back. "All right, I'll go home like a good boy. Will I see you at the hospital later?"

"Around two or so, I thought."

"Okay. Walk me to my car?"

She smiled and walked with him, holding his hand, outside into the yard, where full dawn was staining the sky a spectrum of purples and golds and a faint breeze was stirring the tips of the maple leaves. The hydrangeas in front of the garage were heavy with great white blooms and the scent of heavy summer was rising from the warming earth.

At his car, Michael got in, closed the door and rolled down the window.

She leaned inside and kissed him. "I love you, Michael," she said.

"I love you, too, and I really think we can make it this time."

"So do I." He started the engine, still looking up into her eyes.

She grinned. "It's hell being mature and having to make sensible decisions. For two cents I'd drag you up to our bedroom and ravish you right now."

He laughed and said, "We'll make up for it, just wait and see."

She stood back, crossed her arms and watched him back out of the driveway.

chapter 18

*T*HE BAND QUIT PLAYING at 12:30 A.M. It took them one hour to load up and over five hours to drive back from Bemidji. Randy got home at seven to find his mother still asleep and a note on his bed.

Lisa had a girl, Natalie, 9 lbs. 12 oz, at five this morning. Everybody's doing fine. I'm not going into the store but hope to see you at the hospital later. Love, Mom.

But the way it worked out he was unable to make it to the hospital that afternoon. He was still asleep when his mother got up, and she was gone from the house by the time he rose, groggy, at 12:15 to get ready for his afternoon gig, which started at two in White Bear Lake.

These town celebrations paid well. Every little suburb around the Twin Cities had them at some time during the summer: the Raspberry Festival in Hopkins, Whiz-Bang Days in Robbinsdale, Tater Days in Brooklyn Park, Manitou Days in White Bear Lake. They were all the same: carnivals, parades, bingo, beard-growing contests and street dances. Some of the dances took place at night but many, like today's, were scheduled for the afternoon. Bands liked the bookings not only because they paid well but also because the afternoon scheduling gave them a rare Saturday night off to catch a decent stretch of sleep or to go hear some other band play, which every professional musician loved to do.

White Bear Lake had a pretty little downtown—shady, with trees springing out of openings in the brick sidewalks; fancy, old-fashioned storefronts painted candy colors; flags hanging from the sides of buildings; a little town square.

The entire length of Washington Street was barricaded off, and a bandstand was set up at the south end, facing a turn-of-the century post office building with its surrounding green grass and flower beds. While the band set up, little girls sat on the curb and watched, licking ice-cream cones or chewing licorice sticks. Pint-sized boys wearing chartreuse billcaps and hot-pink shorts maneuvered their skateboards back and forth, deftly jumping the thick electrical cables that snaked across the blacktop. From several blocks away the sounds of a carnival drifted over on the whims of the wind—an occasional tinkle of calliope music, the revving engines from the amusement rides. From nearer wafted the smell of bratwursts roasting on a pushcart in front of a ladies' wear shop midway along the block.

Randy stacked a pair of drums and lifted them from the rear of the van. He turned to find a boy of perhaps twelve years old watching. The kid was wearing sunglasses with pink frames and black strings. His hair was jelled up into a flattop, and his high-top tennis shoes had tongues nearly as big as the skateboard on his hip.

"Hey, you play those things?" the kid asked in a gruff, cocky voice.

"Yup."

"Cool."

Randy smiled at the kid and took the load up the back steps onto the stage. The boy was still there when he returned.

"I play drums, too."

"Yeah?"

"In the band at school."

"That's a good way to learn."

"Ain't got any of my own yet. But I will have someday though, and then look out."

Randy smiled and pulled another load of equipment to the rear of the van.

The kid offered, "Want me to help you carry some of that stuff?" Randy turned and looked the kid over. He was a tough-looking little punk, as tough-looking as it's possible to be at a hundred pounds, without much for muscles or whiskers or body hair. His Dick Tracy T-shirt would have fit Mike Tyson, and he had an I-don't-care way of standing inside it that reminded Randy of himself at that age, about the time his father had left: *Screw the world. Who needs it?*

"Yeah. Here, take this stool, then you can come back for the cymbals. What's your name, kid?"

"Trotter." He had a voice like sand in ball bearings.

"That's all? Just Trotter?"

"That's enough."

"Well, Trotter, see what you think about being a roadie."

Trotter was as good as his name, trotting up and down the steps, hauling anything Randy would hand him. Actually the kid was a godsend. Randy was zoned, operating on four hours of sleep and too much pot last night. God, how he needed to chill out for a solid sixteen hours but that hadn't been possible all week. Their traveling schedule had been horrendous, and they'd been rehearsing a lot, too. All that on top of setup and breakdown—which totaled two and a half, three hours a gig—left damned little time for Z'ing out. Now he faced four hours of playing when his feet would scarcely lift to carry him up the steps and his head felt like a bowling ball balanced on a toothpick.

With the help of the tough little groupie, the last of the equipment got to the stage.

"Hey, thanks, Trotter. You're okay." He handed the kid a pair of royal-blue drumsticks. "Here. Go for it."

The kid took the sticks, his eyes huge and filled with worship behind his shades.

"For me?"

Randy nodded.

"Bitchin'," the kid marveled softly and moved off, already jiving to some silent beat.

"Hey, kid," Randy called after him.

Trotter turned, one of the sticks whirling like a propeller through his fingers. "Stick around. We'll send one out specially for you this afternoon."

Trotter saluted with one drumstick and disappeared.

Pike Watson came around the back of the stage carrying a guitar case. "Who's the punk?"

"Name's Trotter. Just a kid with big dreams, wants to be a drummer someday."

"You give him the sticks?"

Randy shrugged. "What the hell, keep his dreams alive, you know?"

"That's all right."

"I didn't tell him he'd have to learn to sleep and drive at the same time if he wanted to play with a band."

"You droned, man?"

Randy shook his head as if to wake himself up. "Yeah. Major droned."

"Hey, listen, I'll do you a solid. I got some really good shit here." Pike tapped his guitar case.

"Cocaine, you mean? Naw. That stuff freaks me."

"How do you know? One little snort and you're goddamned Batman. You can stop trains and start revolutions. What do you say?"

Randy looked skeptical. "Naw, I don't think so."

Pike gave a mischievous grin. "I guarantee you'll forget you're tired." He spread his fingers and fanned them in slow motion through the air. "You'll play like freakin' Charlie Watts."

"How much?"

"Your first hit's on me."

Randy rubbed his sternum and tipped his head to one side. "I don't know, man."

"Well . . ." Pike threw his hands up and bounced a couple times at the knee. "If you're scared of flyin' . . ."

"What's it do to you—bad, I mean?"

"Nothin', man, *nothiiin'!* You get a little zingy at first—anxious, you know—but then it's strictly superfly!"

Randy rubbed his face with both hands and flexed his shoulders. He blew out a blast of breath that made his lips flop and said, "What the hell . . . I always wanted to play like Charlie Watts."

He snorted the cocaine off a mirror in the back of Pike's van just before they started playing. It made his nose sting and he rubbed it as he headed onto the stage. He felt wildly exhilarated and invincible.

They started the first set and Randy played with his eyes closed. When he opened them a moment later, he saw Trotter out in front of all the others on the street, sitting on his skateboard with his eyes riveted on Randy, playing along on his knees with the blue drumsticks. Yeah, it was hero worship, all right, and it felt sensational. Nearly as sensational as the high that was coming on. Some teenage girls stood at the front of the crowd, too, dressed in shiny biking tights with an inch of their tan, flat stomachs showing below their itty-bitty crop tops. One of them, a blonde with a spectacular mop of curly hair that exploded clear down past her shoulder blades, kept her eye on him without letup. He could spot them every time, the ones who were easy marks. All he had to do was return her gaze a few times, give the little hint of a smile she waited for and at break time stand nearby—not too close, just close enough for her to know he knew—and wait for her to sidle over. The conversations always went the same.

"Hi."

"Hi."

"You're good."

He'd let his eyes overtly explore her breasts and hips. "So are you. What's your name?"

After he'd learn it, he'd make sure he dedicated one song to her and that's all it took to get in her pants.

Today, however, the dedication was for Trotter. Randy put his lips to the mike and said, "I'd like to send this song out to one terrific little roadie. Trotter, this one's for you, kid." Trotter actually smiled, and while Randy rapped out the pickup beat to *Pretty Woman,* he truly forgot about the pretty woman standing behind the kid, and reveled in the genuine admiration he saw beaming up at him from the boy's face.

It happened as they began the second song. One minute Randy was watching the kid idolize him, and the next he was struck by an illogical shock of apprehension. His heart started racing and the apprehension became fear. He turned as if to seek help from Pike but all he saw was Pike's back, in a loose black shirt, diagonally bisected by a wide guitar strap as he stood with his feet widespread, playing.

Sweet Jesus, his heart! What was happening with his heart? It was pounding so hard it seemed to be lifting the hair from his skull. The kid was watching . . . no breath . . . hard to keep playing . . . people everywhere . . . had to make it to the end of the song . . . dizzying anxiety . . . oh-oh, pretty woman!

The song ending . . . "Pike!" . . . everything inside him vibrating . . . "Pike!" . . . and pushing outward . . . Pike's face, leaning close, coming between him and the crowd . . .

"It's all right, man. It always happens at first, you get a little uptight, scared-like. Give it a minute. It'll go away."

Clutching Pike's hand . . . "No, no! This'z bad, man . . . my heart . . ."

Pike, angry, ordering in a fierce whisper, "Let it ride, man. There's a couple hundred people out there watching us right now. It'll be better in a minute! Now give us a goddamn lead-in!"

Tick, tick, tick . . . the sticks on the rim of his Pearls . . . the kid watching from down on the pavement, playing along with the blue sticks . . . dizzy . . . so dizzy . . . kid, get outa here . . . don't want you to see this . . . Maryann, I wanted to change for you . . . his heart fluttering fast as a drumroll . . . everything tipping . . . tipping . . . the floor coming up to meet him . . . the crack of his head as he landed . . . the stool still tangled in his legs . . . looking straight up at the blue sky . . .

The band continued playing for several measures until they realized there was no more drumbeat. As the music dribbled into silence the crowd pressed forward, lifted up on tiptoe and murmured a chorus of concern.

Danny Scarfelli reached Randy first, leaned over him with his bass guitar still strapped over his shoulder.

"Jesus, Randy, what's wrong, man?"

"Get Pike . . . where's Pike?" Danny caught two of his guitar keys on the edge of a drum as he shot to his feet.

Randy lay in a haze of fear with the sound of his own heart gurgling in his ears.

Pike's face appeared above Randy's, framed by the blue sky.

"Pike, my heart . . . I think I'm dying . . . help me . . ."

A jumble of voices.

"What's wrong with him?"

"Has he got epilepsy?"

"Call 911!"

"Hang on, Randy."

Pike leaped off the front of the stage and took off at a run. "Where's a phone? Anybody! Where's a phone!" Before the frantic question left his lips he saw a policeman coming toward him at a run, his silver badge bouncing on his blue shirt.

"Officer . . ."

The policeman ran right past him on his way to the stage, and Pike did an about-face to follow.

"Anybody know what's wrong with him?" the policeman asked, bending over Randy.

Pike said nothing.

The others said no.

Randy mumbled, "My heart . . ."

The man in blue grabbed the radio off his belt and called for help.

Randy lay ringed by faces, looking up at them, terror in his eyes. He grabbed a shirtfront: Danny's. "Call my mom," he whispered.

Blissfully unaware of the events happening at White Bear Lake ten miles away, Bess and Michael met at the hospital, stole one brief kiss in the hall, smiled into one another's eyes and entered Lisa's room together, holding hands. She and Natalie were there alone, the new mother asleep in her hospital bed, and the new baby making mewling sounds in a glass bassinet. The room was filled with flowers and smelled like oniony beef from the remains of Lisa's lunch, which was waiting to be collected.

Bess and Michael scanned the room from the doorway, then tiptoed to the bassinet and stood on either side of it, looking down at their new granddaughter.

They spoke in whispers.

"Oh, just look at her, Michael, isn't she beautiful?" And to the baby, Bess said, "Hello, precious, how are you today? You look a lot prettier than you did last night."

They both reached down and touched the baby's blankets, her downy cheek, rapt in her presence. Michael whispered, "Hi there, little lady. Grandma and Grandpa came to see you."

"Michael, look . . . her mouth is just like your mother's."

"Wouldn't my mother have loved her."

"So would my dad."

"She's got more hair than I thought. Last night it seemed as if she didn't have hardly any but today it looks quite dark."

"Do you think it would be okay if we picked her up?" Bess looked up into Michael's eyes. He smiled conspiratorially, and she slipped her hands beneath the soft pink flannel blanket and lifted Natalie from the bassinet. They stood shoulder-to-shoulder, inundated by love as pure and exquisite as any they had ever felt, stunned once again by a sense of completeness, by the idea of leaving their mark on the future through this child.

"Isn't it something, how she makes us feel?"

Michael kissed the baby's forehead, then straightened and smiled at her. "Wait till you're one or two or so. You'll come to our house to stay and we'll spoil you plenty, won't we, Grandma?"

"You bet we will. And someday when you're old enough, we'll tell you all about how your birth made your grandpa propose to me and brought us back together again. Of course we'll have to edit out the part about the condoms and how your grandpa threw them all over the steps but . . ."

Michael smothered his laughter. "Bess, these are delicate ears!"

"Well, she comes from a randy lot, and if—"

From behind them, Lisa spoke. "What are you two whispering about over there?"

They looked back over their shoulders. Lisa looked sleepy but wore a soft smile.

"Actually, your mother was talking about condoms."

"Michael!" Bess shouted.

"Well, she was. I told her Natalie was too young to hear such things but she wouldn't listen to me."

Lisa boosted herself up. "All right, what's going on between you two? I wake up and you're whispering and giggling . . ." She reached with both hands. "And bring my baby here, will you?"

Lisa pressed a button that raised the head of the bed, and they went to take her the baby, then sit one on each side of her and lean over simultaneously to kiss her cheeks.

"She was awake so we didn't think we'd get in trouble for picking her up."

"She's been a good girl . . . haven't you, Natalie?" Lisa fingered the baby's hair. "She slept five hours between feedings."

They talked about how Lisa was feeling, whom she'd called, who'd sent flowers (she thanked them for theirs), when Mark was expected to return, the fact that Randy hadn't called or stopped by, the probability of his visiting that evening, and Grandma Dorner, too. They admired the baby, and Bess offered reminiscences about Lisa's birth, and what a good sleeper she'd been, and what a lusty set of lungs she'd had when she decided not to sleep.

After all that, while they still sat one on either side of Lisa, Bess glanced at Michael and sent him a silent message. He captured her hand and, resting it on the bedspread covering Lisa's stomach, said, "Your mother and I have something to tell you, Lisa." He let Bess speak the words.

"We're going to get married again."

A radiant smile lit Lisa's face as she lunged forward, the baby still on her right arm, clasping Michael with her left as Bess, too, bent into the awkward, three-way embrace. The baby started complaining at being squashed between two bodies but they ignored her, allowing the moment its due, cleaving to one another, their throats thick with emotion.

Against Lisa's hair, Bess whispered simply, "Thank you, darling, for forcing two stubborn people back together."

Lisa kissed her mother's mouth, her father's mouth. "You've made me so happy."

"We've made *us* so happy." Michael chuckled, drawing a like response from the others as they drew back, all of them a little glisteny-eyed and flushed. They all laughed self-consciously. Lisa sniffed, and Bess ran the edge of a hand under her eye.

"When?"

"Right away."

"As soon as we can get it arranged."

"Oh, you guys, I'm *so* happy!" This hug was one of hallelujah, a near banging together of cheeks before Lisa held Natalie straight out and rejoiced, "We did it, kiddo, we did it!"

Stella spoke from the doorway. "May I get in on this celebration?"

"Grandma! Come in, quick! Mom and Dad have some great news! Tell her, Mom!"

Stella approached the bed. "Don't tell me. You're going to get married again." Bess nodded, smiling widely. Stella made a victor's fist. "I knew it! I knew it!" She kissed Bess first, because she was closer, then went at

Michael with her arms up. "Come here, you handsome, wonderful hunk of a son-in-law, you!" She met him at the foot of the bed as he came around to scoop her up. "I thought that daughter of mine was crazy to divorce you in the first place." Released, she fanned her face and turned toward the bed. "Whoo! How much excitement can a woman stand in one day? All this and a great-grandchild, too! Let me see the new arrival—and Lisa, you little matchmaking mother, don't you look happy enough to float?"

It was an afternoon of celebration. Mark arrived, followed by the rest of the Padgetts as well as two women Lisa worked with, and one of her high-school friends. Bess and Michael's news was received with as much excitement as was their new granddaughter.

At one point Lisa asked, "Where are you going to live?"

They gaped at each other and shrugged.

Bess replied, "We don't know. We haven't talked about it yet."

Leaving the hospital at 4:15 P.M., Bess said, "Where *are* we going to live?"

"I don't know."

"I suppose we should talk about it. Want to come over to the house?"

Michael affected a salacious grin and said, "Of course I want to come over to the house."

They were driving separate cars but arrived at the house simultaneously. Bess parked in the garage and Michael pulled up behind her, went into the garage and waited beside her car while she switched off the radio and collected her purse and turned up the visor. As he opened her door and stood waiting, he found himself happier than he could recall being in years, for simply being with her, feeling certain that the last half of his life was going to be less tumultuous than the first. Everything seemed near perfect—the new baby, the marriage plans, the children all grown up, happiness, wealth and health; he found himself tempted toward smugness as he stood beside Bess's car.

From behind the wheel she looked up at him and said, "You know what?"

She could have announced that she'd taken a job as a palm reader and was going to travel the country with a carnival, and he wouldn't have objected at that moment, as long as he could tag along. Her face looked young and glad, her eyes content. "I couldn't guess."

She got out of the car. He slammed the door but they remained beside it, in the concrete coolness of the garage with its peculiar mixture of scents—mower gas and rubber hoses and garden chemicals. "I've discovered something about myself that surprises me," Bess told him.

"What?"

"That I really don't care about this house as much as I used to. As a matter of fact, I absolutely love your condo."

He couldn't have been more surprised. "Are you saying you want to live there?"

"Where do *you* want to live?"

"In my condo, but I thought for sure you'd have a fit if I said so."

She burst out laughing, draped her arms around his neck and dropped back against the side of her car, taking him with her. With his body fit to hers she smiled up into his eyes. "Oh, Michael, isn't it wonderful, getting older? Learning to sort out what's really important from what's petty and superficial?" She kissed him briefly and told him, "I'd love to live in your condo. But if you'd said you wanted to move back into the house, that would have been all right, too, because it's not so important *where* we live as that we live there together from now on."

He rested his hands on the sides of her breasts and said, "I've been thinking about that same thing, too. Are you sure you aren't saying you like the condo better just because you think it's what I want?"

"I'm sure. In more ways than one we sort of outgrew this house. It was grand while the kids were little but now it's—I don't know—a new phase of life, time to move on. There are a lot of sad memories here, as well as happy ones. The condo is a fresh start . . . and after all, we did decorate it together, to both of our tastes. Why, it makes perfect sense to live there! It's newer, it's got as wonderful a view as this does, nobody has to take care of the yard, it's still close enough for me to get to my store in fifteen minutes and for you to get to downtown St. Paul fast, and there's the beach and the parks, and—"

"Listen, Bess, you don't have to convince me. I'll be overjoyed to stay there. There's only one question."

"Which is?"

"What about Randy?"

She put her hands on his collarbone and absently smoothed his shirt. She let her hands fall still on his chest, lifted her gaze and said calmly, "It's time to cut Randy loose, don't you think?"

Michael made no reply. He had told her essentially the same thing that first night Lisa had tricked them into facing each other at her apartment.

"He has a job now," she went on. "Friends. It's time he got out on his own."

"You're sure?"

"I'm sure."

"Because it strikes me that even though parents think they ought to treat all their kids equally, it's not always possible. Some of them need us more than others, and I think Randy will always need more of our help than Lisa ever did."

"That may be true but it's still time for him to live in his own place."

They let a kiss seal their decision, sharing it leaning against the car with the late afternoon sunlight flooding in, and the sound of condensation dripping off the auto air conditioner, and the smell of gasoline coming from the nearby lawn mower.

When Michael lifted his head he looked serene. "This time I'm staying with you till he gets home, and we'll tell him together."

"Agreed." She smiled and threaded one arm around his waist, turning him toward the kitchen door.

They entered the house to find the phone ringing. Bess answered, unprepared in her radiant state for the voice at the other end of the line.

"Mrs. Curran?"

"Yes."

"This is Danny Scarfelli. I'm one of the guys in Randy's band. Listen, I don't mean to scare you but something's happened to him and he's not . . . well, I think it's pretty serious, and they're taking him by ambulance to the hospital."

"What? A car accident, you mean?" Bess's terrified eyes locked on Michael's.

"No. We were just playing, you know, and all of a sudden he's laying on the floor. He says it's something with his heart is all I know. He asked me to call you."

"Which hospital?"

"Stillwater. They've already left."

"Thank you." She hung up. "It's Randy. Something's wrong with his heart and they're taking him to the hospital in an ambulance."

"Let's go."

He grabbed her hand and they ran out the way they'd entered, to his car. "I'll drive."

All the way to Lakeview Hospital, they sat stiff-spined, fearful, thinking, Why now? Why now? It's taken us all this time to get our lives back on track, and we deserve some unconfounded happiness. Michael ignored stop signs and broke speed limits. Gripping the steering wheel with both hands, he thought, There must be something I should be saying to Bess. I should touch her shoulder, squeeze her hand. But he drove in his own insular parcel of dread, as silent as she, inexplicably reft from her by this threat to their child.

His heart? What could be wrong with the heart of a nineteen-year-old boy?

They reached the emergency room of Lakeview at the same time as the ambulance, catching a mere glimpse of Randy as they ran behind the gurney bearing him along a short hall to a curtained section of the area. An alarming number of medical staff materialized at once, speaking in brusque spurts, in their own indigenous lexicon, focused on the patient with unquestionable life-and-death intensity, ignoring Michael and Bess, who hovered on the sidelines, gripping each other's hands now as they had not in the car.

"Got a sinus tach here."

"What's his blood pressure?"

"One eighty over one hundred."

"Respiration?"

"Poor."

"How bad are the arrhythmias?"

"Bad. Heart is moving like a bag of worms in there. Very irregular and rapid. We put him on D5W."

Three patches were already pasted on Randy's chest, and a blood pressure cuff ringed his arm. Someone snapped leads to them, connected to monitors on the wall. Intermittent beeps sounded. Randy's eyes were wide open as a doctor in white leaned over him. "Randy, can you hear me? Can you hear me, Randy? Did you take anything?"

The doc pulled back Randy's eyelids one at a time and studied the periphery of his eyes. A woman in blue scrubs said, "His parents are here."

The doctor caught sight of Bess and Michael, standing to one side, supporting each other. "You're his parents?"

"Yes," Michael answered.

"Are there any congenital heart problems?"

"No."

"Diabetes?"

"No."

"Seizure disorders?"

"No."

"Is he on any medication?"

"None that we know of."

"Does he use cocaine?"

"I don't think so. Marijuana sometimes."

A nurse said, "Blood pressure's dropping."

An alarm sounded on one of the machines, like the hang-up tone on a dangling telephone.

The doctor shouted, "This guy's coding! Page code blue!" He made a fist and delivered a tremendous blow to Randy's sternum.

Bess winced and placed one hand over her mouth. She stared, caught in a horror beyond anything she'd imagined, while her son lay on the gurney dying and a medical team fought a scene such as she'd witnessed only on television.

More staff came running, two more nurses, one who started a flowchart, a lab technician to help monitor the vital signs, a radiology technician who watched the monitors, an anesthetist who inserted a pair of nasal prongs into Randy's nose, another doctor who began administering CPR. "Grease the paddles!" he ordered. "We have to defibrillate!" With stacked hands, he thrust at Randy's chest.

Bess and Michael's interlocked knuckles turned white.

A nurse turned on a machine that set up a high electrical whine. She grabbed two paddles on curled cords and smeared them with gel. The doctor ordered, "Stand back!" Everyone backed away from the metal gurney as the nurse flattened the paddles to the left side of Randy's chest.

"Hit him!"

The nurse pushed two buttons at once.

Randy grunted. His body arched. His arms and legs stiffened, then fell limp.

Bess uttered a soft cry and turned her face against Michael's shoulder.

Someone said, "Good, he responded."

Through her tears and her terror, Bess looked back at the table, little understanding why these methods were used. Electrical current, zapping through her son's body, making it jerk and flop, that precious body she'd once carried within her own. *Please don't! Don't do that to him again!*

The room fell silent. All eyes riveted on a green screen and its flat, flat line.

Dear God, they've killed him! He's dead! There is no heartbeat!

"Come on, come on . . ." someone whispered urgently—the doctor, who'd made a tight fist and pushed it into the gurney mattress as he stared at the monitor. "Beat, damn it . . "

The line stayed flat.

Bess and Michael stared with the others, linked by wills and hands, in near shock themselves from this quick plunge into disaster.

Tears leaked down Bess's face. "What is it? What's happening?" Bess whispered but no one responded.

The green line squiggled.

It squiggled again, lifting to form a tiny hillock on that deadly, unbroken horizon. And suddenly it picked up, became regular. Everyone in the room sighed and let their shoulders sag.

"All right, way to go, Randy," one of the medical team said.

Randy was still unconscious.

The lab technician, in a businesslike tone, with his eyes locked on the screen, reported, "We're back to an organized rhythm . . . eighty beats per minute now." The nurse with the clipboard checked the clock and made a note.

Bess looked up at Michael and her face sagged, as if made of wet newsprint. His eyes were dry and burning. He put both arms around her shoulders and hauled her close, cleaving to keep his knees from buckling while Randy began to regain consciousness.

"Randy, can you hear me?" Again a doctor was leaning over him.

He made a wordless sound, still groggy.

"Do you know where you are, Randy?"

He opened his eyes fully, looked around at the ring of faces and abruptly grew belligerent. He tried to sit up. "What the hell, let me outa—"

"Whoa, there." Hands pressed him down. "Not much oxygen getting to that brain yet. He's still light-headed. Randy, did you take anything? Did you take any cocaine?"

A nurse informed the doctor, "The cardiologist is on his way over from the clinic."

The doctor repeated to Randy, "Did you take any cocaine?"

Randy wagged his head and tried to lift one arm. The doctor held it down, encumbered as it was by the blood pressure cuff and the lead-in for an IV.

"Randy, we're not the police. Nobody is going to get in trouble if you tell us but we have to know so we can help you and keep your heart beating regularly. Was it cocaine, Randy?"

Randy fixed his eyes on the doctor's clothing and mumbled, "It was my first time, Doc, honest."

"How did you take it?"

No answer.

"Did you shoot up?"

No answer.

"Snort it?"

Randy nodded.

The doc touched his shoulder. "Okay, no need to get scared. Just relax." He lifted Randy's eyelids again, peered down, held up an index finger and said, "Follow my finger with your eyes." To the recording nurse he said,

"No vertical nystagmus. No dilation." To Randy, "Are any of your muscles twitching?"

"No."

"Good. I'm going to tell you what happened. The cocaine increased your heartbeat to the point where there wasn't enough time during each beat for it to properly fill with oxygenated blood. Consequently not enough oxygen was getting to your brain so at first you probably felt a little light-headed, and finally you fell off your stool. After you got here to the hospital your heart stopped beating completely but we started it again. There's a cardiologist on his way over from the clinic right now. He'll probably give you some medication to keep your heartbeat regular, okay?"

At that moment the cardiologist swept in, moving directly to the gurney in brisk steps. The physician speaking said, "Randy, this is Dr. Mortenson."

While the specialist took over, the other doctor approached Bess and Michael. "I'm Dr. Fenton," he said, extending his hand to each of them in turn. He had grand gray eyebrows and a caring manner. "I imagine you both feel like you're going to be next on that table. Let's step out into the hall, where we can talk privately."

In the hall, Dr. Fenton took a second glance at Bess and said, "Are you feeling faint, Mrs. Curran?"

"No . . . no, I'm all right."

"There's no need to be heroic. You've just been through a stressful ordeal. Let's sit down over here." He indicated a line of hard chairs across from the emergency-room desk. Michael put his arm around Bess and helped her to one, where she sank down gratefully. When they were all seated, Fenton said, "I know you have a lot of questions, so let me fill you in. I think you heard what I was saying to Randy in there—he snorted some cocaine, which can do a lot of nasty things to the human body. This time it caused an abnormally high heart rate—ventricular tachycardia, we call it. When the paramedics answered the call, Randy had been playing the drums and had fallen off his stool. That's because there wasn't enough oxygen getting to his brain. When you saw him arrest, there was so much electrostimulus going through his heart it wasn't actually beating anymore, it was only quivering. When a heart does that we have to bring it to a complete standstill so its normal rhythmicity can return. That's why I struck his chest, and that's what we did when we defibrillated him. Once you do that the normal electrical pathway can take over again, which is what's happened now.

"You saw how Randy got a little belligerent when he was coming awake. That often happens when the oxygen is returning to the brain but he should rest easier now.

"I have to warn you, though, that this can happen again during the next several hours, either from the drugs or from the heart itself, which is very irritable after all it's been through. My guess is Dr. Mortenson will prescribe some medication to prevent fibrillation from recurring. The problem with cocaine is that we can't go in there and get it out like we could poison, for example. We can only offer supportive care and wait for the effects of the drug to wear off. It stays in the system long after the high is gone."

Michael said, "So what you're saying is, there's still a chance that he could die?"

"I'm afraid so. The next six hours will be critical. But his youth is a plus. And if he does go into a fast rate, chances are we can control it with the drugs."

The cardiologist appeared at that moment. "Mr. and Mrs. Curran?"

"Yes, sir?"

Michael and Bess both stood.

"I'm Dr. Mortenson." He had steel-gray hair, rimless silver glasses and thick hands with a generous peppering of black hair on them. His handshake was hearty and firm. "Randy will be in my charge for a while yet. His heartbeat has leveled off now—a little rapid but we've administered inderal, which should help stabilize his heartbeat. If we can keep it reasonably steady for—oh, say twenty-four hours or so—he'll be totally out of the woods. Right now the lab people are drawing his blood gases. Our toxologist will do a drug screen and we'll be running a routine battery of other tests as well—blood sugar, electrolytes—standard procedure where cocaine is involved. We'll monitor him here in the ER for a while, then in a half hour or so he'll be transferred to Intensive Care. He's actually very alert now and asking if his mother is here."

"May we see him?" Bess asked.

"Of course."

She gave a timorous smile. "Thank you, Doctor."

Michael thought to ask, "Are there legalities involved, Doctor?"

"No. As I told Randy, we're not the police, neither do we report these cases to the police. Because he's admitted to using cocaine, however, he'll be referred for counseling, and a social worker will more than likely get involved."

"I heard him say he's never used it before. Is that possible?"

"Absolutely. You recall the death of the young basketball player, Len Bias, a couple of years ago? Sadly enough it was his first time, too, but what he didn't know was that he had a heart defect, a weakness too great to endure the effects of the cocaine. That's the trouble with this damned stuff. It can kill you half a dozen different ways, even the first time you let it in your body. That's why we have to educate these kids *before* they try it."

"Yes . . . thank you, Doctor."

The ER medical staff was still watching Randy's monitors as Bess approached the gurney, with Michael lingering several steps behind. A nurse in a traditional white uniform and cap was filling a syringe with blood from Randy's arm. She snapped a piece of rubber tubing off his biceps and said to him, "You've got nice veins." She sent him a smile, which he returned halfheartedly, then closed his eyes.

Bess stood watching, willing her eyes to remain dry. The lab nurse finished drawing her samples and left, pushing a tray containing rows of glass test tubes that clinked like wind chimes as she moved away. Michael hung back while Bess moved to the bed and bent over their son. He looked ghastly, sickly white, his eye sockets gaunt and his nostrils occupied by the oxygen prongs. The leads from his chest draped away to the monitors. She remembered when he was one and two years old how deathly afraid he'd been of doctors, how he'd cried and clung to her whenever she took him into the clinic. Again she struggled against tears.

"Randy?" she said softly.

He opened his eyes and immediately they filled. "Mom . . ." he managed in a croaky voice as the tears made tracks down his temples. She leaned down and put her cheek to his, found his hand at his hip and took it gingerly, avoiding the IV lead-in taped to its back.

"Oh, Randy, darling, thank God they got you here in time."

She felt his chest heave as he held sobs inside, smelled smoke in his hair and shaving lotion on his cheek, and felt his warm tears mingling with her own.

"I'm sorry," he whispered.

"I'm sorry, too. I should have been there for you, talked to you more, found out what was bothering you."

"No, it's not your fault, it's mine. I'm such a rotten bastard."

She looked into his eyes, so like his father's. "Don't you ever use that word." She wiped the tears from his temples but they continued to run. "You're our son and we love you very much."

"How can you love me? All I've ever been is trouble."

"Oh, no . . . no . . ." She smoothed his hair as if he were two years old again, then braved a wobbly smile. "Well, yes, sometimes you were. But when you have babies you don't say I want them only when they're good.

You take them knowing that sometimes they'll be less than perfect, and that's when you find out how much you love them. Because when you've struggled through it, everybody comes out stronger. And that's how this is going to be—you'll see."

He tried to wipe his eyes but she did it for him, with a corner of the sheet, then kissed his forehead and moved back so Michael could take her place.

He moved into Randy's line of vision and said simply, "Hi, Randy."

Randy stared at his father while his eyes filled once again. He swallowed hard and said, "Dad . . . ?"

Michael braced a hand on Randy's far side, bent over and kissed his left cheek. Randy's arms went around his father's back and clung, trailing IV cords and blood pressure paraphernalia. He hauled Michael down as a sob broke forth, then another. Michael held him as fiercely as possible while attempting to keep his weight off the electronic leads taped to Randy's chest. For a long time they embraced in silence, only an occasional telltale sniffle giving away the difficulty they were having holding their weeping inside.

"Dad, I'm so sorry . . ."

"I know . . . I know . . . so am I."

Ah, sweet, sweet healing. Ah, welcome love. When they had filled both their hearts, Michael drew back, sat on one hip and rested an elbow alongside Randy's head. He put his hand on Randy's hair, looking down into his brimming eyes. "But this is the end of all that, huh? You and I have some time to make up for, and we're going to do it. Everything Mom just said goes double for me. I love you. I hurt you. I'm sorry and we're going to work on it, starting today."

Just don't die. Please don't die when I've just gotten you back again.

"I can't believe you're here when I treated you so shitty."

"Aw, listen . . . we just didn't know how to get past our own hurt, so we shut each other out. But from now on we're going to talk, right?"

"Right," Randy croaked. He sniffed and tried to run the edge of one hand beside his eyes.

"Let me help you. Bess, is there a Kleenex over there?" She brought some and passed a handful to Michael and watched as he ministered to his son much as he had when Randy was a toddler, drying his eyes, helping him blow his nose. The sight of the two of them, close and loving again, brought back fresh tears to her eyes.

At last Michael sat back. "Now listen . . ." he said to Randy. "Your mother has something to tell you." He stood and reached for Bess's hand, his eyes saying, *Just in case he doesn't make it through the next twenty-four hours.* He drew Bess forward and stood behind her, his hands resting on her shoulders. She slipped her palm under Randy's and told him quietly, "Your dad and I are going to get married again."

He said nothing. His eyes locked on hers for some time, then shifted to Michael's.

Michael broke the silence. "Well, what do you think?"

"My God, you've got guts."

Michael squeezed Bess's shoulders. "I guess you'd see it that way. We think we've grown up a lot in the last six years."

Bess added, "And besides that, we fell in love again."

A nurse interrupted. "We're going to move Randy to Intensive Care now. Then I think we'd better let him rest for a while."

"Yes, of course. Well, we just wanted you to know, darling. We'll be outside." Bess kissed Randy. "We'll talk about it more when you're out of here. I love you."

Michael, too, kissed Randy. "Rest. I love you."

Together they went out to the ICU waiting room to face the long vigil that would either take or give them back their son.

chapter 19

D URING HIS CRITICAL twenty-four hours, time passed for Randy as phantasm. He would sleep as if for aeons and awaken to find the clock had moved a mere ten minutes. Faint sounds interposed themselves between sound sleep and full consciousness like a background score for his dreams. The *beep, beep, beep* of the blood pressure monitor announcing its new reading became his drumsticks on the rim of his Pearls, beginning a new song. The tinkle of test tubes when the lab technician returned became Tom Little's keyboards. The dim squish of rubber soles on hard floors became a rush of tail feathers on a woman who was dancing through his dream, dressed like a Las Vegas chorus girl in a bright pink flamingo costume while he played backup music with the band. She whirled and he caught sight of her face: it was Maryann Padgett. Somewhere in the room rubber wheels rolled across the floor and through his dream sped a skateboard and on it, the kid Trotter, going faster and faster, on a collision course with Maryann. Randy tried to call out, *Trotter, don't hit her!* but Trotter was watching his high-top tennies, jumping black electrical cables, unaware that he was going to wipe out and take her right along with him.

"Trotter, look out!"

Randy opened his eyes. His own voice had awakened him. His heart was thudding in fear for Maryann.

Lisa was standing beside his bed, holding a baby in her arms.

He smiled blearily.

"Hi," she said quietly.

"Hi," he tried but it came out so croaky he had to try again. "Hi. What are you doing here?"

"Came to show you your new niece."

"Yeah?" He managed a weak grin. Lisa wore her smug Ali McGraw smile, the one with the hard edge that scolded while telling him beyond a doubt how much she loved him.

So I'm going to die, Randy thought.

The realization brought little fear, only an incredible sense of well-being, of giving up the fight at last and doing so content in the knowledge that he was surrounded by love. There was no doubt in his mind he was right, otherwise they wouldn't have let Lisa bring that newborn baby in here.

He grinned and thought he said, "I'd hold her but I'd probably electro-cute her with all these damned wires."

Lisa showed him the baby's face. "She's a beaut, huh? Say hi to your uncle Randy, Natalie."

"Hi, Natalie," Randy whispered. Jeez, he was tired . . . such effort to get words out . . . cute baby . . . Lisa must have made Mom and Dad so happy . . . Lisa always did. He, as usual, had screwed up again. "Hey, listen . . . sorry I didn't come to see you."

"Oh, that's okay. I had about eight midwives as it was."

His eyelids grew too heavy to keep open. When they dropped he felt Lisa kiss his forehead. He felt the baby blanket brush his cheek. He opened his eyes as she straightened and saw her tears glimmering and knew undoubtedly he was dying.

The next time he woke up Grandma Stella was there, in her eyes the same soulful expression as in Lisa's.

Then his mom and dad again, looking haggard and worried.

And then—too unreal to believe—Maryann, which made no sense at all, unless, of course, he'd already died and this was heaven. She was smiling, dressed in aqua blue. Did angels wear aqua blue?

"Maryann?" he said.

"I was here visiting Lisa, and she asked me to come down and see you."

Virgin mother Mary, she spoke. She was real.

He told her, "I'd pretty much given up on you." To his own ears his voice sounded as if he was in a tunnel.

"I'd given up on you, too. Maybe now you'll get some help. Will you?"

She wasn't an easy woman; rather, an exacting one, a throwback to a time when parents taught their daughters to seek a man who was pure in heart and mind. The crazy thing was, he wanted to be that kind of man for her. He didn't understand it but there it was. Lying on his hospital bed, dying, he promised himself that if by some miracle he was wrong and he got out of here, he'd smoked his last joint and screwed his last groupie and snorted his last coke.

"I guess it's time," he answered and closed his eyes because he was so tired not even Maryann Padgett's presence could keep him awake. "Hey, listen," he said from the pleasant darkness behind his closed eyelids, "you'll be hearing from me when I get my act together. Meanwhile, don't go falling in love or anything, will you?"

When Maryann Padgett returned to the ICU waiting room, his entire family was there. She went straight to Lisa.

"How is he?" Lisa asked.

"Weak but making jokes."

Worry sketched drooping lines down Lisa's face. "I got too involved in my new married life and stopped calling him."

"No," Maryann whispered, embracing her friend. "You mustn't blame yourself."

But at one point or another during their vigil, recriminations fell from everyone's lips.

Michael said, "I should have tried harder to get him to talk to me."

Bess said, "I shouldn't have encouraged him to audition all the time."

Gil Harwood said, "I shouldn't have put him in touch with that damn band."

Stella said, "I shouldn't have given him the money for that van."

By ten o'clock that night, everyone was exhausted. Randy's condition seemed stable, his heartbeat regular, though he remained in Intensive Care, where five-minute visits were allowed only once an hour. Michael said, "Why don't you all go home and get some rest."

"What about you?" Bess said.

"I'll stay here and nap in the waiting room."

"But, Michael—"

"No buts. You do as I say. Get some rest and I'll see you in the morning. Stella, Gil, you too, please. I'll be here and I'll call you if anything changes."

Reluctantly they went.

A nurse brought Michael a pillow and blanket and he lay down in the family lounge with the reassurance that they'd wake him if Randy showed the slightest change. He awakened after what seemed a very brief time, drew his arm from beneath the blanket and lurched up when his watch showed 5:35 A.M. He sat up, rubbed his face, finger-combed his hair, stood and folded the blanket.

At the nurses' station he asked about Randy.

"He had a very good night, slept straight through, and there was no sign of any more problems with his heart."

Less than twelve hours to go before he was totally out of the woods. Michael shrugged and stretched and went to find a bathroom. He splashed cold water on his face, rinsed out his mouth, combed his hair and tucked his shirt in. He'd had these same clothes on since yesterday afternoon. It seemed half a lifetime ago since he'd donned them and come up to the hospital, smiling, to meet Bess and to visit Lisa and the new baby. He wondered how they were. Poor Lisa had had a shock, learning about Randy, but she'd handled it like a trooper, getting permission to bring the baby down here to show Randy in case he died. Nobody'd said as much but they all knew that was the reason.

He stood in the doorway of Randy's room, watching him sleep.

Ten more hours. Just ten more.

He walked to the window and stared out, standing with both hands on the small of his back. What irony, both of his children in the same hospital, one bringing in a new life, the other with his life in the balance.

He thought about it as dawn lifted over the St. Croix valley and lit the river and the boats at anchor and the thick maples that rimmed the water and the dozen church steeples of Stillwater. Sunday morning in late August, and the townspeople would soon be rising and dressing for worship services, and the tourists would soon be flooding in to shop for antiques and buy ice-cream cones and walk the waterfront. And the boat owners would be awakening in their cabin cruisers and stepping out onto their decks and watching the mist rise off the St. Croix and deciding at which restaurant they'd eat brunch. At noon Mark would come to the hospital and take Lisa and Natalie home.

And four hours after that—please, God—Bess and I will do the same thing with Randy.

As if the thought penetrated his sleep, Randy opened his eyes and found his father standing at the window.

"Dad?"

Michael whirled and moved directly to the bed, taking Randy's hand. "I made it."

"Yeah," his father said, his voice breaking with emotion. If Randy didn't know he needed ten more hours to be out of the woods, Michael wasn't going to disillusion him.

"You been there all night?"

"I slept some."

"You've been here all night."

Moving his thumb across the back of Randy's hand, Michael gave a quarter smile.

"You all thought I'd die, right? That's why Lisa brought the baby for me to see, and why Grandma came, and Maryann."

"That was a possibility."

"I'm sorry I put you through that."

"Yeah, well, sometimes that's what we do to people who love us—we put them through things without really meaning to."

They took a while to study each other and to reaffirm silently that they were done trying to put each other through anything and were ready to take the next step toward a wholesome relationship with one another.

"Where's Mom?"

"I made her go home and get some sleep."

"So you two are getting married again."

"Is that okay with you?"

"You guys in love?"

"Absolutely."

"Then it's okay."

"We'll have some things to work out."

"Like?"

"Getting you well again. Deciding where we'll live."

"I can live anyplace."

You'll live with us, Michael vowed silently, realizing his and Bess's plans to cut Randy free would have to be waylaid for a while. The idea brought him great hope and a sense of impending peace. "Just so you know—we're not abandoning you. Not this time."

"You didn't abandon me before. That was all in my head but the shrinks here are going to get my head on straight again."

Michael bent low over his son, looking into his eyes. "We'll be there for you. Whatever you need, whatever it takes. But now, I'd better go. Five minutes is up and that's my limit. Anyway, I need a shower and a shave and a change of clothes." Michael stood. "I'll call your mother, then take a run home. But I'll be back in a couple of hours, okay?"

Randy looked up at his tired father, whose rumpled clothes and shadowy growth of whiskers bore witness to his night's vigil. It struck Randy in that moment how damned hard it must be to be a parent, and how little he'd considered the fact until now. *I must be growing up,* he thought. It made him feel expansive, and a little scared, taken in the light of the events of the past twelve hours. *What if I have a kid someday and he puts me through this?*

"Dad?" he said.

Michael sensed whatever was coming would be of import. He waited silently.

"You didn't give me hell for using the cocaine."

"Oh, yes I did. A dozen times while you were fighting for your life. I just didn't say it out loud."

"I won't do it again, I promise. I want to get well and be happy."

Michael put his hand on Randy's hair. "That's what we all want, son." Then he leaned over and kissed Randy's cheek and told him, "I'll be back soon. I love you."

"I love you, too," Randy said.

And with those words another fragment of pain dissolved. Another window of hope opened. Another beam of sunlight radiated into their future as Michael leaned down to hug his son before leaving.

Randy was released from the hospital shortly before suppertime that day. His mother and father walked him out into the sunshine of late afternoon, into a setting crowned by a cobalt-blue sky and a world where people moved about their pursuits with reassuring normality. Down at the public beach on Lily Lake some families were lighting barbecues and calling to their kids to be careful in the water. At the ball diamond across the street, a group of little boys were playing kittenball. A couple of blocks north, on Greeley Street, Nelson's Ice Cream Parlor was doing its usual landmark business, lining the concrete step out front with a row of lickers of all ages. Out on the river the drawbridge was raised, backing up traffic clear up to the top of Houlton Hill. The day-trippers were pulling their boats behind their packed cars, heading back toward the city, and the residents of Stillwater were sighing, looking forward to winter, when the streets would once again become their own.

"Where to?" Michael asked, sitting behind the wheel of his Cadillac Seville.

"I'm starved," Bess replied. "Would anyone like to pick up some sandwiches and eat them down by the river?"

Michael turned to glance at Randy in the backseat.

"Sounds fine with me," Randy said.

And so they took the next halting step in their journey back to familyhood.

Six weeks later, on an Indian summer's day in mid-October, Bess and Michael Curran were married in a simple service in the rectory of St. Mary's Catholic Church. The ceremony was performed by the same priest who'd married them twenty-two years before.

When he'd kissed his stole and draped it around his neck, Father Moore opened his prayer book to the correct page, smiled at the bride and groom and said, "So . . . here we are again."

His remark brought smiles to the assembled faces. To Bess's, which shone with happiness. To Michael's, which radiated hope. To Lisa's, which might have been touched ever so slightly by smugness. To Stella's, which seemed to say, It's about time. To Randy's, which held a promise. And even to Natalie's as she lay on her daddy's arm and studied the glistening silver frames on the eyeglasses of Gil Harwood.

When the priest asked, "Who gives this woman?" Lisa and Randy answered, "We do," bringing another round of smiles.

When the bride and groom repeated the words ". . . until death do us part," their eyes shone with sincerity that had depth far beyond the first time they'd spoken the words.

When Father Moore said, "I now pronounce you man and wife," Lisa and Randy exchanged a glance and a smile.

When their mother and father kissed, Lisa reached over for Randy's hand and gave it a hard squeeze.

The small wedding party went to dinner afterward at Kozlak'a Royal Oaks, overlooking a beautiful walled garden decorated with pumpkins, cornshocks and scarecrows. The personalized matchbooks awaiting them at their table and reserving it for them said *Mr. and Mrs. Curran.*

Spying them, after he'd seated Bess and was taking a chair himself, Michael picked up one of the books and folded it into her hand, saying, "Damn right, once and for all." Then he kissed her lightly on the lips and smiled into her eyes.

There were, as in all relationships that matter most, wrinkles that needed smoothing for all of them in that bittersweet autumn. There was Randy's intense counseling, his loss of a way of life, of friends, of drug-dependency, and his search for inner strength and positive relationships. There was family therapy, and the painful resurrection and obliteration of past guilts, fears and mistakes. There was Lisa's anger when she learned her mother and father were selling the family house. There was Michael and Bess's frequent frustration at living with an adult son when in truth they were impatient to have total privacy. There were Michael and Bess themselves, the husband and wife, readjusting to married life and its constant demands for compromise.

Ah, but there were blessings.

There was Randy, coming home one day and bringing a new friend named Steve, whom he'd met in therapy and who wanted to start a band that would be drug-free and would play for school kids to spread the message "Say no!" There was Michael, turning one day from the kitchen stove as Randy asked, "Hey, Dad, think you could teach me how to make that?" There were suppers for three, with three alternate cooks, and Randy eating healthily at last. And days when Lisa and Mark would come breezing in with the baby, calling, "Yo, Grampa and Grandma and Uncle Randy!" And the simpler homely joys of Bess shouting, "All right, who put my sweatshirt in the dryer and shrunk it!" And of Michael, breaking a radiator hose on his way home from work and calling home to hear Randy volunteer, "Hang on, Dad, I'll come and get you." And of Randy learning to change his niece's diapers and describing what he found inside them in phrases that had the entire family in stitches. And one day when Randy finally announced, "I got a job at Schmitt's Music selling instruments and giving drum lessons to little kids. Pay sucks but the fringe benefits are great—sitting around jamming whenever the place isn't busy."

And one day Bess went out to the County Seat and bought herself a pair of blue jeans.

She had them on when Michael came home from work and found her in the kitchen making Parmesan cream sauce for tortellini—it was her turn to cook. The pasta was boiling, the roux was bubbling, and she was mincing garlic as he stopped in the kitchen doorway and tossed his car keys onto the cabinet top.

"Well, lookit here . . ." he said in wonder, ". . . what my bride is wearing."

She smiled back over her shoulder and twitched her hips.

"How 'bout that. I did it."

He ambled toward her, dressed in a winter trench coat, cocked one hip against the edge of the cabinet and perused her lower half. "Looks good, too."

"Y' know what?" she said. "I really don't care if they do or not. They *feel* good."

"They do, huh?" He boosted himself away from the cabinet and put both hands on her, splayed and inquisitive. "Let's see . . ." He rubbed her, back and front, all over her tight blue jeans, kissed her over her shoulder and murmured against her mouth, "You're right . . . feels very good."

Giggling, she said, "Michael, I'm cutting up garlic here."

"Yeah, I can smell it. Stinks like hell." He turned her fully around and caught her against himself with a two-handed grip on her buttocks. Her arms crossed behind his neck, the paring knife still in her right hand.

"How was your day?" she asked, when they'd shared a nice long kiss.

"Pretty good. How was yours?"

"Crappy. This is the best part of it so far."

"Well, good," he said. "I can make it even better if you'd care to turn off those burners and put down that paring knife."

"Mmm . . ." she murmured against his lips, dropping the paring knife on the floor, reaching out blindly to the side, groping for the control knobs on the stove.

At the other end of the condo the door opened.

Michael dropped his head back and said quietly, "Oh, shit."

"Now, now," she chided gently, "you wanted him back, didn't you?"

"But not when I have a hard-on in the middle of the kitchen at suppertime."

She giggled again. "Just keep your coat buttoned awhile," she whispered at the same moment Randy stepped to the kitchen doorway.

"Mom, Dad . . . hi. Hope we're not disturbing anything. I brought someone home for supper." He drew her forward by a hand, a pretty young woman with dark hair and a smile that had put a boyish look of eagerness on Randy's face. "You remember Maryann, don't you?"

Two parents turned, joy on their faces, their embrace dissolving as they reached out to welcome her.